The Lost Book
of the White

The Lost Book of the White

CASSANDRA CLARE
and WESLEY CHU

Margaret K. McElderry Books

NEW YORK LONDON TORONTO SYDNEY NEW DELHI

MARGARET K. McELDERRY BOOKS
An imprint of Simon & Schuster Children's Publishing Division
1230 Avenue of the Americas, New York, New York 10020

This book is a work of fiction. Any references to historical events, real people, or real places are used fictitiously. Other names, characters, places, and events are products of the author's imagination, and any resemblance to actual events or places or persons, living or dead, is entirely coincidental.

MARGARET K. McELDERRY BOOKS is a trademark of Simon & Schuster, Inc.
For information about special discounts for bulk purchases, please contact
Simon & Schuster Special Sales at 1-866-506-1949 or business@simonandschuster.com.
The Simon & Schuster Speakers Bureau can bring authors to your live event.
For more information or to book an event, contact the Simon & Schuster Speakers Bureau
at 1-866-248-3049 or visit our website at www.simonspeakers.com.
Interior design by Mike Rosamilia
Jacket design by Nick Sciacca
The text for this book was set in ITC Galliard Std.
Manufactured in the United States of America
First Edition
2 4 6 8 10 9 7 5 3 1
Library of Congress Cataloging-in-Publication Data
Names: Clare, Cassandra, author. | Chu, Wesley, author.
Title: The lost Book of the White / Cassandra Clare and Wesley Chu.
Description: First edition. | New York : Margaret K. McElderry Books, [2020] |
Series: The eldest curses | Audience: Ages 14 up. | Audience: Grades 10-12. |
Summary: Magnus Bane and Alec Lightwood must recover a book stolen by warlocks
Ragnor Fell and Shinyun Jung, who are being controlled by a Greater Demon.
Identifiers: LCCN 2020004037 (print) | LCCN 2020004038 (ebook) |
ISBN 9781481495127 (hardcover) | ISBN 9781481495141 (ebook)
Subjects: CYAC: Warlocks—Fiction. | Magic—Fiction. | Cults—Fiction. |
Demonology—Fiction. | Gays—Fiction.
Classification: LCC PZ7.C5265 Lq 2020 (print) | LCC PZ7.C5265 (ebook) | DDC [Fic]—dc23
LC record available at https://lccn.loc.gov/2020004037
LC ebook record available at https://lccn.loc.gov/2020004038

For Steve
—C. C.

To Paula, Hunter, and River
To family
—W. C.

And the angels which kept not their first estate,
but left their own habitation, he hath reserved in everlasting
chains under darkness unto the judgment of the great day.
—Jude 1:6

The Lost Book
of the White

PROLOGUE

Idris, 2007

IT WAS NOT QUITE DAWN WHEN MAGNUS BANE RODE into the low clearing with death on his mind. He rarely came to Idris these days—that many Shadowhunters close together made him nervous—but he had to admit that the Angel had picked a pretty spot for the Nephilim's home. The air was alpine and fresh, cold and clean. Pines shuffled affably against one another on the banks of the valley. Idris could be intense at times, gloomy and Gothic and full of foreboding, but this pocket of it felt like something from a German fairy tale. Perhaps that was why, despite all the Shadowhunters everywhere, his friend Ragnor Fell had built his house here.

Ragnor was not a cheerful person, but he had unaccountably built a cheerful house. It was a squat stone cottage, sharply gabled in rye straw thatch. Magnus knew perfectly well that Ragnor had teleported the thatch directly from a tavern in North Yorkshire, to the consternation of its guests.

As he trotted his horse down to the valley floor, he felt the troubles of the present fade. At the top of the valley, everything was terrible. Valentine Morgenstern was working very hard to start the war he wanted, and Magnus was so much more wrapped up in it than he would have wished. There was this boy, though, with these very hard-to-describe blue eyes.

For a moment, though, it would just be Magnus and Ragnor again, as it had been so many times before. Then he would have to deal with the world and its problems, which would be arriving shortly in the form of Clary Fairchild.

He left the horse behind the house and tried the front door, which was unlocked and swung open at his light touch. Magnus had presumed he'd find his friend engaged in drinking a cup of tea or reading a voluminous tome, but instead Ragnor was in the process of trashing his own living room. He was holding a wooden chair above his own head, in some kind of frenzy.

"Ragnor?" Magnus offered, and in response Ragnor threw the chair against the stone wall, where it broke into splinters. "Bad time?" Magnus called.

Ragnor seemed to notice Magnus for the first time. He held up one finger, as though telling Magnus to wait a moment, and then with great purpose he strode to the oak bombe chest across the room and, one after the other, pulled each of its drawers out, allowing each to fall and smash against the ground in a huge clatter of metal and porcelain. He straightened up, rolled his shoulders, and turned to Magnus.

"You have crazy eyes, Ragnor," said Magnus carefully.

He was used to Ragnor being a relatively dapper gentleman, well-dressed, with a healthy glow to his green skin and a shine on the white horns that curved back from his forehead. The man before him would have seemed in bad shape no matter who he was, but for Ragnor, this was very, *very* bad. He looked lost, his glance flicking around the room as though trying to catch someone hiding just out of sight. Without preamble he said, in a loud, clear voice, "Do you know the expression *sub specie aeternitatis?*"

Magnus was not sure what he'd expected Ragnor to say, but it had not been that. "Something like 'things as they really are'? Though that's not the literal translation, of course." Already this conversation had gone completely off the rails.

"Yes," said Ragnor. "Yes. It means, from the perspective of that which is really true, really and truly true. Not the illusions we see, that we pretend are real, but things with all illusions stripped away. Spinoza." After a moment he added thoughtfully, "That man could *drink*. Very good at grinding lenses, though."

"I have no idea what you're talking about," Magnus said.

Ragnor's focus abruptly snapped and he looked straight into Magnus's eyes, unblinking. "Do you know what existence is, *sub specie aeternitatis?* Not our world, not even the worlds that we know, but the whole of everything? I do."

"Do you now," said Magnus.

Ragnor didn't break his gaze. "It is *demons,*" he said. "It is *evil*. It is chaos all the way down, a bubbling cauldron of malevolent intent."

Magnus sighed. His friend had become depressed. It happened to warlocks sometimes; the absurdity of the universe became somehow both more and less funny as their life spans stretched so far beyond any mundane's. This was a dangerous path for Ragnor. "Some things are nice, though, right?" He tried to think of Ragnor's favorite things. "The sunrise over Fujiyama? A good old bottle of Tokay? That place we used to have coffee in the Hague, it came in those tiny thimbles and you could feel it burn its way to your stomach?" He thought harder. "How stupid an albatross looks when it lands on water?"

Ragnor finally blinked, many times in a row, and then dropped into the plaid-upholstered armchair behind him. "I'm not depressed, Magnus."

"Sure," said Magnus, "total existential nihilism, that's regular old Ragnor."

"It has caught up with me, Magnus. All of it. Now the big guy's after me. The biggest guy. Well, the second-biggest guy."

"Still a pretty big guy," Magnus agreed. "Is this about Valentine? Because—"

"Valentine!" Ragnor barked. "Idiot Shadowhunter business, I've no patience for it. But the timing is good. For me to disappear. Anything bad happening in Idris right now is probably just part of this whole business with the Mortal Instruments. No reason for the agents of the *real* threat to question it."

Magnus was getting fed up. "You want to tell me what this is about? Since you asked me to come here? Said something about the matter's great urgency? Can we have a cup of tea, or have you already smashed the kettle?"

Ragnor leaned in toward Magnus. "I'm *faking my own death*, Magnus."

He chuckled, before turning and heading through a doorway toward, Magnus guessed, more redecorating. With reluctance, Magnus followed.

"For heaven's sake, why?" he called after Ragnor's retreating back.

"I don't know why now," Ragnor called back, "but a bunch of them are coming back. You can't kill them, you know, you can only send them away for a while, but then they come back. Oh yes, do they come back."

Magnus was starting to wonder if Ragnor had finally lost it. "Who?"

Ragnor suddenly appeared directly beside Magnus, emerging from what Magnus had thought was a closet but was, he now realized, a hallway. "He says 'who,'" Ragnor echoed sarcastically, and for a moment he sounded like his usual self. "Who are we talking about? Demons! Greater Demons! What a name. Why did we let them name themselves? They're not so great."

"Have you been drinking?" Magnus said.

"All my life," Ragnor said. "Let me say a name to you. You tell me if it means anything."

"Go."

"Asmodeus."

"Dear old Dad," said Magnus.

"Belphegor."

"Blobby sort of chap," said Magnus. "Where are we going with this? Is one of them after you?"

"Lilith."

Magnus sucked in air through his teeth. If Lilith was on Ragnor's trail, that was very bad. "Mother of Demons. Lover of Sammael."

"Right." Ragnor's eyes flashed. "Not her. *Him.*"

"Sammael?" Magnus said, chuckling. "No way."

"Yes," said Ragnor, with the sort of finality that made Magnus realize, with a sinking feeling, that Ragnor wasn't kidding.

"Can I sit down or something?" Magnus asked.

THEY TOOK REFUGE IN THE WRECKAGE OF RAGNOR'S bedroom. He'd managed to split the whole bed frame in two, which was a pretty impressive trick. Magnus sat on a desktop that had miraculously remained intact. Ragnor paced back and forth.

"Sammael, as everyone knows, is dead," Magnus said. "He did something that started letting demons into our world, and then he was killed, people say by the Taxiarch—"

"You know Sammael couldn't truly be killed," Ragnor snapped impatiently. "Much lesser demons than him come back eventually. He was always going to. And now he has."

"Fine," Magnus reasoned, "but I don't see what it has to do with you. I mean other than in the sense that it has to do with all of us. No, please don't throw any furniture until you've explained."

Ragnor lowered his hands, and a floor lamp that had been spinning lazily toward the ceiling fell to the ground with a clatter. "He's been looking for me. I don't know why, but I can guess."

"Wait," Magnus said, his brain starting to catch up. "If Sammael is back, why isn't he, you know, wreaking havoc?"

"He's not all the way back. He can't spend much time in our world, and he's still just floating out there in some kind of void. I think he wants me to find him a realm."

Magnus's eyebrows went up. "A realm?"

Ragnor nodded. "A demon realm. One of the other dimensions in the cluster of soap bubbles that is our reality. He'll be very weak at the start. He'll need energy to build up his strength, build up his magic. If he can find a realm to claim for his own, he can make it into a kind of dynamo for his own power. And I, Ragnor Fell, am the world's leading expert on dimensional magic."

"And its most humble. Why can't he find his own realm?"

"Oh, he probably would eventually. He's probably been looking all this time. But demon time is not the same as human time. Or even warlock time. It could be hundreds more years before he returns. Or it could be tomorrow." He trailed off. In the corner, a wastebasket slowly tipped over and spilled its contents across the uneven planks of the floor.

"So you're going to fake your own death. Doesn't that seem—hasty?"

"Do you understand," Ragnor roared, "what it would mean for Sammael to return to his full might? If he returned to Lilith, and they joined their power together? It would be war, Magnus. War upon Earth. Total destruction. No more bottles of Tokay! No more albatrosses!"

"What about other seabirds?"

Ragnor sighed and sat down next to Magnus. "I have to go into hiding. I have to make Sammael think I'm gone where nobody can ever reach me. Ragnor Fell, the expert on dimensional magic, must disappear forever."

Magnus processed that for a moment. He stood and walked out of the bedroom to regard the devastation Ragnor had wreaked upon his living room. He liked this house. It had been a place that felt like a second home for more than a hundred years. Ragnor had been his friend, his mentor, for many more years before that. He felt sad, and angry. Without turning back, he said, "How will I find you?"

"I'll find you," said Ragnor, "in whatever new persona I adopt. You'll know me."

"We could have a code word," said Magnus.

"The code word," Ragnor said, "is that I will tell the story of the first night you, Magnus Bane, consumed the Eastern European plum brandy known as *slivovice* in the Czech tongue. I believe you sang a song that night, of your own composition."

"Maybe no code word," said Magnus. "Maybe you can just wink or something."

Ragnor shrugged. "It should not take me long to reestablish myself. I wonder who I shall be. Anyway, if there is nothing more—"

"There is," Magnus said. He turned and found that Ragnor had gotten up from the desk and come to join him in the living room. Magnus said quietly, "I need the Book of the White."

Ragnor began to chuckle and then broke into a heartier laugh. He slapped Magnus on the back. "Magnus Bane," he said. "Keeping me drowning in Downworld intrigue to my fake last breath. Why, why could you *possibly* need the Book of the White now?"

Magnus turned to face Ragnor. "I need to wake up Jocelyn Fairchild."

Ragnor laughed again. "Amazing. Amazing! You not only need the Book of the White, you need to find it before Valentine Morgenstern. My friendship with you has always been a rich tapestry of terrible things happening, Magnus. I think I'll miss it." He smiled. "It's in Wayland manor. In the library, inside another book."

"It's hidden in *Valentine's old house*?"

Ragnor smiled even wider. "Jocelyn hid it there. Inside a cookbook. *Simple Recipes for Housewives*, I believe it's called. Remarkable woman. Terrible choice of husband. Anyway, I'm off." He began to make for the door.

"Wait." Magnus followed and tripped over what turned out to be a statue of a monkey cast in brass. "Jocelyn's daughter is on her way to ask you about the book right now."

Ragnor's eyebrows went up. "Well, I can't help her. I'm dead. You'll have to pass on the information yourself." He turned to go.

"Wait," Magnus said again. "How, um . . . how did you die?"

"Killed by Valentine's thugs, obviously," said Ragnor. "That's why I'm doing this now."

"Obviously," murmured Magnus.

"They were looking for the Book of the White themselves. There was a scuffle; I was killed." Ragnor looked impatient. "Do I have to do everything for you? Here." He stomped past Magnus, pointed at the back wall with his left index finger, and began to write on it in fiery Abyssal script. "I'll *write it on the wall* for you so you won't forget."

"Really? Abyssal?"

"'I . . . was . . . killed . . . by . . . Valentine's . . . goons . . . because . . . they . . .'" He paused and glanced at Magnus. "You never kept up your Abyssal, Magnus. This will be good practice for you." He turned back to the wall and resumed writing. "'Now . . . I . . . am . . . dead . . . oh . . . no.' There. Easy enough for you."

"Wait," Magnus said a third time, but he didn't actually have anything to ask. He grabbed at a random glass jar, tipped over on top of the mantelpiece. "You're not taking your"—he peered at the label and cocked an eyebrow at Ragnor—"horn polish?"

"My horns will have to go unpolished," Ragnor said. "Get out of my way, I'm faking my own death now."

"I didn't know you had to polish your horns."

"You do. Or at least you should. If you have horns. If you don't want them to look dirty and unkempt. I'm leaving, Magnus."

Finally Magnus's composure broke. "Do you have to?" he said, sounding to his own ears like a petulant child. "This is insane, Ragnor. You don't have to *die* to protect yourself. We can talk to the Spiral Labyrinth. You don't have to deal with this alone. You have friends! Powerful friends! Such as myself!"

Ragnor gazed at Magnus for a long moment. Eventually, he walked over and with great solemnity gave his friend a hug. Magnus reflected that this was perhaps their fifth or sixth hug in their hundreds of years of friendship. Ragnor was not much for physical touch.

"This is my problem, and I will deal with it myself," said Ragnor. "My dignity demands it."

"What I'm saying," said Magnus, "is that you *don't have to.*"

Ragnor stepped away and looked at him sadly. "I do, though." He turned to go.

Magnus looked at the letters of fire on the wall, now fading to invisibility. "I don't know why I'm making such a big deal of this," he said. "You just love a dramatic gesture. We'll see if this 'fake death' thing lasts a week before you get bored and show up in my apartment with your crokinole set."

Ragnor chuckled and vanished without another word.

Magnus stood there for a long time, staring at the empty space where Ragnor used to be. His former mentor had taken no luggage, not a change of clothes or a toothbrush. He had simply disappeared from the world.

The front door hung open, as Ragnor had left it. It looked better for the scenario he was trying to portray, but it gnawed at Magnus like a wound, and after a short while he closed it gently.

In the ruins of Ragnor's kitchen Magnus found an enormous clay tobacco pipe, and in the ruins of the bathroom a jar of a rare dried leaf, of Idrisian origin, that had been popular for Shadowhunters to smoke back when Magnus himself was a child, hundreds of years ago. For Ragnor's sake, for old times' sake, he lit the pipe and puffed on it thoughtfully.

From the window he watched the steady footfalls of Clary Fairchild's and Sebastian Verlac's horses as they descended into the clearing to meet him.

PART I
New York

† † †

CHAPTER ONE

The Sleep Thorn

September 2010

IT WAS LATE, AND UNTIL A MOMENT AGO, ALL HAD BEEN quiet. Magnus Bane, High Warlock of Brooklyn, sat in his living room on his favorite chair, open book facedown in his lap, and watched the latch of his top-story window jiggle. For the last week, somebody had been prodding and testing the magical wards protecting his apartment. Now it seemed they had decided to prod more directly.

Magnus thought this a foolish decision on their part. Warlocks kept late hours, for one thing. For another, he lived with a Shadowhunter—who was currently out on patrol, true, but Magnus was fully capable of defending himself, even in his pajamas. He cinched the belt of his black silk robe tighter and wiggled his fingers in front of him, feeling magic gather in them.

He reflected that years ago he would have been much more casual about this kind of break-in, letting it play out naturally and trusting his instincts to lead him through. Now he sat pointing literal finger-guns at the window. Now his infant son was asleep just down the hall.

At just over a year old, Max was sleeping through the night most of the time now. This was a relief, but also an inconvenience, because both of Max's parents kept nocturnal hours. Max, on the other hand, kept military hours, waking every morning at five thirty with a cheerful shriek that Magnus both adored and dreaded.

The window slid upward. Fire woke in both of Magnus's palms, and magic blazed in the dark, sapphire-blue.

A figure pulled its torso through the window and then froze. Framed in the opening was a Shadowhunter in full demon-hunting gear, bow looped over one shoulder. He looked surprised.

"Uh, hi," said Alec Lightwood. "I'm home. Please don't shoot me with magical rays."

Magnus waved with both hands, blue lights paling, then winking out, leaving faint traces of smoke curling around his fingers. "You usually use the door."

"Sometime I like the change of pace." Alec pulled himself the rest of the way in and closed the window behind him. Magnus gave him a look. "Okay. Truth. A demon ate my keys."

"We go through so many keys." Magnus got up to embrace his boyfriend.

"Wait, no. I smell."

"There's nothing wrong," proclaimed Magnus, moving his head toward Alec's neck, "with the smell of the sweat of a hard night's work—you *do* smell. What *is* that?"

"That," said Alec, "is the musk of the common subway tunnel smoke demon."

"Oh, honey." Magnus kissed Alec's neck anyway. He breathed through his mouth.

"Hang on, it's mostly on the gear," said Alec. Magnus gave him a little space and he began taking it off: the bow, the quiver, his stele, some seraph blades, his leather jacket, his boots, his shirt.

"Let me help you with the rest of that," Magnus murmured as Alec finished unbuttoning the shirt, and Alec gave him a real smile, his blue eyes warm, and Magnus felt a wave of love thrum through him. Three years in, he still felt as strongly as ever for Alec. More so every day. Still. He marveled at it.

Alec's mouth quirked, and he shifted his gaze to the hallway past Magnus.

"He's asleep," Magnus said, and kissed Alec's mouth. "Been asleep for hours." He moved to pull Alec toward the couch. Only a quick wiggle of his fingers, and the candles on the end table lit and the lamps dimmed.

Alec laughed, low in his chest. "We have a perfectly good bed, you know."

"Bed's closer to the kid's room. Quieter to stay here," Magnus murmured. "Also, we would have to kick Chairman Meow off the bed."

"Aw," said Alec, dipping his head to kiss the hollow of Magnus's throat. Magnus let his head fall back and allowed himself a little pleased moan. "He *hates* that."

"Hang on," said Magnus, stepping back. With a flourish, he divested himself of the robe, letting it fall into a pool of black silk around his feet. Underneath, he wore navy pajamas covered in small white anchors. Alec's eyes narrowed.

"Well, I didn't know this was happening, obviously," Magnus said. "Or I would have worn something sexier than my fuzzy sailor pajamas."

"They are plenty sexy," said Alec, and then both of them froze, because a sudden scream rent the air. Alec closed his eyes and exhaled slowly, and Magnus could tell he was mentally counting to ten.

"I'll go," said Alec.

"I'll go," said Magnus. "You just got home."

"No, no, I'll go. I want to see him anyway." Still only in his trousers, Alec padded toward the hall to Max's room. He looked over his shoulder at Magnus, shaking his head and smiling. "Never fails, huh."

"Kid's got a sixth sense," Magnus agreed. "Rain check?"

"Stay there."

Magnus opened a little Portal to Max's room to watch Alec pick up their son and rock him. Alec looked over at the Portal from his end and said, "Sure, that seems much easier than just walking down the hall."

"I was told to stay here."

Alec pointed at the Portal and said to Max, "Is that *bapak*? Do you see *bapak*?"

Magnus had wanted to be called something that felt true to his own childhood, but it always felt strange. His own father, the human one, had been *bapak*, and when he said it to Max, he felt a little twinge, as though he were walking on his father's grave.

Max quickly calmed—these days a scream was more likely to be a nightmare than anything requiring more than soothing—and blinked sleepy eyes at Magnus, who smiled and wiggled little glittery sparks from the ends of his fingers at his child. A smile broke on Max's face as his eyes drifted shut. He was already almost asleep again, one chubby blue arm flopping out to the side. Max's skin was deep blue—that was his warlock mark, along with adorable stubs that Magnus suspected would grow into horns. Alec returned him to his crib. Magnus watched, marveling at the strange happiness of his life now, as a beautiful, extremely fit man with no shirt and startlingly blue eyes cared for the baby they had together. He cursed his own sentimentality and tried to think sexy thoughts.

Alec looked up at him, and in the dim light Magnus could suddenly see how weary he looked. "I," Alec declared, "am going to go take a shower. Then I will return to you in the living room."

"Then probably another shower," said Magnus. "Hurry back." He closed the Portal and returned to his book, a study of Scandinavian mythological artifacts and their owners and locations through history. He planned to begin thinking sexy thoughts again when Alec got back.

Two minutes into Alec's shower, which, based on Alec's usual showers, was likely to last around twenty minutes, Max gave a sudden cry in his sleep. Magnus was immediately alert, and then, when no further sound came, relaxed again and returned to his reading.

A few minutes later, he heard footsteps in the hallway. Magnus turned around fast. He wasn't crazy; someone *had* been testing his wards and planning to break in.

When he saw who appeared in the doorway, his heart sank. No matter what she was here for, nobody was going to be having any romantic times tonight.

"Shinyun Jung," he said, affecting a blasé tone. "Are you here to try to kill me again?"

Shinyun Jung's warlock mark was a supernaturally still face, her expression blank and secret no matter what she was feeling. The last time Magnus had seen her, she had been tied to a marble pillar to restrain her, her plot to bring the Prince of Hell Asmodeus to power ruined. Magnus had sympathy for her—she had rage and pain inside her that he could understand all too well. And he had not been upset when she "somehow escaped" Alec's custody and they had not had to turn her over to the Clave.

Now she stood before Magnus, impassive as ever. "It took a great deal of time to break through your wards. They were very impressive."

"Not impressive enough," Magnus said.

Shinyun shrugged. "I needed to talk to you."

"We have a telephone," Magnus said. "You could have just called. It's not a great time, actually."

"I have some very, very good news," Shinyun said, which was not what Magnus had been expecting. "Also, I need the Book of the White. You will give it to me."

That was more what he had been expecting.

Magnus considered whether to go into an explanation of why, despite his wishing Shinyun all the best in her life, nevertheless he was wary of giving her one of the most powerful spell books in existence, because of everything he knew about her and all the things she had done. Instead he said, "I don't have it anymore. I gave it to the Spiral Labyrinth. But what is this good news?"

Before she could speak, a second figure stepped into the room from the hallway.

Magnus gasped.

Ragnor.

Ragnor, who had disappeared three years ago. Who had reassured Magnus he would be in touch soon. Magnus had waited, and then taken up an active search, and in the end he had concluded that Ragnor had been caught after all, that his ruse had failed, that he was dead in truth. Ragnor, who he had mourned for, and said good-bye to in his head, if not in his heart.

Ragnor, holding Max.

Magnus was rendered speechless. Under normal circumstances, he would have gone for his seventh-ever hug with Ragnor. But these weren't normal circumstances. Shinyun was here, and there was something very odd about the way Ragnor was looking at Magnus.

And the way he was holding Max. He held him indifferently, like a sack of flour. Max didn't seem to mind, actually. He was still mostly asleep and blinking very slowly.

"So," said Ragnor, more sharply than Magnus would have

expected, "I see this happened. I always assumed you'd end up with one of these somehow, Magnus. But is it wise?"

"*His* name is Max," Magnus said. He was just going to take this one moment at a time. "Someone had to take him in. So we did. He's ours. How did you get in, anyway?"

Ragnor chuckled, a familiar sound made eerie by its unexpected reappearance. "Magnus Bane. So great in power, so soft in heart. Always taking in the helpless and needy. You've got a whole little shelter here, between the Shadowhunter and this little blueberry."

Magnus was not sure that, given Ragnor's attitude, he had the right to call Max a blueberry. "It's not like that," he said. He looked over at Shinyun, who watched the exchange with silent interest. "We're a family."

"Of course you are," said Ragnor. His eyes glittered.

"So," Magnus said, "are you still fake dead? Or is this officially your return to life? Also, how do you know Shinyun? Also also, I think you should give me the baby."

Shinyun spoke up. "Ragnor and I are collaborating together on a project."

Alec was still in the shower. Magnus considered making a sudden loud noise, although he really wanted to get Max back from Ragnor before that. He decided to stall. "I hope you won't mind," he said, "if I ask you about the nature of that project. Last time I saw you, Shinyun, my boyfriend was releasing you from imprisonment, in the hope that you'd learned an important lesson about working with Greater Demons, Princes of Hell, and the like. Specifically, we hoped that you'd learned *not* to work with them in future." The category of Greater Demons was broad—it included many types of intelligent fiends. Princes of Hell were far more powerful—they were former angels who had fallen when they fought on the side of Lucifer in the rebellion.

"Obviously," said Shinyun with a haughty air, "I no longer serve a Greater Demon."

Magnus let out a slow breath of relief.

"I serve," said Shinyun, "the *Greatest* Demon!"

There was a pause.

"Capitalism?" hazarded Magnus. "You and Ragnor have started a small business and you're looking for investors."

"I serve the greatest of the Nine now," said Shinyun in a gloating, triumphant tone that Magnus remembered well and hadn't liked the first time around either. "The Maker of the Way! The Eater of Worlds! The Reaper of Souls!"

"The Wonder from Down Under?" suggested Magnus. "And Ragnor? Old buddy? Where are you on world-eating?"

"I've come around to being in favor of it," Ragnor said.

"I should have mentioned earlier," said Shinyun. "Ragnor is entirely under the thrall of my master. And my master has given him the gift of the Svefnthorn." From a scabbard at her side she drew a long, ugly iron spike, barbed along its blade and ending in a sharp point that was wickedly twisted like a corkscrew. It looked like a very goth fireplace poker.

Magnus's self-control snapped.

"Give me the baby, Ragnor," Magnus said. He got up and made for his friend.

"It's very simple, Magnus," said Ragnor, shielding Max from Magnus's grasp. "Sammael, ruler of Greater Demons, the greatest of the Princes of Hell, is inevitably guaranteed to finish the job he started a thousand years ago, briefly interrupted by the nuisance of the Shadowhunters, and rule this realm, as he has ruled others. The inevitability of his victory," he went on conversationally, "has—how should I put it—twisted my will with its nigh-infinite strength? Yes, that describes it quite well, I think."

"So faking your own death was basically pointless," said Magnus.

"Shinyun found me," Ragnor admitted. "She was very highly motivated."

Magnus had almost reached Ragnor, but Shinyun closed the distance shockingly quickly and held Magnus at Svefnthorn-point. Magnus stopped short and held up his hands in the classic pose of nonthreatening surrender. His heart was pounding. It was hard to concentrate while Ragnor had his hands on Max.

"You don't understand," Shinyun said. "We're not *stealing* the Book of the White from you. We're giving you something in exchange. Something even more valuable."

And with a jolt she jabbed the Svefnthorn into Magnus's chest.

It sank into his chest without any resistance from bone or muscle. Magnus felt no pain at all, nor any desire to move, even as the thorn pierced his heart. There was only a sort of terrible lassitude. He could sense his heart beating around the thorn. He didn't want to look down, didn't want to see it sticking out of his chest.

Part of him couldn't believe Ragnor was here, watching this. Watching, and not doing anything about it.

Shinyun leaned forward and gave Magnus a kiss on the cheek. She twisted the thorn a half-turn, like the dial on a safe, then withdrew it. It exited as painlessly as it had entered, leaving a trail of cold red flames emerging from his chest in its wake. Magnus touched the flames, which passed through his fingers harmlessly. The wound didn't hurt.

The lassitude was beginning to clear. "What have you done?" Magnus said.

"As I said," Shinyun said, "I've given you a great gift. The first part of it, anyway. And in exchange . . . we'll be taking the Book of the White."

"I told you—" Magnus began.

"Yes, but I knew you were lying," said Shinyun, "because I already have the Book. I retrieved it from your child's bedroom before I made myself known to you. As one would. If one were not stupid."

"Don't take it to heart, Magnus," Ragnor said sympathetically.

"Sammael's very will is bound up with the Book of the White, and his servants feel a constant pull toward its presence."

Magnus had not known that, in fact, and would probably have left the Book of the White somewhere safer than among a pile of his son's picture books if he had. "I could do things to stop you leaving with the Book," he said, and saw Ragnor's eyes narrow. "And also, Alec is here. But you put me at a disadvantage. Ragnor, give me Max, and you can leave with the Book."

"We would leave with the Book regardless," Shinyun said, but Ragnor, who had never had much of an appetite for a physical fight, nodded.

"No funny business," he said to Magnus.

"Of course not," said Magnus.

Ragnor came closer and handed the baby to Magnus, who carefully curled Max into the crook of his left arm. Then, in a sudden outburst of motion, he violently stabbed all five fingers of his right hand into Ragnor's chest, in the general vicinity of his heart. Instantly, through the flow of magic within Ragnor's body and into Magnus's hand, he could sense the presence of Sammael's control: a void, a place where the light of Ragnor's life-essence fell away into blackness. With an effort, trying not to disturb Max, he attempted to draw it out from Ragnor.

"That's funny business, Magnus!" yelled Shinyun. She was pointing the Svefnthorn at Ragnor, manipulating it in subtle movements.

Ragnor made a guttural noise deep in his chest as he struggled against Magnus. Then he tensed, and with a sudden strength cast Magnus away. Magnus was thrown back, lost his footing, and managed to fall onto the sofa behind him, cradling Max. The landing was soft, all things considered, but the fall was certainly surprising enough for Max to wake and immediately burst into tears.

All the adults in the room stopped short where they were. Very quietly Ragnor said, "Don't feel bad, Magnus. The power granted to me by my fealty to Sammael is more than you, or any warlock, could overcome."

"Ragnor!" Shinyun hissed. "Quiet! The baby—"

She shrieked. And fell suddenly to the ground, the shaft of an arrow jutting from her calf. It was so surprising that Max fell silent again.

"Stay where you are!" Alec yelled from the end of the hallway. Ragnor turned to gaze down the hallway with an expression of genuine, curious surprise.

Magnus ought to involve himself in the melee, he knew, but he was sprawled on his couch underneath his infant son. With some effort he began the elaborate movements necessary to stand up and not drop Max. He considered, not for the first time, teleporting his child, and rejected the idea as not safe. He didn't have time to get a Portal open. Maybe if he floated Max to the ceiling . . .

His thoughts were interrupted by the telltale sound and shimmer of Shinyun opening a Portal of her own. Magnus had foolishly assumed she was out of the fight, and Ragnor was already making a beeline for the Portal. There was no way Magnus could catch him in time.

But then Magnus beheld a truly glorious sight. Like a Greek god, Alec stepped into view, his hair wildly out of sorts from the shower, still dripping with water. He had a white towel wrapped around his waist, a leather cord around his neck with a Lightwood ring hanging from it, a huge Sure-Strike rune on his chest, absolutely nothing else on, and an arrow fully nocked in the beautifully polished oak recurve bow that normally hung decoratively on the bedroom wall. It was like something from a Renaissance painting.

Magnus knew that Alec often worried that he was too ordinary for Magnus, that compared to the wonders Magnus had seen in hundreds of years, he must seem comparatively mundane. Magnus did not think Alec understood what it was like to behold, up close, a Shadowhunter in full warrior mode.

It was a lot.

Snapping back to the situation at hand, Magnus noted that Shinyun was already gone through the Portal and Ragnor was now entering it. Magnus, meanwhile, had gotten to his feet and was holding Max in front of him. He needed his hands free to do magic, but he didn't want to let go of his child.

An arrow flew. It missed Ragnor by a hair, but tore a scrap from the back of the warlock's cloak as the Portal closed around him.

There was a sudden silence. Alec turned to Magnus, who was holding and rocking Max. Max had gone quiet.

"Was that Ragnor Fell?" Alec looked stunned. "With Shinyun Jung?" Alec had never met Ragnor, but there were plenty of photos, sketches, and even one large oil painting of the warlock among Magnus's belongings.

"That's exactly who it was," Magnus said into the silence.

Alec crossed the room and crouched down to retrieve the arrow and the scrap of cloth it had pinned to the floor. When he looked up at Magnus, his expression was somber. "But Ragnor Fell is dead."

"No," said Magnus. He shook his head, suddenly exhausted. "Ragnor lives."

CHAPTER TWO

Between Air and Angels

WHILE MAGNUS RETURNED MAX TO BED, ALEC WENT TO put some clothes on. His whole body was still tensed, full of adrenaline and anxiety; he was unsure of what had just happened in his home, or what it meant. Magnus had talked about Ragnor mostly as a figure from his past—his mentor, his teacher, his fellow traveler among the Shadowhunters at various points. He remembered the stoic calm with which Magnus had reacted to Ragnor's death three years ago. At the time, he'd assumed it represented Magnus's great existential wisdom, born of a life lived through so many deaths.

Now he wasn't so sure. When he heard Magnus come into the bedroom behind him he pulled a T-shirt on over his boxers and said, "So you knew about Ragnor? Being alive?"

"Sort of," said Magnus.

Alec waited.

"I knew he was planning to fake his own death, but—he had promised to be in touch. And he had been in deadly danger. That's why he'd gone into hiding. When weeks passed, months, a year, two years, I assumed something had gone badly wrong."

"So first you thought he wasn't dead," said Alec. He turned to face Magnus, who looked oddly vulnerable and uncertain. He'd put the black robe back on. "And then you thought he *was* dead?"

"It was the obvious conclusion," said Magnus. "And I was right, in a way—he *had* been caught. Just by Shinyun." He looked at Alec with intensity. "He was holding Max," he said quietly. He came over and sat on the end of the bed. "I didn't—that's the first—"

He took a moment and then spoke again, the quaver gone from his voice. "There is something quite marvelous about having a child," he said. "In times of danger, it does focus the mind very well."

Alec went over to Magnus and put his hands on his boyfriend's shoulders. "It isn't just us anymore."

"I had to hold it together," said Magnus. "I *had* to. I had no other option. So I did. Otherwise I would be very shaken up right now."

Alec gave him a wry smile. "Because Ragnor Fell is alive? Because Shinyun Jung is back in our lives? Because they're working together? Because they took the Book of the White?"

"Actually," said Magnus mildly, shrugging off his pajama top and robe, "because Shinyun stabbed me with a mythological stick and I don't know what it's done."

Alec looked. There was a fissure in Magnus's chest, from which flowered wisps of scarlet flame that dissipated as soon as they appeared. He wondered why Magnus was not more concerned. He himself was very, very concerned. Before speaking, he bent down and grabbed his trousers from the floor.

"It's called a Svefnthorn, apparently," said Magnus. The lightness of his tone set Alec's teeth on edge. What was wrong with Magnus? Was he in shock? "Why are you putting on your pants?" he asked.

Alec held up the cell phone he'd just withdrawn from his pocket. "I'm calling Catarina."

"Oh, don't bother her in the middle of the night—" Magnus began. Alec held up a finger to silence him.

A voice still half-buried in sleep came over the phone. "Alec?"

"I'm so sorry to wake you up," Alec said in a rush. "But—it's Magnus. He's been stabbed by a . . . well, by a big thorn, I guess. Something demonic, definitely. And now he's got a magical fissure in his chest and there's a light coming out of it."

When she spoke again, Catarina sounded completely awake and alert. "I'll be there in ten minutes. Don't let him do anything." She hung up.

"She says don't do anything," Alec told him.

"Excellent news," said Magnus. He put his robe back on and lay down on the bed. "That was already my plan."

Alec grabbed the arrow from where it lay discarded on his nightstand and pulled the scrap of cloth from it.

He'd missed Ragnor with the arrow on purpose. Even in his panic, his rage that his home had been invaded and Max and Magnus threatened, he had recognized the green-skinned warlock as one of Magnus's oldest friends. He couldn't hurt him.

So he'd gone for a piece of his cloak instead. He closed his hand around it now.

"I'm going to try to Track Ragnor."

Magnus's eyes were half-closed. "Good idea. Great initiative."

"What do you think they want with the Book of the White?" Alec said. He drew a quick Tracking rune on the back of his hand with his stele. He felt the bit of cloak seem to come alive inside his fist, the strange tickle in the back of his mind that said the rune was working to locate Ragnor Fell.

After a moment, Magnus, eyes still closed, said, "No idea. To practice dark magic in Sammael's name, I assume. Any news?"

"Yes," said Alec. "He's to the west."

"How far to the west?"

Alec frowned, concentrating. "Very far."

Magnus opened his eyes. "Hang on." He got up from the bed with an unexpected alacrity, considering how fatigued he'd looked a moment ago, and went into a desk drawer across the room. He waved a folded paper with excitement. "Here we have an excellent opportunity for warlock-Shadowhunter collaboration. You come here with your rune, and—" He unfolded what turned out to be a map of New York City across the surface of the bed and wiggled his fingers around over it. Then he grabbed Alec's wrist and wiggled his fingers under that. Then he leaned over and kissed the back of Alec's hand.

Alec smiled. "How does it feel to kiss an active rune?"

"There's a little scent of heavenly fire, but otherwise it's nice," Magnus said. "Now what do you have, my noble tracker?"

Alec concentrated over the map. "Um, well, he's to the west of this whole map."

"Be right back." Magnus left the room; in a few moments he returned and laid an unfolded map of the whole Northeast over the other map.

"West of all this," Alec said apologetically.

Magnus came back with a map of the entire United States.

"West," said Alec. He and Magnus exchanged a look. Magnus left again and this time came back struggling with a gigantic globe of the earth, easily two feet in diameter.

"Magnus," said Alec. "That's a bar." He opened the globe at the hinge, revealing four crystal decanters inside.

"It's still a globe," Magnus said, closing it. Alec shrugged and began to move his fist slowly over the globe's surface. When it came to rest, Magnus squinted to get a look. "Eastern China. Along the coast. Looks like . . . Shanghai."

"Shanghai?" said Alec. "Why would Ragnor and Shinyun be in Shanghai?"

"No reason I can think of," Magnus said. "Maybe that makes it a good hiding place."

"What about Sammael?"

Magnus shook his head. "The last time Sammael walked the earth, Shanghai was a small fishing village. There's no connection between them that I know of." His dressing gown gaped open as he leaned over the globe, and Alec stared again at the place where Magnus's skin had split open, a grotesque wound, but with no blood, only that eerie light. Magnus caught him looking and primly gathered the collar at his throat. "It's fine."

Alec threw up his hands. "Aren't you concerned at all?" he said. "You have a stab wound. The stab wound is leaking weird magic. That's serious business. You're like Jace sometimes. It doesn't make you weaker to accept help, you know." He softened. "I'm just worried about you, Magnus."

"Well, I haven't become the thrall of Sammael, if that's what you're worried about," said Magnus. He stretched his arms and legs. "I feel *fine*. I just need some high-quality sleep. We'll let Catarina confirm that everything's okay, and then tomorrow morning we'll go to Shanghai, track down Ragnor and Shinyun, and get the Book back. Easy."

"We will *not*," said Alec.

"Well, *someone* has to," Magnus said reasonably.

"We're not going just the two of us. We need backup."

"But—"

"No," said Alec, and Magnus stopped, though he remained smiling. "What happens if I need runes? What happens if Shinyun and Ragnor are too powerful with the Book for us to take on by ourselves? And hey—are we taking Max with us? Because I don't think we are."

"I sort of hoped Catarina could watch him," Magnus said. "For the brief time we'll be gone."

"Magnus," said Alec. "I know you want to solve every problem yourself. I know you hate looking vulnerable—"

"I have help," Magnus said. "I have you."

"I will do everything in my power," said Alec, "and there are lots of things we can do as just us."

"Some of my favorite things," Magnus put in, waggling his eyebrows.

"But this could be serious. If we go, we go with backup. I won't go otherwise."

Magnus opened his mouth to object, but at that moment, mercifully, the doorbell buzzed, announcing Catarina's arrival. Alec opened the door for her, and she strode straight past him without a word. She was wearing blue scrubs almost the same color as her skin, and her white hair was pulled back in a messy ponytail. As Alec followed her back toward the bedroom, she said, "How long ago did it happen?"

"Not long," said Alec. "Twenty minutes, maybe. He says he's fine."

"He *always* says he's fine," said Catarina. She went into the bedroom and barked, "Take that hideous silk thing off, Magnus, let's see this injury." She paused. "Also, why is your bed covered in maps?"

"It's a perfectly nice robe," said Magnus. "And we were planning a post-stabbing vacation."

"We were attacked by Shinyun Jung, the warlock we met in Europe a few years ago," Alec said. "We were Tracking—anyway, we found out where she is. Looks like Shanghai."

Catarina nodded; it was clear to Alec this meant nothing to her. He wondered if Magnus was going to mention Ragnor. It was, he thought, definitely up to Magnus whether to share that news. He looked at Magnus, who said only, "She did it with something she called a Svefnthorn."

"Never heard of it," Catarina said. "But isn't this whole apartment full of books about magic?"

Alec said, a little defensively, "I didn't want to start looking through books before I knew whether Magnus was okay."

"I'm great," said Magnus, as Catarina prodded at his temples and then peered closely into one of his eyes.

Alec watched nervously as Catarina examined Magnus. After a few minutes, she sighed. "My official diagnosis is that this wound is definitely not good, and I don't know how to make it go away. On the other hand, it doesn't seem to be directly harming you at the moment."

"So what you're saying," said Magnus, "is that in your professional opinion, there's no reason for us not to go directly to Shanghai to find Shinyun and get this cleared up."

"I am *not* saying that," said Catarina. "Alec can do some research in your library and the Institute's library, and I will look at my own sources in the morning and see what I can find. You should *definitely not* go haring off to Shanghai with a glowing magical hole in your chest."

Magnus put up a bit more of a fuss, but in the end, as Alec had known he would, he deferred to Catarina's wisdom. Once Magnus had promised to take her assessment of the situation seriously, she sighed, ruffled his hair, and headed out.

Alec walked Catarina to the door, where she gave him a long look. "Magnus Bane," she said, "is like a cat."

Alec raised his eyebrows.

"He'll never let you know how much pain he's in. He'll put on a brave face, even to his own detriment." She put her hand on Alec's shoulder. "I'm glad you're here to take care of him now. I worry about him a little less these days."

"If you think I can make Magnus do what I say," Alec said with a smile, "you have been sadly misinformed. He'll listen to me, but he does what he likes. I guess that's another way he's like a cat."

Catarina nodded and said, deadpan, "Also, he has cat eyes."

Alec gave her a quick hug. "Good night, Catarina."

Back in the bedroom, Alec found Magnus with his robe back on, digging around under the bed. "What are you doing?" Alec cried.

"Obviously," said Magnus, eyes gleaming, "we are haring off to Shanghai to find Shinyun and Ragnor."

"No, we are *not*," said Alec. "You promised Catarina you'd take this injury seriously."

"I am," said Magnus. "I'm feeling very seriously that getting hold of Shinyun and Ragnor is the best way to start healing up."

"Maybe," said Alec. "But right now, we are getting the four hours of sleep we can get before Max wakes up."

Magnus looked mutinous, but then sighed and sat back down on the edge of the bed. "Hell. We didn't ask Catarina if she would watch Max while we're gone."

"Another reason to wait for morning. We can figure out the plan for Max and gather at least a *little* information before we go." Alec waited a moment and then said, carefully, "We could be gone for days, you know."

Magnus hesitated, then nodded in acceptance. "That's true. Okay. Tomorrow morning we see who can watch Max for . . . for days." He gave Alec an incredulous look that he knew well by now, as it was a look that he gave Magnus too. It was a look that said, *How is this our life? How is it so strange, and difficult, and exhausting, and wonderful?*

"How has this not come up before?" Alec said. "Having to find someone to watch Max?"

"Well, things have been quiet," said Magnus.

He was right. It had been a relatively peaceful year—aside from the Cold Peace, of course, which continued to loom over all of Downworld. They had both barely been called away from New York, and certainly not overnight. They had left Max with others, but only for a few hours—a Conclave meeting, a fight breaking out somewhere locally, Downworlder politics gone awry. They had never been away from Max for longer than that. Max had never gone to sleep without them there.

Through force of will, Alec stopped his train of thought before it got too far out of the station. "We will make a plan for Max," he said, "in four hours." He threw himself onto the bed and reached out to pull Magnus down next to him. The warlock lay on his side, and Alec curled himself around Magnus, feeling a long exhale leave Magnus's body as they nestled comfortably together.

The thrum of tension in Alec's stomach slowed and eventually came to a rest. By the time Chairman Meow appeared from under the bed and perched smugly on top of Magnus's hip, Magnus's breathing was even and low. Alec planted a soft kiss on the top of his boyfriend's head and allowed himself, too, to finally sleep.

IN HIS DREAM MAGNUS RULED OVER A RUINED WORLD. He sat on a golden throne at the top of a million golden stairs, calling orders in a language he didn't understand to scurrying gray creatures far below him. He was so high that clouds floated by on the stairs below his throne, and beyond the stairs he could see the sun, bloated and red, reflected in flames on the surface of a vast flat ocean.

No other people were there. Other than the bedraggled, beaked gray things that lurched below him, he was alone. Slowly he stood up and walked, curious, down a few of the stairs. He thought that if he descended far enough, he would be able to see himself reflected in the ocean below.

He kept walking down the stairs, although when he glanced over his shoulder the throne barely seemed to recede behind him. Eventually he looked down at the surface of the sea and beheld himself. He was gigantic, he realized—fifty feet tall, a hundred feet tall. His cat's eyes were huge and luminous. There was no sign of the wound in his chest that the Svefnthorn had made. Instead the skin of his chest was rough, textured, thick like the hide of an animal. He raised his hands up in front of him, palms out, and noted with some interest the huge curving claws at the ends of his fingers.

"What is this for?" he yelled. "Why would I be in this place?"

The gray creatures all stopped as one and turned to gaze at him. They spoke to him, but he couldn't understand them. They seemed either to greatly love him or to be greatly frightened of him. He couldn't tell which. He didn't want either.

MAGNUS KNEW HE HAD SLEPT LATE WHEN HE AWOKE AND saw the angle of the sunlight on the wall. He found the other side of the bed empty and concluded that Alec had decided to let him sleep in before their departure.

He found his robe, blinked the sleep from his eyes, and went into the kitchen, where Jace Herondale was pouring coffee into Magnus's I'M KIND OF A BIG DEAL mug.

Magnus was glad he had not wandered out into the kitchen naked. "Don't you have your own coffeepot?" he said blearily.

Jace, blond hair in its usual, preternaturally excellent state, flashed him a winning smile that Magnus was not prepared to deal with before he, too, had some coffee. "I hear you got stabbed by a weird Norwegian thorn," Jace said. "Also, do you have any soy milk? Clary's doing a whole soy milk thing now."

"What are you doing in my apartment?" said Magnus.

"Well," said Jace, now rummaging in the fridge, "I'd like to think I'd be welcome anytime, what with my close relationship with all three of you. But in this case, Alec called us. Said something about Shanghai."

"Who is *us*?" Magnus said suspiciously.

Jace waved his coffee cup around. "Us! You know. All of us."

"*All* of you?" Magnus repeated. He held up a hand. "Wait. Stop. I am going to go put on something more substantial than a robe. You are going to use your angelic powers to pour me as large a mug of black coffee as you can find, and I will be right back, and then we can talk about terrible concepts like who 'all of us' are, and what Alec told you about last night."

When he entered the living room, now suitably dressed, he found Alec, arms folded, looking long-suffering. In the far corner of the room, next to the ceiling, Max floated, tumbling in the air. He didn't seem to be in peril—indeed, he was yelling, "*Wheeeeeeeeeee*," and appeared to be having an excellent time. Under him, Clary Fairchild and Isabelle Lightwood attempted to nudge him back to the ground with a broom handle. With her free hand, Clary was waving a red braid, trying to get Max interested as though he were Chairman Meow. Max was upside down and obviously feeling good about it. Everyone other than Isabelle was in T-shirts and jeans, but she, of course, had shown up in a fitted black sweater over a tiered velvet maxi skirt. She was one of the few people who could occasionally make Magnus feel underdressed.

He went over to Alec. "Antigravity spell, I bet," he said.

"He knows it drives us crazy. He's loving Clary and Isabelle right now." Alec seemed both annoyed and admiring, a tone of voice Magnus had not realized he would so closely associate with having a child.

"I thought we were haring off to Shanghai," Magnus said quietly.

"We are," said Alec. "But I told you. If we're going to be fighting evil warlocks, we can't go alone. I called Jace this morning."

"And invited the whole gang?" The door opened and Simon Lovelace entered. He was wearing a black T-shirt that said, in large white bubble letters, GOOD LUCK WITH YOUR THING. But he had an unexpected look on his face—distracted, unhappy—and Magnus wondered why.

Maybe it was just the weight of the last few years on his shoulders. Even among their group, Simon had been through a lot. He'd been a mundane, been a vampire, been in Shadowhunter prison, become invulnerable, killed the Mother of Demons, met the Angel Raziel, lost his memories, gotten them back, and graduated from Shadowhunter Academy, and they'd all expected that would be it—a happily ever after for Simon.

But it hadn't turned out that way. Four months ago, Simon had indeed gone through the ritual of Ascension to become a full-fledged Shadowhunter. And what should have been a time of triumph and celebration for all of them had turned tragic, as Simon's closest friend at the Academy, George Lovelace, had died during the ritual. Died horribly, as a matter of fact, in front of all of them. The memory sprang to his mind unbidden, of Simon throwing himself hopelessly at George's burning body and being held back by Catarina. Simon had taken George's name in honor of his memory.

Considering this, Magnus had to admit it was actually stranger to see Simon break into a wryly amused smile as he took in the situation at the far end of the room. He ran to help Clary and Isabelle, and Magnus gave Alec a look. "So, the *whole* gang?"

"Well," Alec said, "Jace thought Clary should come, and that seemed fine to me. And then Clary suggested that Simon should come along as well—he's her *parabatai*, after all, and with demon activity being pretty minimal these days, he could use some more on-the-ground experience. And then Isabelle found out and she was offended that I hadn't asked her first thing, and said she was coming too."

Magnus had to wonder whether it was wise for Simon to come along on this trip, and why Clary had insisted. She knew better than anyone, except maybe Isabelle, how Simon was doing, and it was obvious that he wasn't doing well. He would have to remember to ask her about it later.

For now he clapped his hands, very loudly, and the three Shadow-hunters stopped in their tracks. Simon was holding on to Max's arm as Max hung upside down above him, laughing delightedly. "All Shadowhunters in my house," he called out. "If one of you would please put your hands out to catch my son, I'm going to deal with the spell. And where's the blond kid with my coffee?"

Magnus quickly annulled his son's spell with a few gestures, and Max returned to the ground (where he immediately crawled over to Alec and threw his arms around Alec's leg in excitement). Jace returned from the kitchen with the promised coffee, and Magnus finally sat down on the couch. "All right, so what's going on?" he asked.

Isabelle raised her eyebrows. "First—does that happen with Max a lot?"

Magnus shrugged. "Not a *lot*. Warlock babies do some magic sometimes. By accident."

"It's not so bad," Alec said. "You just keep more extra clothes around, and you keep a fire extinguisher close by."

Jace hopped up to sit on the window ledge, somehow managing not to spill any of his coffee. "I thought you were changing."

"I did change," Magnus said, puzzled.

"You're still wearing a robe," Jace said.

"I was wearing a *yukata*," said Magnus. "Now I'm wearing a dressing gown."

"Well, they both look like robes," said Jace.

"Let's talk about last night," Magnus said. "What did Alec tell you?"

"Can we see the glowing fissure in your chest?" Simon asked.

"Simon, it's rude to bring up glowing fissures in other people's chests," said Clary. "What do you think they want with the Book of the White, Magnus?"

Magnus turned to look at Alec. "So, you told them everything? Did you say the *S*-word? The *R*-word?"

Alec rolled his eyes. "If you're asking if I told them about Shinyun and Ragnor, I did."

"So you knew Ragnor wasn't dead, that day I came to his house in Idris?" Clary said. "When I was with—with Sebastian? You lied to us?"

"I had to," said Magnus. "I couldn't risk anyone tracking Ragnor down and hurting him." He looked at the ceiling. "But then he dropped out of contact and I thought he was dead anyway."

"How do you feel now?" said Clary. She looked concerned, more so than Magnus would have expected.

"I feel fine," he said, and realized he was telling the truth. He felt good, even, as if he'd had a full night's sleep and a proper breakfast instead of barely any sleep and Jace's too-strong black coffee. "That's not me putting on a brave face," he felt obligated to add. "I really do feel good. I'm not *happy* to have a magical glowing chest wound, but it doesn't seem to be doing me any harm. Other than the aesthetics, of course."

Simon looked up from where he had gotten down on the floor with Max. "It's kind of working for you, actually. Adds to your overall mystique."

"What Alec told us," said Isabelle, "is that Ragnor Fell is alive, he's working with that warlock you dealt with in Europe a few years ago, and they took the Book of the White to do something that will be good for whatever Greater Demon they're working with."

"And therefore bad for us," put in Simon.

"Bad for the earth," said Magnus.

"That's bad for us," Simon confirmed. "We live here."

"Did you tell them which demon it is?" Magnus demanded of Alec. To the others he went on, "What does the name Sammael mean to you?"

There was a silence. "Oh," said Jace. "That's why you called," he added to Alec, who nodded.

"He's a Prince of Hell, right?" said Clary.

"A *long-dead* Prince of Hell," said Jace. "He was the consort of Lilith. Pity they missed each other by a few years." Lilith's power was much diminished since the Dark War, shattered by the Mark of Cain while Simon bore it. Little had been seen of her since.

"He's more than that," said Simon quietly. He was looking at the floor, very unlike himself, and Magnus figured he was recalling his ordeal with Lilith. "Remember, I only got out of the Academy a few months ago. I've studied this stuff more recently than any of you." He rose to his feet and leaned against the wall, as if he needed bracing for what he was about to say. "Sammael is the oldest of the Princes of Hell, other than Lucifer himself. He is supposed to have been the Serpent in the Garden of Eden. He's known as the Father of Demons, just like Lilith is called the Mother."

"Everyone's got father issues," said Jace. "Even demons."

Simon ignored him. "Shadowhunter history teaches that for thousands of years before the Shadowhunters, demons would make their way to our world, but only occasionally, and in tiny numbers. Sammael changed that. He did something—we don't know what—that weakened the barriers between our world and the demon worlds. Sammael opened the path for demons to invade Earth. And when he came himself, devastation followed him.

"He couldn't be defeated by any human being, no matter how powerful. So the story says the angels themselves intervened, and the Archangel Michael came down and defeated Sammael—"

Jace was nodding and picked up the narrative. "And Raziel came down and created *us*. But nobody could undo what Sammael had done, so the walls between the worlds remain thin and demons keep coming."

"I guess defeating Sammael at least prevented the problem from getting worse," said Clary. "I know Princes of Hell can't be killed—"

"The blow that defeated him was dealt by an Archangel," said Magnus. "I think everyone at least *hoped* it might actually kill him. Seems not."

"How do we get Michael to come back and defeat him again?" said Isabelle. "It'd buy us another thousand years."

"We can't," said Simon. "We're on our own. That's the whole thing with us, right? Shadowhunters. The angels aren't here to deal with our problems. It's just us."

He looked grim. Magnus felt a stab of renewed concern for Simon. He'd been fighting demons just as long as Clary had, had been a Downworlder himself, had been face-to-face with Raziel, and through all of it Magnus had grown impressed with his morale, his willingness to persevere and keep a brave face even when the situation seemed worse than impossible. Simon had faced down Lilith and walked away—why was just the idea of Sammael enough to rattle him now?

Simon had wanted to become a Shadowhunter so badly, to fight demons directly, to be a colleague to Clary, to Isabelle, to all of them. But just now, he didn't look like it had been good for him.

"I know I'm the guy acting casual about a magical hole in my chest," said Magnus, "but can I provide some context here that might make us feel a little better? Shinyun and Ragnor mentioned Sammael, but other than this weapon Shinyun has, which she claims is his, we have no idea whether Sammael is even coming back. Shinyun and Ragnor could be involved with a mundane cult, or a Greater Demon pretending to be Sammael. The important thing is, Sammael is definitely, *definitely* not in our world. If he was, we'd know. He'd be doing things. Armies of demons would be ravaging the planet. And they're not." He smiled brightly. He really was feeling surprisingly positive about the situation. "So Alec and I will go to Shanghai, and we'll track down Ragnor and Shinyun, and we'll get the Book of the White back, and everything will be great."

"So what you're saying," Isabelle said slowly, "is that the good news is that Sammael hasn't destroyed Earth *yet*?"

"Even if it is the real Sammael, we probably have *days* to stop him!" Magnus said.

Clary and Isabelle exchanged worried looks.

Alec also looked worried. "Um, so, Magnus, who's going to look after Max for *days*?"

Magnus waved his hands at the assembled group. "Some of these fine people."

"Are you kidding?" said Clary, jumping up. "Obviously we're all going to Shanghai. This is a big-deal situation, right? You need the whole team."

Jace looked amused. "Sure. It can't possibly be that you're bored patrolling New York and want to go someplace new."

"Okay, I am," Clary admitted. "But *also* we have to stop the Father of Demons from, you know—fathering more demons, I guess."

"A *lot* more demons," said Simon. "Why not? Let's go fight two powerful warlocks and a demon so bad it took an angel to kill him last time. I'm sure all my classroom experience will come in handy."

Isabelle came over and affectionately tousled Simon's hair. "Sure, sweetie, you're just a newbie. You were never an invulnerable Daylighter vampire who's been to a hell dimension or anything."

"You'll note the word 'invulnerable,'" Simon grumbled, but he smiled a little, at least.

Magnus stood up and clapped his hands. "All right, my lovelies. Alec and I will need to pack our things and figure out what we're doing with this one." He gestured at Max, who Jace had hoisted onto his shoulders. Dutifully Jace put Max back on the ground. "You all no doubt need to return to the Institute to collect your gear, so—" He waved his arms. "Get out of my house."

* * *

THEY HAD ALL LEFT BUT CLARY. ALEC HAD TAKEN MAX into the bedroom, and Magnus was headed to join them when Clary suddenly grabbed his arm and said, in a quiet but intense tone, "I need to talk to you for a moment."

Magnus regarded her. It was so strange to see her now, a proper adult. For years, she had been a quiet, wide-eyed child whom he'd met over and over for the first time. She knew nothing of the Shadow World—and it had been Magnus's job to make sure that remained true. And so when her mother would bring her over, she always had the same reaction—awe, uncertainty. Each time, she noticed his eyes, luminous and slit-pupiled—each time, he expected her to be frightened, but she was only ever curious. When she got old enough, she would ask him, "Why do you have cat eyes?" He got to try out plenty of responses.

"I traded them with my cat. Now he has human eyes."

"The better to see you with, my dear."

"Why do you *not* have cat eyes?"

It was strange to know that Clary didn't share those memories. To have watched someone grow up without them remembering it. Until, of course, the day he saw her at Chairman Meow's birthday party, surrounded by New York's Shadowhunters, and without warning, transformed into the warrior she had been born to be, already the spitting image of Jocelyn at her age.

Now she looked uneasy, as though she was thinking about how to deliver bad news. A few years ago she would just have blurted it out, but now she was his friend and she was concerned about his feelings. It was nice, but strange.

She said, "I had a dream about you, this morning. Just before Alec's call woke us up."

"A funny dream?" Magnus said hopefully. "And *not* an ominous, prophetic dream, right?"

"I stopped having those after the Dark War, so I hope not. You seemed to be having a good time, actually," said Clary. "You were on a big golden throne."

"I had that dream too," said Magnus. "At the top of lots of stairs? I was being attended by gray creatures with beaks?"

"No," said Clary, looking concerned. "But you had become a hundred-foot-tall monster."

Magnus nodded thoughtfully. "Are we talking a Godzilla-type situation?"

"More like a . . . demon situation. You had huge sharp teeth, and long claws coming out of your fingers. There was something wrong with your eyes. And there was—" She paused. "There was a red fire, in the shape of an X, burning from within your chest."

"Well," said Magnus heavily. "I have some good news. There is only one line of fire burning on my chest right now, not an X. Prophetic dream understood. Avoid getting another cut in the shape of an X. Excellent advice."

"There's more," said Clary. "The confusing part."

"So far, this has been very straightforward," agreed Magnus.

"You were in chains. Like, in *lots* of chains. Your legs were chained to the ground, your arms and your shoulders and your waist all chained to the wall. Huge chains, with huge iron links. You were weighed down by them. It was amazing you weren't literally crushed to death under their weight."

Magnus had to admit that did seem bad.

"But here's the thing," Clary said. "You didn't look like you were in pain. Or even bothered. You looked happy. More than happy. You looked ecstatic. You looked . . . triumphant."

She fixed her gaze on Magnus. "I don't know what it means. Like I said—I don't have prophetic dreams anymore. Usually. But I thought I should tell you anyway."

"Better safe than sorry," said Magnus. "I hope it's totally abstract, like, I will be sad, but happy about being sad. Something like that. Rather than involving actual iron chains or having bigger teeth."

"Well, here's hoping," said Clary.

"Run along to the Institute," Magnus said. "I should go check on my family."

Clary departed, and Magnus, uneasy for the first time since the morning, went to find Alec and their son and hold them close for a moment. Just to warm himself up.

CHAPTER THREE

A Brief Farewell

ALEC WAS GETTING A LITTLE FRUSTRATED. HE'D CALLED Catarina and asked if she could look after Max for a couple of days, only to find out that she was working double shifts at the hospital and would barely be home (though she did agree to stop in and feed Chairman Meow in the evenings). He'd called Maia, who turned out to be hosting friends of Bat's. He'd considered, but rejected, calling Lily. Lily often spoke of how Max was "so delicious" that she just wanted "to eat him up," and while Alec trusted Lily, he was not completely sure she was speaking figuratively.

"What about your mother?" Magnus said. He had put Max into an iridescent magical bubble and was rolling him around the bedroom while Alec fetched suitcases from the back of their closet.

"What? No," Alec said. He watched Max for a moment. "Is he in a magical hamster ball?"

"No! Well, kind of, yes," said Magnus. "He likes it. Why *not* your mother?"

"This kid floats up to the ceiling sometimes," said Alec. "He sets a blanket on fire in his sleep every three weeks or so."

"Another advantage of the magical hamster ball," said Magnus. "Magic shield. I didn't want Max knocking out the neighbors' cable again."

"Well, my mother doesn't *have* a magical hamster ball," said Alec.

Magnus rolled Max out into the hallway, to squeals of delight, and called back, "She's a Shadowhunter! She's supposed to be able to handle warlocks. She raised you!" He ducked his head back into the bedroom and raised his eyebrows. "She raised *Jace*."

"All right!" said Alec, laughing. "You win. I'll call her."

IT TOOK THEM TWENTY MINUTES TO PACK THEIR THINGS, and then two hours to assemble Max's gear, which was strewn all over the apartment. It hadn't seemed like a lot of stuff, but when it was all in one place, it made quite a haul: his stroller, his Pack 'n Play, a huge stack of clothes, a cardboard box of baby food, and a black satchel into which Magnus stuffed a few of Max's favorite picture books and toys, and also some components for the more useful wards to handle Max's accidental magic.

Eventually, after fishing a recalcitrant Chairman Meow out of the satchel, where he'd gone to sleep, they departed and made their way to the Institute.

The New York Institute was a solemn stone castle amid towers of metal and glass. Magnus liked the churches of New York, the way they carved a hushed and sacred space into the bustle of the city. Maybe that was why he had always found the self-seriousness of the Shadowhunters oddly charming. They tended to be flippant about it if you asked—even Alec—but the Institute was a reminder, even when it would be easy to forget, that theirs was a divine assignment.

It could be both good and bad that warlocks were so much more idiosyncratic and disorganized. Even the idea of High Warlocks had started as a joke, an affectation among the rare warlocks of the sixteenth and seventeenth centuries who were able to achieve some prestige in the mundane society that mostly rejected them as monsters. Magnus would estimate that a good half of the "High Warlocks" in the world today had appointed themselves to the position. Even cities with a long history of High Warlocks, like London, still mostly named them as a result of dares at parties.

Magnus was, in fact, one of those self-appointed warlocks; the whole joke about his being the High Warlock of Brooklyn was that no other New York borough had a High Warlock at all. He'd hoped to popularize the idea, but so far nobody had stepped up, except for a young woman with a unicorn horn sticking out of her forehead who had declared herself the "Medium Warlock," also of Brooklyn. But over the years, he'd come to feel it as a kind of real responsibility. And the Shadowhunters, he'd learned fast, were *thrilled* to have a warlock they could reliably call upon—even the Lightwoods, who, when they came to run the Institute in New York, Magnus had known only as members of a famous Shadowhunter hate group. And Magnus, for his part, was thrilled to have a steady, recurring revenue stream.

When he'd heard they were coming, Magnus took a deep breath, added a 15 percent "Nuisance Fee" to his already monstrous rates, and, when it was absolutely necessary, breezed into the Institute and tried to keep things light. *How have you been; lovely non-apocalyptic weather we're having; enjoy this beautiful spell you don't deserve; please pay my absurdly high bill promptly; am I providing regular protection spells for fugitives in hiding from the Nephilim? Why, no!*

It was strange to walk into that same Institute, with a Lightwood next to him, holding their child. To have Maryse Lightwood as something more like family and less like a business partner he could never fully trust. He was glad that Robert, at least, was busy with Inquisitor business in Idris. Inquisiting some folks, he assumed.

The entrance hall of the Institute stretched high above them, silent and dim and imposing. It always seemed to Magnus that the small group of Shadowhunters who lived here really rattled around the place. He knew it well, but in the manner that he might know a hotel lobby he'd passed through many times. It was not his place, and despite the efforts of the Lightwoods and Jace to make him feel comfortable here, he remained almost unconsciously on guard. Three years of close collaboration and friendship with the local Shadowhunters did not erase decades of more tense times spent here.

For one thing, it meant that he whispered to Alec, even though there was no reason at all to whisper. It just felt true to the aesthetics of the place. "Where is everyone?"

Alec shrugged, striding across the hall as if he owned the place, which Magnus supposed he sort of did. "I expect everyone's off gathering gear and weapons. We should just go find my mother."

"How do you propose to find her?" Magnus said.

"Ah," said Alec, "the Institute has a very old magic woven into its walls. I shall now use it to commune with my mother, wherever she might be found." He put his hands around his mouth and bellowed at the top of his lungs. "MOOOOOOOOOOOM!"

Alec's voice reverberated impressively against the stone walls. Max giggled and yelled, "Maaaaaaaaaaaaaaaaaaaa!" alongside Alec. The sound faded away and Magnus waited.

"Well?" he said, and Alec held up a finger. After a moment, there was a flare, and a fire-message appeared in front of him. He plucked it from the air and opened it, giving Magnus a superior look. "'She's in the library,'" he read.

A second fire-message appeared, in the same spot as the first. Alec opened it. "'Did you know you can send fire-messages within the Institute?'" he read. "'I just found out.'" He looked at Magnus in bewilderment. "Of course I knew that."

"To the library, then?" said Magnus.

A third fire-message appeared. Max lunged to try to grab it, but it was too far above his head. Magnus grabbed that one and read, "'I love fire-messages, have a great day, your friend, Simon Lovelace, Shadowhunter.' Can we go?"

They heard a fourth one burst behind them as they left by the hall door, but neither of them looked back at it.

"I PROMISE YOU," SAID MARYSE, "I CAN COMPLETELY handle Max for a few days."

Alec's mother was standing in the center of the library, near the desk where their old tutor had once sat. She was tall in the same way Isabelle was tall, unapologetically taking up space in the world, standing so straight she seemed even taller than she was. She folded her arms as though daring Alec and Magnus to disagree.

"Mom," Alec said, rubbing the back of his neck, "I just don't want you to have to deal with any . . . emergencies. He's a warlock."

"You're kidding," said Maryse. "I thought he had a terrible accident with a fountain pen."

Max lay on his stomach on the rug between them, doodling with Maryse's stele on an old, beaten-up shield she had found in the cellar the last time Max was over. The stele left sparking bright lines across the steel surface that faded slowly to black. Max was extremely into it.

"You know, you've gotten sassier recently," said Magnus, eyes twinkling. He had opened the satchel and was unloading toys and books onto Maryse's desk. She didn't seem to mind.

"I'm just saying," Alec pressed on, "he was floating on the ceiling this morning. He doesn't really have any control yet over the magical stuff he does."

"Alec, I raised you, Jace, Max, and Isabelle and you were plenty of trouble. I will be fine. Also, most of the time Kadir will be here."

As though he'd been waiting for his cue, Kadir Safar swept into the room. He was a tall, dark-skinned man with elegant features and a sharply defined goatee. Alec was not exactly clear on Kadir's official title at the Institute, but in recent months he had evidently become Maryse's second-in-command. He had helped train Alec, Isabelle, and Jace growing up, and was a man of few words and fewer expressions. Alec had always felt they understood each other. "Did you need me?" Kadir said to Maryse, hands behind his back. His eyes scanned the desk and its new pile of colorful objects. "Your grandchild's belongings, I assume. What do you have there, Magnus?"

Magnus held a stack of picture books in his hands that he'd just withdrawn from the bag. He waved them at Kadir. "I hope you're prepared for all the reading this kid will demand." He began placing books on the desk one at a time. "*Goodnight Moon. The Poky Little Puppy. Where the Wild Things Are.* Huge right now in our house. Main character is also named Max."

"I am familiar," said Kadir, drawing himself up with dignity, "with *Where the Wild Things Are.*"

"There's this one, which I guess is called *Truck*? It has a different kind of truck on each page with its name," Magnus went on. "Max is very enthusiastic about it, but I warn you, it has no narrative propulsion."

"Truck," confirmed Max. Warlocks tended to talk early, and Max was no exception. He'd said his first word, "newt," when he was only nine months old, causing Magnus to hide his spell components.

"And of course," said Magnus, "there is *The Very Small Mouse Who Went a Very Long Way.* By Courtney Gray Wiese."

Alec let out a long groan.

"Not a favorite?" said Maryse. "I don't know that one, but it doesn't sound bad."

"Lily brought it to us," Alec said. "I have no idea where she found it. It must have been in the Hotel Dumort."

"For decades," agreed Magnus. "The very small mouse does indeed go a very long way, but she does so in order to learn very outdated moral lessons about personal hygiene."

"Hmm," said Maryse and Kadir.

"It is his favorite," Magnus said, shaking his head. "Unfortunately."

Alec took a dramatic breath and proclaimed, "'Now wash your feet, O little mouse / Or you will never find a spouse.'"

"Mouse?" Max said, perking up.

Kadir held up his hand. "I look forward to discovering it for myself. Now, if there's nothing else, Maryse—"

"Stay a moment," Maryse insisted. "I wanted to tell Alec the news. Alec, I've asked Jace if he would take over soon as the head of the Institute. I hope you don't mind."

Alec tried to hide the surprise on his face. Not that his mother would ask Jace to run things, but that she would stop running the Institute herself at all. She'd given no hint of it. He wanted to ask why but held himself back, uncertain.

Magnus had no such qualms. "But why would you step down?"

Maryse shook her head. "Running an Institute is a young person's job. It needs someone with the energy to be a full-time Shadowhunter and *also* keep up relationships with the Downworlders, manage the members of the Conclave, stay in touch with the Council . . . it's a lot."

"But it's gotten easier," said Alec. "Not that you don't deserve a rest. The Alliance has really changed how closely in communication Downworld and the Conclave are." He felt himself flush a little. He always felt like he was bragging when he mentioned the Downworlder-Shadowhunter Alliance that he had put together with Maia Roberts, who led New York's largest werewolf pack, and

Lily Chen, who was the head of New York's vampires. But he *was* proud of the work they'd done.

"It has," said Maryse, "and Alec, I appreciate all the effort you put in there—that's why I didn't ask you to run the Institute. You've got plenty going on already. Not to mention the little blue-bell here."

Max looked up, sensing that someone wished to admire him. He grinned winningly at Alec, and his head burst into blue flames.

"Oh dear," said Maryse, blinking and jerking back. Kadir's expression did not change at all as he took a glass of water from Maryse's desk and poured it over Max, putting out the flames. Max blinked in surprise, then began to cry.

Kadir raised an eyebrow at Alec. "Sorry about that." Maryse scooped up Max, who quickly forgot that his head was wet in favor of grabbing for Maryse's earrings.

"It's as good a solution as any," Magnus said. "Better a crying kid than a house on fire."

"An apt aphorism," said Kadir. For Kadir, this was close to a declaration of undying love.

"What did Jace say?" said Alec. "Is he going to do it?"

"He said he needed time to think," said Maryse. She looked uncertain. "I'm sure he'll accept," she said. "I'm surprised he hasn't mentioned it to you, actually. I half thought you'd already know my news."

"He hasn't brought it up at all," said Alec. He was troubled. Why *hadn't* Jace mentioned it? Even if he had doubts, who else would be better to talk about them with than his *parabatai*? And what would Jace have to worry about, anyway? Alec knew he would kill it as head of the Institute.

"I can't imagine he wants to be the guy who has to uphold the Cold Peace," said Magnus mildly.

"Has he talked to *you* about it?" said Alec. Magnus had a good point, though. The Cold Peace was the name for the terrible relationship between faeries and Shadowhunters at the moment. After a good number of the fey had sided with the enemies of the Nephilim a few years back, the Shadowhunters had sanctioned them harshly and strong-armed them into signing a treaty that left them unprotected and badly weakened. Things had been somewhat more than tense ever since. Many Shadowhunters—and especially the Shadowhunters of the New York Institute—hated the Cold Peace and would have happily seen the restoration of normal relations. But it was the job of the Institute to uphold the Law, which was hard, but it was the Law, and so on.

"He hasn't said a word to me," said Magnus. "It's just a guess."

Maryse shrugged. "I've been juggling the Clave's expectations about the Cold Peace and the realities of New York's Downworld for three years. It can be done. Jace can be good at politics if he decides to be. And I won't be *dead*. I'll still be living here and have plenty of advice on the subject of the Cold Peace." She sighed. "I admit I'd hoped that you would have some insight into Jace's thinking."

"I don't, yet," said Alec, though he wasn't sure when in their big group outing he would be able to get a few minutes with Jace to ask him in private.

"Much of *my* advice," put in Kadir, "about working around the Cold Peace would involve going through you and your Alliance."

"Uh, speaking of which, should you tell them you're going to China today?" said Magnus.

Alec hadn't thought of that. "I really should," he said. He dug out his phone, and one text later, he got a quick response from Maia: I'M IN THE SANCTUARY.

Alec got up. "Maia says she's . . . in the Sanctuary? Did any of you know she was here? Or even that she was coming?" He exchanged a glance with Magnus that he'd developed over the past months: the wordless question, *Is it okay to leave Max with you while*

I do a thing? And the wordless nod back. It was strange to have created a new language between himself and Magnus, one that was just for their family.

"Maybe she's here to tell you she can see the future," said Magnus. "Ask her how Shanghai's going to go."

Alec excused himself and headed out into the hall, then down the stairs to the Sanctuary. There he found Maia waiting, looking very proud of herself.

"Alec!" she said. "Good to see you." She stuck out her hand for him to shake. Alec took her hand in some confusion; they were not big hand-shakers, the two of them.

He realized what was going on as his hand passed through Maia's and she yelled a delighted "Ha!"

Alec recovered his balance and gave her a disapproving look. "You're a Projection."

"I'm a Projection!" said Maia, throwing her hands over her head. "So exciting."

"So that means—"

"We finally have Projections working in the Den."

"The 'Den'?" said Alec, raising an eyebrow.

"New name for headquarters," said Maia. The werewolves of Manhattan were based in an abandoned police station in Chinatown. "I'm trying it out."

Alec nodded thoughtfully. "I'm cautiously in favor of it."

"Good to know. So, *apparently*, there's a faerie ring directly under the station, and that's why things weren't working. I guess it's been there since, like, the founding of New York."

"A faerie ring? Uh—" Alec wasn't sure how to ask the next question, which was: *How do we deal with that problem, given that the Alliance isn't technically supposed to be in communication with faeries?*

"Look, I never talked to a faerie about the situation," Maia said. "I talked to a warlock, she talked to someone at the Shadow Market, then one day Projections work and someone leaves a wicker basket of acorns on the front stoop."

"That's very autumnal," said Alec.

"One thing about faeries, they are *committed* to the aesthetic," Maia agreed. "Anyway. What's this about Shanghai?"

"Missing magic book, Magnus feels responsible, we've both got to go. It shouldn't be more than a few days. And it might be a dead end and we'll be back in an hour," Alec added, although he didn't think that was likely.

"So is there Alliance stuff you need to tell me?"

"God no," said Alec. "You and Lily can certainly handle Alliance business for a few days. I might miss game night, though."

Maia sighed. "Without you there, Lily's going to make us play charades. Or whist or something. She's such an old lady sometimes. A drunk old lady."

"Maia," Alec said disapprovingly.

"Oh, you know I love her," Maia said. "Did you consider bringing her along? She speaks Mandarin, for one thing."

"Just last week I heard Lily say, in my presence, the full sentence, 'I want to never again in my life set foot within the borders of China,' so, you know. . . . Magnus also speaks Mandarin."

"Of course he does," said Maia.

"There is one thing," said Alec. "My mom is watching Max while we're away. She's never watched him for more than, like, a few hours. Can you . . . keep an eye on them?"

"I'm sure Max will be fine," said Maia.

"Honestly, I'm more worried about my mother," said Alec.

"I'll stop by a few times," Maia said. "I'm sure I can come up with some boring bureaucratic reasons I need to come to the Institute anyway. Um, anyway—" She suddenly looked up and past him. "You have company."

Alec turned in surprise to see Jace, Clary, Simon, and Isabelle, all in gear and fully armed. They were mostly holding their usual favorite weapons—Simon his bow, Clary her sword, Isabelle her whip. Jace, for some reason, was carrying a kind of spiked flail on a chain. They and Maia waved—Jace waved very carefully, due to the flail—and exchanged hellos.

"We made a pile of our luggage," Clary said, gesturing vaguely behind her. "So Magnus can teleport it later if we need to stay overnight."

"Got the Projection working, I see," Simon said to Maia approvingly. He gave her a thumbs-up.

"Wait—how can you tell she's a Projection?" said Alec.

"You can totally tell," Jace said. "You just get a feel for it."

"You do?" said Alec.

"Yeah." Simon nodded.

"Huh. What's with the, uh, flail, Jace?"

"It's a morning star," said Clary, in deeply mournful tones.

"Morning stars don't have chains," said Alec. "It's a flail."

"He wants us to call it a morning star," said Clary, even more gloomily. "You're not even a Morgenstern," she said to Jace. "*I'm* a Morgenstern."

"I'm still closely associated with the name," Jace insisted. "I was just feeling like—can I pull off having a morning star as my signature weapon? Is it *me*?"

"You mean, can you avoid looking like a heavy-metal album cover?" said Simon.

"I don't know what that is, and I don't want to," said Jace. "I just mean, am I cool enough?"

"Of course you are, honey," said Clary. "Look," she added to Alec, "I see the concern on your face. I figure we let this run its course for a week or so. If it doesn't burn out by then we can step in."

"Fair enough," said Alec.

"It's a trial run," agreed Jace. "Maybe I won't like it and I'll stop using the morning star. I've got seraph blades too, obviously. And, I don't know, probably four or five knives on my person that were already in the pockets of my clothes when I put them on."

Alec felt a rush of fondness for his *parabatai*. "I wasn't worried."

They said their good-byes to Maia, and she disappeared just as Magnus appeared at the door of the Sanctuary. He'd changed clothes—only the Angel knew where he had gotten the new outfit from—and was now in a velvet suit in dark navy, with a matching navy shirt and tie. Alec had always secretly found Magnus to be at his absolute most handsome in a suit and was pleased that his boyfriend had gone in that direction. He also noted that it prevented any possibility of his glowing wound being visible.

Behind Magnus was Alec's mother, holding Alec's son. It still felt strange, even after half a year, to think, *my son*. Strange but good. Maryse and Max were both waving excitedly.

"Wish your daddies luck on their mission," Maryse said. "Let's hope they get the magic book back from the bad woman who stole it." Alec nodded. They had all agreed, at Magnus's pleading, not to tell the Clave about Ragnor. So all Maryse knew was that a warlock named Shinyun Jung of Magnus's acquaintance, who was bad news, had stolen the Book of the White, and that they were going to Shanghai to find her.

Alec went over to them and kissed Max's forehead. "Be nice to your grandma, okay, kiddo?" Max put his hand on Alec's nose and Alec quickly turned, gave his mother a kiss on the cheek, and retreated successfully without choking up.

"You kids be careful out there," Maryse said.

Isabelle said, "Mom, we're grown-ups."

"I know," said Maryse, leaning forward to embrace her daughter. She turned to Jace and, after a brief standoff, he also allowed her to hug him. "But be careful anyway."

She blew Magnus a kiss and retreated, closing the door behind her.

Alec began to laugh. "This is not the way I'm used to launching a mission. It's very emotional compared to the old way."

Jace said, "You mean sneaking out under cover of darkness? I myself don't miss it."

"So, we're already in the Sanctuary," Magnus said. "I may as well make the Portal right here." With some flourishes, he applied himself to the Portal's construction. Alec watched him. Magnus could be extremely elegant even when he was giving it the least thought; the dexterity with which he went through the gestures and words that made up the Portal summoning was a beautiful thing to behold, a reminder that Alec not only loved Magnus but also continued to admire so much about him.

His reverie was interrupted when the Portal opened and Magnus's expression changed from concentration to alarm. The view through the Portal definitely did not look like it was of a place on Earth. The colors were wrong.

Out of it swarmed a dozen demonic beetle-creatures, each about the size of a basketball.

Magnus yelled in surprise and began to wave frantically, working to shut the Portal. Alec drew a seraph blade, murmured, *"Kalqa'il,"* to it, and leaped at the nearest beetle.

"They're Elytra demons," called Simon. "I think."

"Any further insights to share about them?" said Jace, drawing his flail. "Other than their name? Greetings, Elytra demons! Welcome to our dimension. Your time here will be instructive but short."

"I have an insight," said Isabelle. She swiftly gave a kick to the nearest beetle. When it flipped onto its back, she plunged a blade into the soft body under its hard carapace. "Kick 'em over."

"Roger that," said Jace. He spun his flail and, after a moment's winding up, smashed it into the side of an Elytra, which promptly crumpled and vanished. "That also works, by the way. If you've got a flail with you."

"Ha! I told you it was a flail!" yelled Alec, kicking over a beetle of his own.

They made quick work of the demons. When things were quiet again, Alec immediately made for Magnus, who had barely gotten a wrinkle in his suit, though Alec had seen him dispatch two of the beetles himself with bolts of blue fire. "What happened?" he said.

Magnus shook his head. "I have no idea. That was Shanghai, but . . . not our Shanghai. That doesn't usually happen. And by that I mean, that doesn't ever happen. You don't open a door to an alternate world by accident. It's hard enough to do on purpose." He looked around at them. "Clary, can you try? Just try reactivating the one I closed."

Clary looked at Magnus in surprise. Alec schooled his own expression, but he was just as taken aback. "Of course," Clary said. She took out her stele and went to work.

Into the ensuing silence, Alec said, "Could it be because of the thorn?" Someone had to, after all.

Magnus hesitated. "I don't know," he admitted. "We've been rushing around getting ready to leave, and I haven't so much as googled the word Svefnthorn."

"I googled it," Jace said, to Alec's surprise. "While we were getting our stuff together."

"You," said Alec, "*googled* it."

"Yeah," said Jace. "It sounded Norse, so I went into the library and looked it up in the Saga Concordances. Like a normal person. That's *googling*, right?"

"More or less," said Simon.

"And?" said Isabelle.

Jace shrugged. "It means 'thorn of sleep.' It shows up a few times. Some god uses a Svefnthorn to put another god into a magical slumber. You know, usual god stuff."

"It didn't put me to sleep," Magnus said doubtfully. "Nobody mentioned sleep."

"Well, that's just mundane mythology," Jace said. "I didn't have time to go into our own texts, or anything demonic."

"Unluckily," said Magnus, "I fear that the library of the Shanghai Institute may mostly be in Chinese. Luckily, we happen to be traveling to a city that is home to one of the greatest wonders of Downworld: the Celestial Palace."

"How is a palace going to help?" said Simon.

"Because," said Magnus, clearly relishing this, which Alec found adorable, "the Celestial Palace is that greatest of things: a bookstore."

From where she was working a few yards away, Clary waved her arms; she had the Portal open. "It looks okay?" she said uncertainly.

Magnus came to peer through it and shrugged. "Sky's the right color, there are stars, moon's out, buildings look right, no giant beetles. I say we go for it."

"That's a very inspiring speech, Magnus," said Jace.

"What the hell," said Isabelle.

They gathered together and walked through the Portal. The cool breeze became a soft enveloping cloud of humidity. The low rumble from outside the Sanctuary windows was replaced by a cacophonous, honking orchestra of cars and the steady clamor of a crowded city street at evening. Bright colored lights flickered, animated and swirling in the night sky.

And Alec's world tilted; that sky was in the wrong place. And he was falling. They were all falling. They were falling quite awhile.

PART II
Shanghai

† † †

Heavenly Places

IT WAS A WONDER THEY DIDN'T HURT ANYONE. THE SHAD-owhunters emerged through the pearlescent frame of the Portal into thin air, twelve feet off the ground, and fell to the pavement amid an enormous bustling crowd of people.

They all landed safely, or at least cushioned themselves well enough to suffer only a few bruises. Alec carefully got to his feet, glad to be glamoured into invisibility. Wherever in the city they were, it was *crowded*.

It was full evening in Shanghai, a pleasantly warm one, and as he straightened up, Alec realized they stood on a massive pedestrian thoroughfare that extended in both directions beyond the distance he could see. The crowds were thick—Manhattan thick—and both sides of the street were lined with buildings shining with huge, brightly lit signs. Every wall was flooded with neon color and vivid advertisements. Large vertical signs in Chinese characters hung from each building into the streets, painting the walls in an electric rainbow of blue, red, and green. In the distance, a needle-shaped structure shot up into the night sky, glowing in waves of dazzling purple. Around it was the rest of the Shanghai skyline, some of it half-finished and surrounded by cranes, other parts lit up to stand as totems above the teeming city below.

There were English signs among the Chinese. "It looks like Times Square!" Isabelle said brightly. "Shanghai Times Square."

"It's much cooler than Times Square," Simon said, gazing around at the spectacle before him. "More neon and lasers and banks of colored lights, fewer giant video screens."

"There are plenty of giant video screens," said Clary. "And it's not Times Square. Well, I guess it kind of is, but it's more like Fifth Avenue. We're on East Nanjing Road—it's a big shopping area with no cars."

"So," said Simon, "you thought, better hit up the sales before we find the evil warlocks?"

"They're not necessarily evil," Alec said. "The, uh, misguided warlocks."

"The misguided warlocks who make terrible decisions," amended Isabelle.

"No," said Clary. "I mean—I was reading about this place on my phone this morning. I was just looking up the famous places to go in Shanghai. I wasn't trying to end up here. I was trying to go to the Institute, and this is nowhere near it."

"Also," said Alec with a jolt, "where is Magnus?"

They looked around. Alec was keeping a clamp on his feelings, the way you might put pressure on a bleeding wound. He couldn't panic now. That wouldn't be helpful to Magnus.

"Clary, can you see through the Portal?" he demanded. "Is Magnus still back on the other side?" He squinted at the small glowing square floating well above their heads.

Clary backed up and shook her head. "No, nothing."

Alec took out his phone and called Magnus. He did not pick up. Alec continued not to panic. Instead, he sent a text: WE ARE IN NANJING RD SHOPPING AREA, WHERE YOU?

They stood there, waiting, with the unseeing crowd streaming around them, hidden within their glamours. Alec wasn't sure what they would do if they couldn't find Magnus. Would they just have to keep going through with the mission? How would that even work? Magnus was the only one of them who spoke Mandarin. Magnus had the scrap of Ragnor's cloak that was necessary to Track him. They could go to the Institute—itself a project involving getting cash, finding a taxi, and so on—but even there, Magnus had spoken of his long relationship with the Ke family, who ran the place. Alec had expected to have Magnus's help when they arrived.

The others were all looking at Alec worriedly. Jace had come a little closer, not quite putting his hand on Alec's shoulder, but as if he were about to. And indeed, Alec knew, if Magnus didn't appear, and soon, there would be no more mission, no matter how many intellectual exercises he ran about it in his head. Even if the danger of a Prince of Hell loomed in the future, Alec would abandon everything else and go after Magnus first, wherever he might be.

Alec's phone beeped.

He grabbed at it, flipping it over. It was a message from Magnus. They all crowded around to read it: TOOK AN UNEXPECTED SWIM. MEET ME IN FRONT OF THE MCDONALD'S NEAR GUIZHOU ROAD.

Alec felt Jace's hand graze his back lightly, a silent reassurance: *See, brother, everything is fine.*

"Of course there's a McDonald's," said Isabelle, and they headed off, using the GPS on Simon's phone to guide them.

Sometimes Alec thought that eventually the modern world would overtake the Shadowhunters, despite their best attempts to stay out of it. It was inevitable, if you lived in a big city; just navigating your way around took a certain understanding of the mundane world and how it worked. Here Alec had been dropped into one of the most crowded spots in one of the biggest cities in the world, about as far from his home as he could get while remaining on the planet. And yet he felt a certain familiarity: big city shopping streets were big city shopping streets. The signs were in Chinese, and the aesthetic wasn't the same, but the feel was the same: the night and the lights and the people, families, strange pairings, solo workers just trying to get through the crowd to get home. It should have been totally alien to Alec, but it wasn't. It was new. But there was something there he already understood. He was surprised to find how many things in his life worked that way, when he gave them a try.

They met Magnus at the point where the pedestrian part of the road ended and car traffic began. The warlock's hair was, strangely, soaking wet, and spiked angrily up above his head. His clothes were dry, but they were not the same clothes he had been wearing when they went through the Portal. Alec was a little disappointed—he loved Magnus in a suit—but Magnus had perhaps wisely chosen to blend in, in black jeans, a sleek black button-down shirt, and a black leather motorcycle jacket. He looked like a sexy urban race-car driver. Alec was in favor of it.

He swept up to Alec, put his arms around his neck, and kissed him. Alec kissed him back, passionately, relief coursing through his veins. He would have liked to grab handfuls of Magnus's shirt and drag him closer, kiss him until they were both staggering, *but*. He was standing in front of his sister and his *parabatai* and his *parabatai*'s girlfriend and her *parabatai*. He had to draw a line somewhere. He did kiss Magnus back as strongly as he was able; Magnus was here, he was fine, and Alec could feel his body relax.

"I guess you didn't get to the Institute either," said Clary, when a significant amount of time had passed.

Magnus broke the kiss.

"Is it all right? For two men to kiss in a crowded street in Shanghai? I don't know if I'd kiss you that way in Times Square," said Alec.

"Darling," Magnus said quietly, "we're invisible."

"Oh," said Alec. "Right."

"I did not go to the Institute, no," said Magnus to Clary. "I went to thirty or so feet above the Huangpu River." He saw Alec's look of alarm. "Then a few seconds passed, and I was in the Huangpu River."

"What did you do?" said Jace.

"I tumbled through the air gracefully and landed on my feet on the back of a friendly porpoise," said Magnus.

"That is *very* believable," said Simon, encouraging as always.

Magnus waved his hand. "That is how I wish you to think of me. Riding a porpoise to shore, and straight to join you. I don't understand it. That's two Portals in a row that have gone wrong, in ways Portals should not go wrong. How did we get split up?"

"I think," said Jace, "we were all hoping you would know."

"I just draw 'em," said Clary. "That doesn't mean I understand the magic behind them."

"No more Portals for a while, anyway," said Magnus. He pulled the scrap of Ragnor's cloak from his pocket with a flourish and handed it over to Alec. Jace took out his stele and gestured to Alec, who dutifully held out his hand for Jace to refresh the Tracking rune.

"The rune is still just going to pull us in a direction, and Shanghai is huge," said Alec. "How are we going to handle this?"

"We're going to take a taxi," said Magnus, holding his arm out to the street. "So un-glamour yourselves." The taxis in Shanghai appeared to be an assortment of colors, but they were all silver on their bottom half and the same model of car, so it was pretty easy to spot them in traffic. One, a vivid shade of violet, quickly pulled over for them.

Magnus eyed the size of their group. "Two taxis."

Alec waved down a second taxi, and Magnus quickly spoke to

the driver of the new taxi, then went to get into the first one.

"Wait, what did you tell him?" Alec said.

"I told him to follow the first cab. And that the dark-haired man with the bright blue eyes would be handling the fare." He hesitated. "Alec—if Ragnor doesn't know we're Tracking him, and he's in Shanghai, he'll still be here tomorrow morning. If you don't want to go racing off without anything to go on but this Tracking rune, I totally get that. We can take a couple of hotel rooms—I know some great places—and tomorrow morning we can go to the Institute and do this through the proper channels."

Alec tried not to be thrown by this total about-face. "Magnus, I'm touched, but I have to wonder—are you avoiding catching up to Ragnor because you don't know what to do when you find him? Is that what this is about?"

"This conversation is a real roller coaster," said Isabelle, sticking her head out of the back window of the second taxi, "but my Mandarin is nonexistent, and Jace's is really poor, and this taxi driver has started the meter."

"No," said Magnus. "It's just—finding Ragnor is better than having no leads, but it's absolutely backward from how I would want to do this. I don't want to go through him to get the Book. I don't even want to go through Shinyun."

"They're the only leads we have, my love," Alec said, "so I think we're getting in the cabs."

"Okay," said Magnus. He kissed Alec. "Let's go."

They both got into the back of the first cab, joining only Simon, who had the map open on his phone and gave a thumbs-up, though his expression was distant. Magnus turned to Alec. "Okay, so what direction?"

Alec gripped the scrap of cloth. "Still west."

Magnus leaned forward and spoke to the driver in Mandarin, pointing in a direction. The driver seemed surprised but, after a brief negotiation, acquiesced. "Just tell me when we should turn," Magnus said, and Alec nodded, and the taxis took off into the night.

THE LAST TIME MAGNUS HAD BEEN IN SHANGHAI WAS twenty years ago. It had been only months into the rebirth of the city, its sudden strange second life, in which it would become the biggest city in China, flooded with money and new growth. Even now there were new skyscrapers going up, new shining lights wherever Magnus looked. It was still itself, it was still Shanghai. But it had changed so much, in such a short time.

They made their way out of the center of the city, leaving the fancy lights of Nanjing Road behind. They made their way through the lively district of Jing'an, until they were in the vast residential blocks that rolled away forever into the distance, new high-rises and a few garden apartment complexes. Another few turns and they were entering an older neighborhood, a place left over from the Shanghai that the international luxury brands and skyscrapers were busily replacing with a bright sheen of modernity.

While they rode, Magnus tried to explain the unusual Downworlder situation in Shanghai. "Back in the nineteenth century," he said, "Shanghai was divided into a bunch of international concessions—land that was leased to other countries, within the city. Britain had one, France, the United States. They were still officially part of China, but the other countries could kind of do whatever they wanted within the concession borders. When that happened, the Downworlders of Shanghai struck their own deal, and were given their own concession."

"What?" said Alec, turning to look at Magnus. "There's a permanent Downworlder-run neighborhood here?"

"There are a few Sighted mundanes living there as well, probably," said Magnus. "But yes."

"If they have a permanent neighborhood, does that mean there's no Shadow Market in Shanghai?"

Magnus laughed. "Oh, there's a Shadow Market all right."

Quickly the streets became too narrow for the taxis, and Magnus and the others abandoned them to continue on foot. Simon looked oddly pale, although not in the vampire way he once had.

"Shadowhunters don't get *carsick*," Jace was saying.

"Did your dad teach you that?" Simon said, wobbling slightly from foot to foot. "Was he ever in a car in his life? Was he ever in a car *in Shanghai* in his life?"

Clary and Isabelle exchanged looks. "You all right, Simon?" said Clary.

"Hey, they who don't do well in stop-and-go traffic also serve the Angel," Alec called over. "Can we go?"

Sometimes Magnus wasn't sure being a Shadowhunter was better for Simon than being a vampire had been. He was no longer undead; that was definitely good, of course. But there was a certain blood-and-thunder machismo that could creep in uncomfortably around the edges of Shadowhunter culture. Valentine had wielded that narrative of inborn strength, of supremacy, like a weapon. It was an attitude that always threatened to resurface among the Nephilim. Bending and twisting himself to fit inside it had nearly broken Jace. If it hadn't been for Alec, Isabelle, and Clary . . .

The Tracking rune had led them into one of the remaining pockets of old Shanghai, from before the wide boulevards and the shining silver malls. They had to walk in single file to avoid blocking the way for pedestrians and cyclists. And it was still crowded here, too, everywhere a flow of people, bicycles, animals, like a rushing river, in a way that reminded Magnus of a dozen cities he'd been to that were always the same and yet always new. Shanghai, Singapore, Hong Kong, Bangkok, Jakarta, Tokyo, New York . . .

Magnus hadn't told anyone yet, but he felt something within the glowing crack in his chest, a swelling node of magic. Not evil magic, he thought. Not even alien magic. His own magic, pooling within him. It was creating a kind of aura at the edges of his vision, bright blue and sparkling. The aura seemed to pull and bend in response to other auras that Magnus wasn't otherwise aware of.

He wasn't sure how to bring it up. He guessed they would find Ragnor, then through Ragnor find Shinyun, and hopefully she would explain the phenomenon to him. Or he hoped it could wait until they could do some research tomorrow.

Clary was examining a series of signs covered in felt-tip handwriting, tacked up to the windows of a closed storefront. Magnus gestured above them. "It's a hair salon. That's just their menu."

"Isabelle," Simon stage-whispered. "Can we take home one of the chickens?"

"Yes," said Isabelle. "You can take home as many as you can catch."

"Don't encourage him," said Clary. To Magnus she said, "Is this the kind of place Ragnor would be?"

Magnus looked around at the narrow lanes, the concrete walls tacked with notices and ads and stenciled graffiti; he could smell animals and food and garbage and people living too close together, everything unchanged for decades in a place that seemed to be transforming itself hourly. "This is not really where Ragnor would live," he said slowly. "But it *is* exactly where Ragnor would hide."

"Unless he knows we're coming," said Jace.

"If he knows we're coming," said Magnus, "why would he stay in Shanghai at all? He's an expert in dimensional magic. He could Portal anywhere. He could go to the Spiral Labyrinth and hide, if he wanted to. They don't know he's being . . . controlled, or whatever it is."

"But the Tracking rune makes it clear he *is* still in Shanghai," said Alec. "So he doesn't know we're coming."

"Or," said Jace, "he wants to be found."

Magnus hadn't thought of that, but he agreed it was a possibility. Being in thrall to Sammael and being friendly toward Magnus were not necessarily incompatible, at least not in the mind of Shinyun, and maybe not in the mind of Ragnor, either.

On the other hand, did Ragnor expect him to arrive with five Shadowhunters? One, sure, but five?

He was getting jumpy. His wound tickled.

The Tracking rune led them to a shabby white apartment building. Spiky black graffiti was splashed across one side, over the peeling paint. Alec in the lead, they went in, following him up two flights of stairs to a dingy apartment door in a dingy carpeted hallway. Magnus was about to knock, but then hesitated.

Alec gave him a look and banged on the door for him. After a moment, it opened, revealing a bald, bearded, goat-legged faerie gentleman who gawked in openmouthed horror at discovering an entire squad of Shadowhunters at his door.

"You can't come in!" he yelped in Shanghainese, much louder than Magnus would have expected.

"They don't speak any Chinese," said Magnus politely in Mandarin. "English, if you please. It's not like it's any effort for a faerie."

The faerie didn't take his wide eyes off the Shadowhunters. "You can't come in!" he said in English.

"Hi," said Alec. "We actually don't have any business with you at all, and we're sorry to bother you. We—"

"You'll never find anything!" the faerie shrieked. "My hands are clean, do you hear me? Clean!"

"I'm sure they are," said Alec. "We're looking for a warlock. He's very easy to recognize. He's green—"

"All right," said the faerie. He leaned closer. "If I confess to some of what I've done, will you give me leniency? I can help you take down some big names. *Big* names."

"Do tell," said Jace.

Alec gave Jace a dark look. "You don't need to do that," he said. "If you could tell us whether you've seen our friend? We think he might have gone into your apartment."

"We're not interested in big names," put in Magnus.

Jace piped up, "We're a *little* interested, right?"

"I can give you Lenny the Squid," said the faerie fervently. "I can give you Bobby Two-Legs. I can give you Socks MacPherson."

Alec rubbed his face with his hands, and Magnus restrained a smile. Truly, his boyfriend's patience and professionalism was a beautiful thing to behold.

"Let's take a step back," Alec said. "Have you ever heard of a warlock named Ragnor Fell?"

The faerie stopped and squinted suspiciously at Alec, as though trying to perceive a trick. "I don't have to answer any of your questions."

"Have we considered the 'bad cop' option?" Jace said, a light growl in his voice. "I'm feeling better and better about it."

"Fine," said the faerie. "I've never heard of anyone by that name."

"Hang on a moment," Alec said, turning to the group. "Can we give this guy some space, actually? He's scared to death. If five faeries came unannounced to your door, you'd be pretty freaked-out too."

"Sure," said Jace, exchanging a look with him. "Come on, guys. Let's give him some room." They went down the hallway a bit; Magnus went with them. Alec leaned into the front door and spoke with the faerie. After a minute or so, he emerged back in the hall-way, his expression neutral. "I'm going to go inside and speak with Mr. Rumnus for a minute. Magnus, could you come with me?"

Somehow Alec had calmed the faerie down enough to let him inside. Magnus had to remind himself that Alec knew something about talking to untrusting Downworlders. Some of those untrusting Downworlders had become Alec's close friends.

Simon called, "Does he know his name is—"

"He knows," said Alec.

Simon nodded, satisfied.

Magnus followed Alec inside. It was a shabbily kept little apartment, quite normal. Perhaps too normal for a goat-legged faerie to be living in, Magnus thought. He began extending his magic outward into the room, trying to keep his expression and his hand motions as neutral as possible.

"Mr. Rumnus says there's been some bad warlock business in Shanghai of late," Alec said.

"What kind of bad warlock business?" said Magnus. "Like turf wars?" He was distracted. He had expected some magical signature, some residue at least; the Tracking rune had led them here, so Ragnor *had* been here, the Tracking rune said he *was* here. But there was no place for him to be. The apartment was one room, the whole place visible at once; the bathroom door was open and revealed nobody. There was definitely no other magical being in the room other than himself and this faerie. How could this be a dead end?

"What are you doing with all these Shadowhunters?" said Mr. Rumnus abruptly to Magnus.

"He's my boyfriend," Alec said. "He's also a High Warlock."

"Punch above your weight a little, huh?" said the faerie to Alec, leering.

"Ugh," said Magnus.

"This isn't your apartment, is it, Rumnus?" Alec said sharply.

"What?" the faerie said.

"You don't live here. Look at that." He gestured at a large sculpture, more than six feet tall. It looked like a school of abstract fish colliding with a flock of abstract birds. It was marvelously hideous.

"That's wrought iron. You have a giant wrought-iron sculpture in your living room?"

"Also," said Magnus, "that big plastic chair shaped like a hand is very non-faerie." And then he doubled over in pain.

His head suddenly hurt as though he had been hit hard. A high-pitched scream, quiet but growing louder, began to throb in the back of his head.

He felt hands grasp him, and Alec's voice yelled, "Magnus!" as though from a long way away. With an effort, he lifted his head, in time to see the ceiling tear open and the whirling clouds of a demon world appear behind a shining Portal.

AS SOON AS THE PORTAL OPENED AND THE WIND BEGAN to whistle, Alec knew demons were coming. He drew his bow and yelled, "It's a trap!" at the open front door.

Isabelle was first to arrive, her whip at the ready. "Of course it's a trap," she said.

"Of course we didn't put on combat runes," Jace said, joining her.

Demons began to fall into the room through the Portal. These were demons Alec hadn't seen before, massive snakes with shiny black scales and silent screaming human faces. As soon as they appeared, he began to shoot. Simon entered, an arrow nocked in his bow, looking more alarmed than Alec would have expected. Clary came in laying about her with glowing seraph blades.

It was a strange fight. Rumnus had crawled under a table and was scrunched up with his eyes closed as though he wished it all would just go away. Magnus had one hand extended, and sparks were haphazardly flying from it, sometimes hitting demons and sometimes leaving little scorch marks on the walls and the furniture. His other hand was at his temple and his eyes were squinted closed; he looked like he was fighting through a migraine, though Magnus was not known to get migraines. Alec wanted to go to him, but the room had become an overcrowded mess of snake demons and sharp objects.

Whatever was causing the snakes to appear, it wasn't pursuing any kind of battlefield strategy. They continued to fall into the room as if dropped haphazardly by a giant unseen hand. Some landed upright, but others sprawled into a tangled mess or came down on their own heads, leaving them open for easy kills. Clary went around the room delivering those kills gleefully.

Alec spun to avoid a demon's bite and found Jace, arms pinned by two of the snakes. He quickly put arrows in both of them, and the second Jace was free, he leaped forward and buried a seraph blade in the face of the demon that Alec had spun away from, which had been coming up behind him.

They exchanged a quick look, each confirming the other was all right, and turned back to the battle.

It was over quickly, considering the number of demons and the Shadowhunters' lack of preparation for a fight. From Alec's perspective there were lots of snakes, and then there were no snakes, only his own heavy panting and that of his friends as they caught their breath, no longer in immediate danger.

Abruptly a gigantic version of the screaming human face of the snakes, this one easily ten feet across, appeared in the Portal. It opened its distended mouth and *screeched*, its eyes searching. It caught sight of Magnus, who was still clutching his head, his teeth gritted, his fingers sparking at the end of his outstretched hand, but not to any noticeable effect.

Simon fired an arrow into the Portal; it passed through the face and vanished into nothing. He looked at Alec with a panicked expression. Alec shrugged.

And just as suddenly as it had appeared, the demon face vanished. The Portal, too, quickly faded away, leaving only the bare, cracked ceiling of the apartment and the sound of Alec's own heart-beat in his ears.

He went over to Magnus immediately and put his hand on his boyfriend's shoulder. He leaned in and said, "I'm here. Are you okay?"

Magnus took his hand off his forehead and blinked at Alec. "I'm okay," he said. He looked oddly unstable, like a reed caught in a wind. "The headache is going away. That was . . . that was some-thing. I don't think I've ever—"

He stopped himself and a steely look came over his face. "You," he said past Alec, to the faerie, who was scuttling out from under the table.

"I think we can—" began Rumnus.

"You!" Magnus roared. Alec was surprised—not that Magnus was angry, but at the force in his voice. Magnus kept his cool, in almost all situations. It was one of the great consistencies in Alec's life. Now, Magnus extended a hand and Rumnus went tumbling over, falling to the ground in a heap.

"This isn't your apartment," said Magnus dangerously. "This isn't Ragnor's apartment either. In fact," he went on, "this isn't *anybody's* apartment." He put his arms above his head, and a great electrical storm came from his hands, crackling as loudly as the demon face had screamed. The bolts of blue energy flew jagged and chaotic around the room, and when they cleared, Alec could see that Magnus had dispelled some powerful illusions, stronger than any glamour Alec had seen before. The apartment was, in fact, empty—abandoned, even. No furniture, no rugs, cracked white walls with unknown dark residue on them, a broken bare lightbulb dangling from the single socket in the ceiling. Magnus turned his gaze on Rumnus, who had gotten to his feet. "What do you have to say for yourself?" he bit out.

Rumnus considered his options, and then, making a decision, yelled, "You'll never take me alive, narcs!" He ran to the window and threw himself out of it before anyone could stop him.

They watched him plummet toward the ground. Before he hit, huge brown bird's wings sprang from his back, and he flapped them and flew off into the night.

"How about that," said Alec mildly into the silence.

Magnus was breathing hard. His hand was gripped tightly on his chest. Just over his wound, Alec noticed. He approached Magnus cautiously.

"Okay," said Clary, "so what was *any* of that?"

Magnus went to sit down on the chair, seemed to remember there was no chair, and lowered himself slowly to the floor, exhaling. "I'm not sure."

"Let's start with the part that wasn't snake demons," said Alec. He folded his arms and looked at Magnus. "What was *that*? That wasn't like you. You don't get angry like that."

"I often get angry like that," Magnus retorted, "when encountering lying Downworlders who are collaborating with demons."

"And we assume he's collaborating with demons," said Jace, "due to all of the demons that fell out of the ceiling? And the yelling demon face?"

"Yes," agreed Magnus. Some of the fight seemed to be draining from him. He looked at Alec. "I'm sorry. I'm just frustrated."

"No kidding," said Isabelle. She started ticking things off on her fingers. "Where's Ragnor? Why did the Tracking rune lead us here instead of where he actually is? How did he know we were Tracking him? Did he send those demons? Did Shinyun Jung? Did someone else they're working with who we don't even know about?"

Alec thought. "There were a bunch of the snakes, but there definitely weren't enough to be a real threat to all of us. Which means this was either a warning—"

"Or," Jace put in, "they didn't realize you were bringing four other Shadowhunters with you."

"So where next?" said Simon. He had his hands tucked under his crossed arms and was looking squirrelly.

They all looked at Magnus, who sighed heavily. "What does the Tracking rune say?"

Alec took the scrap of cloth back out of his pocket and tried the rune again. He shrugged. "It says we're in the right place."

Simon said, "We could try the Institute. See what they know about this 'bad warlock' stuff the faerie mentioned."

"No," said Alec sharply, and Simon jerked back. "Let's not raise any more alarm bells than we have already. We need to try to control the flow of information to the Clave."

"We *are* the Clave," said Isabelle. "This isn't like a few years ago, when we were too young to have a voice."

Jace shook his head. "Alec's right. We're a very small part of the Clave, and our approach to Downworlder business is far from universal or even normal, by Nephilim standards. We don't know what we're getting into."

"We do, actually," said Magnus. He seemed to be recovering; he picked himself up off the floor and carefully wiped dust from his jacket. "The Shanghai Institute is run by the Ke family; it has been for years. They're good people. They're the family of Jem Carstairs—of Brother Zachariah. But," he added, as Jace opened his mouth to respond, "we have nothing for them to do right now, it is getting late, and I am *not* sleeping on a cot in a spare room in an Institute. I am going to make a call, and then we are going to stay at my favorite hotel in the city." Alec felt a warm rush of relief; this was more the Magnus he knew. "When you travel with me," Magnus reminded them, "you travel in *style*."

CHAPTER FIVE

The Chessboard

MAGNUS ALWAYS STAYED AT THE SAME HOTEL IN Shanghai, mostly out of nostalgia. He had largely found nostalgia to be a dangerous drug well kept away from—otherwise he would spend too much of his time nostalgic for when Manhattan still had farmland, or for the court of the Sun King, or for the days when Coca-Cola had real drugs in it. He indulged himself in this case because he had slept in the hotel a few times before it was ever a hotel, when it was the private residence of the notorious mob boss Du Yuesheng. It was a lavish Western-style villa in the French Concession, all classical white columns, stone wreaths, and pillared balconies curled around with gold. Du had bought it in the 1930s for, Magnus was sure, the main purpose of throwing the city's most scandalous parties, and Magnus made it to quite a lot of cities' most scandalous parties in the 1930s. Du Yuesheng had been a danger- ous, violent man, but extremely intelligent: far too intelligent to suppose Magnus had any interest in opium. They usually talked about opera, and opera singers.

Now, decades after his death, it was the Mansion Hotel. It

reminded Magnus of an earlier time—not a better time, just an earlier time. But who might stay in the Mansion Hotel today who remembered it as it was? Only the very oldest mundanes, if any remained. The place was decorated with relics of bygone, more decadent days: an old opium pipe, a phonograph that still played opera from crackling speakers, sepia photographs on the walls that Magnus had magically removed himself from, deep velvet chairs, and carved ebony cabinets. It was a great pleasure to sweep in through the gates and up the steps, past small stone guardians and fountains, and approach the opulent crystal-white facade with anticipation.

Magnus looked over at the others. They had *iratzed* and otherwise cleaned themselves up, but were still bedraggled enough from the fight that they'd kept their glamours on and waited outside as he went by himself to check in.

Magnus returned with keys dangling from his fingers, and they split into three groups. Magnus had booked a balcony suite for himself and Alec; he opened the door with a flourish.

Alec looked around consideringly. Magnus couldn't help but remember the young man Alec had been when they'd first visited Venice, the way he'd touched everything in their hotel room with wondering, surprised fingers.

Now he smiled. "It's very you."

Magnus laughed. "Because it's opulent yet tasteful?"

"That, but—I'm sure there are plenty more over-the-top hotels in Shanghai. More jewels, more gold, more glitter."

"I'm not always over-the-top," Magnus protested, sitting down on the end of the bed.

"Exactly," Alec said, and leaned over to kiss him. "This hotel feels like a piece of the past. Not modern glass-and-steel Shanghai, a different place. Not quieter or less, just—different."

Magnus felt his heart swell up with love for this man who

understood him so well. But all he said was, "It's way better than whatever barracks the Institute would put you in—"

Alec had thrown his jacket over a chair as they came in, and now whipped his shirt off. He grinned as it came over his head.

"Well," said Magnus, "my evening is looking better and better."

"It's a good thing you think scars are sexy," Alec said. He brushed at his arm and made a face. "I feel like I rolled in snake demon. I need a shower. Be right back? Hold that thought?"

Magnus pulled him down for another kiss, then, just for good measure, planted another one on the side of his jaw. Alec inhaled, his eyes closing. He bit Magnus gently on the lower lip and drew away. *"Shower."*

Relenting, Magnus fell back on the bed and let his eyes close.

The last time he'd been in Shanghai, it had been in 1990, with Catarina. It was the first time he'd set foot in the city since things had become bad there, in the 1940s, and stayed bad through the fifties and sixties and seventies. A family of Sighted mundanes had found and adopted a young warlock, only a toddler, and they desperately needed someone to teach them how to parent a Downworlder. The warlocks of Shanghai at the time were a strange lot, scholars obsessed with Chinese astrology and disinterested in the problems of a stray child; they would have just taken her away from the mundanes and left her to run in the streets of the Shadow Concession, taken care of by whatever Downworlders were around. Concerned parties had found Catarina, and she had convinced Magnus to come with her as an interpreter, and, Magnus suspected, because she was worried about him.

The warlock child was a scared-looking girl with huge bat ears, maybe three years old. When she saw Magnus for the first time, crowded into the tiny kitchen with her new parents and Catarina, she burst into tears, which did not strike him as a great start.

So he kept his distance while Catarina talked with the parents.

Luckily, they knew about Downworld already, and Magnus found himself writing down lists in Chinese of magical supplies as Catarina rattled off her recommendations in English. When there was a pause, he tried to flash a smile at the child—apparently named Mei—who ducked behind her mother's leg.

Was it his eyes? He returned to translating for Catarina, feeling self-conscious. A rare experience for him.

At some point the parents went into a different room of the house, apparently to discuss the situation with an older relative who wasn't in good enough health to emerge. They asked Catarina if she would watch Mei, and of course she agreed.

Mei slowly made her way over to Magnus, her eyes wide and her ears twitching slightly. Magnus tried to look as unthreatening as possible. He thought it was going fairly well, but then she suddenly shrieked and retreated.

Magnus held up his hands in surrender, and Mei moved back even farther and began to sob.

Catarina made a disapproving sound at Magnus. "What are you doing? Talk to her! Interact with her!"

"She doesn't like me," Magnus said. "I think she's scared of my eyes."

"Oh, for goodness' sake," said Catarina impatiently. "She isn't scared of your eyes. She just doesn't know you."

"Well," said Magnus, "I'm giving her space."

Catarina rolled her eyes. "You don't give toddlers *space*, Magnus. She's been alone enough already." She went over to Mei and got down on her knees to embrace her. Mei immediately stuffed her head into Catarina's chest, and Catarina just held her there. "This child is very lucky," she said quietly. "A warlock raised by loving mundane parents is . . . well, she's lucky."

"You're very lucky, Mei," Magnus said to Mei in Mandarin, in as gentle a voice as he could muster.

Mei peeked out from where she had buried her face against Catarina and looked at Magnus sideways, considering.

"And one day, you will wield great power!" Magnus said cheerfully.

Mei laughed, and Catarina gave Magnus a long-suffering look. But Magnus was pleased with himself.

"You see?" said Catarina. "It isn't so hard."

Magnus sometimes wondered if the girl remembered him. Probably not; he didn't remember much from when he was only three years old. Why did he care, anyway? He'd spent an hour with her, decades ago.

Strange, to touch someone's life and for them not to remember it.

NOW HE FELT THE BED SINK DOWN NEXT TO HIM, AND opened his eyes to discover Alec beside him. Alec's hair was wet, dripping onto his shoulders, blacker than a spill of ink. "First night without Max in the next room," said Magnus softly. "For a while."

"So I guess we can take our time," said Alec, running his finger under Magnus's waistband.

Magnus shivered. Clever repartee had deserted him; only Alec had ever been able to undo him so completely, reduce him to stammering component parts that all wanted only one thing.

"I guess we can," he said. And then there was no talking, for a time. Alec flowed into Magnus's arms, and he was all warm bare skin and damp hair and kisses that tasted like rain.

They kissed, at first gingerly, like they had when they were newly together, and then with a deepening sense of want. Magnus slid his hands down Alec's back, palms following the slope of his spine, the hard muscle of his latissimus dorsi. His lips grazed Alec's cheek, the little place behind his ear that Alec liked. There was something urgent in their connection, something that had been constrained and held back. Magnus reminded himself that there was no child in the next room, no chance that a siren-like wail would pierce the moment and declare it to be abruptly over. He missed Max, very badly. But he had also missed this.

Alec reached for Magnus's shirt buttons and started to undo them. Magnus focused on distracting Alec while Alec tried to concentrate on fine motor movements. Normally this led to a frustrated tearing off of the shirt, with buttons flying everywhere, which Magnus always enjoyed. This time, however, Alec managed to keep it together, and Magnus shrugged the shirt off one shoulder, then the other. Alec moved down to kiss Magnus's throat and the top of his chest, and then he stopped.

Magnus opened his eyes. Alec was looking at the wound that the Svefnthorn had given him, a diagonal slash across his heart glowing lightly in a shifting reddish-pink. Alec had seen the wound the night Magnus got it, but he hadn't been face-to-face with it like this.

Alec continued looking at Magnus's chest, his head tilted. Magnus regarded him with bemusement. Slowly, thoughtfully, Alec licked his finger, then brought it down, keeping eye contact with Magnus, and traced his wet finger along the length of the wound.

"Does it hurt?" he said hoarsely.

"No," Magnus said. "It's just the remnants of magic. It doesn't feel any different than if it weren't there."

Alec reached his hand up to touch Magnus's face, fingertips brushing from the curve of his eye, trailing down his cheek, curling under his jaw so Magnus was held still for a moment. Then Alec let out a long breath. Magnus hadn't even noticed the tension Alec was holding, but he felt when it dissipated and the taut line of Alec's shoulders eased.

Magnus found himself sitting up again. He balled up the shirt, now totally free of his body, and tossed it aside. He reached for Alec and gathered him into his lap, and Alec kissed him again. Magnus wove a hand through Alec's hair and tugged a little to bring him even closer, catching Alec's sharply torn breath in his own mouth. The kiss went from light to heat. Magnus curled two fingers into the knot holding Alec's towel together, and sealed the space between them, so not even the moonlight through the curtains could slide between their bodies. Alec didn't break that craving, clinging kiss as his hands slid up Magnus's arms and their kisses grew wilder, a savage accompaniment to the sweet interplay of touch and heat and pressure.

Their bodies pressed together hard. Magnus's head was full of smoke and his skin alive with fire as he reached down and deftly peeled away Alec's towel. The towel quickly went the way of the shirt.

"We're still us," Alec whispered to Magnus, and Magnus felt a wave of love and desire go through him, fervent desire. They loved Max, they loved him more than life itself, but it was also true: they were still them.

"To always being us," Magnus murmured, and pulled Alec down onto the bed with him.

AFTERWARD, THEY LAY IN EACH OTHER'S ARMS, BREATH-ing together quietly. Moonlight came in through the window, and the ambient glow of the French Concession outside. An unknown amount of time passed, and then Magnus heard Alec's muffled voice: "I hate to spoil the mood, and I would honestly be happy just staying here and not moving ever again, but . . . I need to sleep, or we're going to have to fight through demons *and* jet lag."

"I've got it," Magnus said, and he raised his hand in the air and waved it, making whorls of golden dust in the air that, he knew, would settle upon them gently and lull them into an easy slumber.

Or that was the plan, anyway. Instead Magnus felt a jolt of magic burst into his hand from the warm node in the center of his chest, and way more sleep dust than he'd intended appeared in the air, then fell in a clump directly onto their faces. Alec sputtered and laughed. "What was *that?*" he said, his eyes already closed, and then he went limp against the pillow and began to snore gently.

"I seem to be having some issues with calib—" said Magnus, and then he too was asleep.

THE NEXT MORNING MAGNUS WOKE TO FIND HIMSELF alone. Alec had gotten up at daybreak, along with the other Shadowhunters, and they had all gone to the Institute. Alec left a note saying he had let Magnus sleep because he seemed to need it—which made Magnus immediately suspicious. After all, he had a more direct connection to the Ke family than any of them; why had they not wanted him to come with them?

He trailed wearily into the bathroom. He splashed water on his tired face and stared into the gold-framed glass above the porcelain-and-walnut sink. The jagged line carved into his chest stared back at him, still emanating its strange light. He was being ridiculous, he told himself—Alec was always forthright with him, and if he said he let Magnus sleep because he seemed to need the sleep, then he was surely telling the truth.

The velvet curtains were tightly shut across the tall balcony doors, the rattle and purr of the busy city morning muffled. The dimness made everything look shadowy, even Magnus's eyes. He opened the curtains and squinted into the light.

He put on clothes—Shanghai was hot and muggy, as always, so Magnus opted for white linen pants, a guayabera, and a white Panama hat—and went downstairs, wondering if it was too late for breakfast. Attached to the hotel was an enclosed garden, its walls tall, white, and adorned with loops of white stone made to resemble wrought ironwork. He found himself wandering out into it, enjoying the sun on his face. Tourists wandered the graveled paths, elegantly dressed; Magnus counted at least ten languages being spoken in his immediate vicinity. Deep red flowers grew on bushes here, dark green leaves offering up their hearts to the sky. Branches from other trees curved over the walls as if they wanted to enter the garden too. There were benches scattered about, and a stone bridge in an angular geometric pattern, leading to a little green-and-yellow pagoda open to the elements and guarded by a stone creature.

On the bridge was Shinyun.

In a major change from her usual, more traditional clothes, she had gone for razor-sharp tailoring and a blood-red business suit. The Svefnthorn was strapped to her back, its ugly twisted point jutting out behind her head.

This, Magnus thought, was a lot to deal with before coffee.

"Magnus!" Shinyun called to him sharply. "Stay there." She glanced around. "Or I'll have to hurt one of these nice little traveling folks. What does one call them? Tourists."

Magnus weighed his options. They were grim. None of the tourists had turned to look at Shinyun when she spoke: he expected she was glamoured. He could try to lunge in with some warding magic, but at least a few mundanes were likely to be hurt or killed even so, and he wasn't sure of the current extent of Shinyun's powers.

He didn't move as Shinyun approached. Quietly, he began to surround himself with wards. He could at least protect himself from another thorning.

"If you want to fight," said Magnus lightly, "I'll have to put you on my calendar. I can't possibly do anything before I've eaten."

"It needn't come to that if you don't do anything stupid," she said. "I just want to talk."

"If you want to talk," said Magnus, "you'd better be ready to talk over breakfast."

Shinyun drew herself up with dignity and said, "I am." She brought out a plastic bag from within her purse. "Do you like *ci fan?*"

"I do," said Magnus, eyeing the little parcels of glutinous rice. "I like them very much."

A few minutes later found them seated on benches in the garden. It was a fine morning, sunny and breezy. The osmanthus flowers were blooming in Shanghai, and the wind brought their gentle scent, a little like peach or apricot. He chewed a mouthful of pork and pickled vegetables and felt a little better. Unfortunately, this reminded him that he was breakfasting with an unstable person, who had stabbed him the last time they'd met, with a weapon she currently had with her, and who, if Clary's dream meant anything, might try to stab him again. On the other hand, at least he was pretty sure the breakfast was not poisoned.

Magnus popped another *ci fan* into his mouth and checked his protective wards. They were still in place. A charging rhino shouldn't be able to get through them.

"How did you find me?" he asked around a mouthful. "I ask only out of professional curiosity."

"We have been in Shanghai for months," Shinyun said. "Obviously by now we've assembled a team of secret informants throughout the city."

"Obviously," murmured Magnus. If it turned out that he and his friends hadn't been able to find Ragnor only because he was more successfully tracking *them*, he was going to be very annoyed. He hoped the others hadn't encountered Ragnor on their way to the Institute or anything. On the other hand, he also hoped they didn't come back before he figured out how to get rid of Shinyun. "So, uh—how's your evil master? How are his evil plans going?"

"Sammael's only counsel is his own," said Shinyun. "I follow his lead without question. It's very relaxing, actually."

"So you don't even know what he's trying to do? Do you know why he wanted the Book of the White? Do you know why he wanted *Ragnor*?"

"Oh, that's easy enough." Shinyun took a bite. "He wanted Ragnor to find him a realm. And Ragnor did. A while ago. But by then he'd come to accept Sammael's victory and became his willing minion."

"His *willing* minion?" said Magnus, eyeing the Svefnthorn. "That doesn't sound like the Ragnor Fell I know."

"Sammael is not like other demons," Shinyun said. She regarded Magnus thoughtfully. "You think I'm a fool, tying my fortunes to the Serpent of the Garden."

"No, no," Magnus protested. "Serpent of the Garden, he sounds very trustworthy."

"It's not a matter of trust," Shinyun said. "I know what I'm doing."

"Okay," said Magnus. "What are you doing?"

"Here on Earth," Shinyun said, "power is a complicated, strange thing. Humans grant one another power; it's exchanged, it's gained and lost—it's all very abstract. But *out there*—" She gestured above her.

"In the sky?" said Magnus.

"Out beyond our own world, in the worlds of demons and angels and whatever else is out there. Out there power is not some abstract piece of human culture. Power is *power*. What we here on Earth call magic is just power by another name, power wielded here in this realm."

"And you want power," Magnus said. Despite himself, he was a little interested. He had always known there were Princes of Hell and mad archangels out there, playing with humanity as if with a chessboard. This was like a peek into the gaming room.

"Power is all anybody can ever want," said Shinyun. "Power is the ability to choose what happens, to will something and have it come to pass. Ideals humans talk about—having freedom, meting out justice—these are all just power by other names."

"You're wrong," Magnus said, but gently. "And even if somewhere, out in some primordial abyss, you'd be right, it doesn't matter. Because we live here on Earth, where power is complicated and interesting, instead of cosmic and boring."

Shinyun bared her teeth, a strange sight given the blankness of her expression. "That may have been true of Earth once," she said, "but then Sammael released cosmic, boring demons all over it, and Raziel released cosmic, boring Shadowhunters to fight them." She shook her head. "Maybe you can't understand. You were born to great heritage. You don't know what it's like to go through this world in weakness."

Magnus laughed. "I was born to dirt-poor farmers in an oppressed imperial colony. I'm doing all right now, but—"

"Of course I'm not talking about your mundane parent," hissed Shinyun. "I'm talking about *Asmodeus*."

Reflexively, Magnus looked around; no one was looking at them. No one had tried to sit on their bench, either; glamours were useful that way.

"Any warlock," Shinyun went on in a quieter but no less intense voice, "who thinks he is more similar to humans than he is to demons, that humans deserve his protection—that warlock is deluding himself. He is not a human. He is a demon gone native."

"Look," Magnus said, as she stared bug-eyed at him, "I get it. I get why you would try to find the biggest, baddest demon you can, and make him your protector. But you don't need to do that. You don't need to find *any* demons. You're a warlock: you already wield magical power that humans couldn't dream of. And you're immortal! You've got it pretty good, Shinyun. You're the only one who doesn't know it. Settle down. Start a family! Adopt a kid, maybe."

Shinyun said, "Living forever isn't a *power* when your life is a tragedy."

Magnus sighed. "*Every* warlock's life starts as a tragedy. There are no love stories in any warlock's origins. But you get to choose. You choose what kind of world you live in."

"You *don't*," said Shinyun. "Fish eat smaller fish. Demons eat smaller demons."

"That's not all there is," Magnus insisted. "Shinyun." He put his hand on her shoulder. "Why did you come to see me? It can't have been to win this argument."

Shinyun giggled, a disconcerting segue from her previous attitude. "I came to give you the present I promised you back in Brooklyn. *And* I wanted to win this argument. And now I can do both at the same time."

She lunged, her hand a blur of motion; Magnus was already on his feet, his hand upraised, blue fire humming from his palm.

Something stabbed through and through him. He gasped.

He had been ready for Shinyun to thrust with the Svefnthorn, had been braced with magic to block her, but his wards shattered apart like glass as the Svefnthorn drove directly into the wound it had already made in his chest.

A spasm of magic, not quite pain and not quite pleasure, but overwhelming whatever its valence, drove Magnus to his knees. He looked down at the spike sticking out of his chest for the second time. He took a shuddering breath. "How—?"

Looming above him, Shinyun said, in a tone of both satisfaction and pity, "The thorn is already part of your magic, Magnus. Your magic cannot ward against itself."

She twisted the thorn in his chest, like a key opening a lock.

"You cannot guard against the Svefnthorn." She twisted it again before finally withdrawing it from his chest. There was no blood on the spike, but Magnus thought he saw it glitter with blue light as she returned it to its scabbard. "Don't tell me you haven't looked it up since I told you about it."

"It's from Norse mythology, and it puts people to sleep," said Magnus. "Except obviously it's somehow connected to Sammael, who isn't part of Norse mythology, so no, I guess we have only done the barest minimum research so far, now that I say it out loud."

"Outside of mundane myth," Shinyun said, "it has quite a history. My first task from Sammael was to recover it from its hiding place and attune it to my master. It was quite an adventure, actually. I faced many perils, and engaged in many small intrigues—"

"Please," said Magnus, holding up his hand. "I don't care." He put his hand to his chest, felt the heat emanating from the wound. The node of magic in his chest continued to thump and beat like a second heart, stronger than before. It felt—well, actually, it felt pretty good.

Shinyun sat herself down next to Magnus where he knelt on the grass. She seemed quite calm. "You'll come to understand," she said, as though confiding a secret. "I thorned myself as soon as I was given permission to do so. I have never regretted it. Soon you'll appreciate what I've done for you."

"If I don't," said Magnus, "are you going to stab me again?"

Shinyun shook her head. She seemed excited, as though she'd had to wait a long time to tell Magnus something, and now she was finally getting to do so. "No," she said. "Now you have a choice. Now *you'll* choose to be struck again by the thorn."

Magnus could tell that she desperately wanted him to ask what she meant. He refused to give her the satisfaction, and just waited silently while Shinyun watched him eagerly.

Finally she said, "Once you've tasted the thorn twice—"

"Please don't say 'tasted,'" said Magnus, put off.

"—you are connected to the power of my master. A third taste—"

"Please," said Magnus.

Shinyun made an impatient gesture, but she said, "A third *wound* with the thorn will make you his entirely. He shall become the master of your will, and with your newfound gift, you will serve him."

Magnus goggled at her. "Why would I ever do that?"

"Because," she said, almost bouncing on her knees with glee, "if you aren't wounded a third time, the thorn will burn you from the inside out. You'll be consumed by its flame. Only by accepting Sammael into your heart can you avoid death."

Magnus put his hand to his chest again, alarmed. "What?" he said. "So I have to accept Sammael into my heart *literally*? Or I die?"

"That's how it works," Shinyun said. "No magic can reverse the course of the thorn once it has burrowed into you." She playfully pointed at Magnus's chest. He slapped her finger away. "Soon enough," she said, "you'll realize this is the best thing that's ever happened to you."

"I would be very surprised," said Magnus, forcing himself to stand up, "if it made it off the 'worst things that have ever happened to me' list. But I'll keep you posted." He took a deep breath around the wound and looked at Shinyun. "I thought you'd learn. We tried to help you, we really did."

"And now I'm helping you," she said. "The next time we meet, you'll feel differently. I promise."

"And when will that be?"

"The time is closer than you think. The time may be closer than even I think." Shinyun was almost dancing, she was so pleased with herself.

"What does that mean?" Magnus yelled in exasperation. "Why are you so crazy?"

But a blood-red fog had appeared beneath Shinyun's feet, and it swiftly swirled in a rising cloud to cover her completely. When it dissipated into the morning breeze, she was gone.

CHAPTER SIX

Tian

IT WASN'T SOMETHING HE WOULD ADMIT TO ANYBODY but his closest friends, but Alec kept a list in his head of the Institutes he most wanted to visit.

Obviously there were hundreds of Institutes that he would *like* to visit. This was just a simple top ten.

There was the Maui Institute, of course, where there were no external walls and little ceiling and, it was said, very minimal demon activity. The Amsterdam Institute, a huge invisible boat permanently anchored in the IJ. The Cluj Institute, a great stone castle jutting into the sky, high above the timberline in the Carpathian Mountains. And there was the Shanghai Institute.

Unlike any other Institute Alec could think of, Shanghai's was in a place that had been well-known and sacred to mundanes long before the Shadowhunters were even created. Once the building had been part of Longhua Temple, a complex of Buddhist monasteries and shrines that had stood for almost two thousand years. The complex had been constantly worked on, repaired, and updated over the centuries, and early in their history the Shadowhunters had taken the opportunity to claim some of the unused grounds to make their home.

Walking with his friends through the warm, sunny morning, Alec stopped outside the temple complex to look at its most famous sight, the Longhua Pagoda, a tower of six roofs with upturned eaves, stacked around a crimson-and-ochre octagon that rose into the sky. Alec had seen pictures of it dozens of times. "I can't believe I'm actually here," he said out loud.

"You could have come anytime," Isabelle noted from behind him. "We have Portals."

"I just didn't take the opportunity before," said Alec. "I should visit some of the others on my list, when we get home." The brief, disloyal thought, *I should have visited these places before I had a kid,* flitted through his mind, and he rejected it. It wasn't like he and Magnus were going to have to fly in a commercial mundane airplane with Max. They could just carry him through a Portal. Assuming Portals didn't continue going to the wrong places, or being infested with beetle demons.

The pagoda was beautiful, but the crush of mundane tourists suddenly felt oppressive. He turned away. "Let's go."

The Institute was made of the same brick as most of the other temple buildings, with the same upturned eaves and hexagonal windows. In a tower off its central axis was a copper bell, the twin of the one in the mundane bell tower close by. The bells had been a set, created to ward off demons, and while the mundanes rang theirs only occasionally, the Shadowhunters welcomed the dusk by tolling theirs. Alec wondered if he'd get to hear it. He was already thinking about how to find an excuse to return here before they left.

Going up the stairs to the massive double doors, he hesitated. Leaving Magnus behind had been a hard choice, but his boyfriend needed a break. Magnus dealt with the stress of adding parenthood to his existing life simply by sleeping less and pushing himself more.

It was the least Alec could do to let him sleep in today. It was true that Magnus knew the Ke family, who ran the Institute, and no doubt he would join them soon, but Alec was sure the rest of them could handle going to a friendly Institute without assistance. They were all in gear, and wearing runes, so they'd be immediately recognizable.

He started back up the stairs but froze as one of the giant doors creaked loudly on its hinges, then swung open fully.

Alec was somewhat surprised to discover that behind the door was a very young man—perhaps eighteen, a few years younger than Alec himself—tall and wiry, with straight-cut black hair and dramatic eyebrows. He was wearing gear in a dark, shiny burgundy—the famous oxblood lacquer of the Shadowhunters of China, which went in and out of fashion every few generations. He reminded Alec of someone, but he couldn't think who it was.

Clary raised her hand in greeting and began to speak, but the young man was looking at Alec.

"Are you Alec Lightwood?" he asked, in accentless English.

Alec raised his eyebrows in surprise.

Isabelle said, "Oh *no*, Alec's famous now."

The man turned to look at her. "And you must be Isabelle, his sister. Come," he said, waving them inside. "All of you are expected."

THE INSTITUTE FELT SURPRISINGLY EMPTY. THERE WERE only, it turned out, four Shadowhunters at home, the man explained: the rest were out "investigating the Portal situation."

"Forgive me," he said when they had all filed in and he had closed the door after them. "I don't mean to be mysterious. I am Ke Yi Tian—you should call me Tian—and I was told to expect you. Alec and Isabelle Lightwood, as well as Clary Fairchild, Jace Herondale, and Simon Lovelace."

"So Alec isn't famous?" Isabelle sounded disappointed.

"Told by whom?" Jace said. He sounded guarded; Alec didn't blame him.

"A member of my family," Tian said. "No longer a Shadowhunter, but he continues to . . . keep an eye on those he considers persons of interest."

"That's not ominous at all," muttered Simon.

"It's not," said Clary. "He means Brother Zachariah."

"Former Brother Zachariah," said Tian. He looked around at them and gestured to a door. "Shall we walk and talk in the peach orchard?"

They all looked at each other. Alec said, "Yes. Yes, that seems like it would be very nice."

The peach orchard was a fine and pleasant space, well-shaded and equipped with small wooden tables and stools placed here and there for sitting. Tian led them to one, and Simon and Clary sat down, while the rest of them remained standing. "So are you here about the Portals?"

"Sort of," said Alec. "What's going on with the Portals, exactly?"

Tian looked surprised. "Portals are misbehaving all over the world. It only started a few days ago, but it's quickly become a real mess. I assumed you'd know—didn't you travel to Shanghai by Portal?"

"Yes," said Clary, "and they were definitely . . . misbehaving. We assumed it was just us."

"Everyone thought it was just them," said Tian. "But it's everyone. Portals go to the wrong place, or don't open at all, or they're full of demons. Everyone is out looking into it."

"We think our mission might be indirectly related to the Portals somehow," Alec said carefully, "but actually we're in Shanghai to look for a couple of warlocks, one man and one woman. They stole a powerful spell book from New York recently, and we think they're too dangerous to be allowed to keep it."

Tian tugged idly at a branch, his dark hair falling into his eyes. "Well, the good news—and the bad news—is that almost all the Downworlders in Shanghai live in the same neighborhood."

"The Downworlder Concession," Alec said.

"Exactly. But there are a *lot* of Downworlders in the city. A *lot*. I should know—that's my patrol area."

"They let you patrol there?" said Isabelle.

Tian nodded and said, with some pride, "Relations between Shadowhunters and Downworlders have always been very good in Shanghai."

"Even now?" said Alec.

Tian grimaced. "We do our best. It's about knowing the people, building relationships with them, trusting them, so when it matters, they'll trust you."

Alec found he liked this guy. "Do you have any suggestions?"

Tian nodded. "If you can wait, you should go to the Shadow Market tomorrow. There are a few people you could talk to . . . but really the best place to start would be with Peng Fang. He's a vampire blood merchant—"

"We've met," Alec said glumly. Isabelle and Simon exchanged puzzled looks.

"And there are others." Tian hesitated. "Would you be offended if I escorted you? Things are better in Shanghai than elsewhere, but many Downworlders would still be wary of Nephilim strangers. Especially obviously foreign Nephilim strangers."

"Hey," said Simon defensively, "Alec here is the *founder* of the Downworlder-Shadowhunter Alliance. He's got a Downworlder pass."

"I don't," said Alec, "have a 'Downworlder pass.'"

"If any Shadowhunter does, you do," Simon insisted.

"I'll take you and make introductions," Tian said. "They know me. And you'll want to split up when you walk around. Six Shadow-hunters together in a Shadow Market looks like something's about to go down." He smiled at them. "Come to my family home tomorrow. We can have breakfast and then go to the Market."

"But the Market is at night," said Simon.

Tian smiled more broadly. "Welcome to Shanghai, home of the one and only Sunlit Market."

"What do—" began Simon.

"Vampires have a blacked-out section of the Market that's been enclosed for their use," said Tian.

Simon nodded, satisfied.

"I heard something about a bookstore," Alec said. "The Celestial Palace."

Tian's eyebrows went up. "It's nearby. We can stop there as well. It is . . ." He hesitated. "It is faerie-owned and staffed. You'll attract attention. The whole concession will know in minutes that a gang of foreign Shadowhunters has come to the Palace."

"Will it cause trouble?" Jace asked.

Tian shrugged. "Probably not. Just gossip. If you don't want faerie monarchs or vampire clans or the Spiral Labyrinth to know you're in Shanghai, that'll be blown the moment you walk in."

"Why wouldn't we want them to know we're in Shanghai?" said Alec.

Tian hesitated. "May I speak frankly?" he said. When they nodded, he went on. "One of the ways things stay friendly between all of us here in Shanghai is that we Shadowhunters try to take situations as they come, and find solutions where we can."

"I'm not sure what you're getting at," said Clary.

Tian cleared his throat. "Our goal is the overall stability of the Shadow side of the city. That means sometimes allowing some Downworlder activity that might not normally be considered acceptable. Always because of important extenuating circumstances, you understand."

"Oh, I get it," said Jace. "You're saying, if we go to the concession together, we might see some illegal stuff, and you want to know if we can let it slide."

"*Is* that what you're saying?" Alec said.

"I wouldn't put it in quite those terms, but—yes," said Tian.

They exchanged looks. Carefully, Jace said, "While all of us are known primarily for our strict adherence to the letter and spirit of the Law . . ."

"Obviously," agreed Isabelle.

". . . we are also visitors here, and we understand that circumstances are often complicated and have a lot of history. Also, we are from the New York Institute, and we are past masters of letting it slide."

Jace winked. Tian looked puzzled.

"We're not here to interfere with the way you do your Shadowhunting," Alec clarified, by way of reassurance.

Tian's brow furrowed. "Do you say that in English? 'Shadowhunting'?"

"No," said Isabelle. "No one says that."

"Well, maybe we should start," returned Alec. Isabelle stuck out her tongue at him.

"So what's the demon situation like here?" Clary asked.

"Not great. Getting worse." Tian straightened up. He seemed uneasy. "Let's go back inside. I'd like to see if my father has returned from his rounds."

As they walked, he elaborated. "For one thing, in a city this big, there are always going to be idiots who summon new demons, and old demons that showed up centuries ago and are still hanging around. In fact, we've been getting a lot of the latter lately. Strange demons, things that haven't been seen in Shanghai for a hundred years. Things you have to look up in a book when you get back from fighting them."

"Any idea why?"

"A bunch of theories. Nothing really solid. It's funny: for decades Shanghai was known as this very safe city, very few demons, safe for Downworlders. In the time after Yanluo—"

They were back in the entry hall of the Institute, and Tian was about to continue speaking when there was a sudden loud knock at the front doors. Tian looked sharply at the doors, then went to answer the knock, his brow furrowed.

"What's wrong?" said Alec.

"You can't *knock* on this door," Tian said. "It's half a meter thick. No one could knock hard enough."

He pulled the door open and behind it, in the glare of the morning, was Magnus. He was doubled over, hands on his knees, panting, as though he'd been running hard.

"Magnus!" Alec started toward him.

Magnus looked wild-eyed, not like himself at all. He looked around at the group, then at Tian. "You must be Tian," he said. "I'm Magnus Bane, good to meet you. All of you," he added, "get out here and bring weapons. Now."

ALEC FOLLOWED MAGNUS THROUGH THE DOORS. BEHIND him, Isabelle gasped.

Black curtains of shadow hung from the sky under what appeared to be a small, low-hanging storm cloud. There was no rain, though thunder rumbled. The area under the cloud was dark as night, and out of the boiling fog at the bottom of the cloud tumbled demons, dozens of them.

In the center of the rain of falling demons, a hundred feet above the ground, Shinyun floated, her hands raised. Light glowed around her, crimson and rippling.

"So, a few things," said Magnus.

Tian emerged from the Institute, now holding something on a

silver cord, which he whipped around beside him. "Who is that?"

"That is a very bad warlock who doesn't like me," said Magnus. "That's the first thing. The second thing is, I'm not a hundred percent sure, but I *think* she may be in command of some demons."

The demons who landed were rolling and coalescing into their various different forms. There were creatures that seemed made of the cloud bank itself, with cold, bone-white eyes. There were more of the snake demons that they had fought in the faerie's apartment, and grinning skeletons.

Alec had come up beside Magnus and was sticking close to him. "How did she find us?"

"She found me," said Magnus. "At the hotel."

"How?" said Clary.

He rolled his eyes. "She has spies everywhere, apparently."

"She attacked you?" said Jace.

"Yes, but then I left the hotel to come to the Institute and she showed up when I was halfway here and attacked me *again*, with demons this time."

"Does that mean she stabbed you with the thorn again?" Alec said in alarm.

"There's no time to go into that—"

Alec turned to face Magnus and grabbed him by the shoulders. "Did she stab you again?" he said again, more intently.

Magnus said, "Yes."

It was like being stabbed himself. Alec closed his eyes.

"And it gets worse. But we really *don't* have time for that yet. Right now we need to deal with her little army. They followed me here."

"You led her to us?" Simon looked surprised.

"Well," said Magnus in irritation, "I didn't think I could handle her and all the demons by myself. What would you have suggested I do?"

Alec didn't say anything. Normally, Magnus would have been able to neutralize Shinyun easily; he was a much more powerful warlock than her. Either she had grown more powerful or Magnus had become weaker. Or both. And now he'd been wounded again.

He drew his bow and fired a couple of arrows at the balls of fog; they stuck, so there was *something* solid in there. "Tian!" he called over. "Are these your locals? What am I shooting at?"

"The snakes are Xiangliu—do you not have them in America?" There was a flash, and the rope Tian was whirling suddenly burst forward, at an angle, and Alec saw that at the end of the rope was a diamond-shaped blade of *adamas*, which lopped the head off one of said Xiangliu. "The clouds are Ala, they're mostly annoying."

"Oh man," said Isabelle, running to Tian, a slender staff in her hand. "What *is* that weapon? It's awesome."

Tian looked pleased. "Rope dart." Expertly he spun the returning rope around his body, catching it near the blade to regain control.

"I want one," said Isabelle. She whipped the end of the staff and a long curved blade, like a scimitar, unfolded and snapped into place at its end.

Simon had dropped his bow and drawn two seraph blades, which glowed in his hands like beacons in the unnatural dark. "Is that a guisarme?" he called to Isabelle.

Isabelle impaled a skeleton on the end of the weapon, then whipped it around and impaled a second skeleton before the first had even fallen. "It's a *glaive*," she said, with a wicked grin at Simon.

"God, I love you," said Simon.

"Can someone throw some water on those two?" said Magnus. "Look, I'm sorry for bringing her here. I didn't know what to do. Shinyun—I'm going to go and try to talk to her."

"Can you fly up to where she is?" said Alec.

"Yes, but I'm going to need help if I don't want to get knocked out of the sky."

"We'll keep everything else off you," said Alec.

"I'm going to engage with the skeletons," said Simon.

"I'm already engaged with the skeletons," Isabelle said. She looked Simon up and down, concern showing through her battle-ready expression. "You got this?"

"I," said Simon, "may only have been a Shadowhunter for a short time, but I have been preparing my *whole life* to fight skeleton warriors. I got this."

Jace had disappeared. Alec cast his eyes over the swarm of demons and knocked an Ala out of the sky with two quick arrows. He soon caught sight of Jace, who was taking high leaps into the air, much higher than any mundane could, and whipping his flail into anything near him. Tian's rope dart was making the Xiangliu dance and dodge to stay away from its unpredictable arcs, and as Alec laid down more arrow fire, he noted that Clary had placed herself so that the disoriented Xiangliu dodged away from Tian and directly into her seraph blades.

Behind Alec, sparks flew from Magnus's fingers toward the ground, and he rose into the air toward Shinyun. Alec watched him, bow at the ready. There was something different about the sparks—they seemed . . . sharper? And there was an odd haze over the whole battle, like looking through a hot fire.

Around Alec the five other Shadowhunters laid waste to the demons on the ground. Alec kept his eyes on Magnus, knocking the cloud demons away with a well-placed arrow if they drifted toward him.

"Alec, behind you," Simon yelled, and Alec whirled just in time to see a surprised-looking Xiangliu shatter its way out of existence. Tian's rope dart hovered a few inches in front of Alec's face, then whipped away. Alec looked over at Tian, who winked.

Alec returned his gaze to Magnus.

* * *

MAGNUS FLEW TOWARD SHINYUN AND WONDERED IF she'd try to blow him out of the sky. He kept his gaze on her; he had to trust Alec to keep his path clear. He *did* trust Alec to keep his path clear.

"Shinyun," he yelled as he got closer, to be heard over the wind and the rumbling backdrop of thunder. But also because he was mad. "You give me a beautiful gift and then you attack us? I thought our conversation went well!"

Shinyun gazed at him impassively. "You could summon just as large an army, you know."

"I couldn't," said Magnus, "but also I wouldn't. For one thing, it's extremely illegal." Shinyun barked a laugh. "For another, then we would have *twice* as many demons, rather than *no* demons, which is my preference."

"Oh, but you could," Shinyun said. There was a rush of wind and Magnus became aware of two Ala demons rushing at him, one from each side. Shinyun, he thought grimly, was trying to make a point.

Well, fine. How about this *point?*

With a roar, Magnus thrust out his arms, letting the simmering bubble of magic deep in his chest come to a full boil. Bolts of lightning crackled out from both of his hands, bright blue and knife-edged. The Ala demons were split clean in half by the two bolts and fell away. Magnus lowered his hands—to his surprise, he had had no trouble keeping himself aloft during his attack.

While Shinyun's face was as unexpressive as ever, Magnus got the distinct impression that she was smirking at him. "You see? Whatever you may think of my master, the Svefnthorn's power is undeniable."

"What does your master think of *me*?"

She laughed. "He doesn't know anything about you yet. But I think he's going to be very pleased when he does."

"Why would he be pleased?" Magnus said incredulously. "Because you're strengthening one of his enemies?"

She laughed. "You don't know Sammael at all."

"I agree," said Magnus. "I do not." He looked around. "Looks like my friends are almost finished mopping up your demon army."

Shinyun shrugged. "There are more where they came from. But I'll go. I just wanted you and your friends to see a little demonstration of what the thorn makes possible."

She raised her hands, and as one, the demons far below them froze. As one, they turned to look at Shinyun. Magnus saw one of them crumple and vanish as a Shadowhunter, he couldn't tell who, took the opportunity to thrust a blade through its back.

Another gesture, and all the remaining demons rose into the air. They rose until they began to be drawn back into the black cloud whose shadow they had been fighting in.

"Wait," said Magnus. "Where's Ragnor? I want to—I *need* to speak to him."

"I'll pass on the message," Shinyun drawled, "but he's very busy."

Magnus yelled, "How did he evade our Tracking magic? What are you trying to accomplish? *Where's the Book?*"

Shinyun just laughed. She rose into the storm cloud above her, still laughing. Magnus had to grant her a certain classic villainous style.

After Shinyun entered the cloud, all was still. In silence, over about two minutes, the storm cloud faded, lightened, dissipated into wisps of curlicue mist. It was gone; Shinyun and her demons were gone.

It was, again, a sunny day.

ALEC WATCHED MAGNUS DESCEND, MAGNUS'S CURLING black hair tousled by the harsh wind. He touched down lightly, graceful as a cat, and looked toward Alec.

Alec was relieved. He was terrified. He had questions.

He also noticed Tian's expression. He looked stricken, and Alec wondered whether he hadn't been around warlock magic much before. But Tian wasn't looking at Magnus.

"Baigujing," Tian said. He looked at the sky, then back to Alec. "The skeletons. They were the daughters of Baigujing."

"Who?" said Isabelle.

"Ooh, I know this, I know this," Simon said, raising his hand and bouncing up and down. Isabelle gave him a look and he put his hand down. "Sorry. I just Ascended this spring," he said to Tian.

Tian made a go-ahead gesture. "No, feel free, if you want to explain."

"Baigujing is a Greater Demon. She's in *Journey to the West*," he added. "The novel. Uh, she's a shape-shifter, but her real form is a skeleton. And she has these . . . attendants."

"Her daughters," Tian said. He took a deep breath. "Baigujing herself is . . . well, neither she nor her attendants have been seen in our world in a long time."

"Like you were saying," said Clary, "demons nobody's seen for a long time."

"These demons were part of an army," Tian said, shaking his head. "Baigujing was a captain in that army. But that army was destroyed and scattered generations ago. This should be completely impossible. And there's more—"

"A lot of impossible things have been happening lately," said Magnus, joining the others.

Simon folded his arms and regarded the warlock with narrowed eyes. "So, flying? You can just fly now? That's a thing?"

"I . . . don't really know," Magnus said. He sounded distant. He gave Tian a wan smile. "Ke Yi Tian, is it? I'm Magnus Bane. High Warlock of Brooklyn."

"You've already been higher today than any other warlock I know," Tian said.

Magnus pointed a finger at him. "Good one. Do you think there might be somewhere I could lie down for a minute?"

Alec was at Magnus's side in under a second, his arm around him, letting Magnus lean on him hard. Magnus was pale, his breath short. "He needs to rest," Alec said to Tian. "Can we take him into the Institute?"

Tian shook his head. "That will lead to more trouble, not less. My family all knows Magnus, but there are other people coming in and out of the Institute constantly now that this Portal business is happening. And this warlock who doesn't like you could find you here again."

"What do you suggest?" Alec said.

Tian smiled. "How would you like to meet my grandmother?"

CHAPTER SEVEN

Ke House

MAGNUS WANTED TO OPEN A PORTAL TO KE HOUSE. Everyone else voted *not* to open a Portal, considering what was going on with the Portals, but Magnus was feeling lucky.

Magnus knew he had to sleep, and very, very soon. But he also felt surprisingly good. He opened the Portal with a flourish. Beetle demons immediately began to drop out of it; each had just enough time to register surprise that it was in broad daylight before exploding into ichor. After about a minute and fifty or so beetle demons, Magnus closed the Portal with a sigh.

"I just couldn't stand their sad little feelers anymore," he said.

His friends looked at him with concern. Tian raised an eyebrow and waved a phone at Magnus. "I've called some taxis."

Soon Magnus was watching the city go by out the window as they drove past Jiao Tong University and into more residential areas. Magnus hadn't been to Ke House in . . . more than eighty years. Shanghai had gone through not just a transformation but many transformations piled atop one another since then.

He thought of the first time he came to Paris after Haussmann's renovations. He stood on the Île de la Cité in bewilderment, unable to get his bearings. He could see the river; he could see the spires of Notre Dame a few blocks away. He had stood in this geographical location dozens of times before, but he had no idea where he was.

So it was today. The new houses of modern Shanghai smeared by in the windows.

No, Magnus thought as they helped him out of the car. *That isn't the strange thing.* This *is the strange thing.* Tall double doors, gleaming metallic red, set in simple gray concrete walls impossible to see over. These doors were the same as he remembered. It was so strange, to see something that hadn't changed.

The wards allowed Tian through, and he waved to his guests to follow him. They did so a bit warily. Magnus had seen how surprised Jace and Isabelle had looked when Tian had explained that the ancestral home of the Ke family wasn't the Institute. It seemed the Ke family was a large one, and a traditional one. Ke House was older than the Institute, and those family members who had retired from Institute work, or were simply part of the Shanghai Conclave, had always lived here.

The property itself was large, Magnus remembered, but the main house itself very modest. He was sure there had been renovations since the 1920s, but the core of the house seemed much the same: brick-red columns, dougong brackets, and straight-lined roof, simple and modest, but protected, of course, by the traditional ridge beasts on the corners of the roof, beautifully carved lions and horses commemorating the joining of the Ke family and some other household, centuries ago. The brackets were painted blue now, Magnus thought. A blue that seemed to darken even as he looked at it. He heard Alec's voice and closed his eyes.

He really was very tired.

* * *

HE AWOKE TO FIND HIMSELF IN A SMALL, COMFY BED-
room; out the window the sun was beginning to think about getting low in the sky. He felt refreshed, as though he had slept for a
day. He wanted to find Alec.

He pulled himself out of bed and looked at the wound in his
chest where it was exposed above the fold of his dressing gown. (He
noted that he had apparently been put into a dressing gown, he presumed by Alec. He *hoped* by Alec.) Now, with two cuts, it formed an
X over his heart, and he thought with a wince of Clary's dream. No
chains yet, at least. The X was warm to the touch, like an inflamed
cut, but he felt no pain if he pushed at it. The little flames of light
that wafted out of the wound didn't feel like anything. The fact was,
the wound felt good. Behind it was a warm core of magic that was
clearly his own, but he felt tendrils of it reaching out through the
wound, reaching for . . . what? The thorn?

Sammael?

He found his clothes folded on a chair beside the bed and
changed out of the dressing gown. Then he padded down the hall.
At the end of the hall was a small sitting room, decorated mostly in
weapons—*Shadowhunters,* thought Magnus with a sigh—and a man
seated in one of the chairs. He was leaning forward, as though deep
in thought or, possibly, napping, and Magnus couldn't see his face.
That's funny, he thought, *the Ke family still look like—*

The man raised his head, and Magnus startled.

"Jem?" he said. He whispered it, like maybe it was supposed to
be a secret.

Jem got up. He looked good, Magnus thought, for being 150
years old, for having been a Shadowhunter and a Silent Brother
and then, after all those years, suddenly a mundane. Even in modern times, Jem still favored clothes a bit like what he'd worn as a
much younger man—he was in a simple white shirt with pearl buttons, but over it was a brown riding coat cut in a vaguely Victorian

shape. Under other circumstances, Magnus might have asked him the name of his tailor.

Without a word Jem stepped forward and embraced Magnus. They had been friends a long time. There were a lot of downsides to being a warlock, but the feeling of embracing a friend who you'd known for more than a century was not one of them.

"What are you doing here?" Magnus said. "Not that I'm not pleased to see you."

"I have a perfect right to be here," Jem said with a twinkle in his eye. "I'm a member of the Ke family, after all. Ke Jian Ming, in case you've forgotten."

"So . . . a coincidence? You just happened to be visiting family? Is Tessa with you?"

Jem's expression suddenly turned serious. "Tessa is not with me, and no, it's not a coincidence that I'm here."

He led Magnus outside, and they walked over to the pond. It seemed to Magnus that it was a bit different in shape than the last time he'd been here, but it had been beautiful then and it was beautiful now. Firs and willows leaned over the water, their branches so low they dipped into it. They shaded the gold, black, and white koi hurrying underneath, visible only as shifting shadows in the green water.

A red bridge, paint flaking away with age, arched over the pond, leading to a dirt-floored courtyard where a girl in gear, only eleven or twelve, ran through stick-fighting forms.

"I was born here, you know," Jem said. "Before my parents ran the Institute." He looked out at the sun's reflection on the still water of the pond.

"Where's Tessa?" said Magnus.

"The Spiral Labyrinth," Jem said, and Magnus breathed a sigh of relief. "But not of her own choice. She was being pursued by a warlock. Of your acquaintance, I think. One with an unmoving face."

"Shinyun Jung," Magnus said. "I should say she's of my acquaintance; I came here straight from fighting her and her monster squad."

"So I heard from the others," said Jem.

"Why would Shinyun be after Tessa?" Magnus said.

Jem looked at him in surprise. "Well—because she's an eldest curse, of course. Like you."

Magnus blinked. "You mean, because she's the daughter of a Prince of Hell? Like me?"

"No. It's more than that. Tessa went to the Labyrinth not just to hide but to research. Eldest curses are not just children of Princes of Hell. They're the oldest living children of those princes. There can only be nine of them alive at any one time, and I know of only two. And I'm talking to one of them and married to the other."

Magnus started. "I didn't know you got married." It had been a long, strange road for Jem and Tessa; he was glad if they were reaching a place they could finally rest together. "Congratulations."

"Well, not really," said Jem. "We got married by mundane laws—in private, you understand, in secret, no one there but us and the necessary officials." He gazed at the water. "We want desperately to have a proper wedding, with all our friends and family, but—we lead a dangerous life. We have been searching a long time for something many bad people also want to find. More than just Shinyun has pursued us. I couldn't ask my friends, or Tessa's descendants, to come to a wedding ceremony where they might be in peril."

"Sounds like an interesting party to me," said Magnus, but the deep sadness in Jem's eyes plucked at his heart. "Look—I can think of a way I could help you hold a wedding, safely, with everyone you want there. When we make it out of this whole situation, I'll show you."

"Thank you," said Jem. He caught at Magnus's hand. "Thank you. I'll do whatever I can to help you with the Shinyun problem.

When we learned from the Labyrinth that she was in Shanghai, I came here to see if the Institute had seen anything. They hadn't, but then you showed up. I've been here only a few more days than you."

"Well," said Magnus, "what have you found out?"

Jem sighed. "That Portals aren't working."

Magnus said, very quietly, "Shinyun is working on behalf of Sammael. *Sammael* Sammael," he added significantly.

Jem's eyebrows went up. "Well, that's not a name you hear every day. Since Earth isn't currently in an apocalyptic demon war, I assume he's not actually here."

"I assume that too, but I don't know how Shinyun has been communicating with him, or where he is. Or what form he's in, for that matter." Magnus thought. "If it makes you feel any better, I don't think Sammael has any interest in Tessa. Shinyun told me that she hasn't even told Sammael about *me* being part of this."

Jem considered this. "It doesn't make me feel all that much better." He sighed. "I guess it was inevitable. We both know Princes of Hell can't really be killed. They just go away and then come back eventually. It's been a thousand years; it's surprising it took this long."

Magnus laughed. "You know, the funny thing is, he *just* missed Lilith by a bit."

Tian appeared from around the corner in the courtyard beyond, where the girl was practicing. He was in his distinctive burgundy gear, with the silver lines of his rope dart in loops around his body. He leaned down to talk with the girl.

"I should find Alec," Magnus said. "Do you know where the others are?"

"The coach house, I should think," said Jem. "They were freshening up—"

He stopped as an older woman with long gray hair in two braids appeared from the house and stared them down. She was holding a wooden spoon the size of a longsword and a bowl twice the size of Magnus's head. On each of her upper arms was a gigantic Balance rune.

There were also runes on the spoon.

"Mother Yun," said Jem mildly. "Tian's grandmother."

"Your friends are sitting at the table for dinner," apparently-Mother-Yun snapped at Jem in Mandarin. "Which is more than I can say for you. Or her." She waved the spoon at the training girl. "LIQIN!" she hollered at the top of her lungs. "Come and eat, girl! You too, *xiao* Tian."

The girl literally stopped her leg in the air mid-kick and slowly lowered it. She turned and saw that Magnus and Jem had been watching her, and suddenly became self-conscious. "That's another Ke cousin," Jem said. "Liqin. Tian's kind of an older brother to her, since he's an only child."

The girl, with the same serious-minded expression that Tian seemed to default to, nodded to Jem and hurried past to heed Mother Yun's warning.

"Hi, Liqin," Magnus said, waving.

The girl stopped and rolled her eyes. "It's Laura, actually. I'm from Melbourne. Auntie Yun won't call me anything but my Chinese name, even though she speaks English *perfectly well*." These last two words were directed somewhat more pointedly in the direction of their target.

"Hi, Laura," said Magnus, waving again.

She blushed and ducked her head, heading in for food.

"And *you*," Yun said to Jem, still in Mandarin. "Jian. You come in at once too. With your friend."

"Yun, *mei mei*," Jem said, drawing himself up to his full height and bearing. Magnus smiled to hear Jem address Yun as *little sister*: technically, she *was* younger than Jem, though she looked decades older. "I am your great-great-uncle-cousin, or something like that, and I will not be spoken to in that manner. But yes, Magnus," he added under his breath, "let's go. You don't want to see her get mad."

IT HAD TAKEN ALL OF ALEC'S WILLPOWER TO NOT SPEND his whole time at Ke House watching Magnus sleep. Once they had found that Brother Zachariah—now just Jem Carstairs—was in residence, they had let him examine Magnus, and he proclaimed that, for the moment, what Magnus needed most was rest. So Alec had let him sleep.

He'd felt awkward, at first, in these strangers' home, without Magnus to be breezy and friendly and make everyone comfortable. Luckily, Alec had a tendency to stick close to outgoing and confident people, and Jace and Isabelle had made all the introductions and explanations, while he, Clary, and Simon had hung back. At least until Jem arrived, at which point Clary and Simon had perked up and gone to chat with him and explain the situation.

Alec still didn't think he knew Jem all that well, even though he'd met him a number of times now. As with so many of Magnus's old friends, the literal centuries—well, one and a half centuries, in Jem's case—seemed an unbreachable hurdle. But Jem himself was preternaturally kind, and he had come over to speak with Alec himself—to assure him that Magnus was all right, that he had burned through a lot of magic in a short time, that he would feel better after a good rest, and that in the meantime Alec should enjoy the grounds and come meet the family.

The only ones in residence today turned out to be Tian's grandmother, who Jem called Mother Yun, and his cousin Liqin, who stared bug-eyed at Clary for a few seconds and then ran away. The guests had been given tea and shown around the property, which was as dense with Shadowhunter history as the Institute itself. It was unfortunate, he felt, that none of them could pay proper attention to the place. They were all still shaken up from the encounter with Shinyun and her demon army.

While Magnus slept and Yun prepared dinner, Tian took his guests into the dining room, where a long rosewood table dominated the space. He sat down with a sigh, running his hands through his hair.

"Please sit," he said. "I know I've been dragging you all over this house without engaging in the discussion we really need to have, but I needed time to think."

Alec and Jace exchanged a look of shared relief. Alec knew Jace had barely been holding himself back from demanding answers about supposedly extinct skeleton warriors. They all took seats, their attention fixed on Tian.

"I need to know," Tian said. "Who was that warlock? The one commanding Baigujing's daughters?"

"Shinyun Jung," Alec said. "A warlock who only makes bad decisions. What would it mean for her to be commanding Baigujing's daughters?"

"They are fiercely loyal to Baigujing herself. And this Jung Shinyun—a warlock who could command Baigujing—would be a powerful one indeed." Tian looked at Alec. "I assume she is the warlock who stole the book you're looking for."

Alec nodded.

"I may have to explain something of the history of demons in Shanghai," said Tian. "I'll try to keep it short."

"I recommend the use of dioramas," said Jace. Clary kicked him under the table.

The Nephilim of China, Tian explained, and especially of Shanghai, had been tormented for years and years in the eighteenth and nineteenth centuries by Yanluo, a Greater Demon known to mundanes across East Asia as the King of Hell. He had banded together with other powerful demons as well, including Baigujing, and together they waged a terrifying war against mundanes, Downworlders, and Shadowhunters alike.

When Yanluo struck at the Shanghai Institute in 1872 and murdered several Shadowhunters, he became the nemesis of the Ke family. They tracked him across China, finally slaughtering him in 1875. (Tian seemed rightfully proud of this fact.)

"He's dead," said Jace. "So he's not our problem, I take it?"

"What about Baigujing?" asked Isabelle.

"That's the thing," said Tian. "Yanluo is not the actual King of Hell, of course. He isn't even a Prince of Hell. Mundanes called him the King of Hell because his realm, Diyu, was believed to be the human underworld. It *was* a horrible place. No one seems to know how Yanluo came to rule over Diyu, but he used it to torture mundane souls and entertain his demon cohorts with scenes of bloody massacres and torment." He sighed. "For a very long time, the only permanent passage between Diyu and our world—or any world—was a Portal right here in Shanghai. This was before humans could make their own Portals, of course, and Yanluo would pass back and forth between the worlds without anybody being able to do anything about it. The moment he died, though, the Portal was closed—forever—and his cohorts were trapped in Diyu. Baigujing and her daughters were among them."

"Well, they're out now," said Simon grimly.

"Could the Portal that closed have opened again?" demanded Clary. "Should we go check on it?"

"No one knows where it is—or was," said Tian. "Around the time of Yanluo's death, Shanghai was in the middle of a huge expansion, with all the European countries establishing territory here and trade exploding. It's not clear what happened to the Portal. Nobody's stumbled across it since Yanluo's death, in any event. Most of us believed it vanished when he died. He was the sort who wouldn't have wanted anyone else to use it if he couldn't."

Liqin entered abruptly and sat herself down at the table with a kind of military discipline, and Tian interrupted his story to ask her how her training had gone. Alec noted with some surprise that when she responded, she did so in a definite Australian accent. And then Jem arrived, with Magnus.

The Shadowhunters sprang up from the table as one to greet them and check on Magnus, but Alec made sure he got there first. He grabbed Magnus around the waist and held him fast. "I didn't even know you were awake," he said in a low voice. "How are you feeling?"

"Hungry," Magnus said. "Otherwise fine." He half-consciously brushed at his shirt, over his wound.

Alec kissed him, hard and fierce, as if to prove to himself that Magnus was okay. Magnus returned the kiss, and Alec could feel some tension leave his body as he did.

After a few seconds, Isabelle delivered a loud wolf whistle, and Alec pulled away, smiling in embarrassment. Magnus gave him a sympathetic look and a peck on the cheek. "That was lovely," he said.

Alec hugged him a little tighter, and Magnus said again, "I'm all right." But Magnus, Alec thought wryly, would always say he was all right.

"You're not," said Alec quietly. "You said Shinyun stabbed you again."

Magnus sighed and unbuttoned his shirt, revealing that the wound was now a harsh X across his chest. There was a sharp intake of breath from the assembled Shadowhunters. Clary put her hand to her mouth; she looked surprisingly more alarmed than the others.

"I have even worse news," said Magnus. "But I believe Tian was telling a story, and I hate to interrupt."

Tian looked stunned. "No, please. This seems more urgent."

"If she gets me a third time," Magnus said, "I become Sammael's servant."

"Well," said Alec, "then you are going straight into hiding right now. Or to the Spiral Labyrinth."

"You're safe here," said Jem. "This house is very well-warded."

"I can't go into hiding," Magnus went on doggedly, "because if I *don't* get stabbed a third time, the thorn's power will burn me from the inside out and I'll die."

There was a terrible silence. All Alec could hear was his own breathing, intense and unsteady in his ears. He saw Jace look at him with his eyes full of concern, but his own fear was too deep for even his *parabatai's* reassurance to reach it.

"So what are we going to do?" said Simon. He sounded bleak.

"Defeat Sammael," said Jace, his voice hard.

"Destroy the thorn," suggested Isabelle.

Alec looked at them carefully, but they didn't seem to be joking.

Magnus said, "I'm not sure how easy either of those things will be."

Clary, with a mulish look, said, "I didn't think you brought us here to do *easy* stuff."

"We'll take care of it," Magnus said. He looked at Alec, who returned his gaze evenly. "We *will*," he said again.

Alec's further thoughts on the matter would have to wait, though, as through the door to the kitchen came Yun, carrying an enormous platter of food. Alec noted that she had put her giant spoon in a scabbard on her back, which seemed appropriate.

"None of you are sitting down!" she shouted, and they all hurried to return to the table. "Welcome!" she added to Magnus in the same shouting tone.

Magnus spoke to her in Mandarin, and she seemed to soften a bit. He had that effect on people. She responded in Mandarin at some length and then continued in English. "Jian says you are excellent people, and he is *mostly* a good judge of character, even if he is not a Shadowhunter anymore." She winked at Jem and began setting plates out.

"Should we keep talking about Yanluo?" Simon said to Tian. Magnus violently shook his head *no* at Simon. "Or . . . not?" Simon added.

"It's all right, Magnus." Jem smiled faintly. "I have my own personal connection to Yanluo, that's all."

Tian began serving himself fried bean curd and vegetables from one of the plates. He gestured for the rest of them to join him. "Eat, before my grandmother starts to take offense," he said. "I'm happy to help you with any of the dishes if you—"

But the Shadowhunters needed no further invitation and dug into the spread, which Alec noted was different from the Chinese food he was used to in New York, but had some definite similarities. The most familiar thing at the table were soup dumplings, which Tian's reaction made clear were a sign Yun had pulled out all the stops for her guests. He had begun to explain how to eat them but quickly stopped once he realized that everyone at the table had grabbed spoons and were gently biting open the top of the dumpling to let the steam escape so they could drink the soup inside.

Simon grinned at Tian's surprise. "*Xiaolongbao*, right?" he said. "It's, like, the only Chinese I know. Oh! Also *char siu bao*. Most of my knowledge is *bao*-related."

"*Char siu* is Cantonese," snapped Yun over her shoulder as she returned to the kitchen.

"I didn't intend any offense," Simon said, looking mortified.

Jem rolled his eyes. "She isn't taking offense. That's just how she conveys useful information."

"She trained me," said Tian, "and a generation of Shadowhunters before me."

"She's terrifying," said Magnus with sincere admiration.

"You should have seen her in her prime," said Jem. "That was a different Shanghai, though. She has quite the pedigree—she's Ke Yiwen's youngest granddaughter."

Magnus looked impressed. Isabelle interrupted herself from cutting half of the gigantic lion's head meatball on Simon's plate for herself. "Who's that?"

"She's the one who killed Yanluo," Tian said through a mouthful of food. "Though Jem knows more about it than I do."

Jem's expression was somber and a little distant. Alec knew it well. It was the look Magnus got when he thought of something that had happened a long time ago whose memory still pained him. "A few years before Yanluo was killed, he invaded the Shanghai Institute, captured my parents and me, and tortured me in front of them. To pay them back."

His voice was steady, but then, Jem had lived two lifetimes since then. Alec wasn't surprised to see Magnus reach out and put a reassuring hand on Jem's arm.

"Pay them back for what?" said Clary, her green eyes wide and full of concern.

Jem's mother, Magnus explained, had destroyed a nest of Yanluo's brood, and so Yanluo had sought revenge against her child. He told them about the demon drug *yin fen*, how Yanluo had injected Jem with it for days on end, so his body would be dependent on the drug and he would have to take it forever or die—only his becoming a Silent Brother had ended the addiction, and only heavenly fire, pouring through Jem as he held on to Jace while Jace burned with it, had cured it permanently.

"I remember that part," Clary said grimly.

"I remember it a *little*," Jace said. "That was kind of a weird time for me."

"How strange. You're *never* weird," said Isabelle innocently.

"We still see *yin fen* around occasionally," Tian said, "though nothing like it used to be in Uncle Jem's time. Young werewolves bring it in from Macao or Hong Kong. The Downworlder community is pretty good at shutting it down, though; they know the dangers."

"In Singapore," Magnus put in, scratching at his wound without seeming to notice, "the Shadowhunters will just kill you on the spot if they catch you with it."

"Isn't that against the Accords?" Simon said incredulously. Magnus shrugged.

"At least I survived," said Jem, picking the story back up, "unlike my parents. My mother's sister, Yiwen, dedicated herself to revenge, and a few years later—I had gone to live at the London Institute, of course—she and my uncle Elias Carstairs tracked Yanluo down and killed him." He nodded at the kitchen door, where Yun had disappeared. "Mother Yun is Yiwen's youngest granddaughter, the only one still alive." He smiled. "The second-oldest living Ke."

Alec took another serving of red-cooked chicken and felt out of place. It was a feeling he still had, sometimes, when Magnus's life before him, long before his birth, in fact, loomed into view. Magnus and Jem had so much shared history, their relationship was so long and complex—for a moment he felt a tinge of jealousy, and then stopped himself; obviously his relationship with Magnus was of a totally different kind than Jem's, and it was silly of him to envy them their shared history. . . .

And then his mind flipped, and instead he thought about Jem, so young, terrified, screaming; about Jem's parents, watching in helpless horror as their child was tortured in front of them for days. And he realized that the greater horror for him, now, was the parents' horror: he could imagine withstanding his own torture, his own pain, but the idea of Max suffering, of his cries, of Alec's helplessness . . . he shuddered and caught Magnus's eye. Magnus was gazing at him with what Alec thought of as his cat's gaze—heavily lidded, serious, enigmatic. He gave Magnus a smile, and Magnus gave him one back, although it was more wan than usual.

After dinner, Magnus disappeared abruptly, but Alec was stuck with his friends for a few minutes more. Liqin very shyly approached Clary to ask her advice on something; the conversation turned to training and weapons and runes, and Alec snuck away into the rapidly fading twilight of the house's back patio, where he found Tian, Jem, Yun, and Magnus standing in a small circle, gazing up at the sky. Magnus's arms were crossed tightly over his chest protectively, and Alec couldn't tell why—the conversation was entirely in quiet, rapid Mandarin.

Magnus caught sight of him and beckoned him over. Alec slid in next to him and put his arm around Magnus's shoulder; he was relieved to feel Magnus lean his weight against him, though he kept his arms crossed.

"Yun was just telling us that the Shanghai Institute fire-messaged her this evening," said Jem. "They're concerned, because a lot of the demons they've been seeing in the city are from Yanluo's time and are associated with Diyu. But Yanluo has been dead, and Diyu shut down, for a long time."

"Those children of Baigujing we fought today," Tian said. "They are more like legends to my generation; nobody's battled them in years."

"To my generation, even," Yun agreed in a quiet but still-intense voice. "The Xiangliu, too, were rare for my whole life, but the Institute says that now they seem to be in every dark alley."

"Do you think Yanluo could have returned?" Alec said, not looking at Jem.

But Jem himself spoke up. "I don't. Yanluo wasn't a Prince of Hell; he could be killed and he *was* killed. But someone else could be accessing Diyu and letting its demons back into our world."

"A million yuan says it's Shinyun," Magnus said grimly. "And Ragnor."

"But why?" said Tian.

"Several reasons," Alec agreed. He had come to much the same conclusion himself, earlier. "We know they've declared their fealty to Sammael"—Yun looked sharply at Alec, her eyes suddenly wide—"but we don't know where Sammael is now, or what power he has, or even whether Shinyun and Ragnor have direct access to him," he continued. "Maybe it's a distraction from their own activities. Maybe Sammael has some interest in Diyu."

Magnus let out a long exhale. "Ragnor found Sammael a realm, apparently."

"A million yuan—" began Alec.

"No bet," said Tian. "If Sammael has taken Diyu, then he is one step away from walking in our world again."

"He's one *realm* away," Jem said. "There is warding that keeps Sammael away from Earth, in place since the Taxiarch defeated him. But it would only be a matter of time."

"Maybe less time than we'd like," said Magnus. "They have the Book of the White, and we don't know what they want it for. We don't know where this old Portal was, or if Sammael might be trying to reopen it. Maybe he already has reopened it, and that's how these demons are getting here."

"We don't know *anything*," said Alec in frustration. Out of the corner of his eye, he saw his friends, with Liqin, marching in the dusk out to the training ground. He didn't want to leave Magnus's side, but he itched to join them, to lose himself in the regularity of sparring and training. He knew the others were trying to give Magnus and him some space, and to let Magnus reconnect with Jem and Yun. Alec couldn't help worrying that Magnus was more vulnerable than they guessed—he always projected an image of unassailable confidence, but Alec understood that as close as Magnus might be to Clary, to Jace, to Simon, there was a private Magnus that only he and a few others ever saw. Catarina. Jem and Tessa. Ragnor. "We have to try to find Ragnor," Alec said. "He'll talk to you, Magnus, I know he will—even if he's trying to convert you to his side, he'll still talk to you."

"Ragnor is very good at not being found, if he doesn't want to be," said Magnus. "I'd have to look into some unusual magic to try to find him, given how easily he sidestepped the Tracking rune."

"Then I think our next step is research," Tian said. "Tomorrow we go to the Sunlit Market. I have contacts there. We can start with Peng Fang—"

Magnus let out a loud groan.

"He's not so bad," Alec said.

"I guess I'd take him over *Sammael*," Magnus allowed.

"There are a few others," Tian said, "and the Celestial Palace, for research materials."

"Not the Institute library?" Alec said in surprise.

Tian shrugged. "The Institute library has been carefully curated and contains useful books known to be true. The Celestial Palace contains dark corners with books full of rumors and innuendos. I suspect we'll have a better time there."

"I do love rumors and innuendos," said Magnus.

"You should go to see Mo Ye and Gan Jiang," put in Yun. Tian furrowed his brow.

"What?" said Alec.

"Faerie weaponsmiths," Tian said. "They work by . . . appointment only. Grandmother, I don't know if weapons are what is—"

"If the horde of Diyu is returning," said Yun severely, "then you will need more than seraph blades. Mo Ye and Gan Jiang knew the fight against Yanluo and his brood for hundreds of years before any of us were born. Even you," she added with a nod to Magnus.

"They may know about the Svefnthorn, also, if they're weaponsmiths. So here's the list of things we need to look into, if I have this correct," said Alec, ticking them off on his fingers. "Shinyun, Ragnor, Diyu, Yanluo, Sammael, the Portal to Diyu, the Svefnthorn, the Book of the White, some other magic book maybe."

"Well," said Magnus pleasantly, "that sounds like a very busy day, and I will need a good night's rest for it. Alec and I must call home now to check on how our son is doing, so I take my leave of you for the night. Alec?"

They thanked Yun for her hospitality again, and Magnus, still not uncrossing his arms, led the way across the courtyard to his bedroom. Alec followed, an uncertain foreboding in his chest.

AS SOON AS THE BEDROOM DOOR WAS CLOSED, MAGNUS turned and pushed Alec against it, hard. He kissed him fiercely, drowning himself in the taste of Alec, the feel of Alec's stubble against his mouth (Alec thought it was messy, but Magnus was kind of a fan), the strength of Alec's arms as they reached up to hold the back of Magnus's head and help deepen the kiss.

When he pulled away, Alec's bright blue eyes were surprised and glinting, his mouth an adorable curl. "That was unexpected."

"I missed you," said Magnus, out of breath, and Alec, bless him, didn't ask him what that meant, didn't say that they had been together this whole time, but only kissed him back. Without breaking the kiss, Magnus reached for the base of Alec's throat and started unzipping his gear jacket. Alec, laughing, reached for the buttons of Magnus's shirt and began undoing them. Magnus kissed Alec's throat, and Alec let out a small pleased moan, but continued to carefully and fastidiously undo the buttons, his hands trembling slightly. That was Alec all over. Magnus thought with amusement of the first time Alec had torn his shirt open, early in their relationship. He always remembered Alec's adorable look of surprise, as if he hadn't been able to believe he'd ripped someone's shirt off.

Alec began to kiss his way down Magnus's neck, gentle but urgent. Magnus wondered, distantly, what he would do when he reached the wound the thorn had made, which continued to roil with scarlet magic. He pushed the thought down and bent his head to ruffle his hands through Alec's beautiful black hair and plant a kiss on the sensitive spot behind his ear. Alec murmured wordlessly and pulled back to take his jacket fully off and drop it to the floor. He grinned at Magnus and helped him shrug off his shirt as well.

Alec stopped and stared. But not, Magnus realized, at the wound. Instead he looked back and forth with sudden alarm at Magnus's arms. The warm, tugging insistence that had been spreading through Magnus's body as he kissed Alec was replaced abruptly by a cold feeling, like an ice cube slowly sliding down his throat and into his stomach.

"What?" he said. And extended his arms to look, and saw.

In the middle of each of his palms was the outline of a star, like the spiked end of—well, a flail. Extending from each star, interlocking loops ran down the insides of both his arms, angry and red and blistered.

Alec reached out, unsettled and breathing hard, and with great gentleness ran his fingers over the loops. They were raised from the rest of the skin, rigid and swollen. They extended all the way past Magnus's biceps and down the smooth planes of his chest to the wound itself.

"Chains," Alec said to himself, then looked up at Magnus's face, his expression intense. "They look like chains." He hesitated, then added, "Did you know?"

"No," said Magnus. "They don't . . . feel like anything. I mean, nothing more than how the wound feels—"

"How does the wound feel?" Alec said. He was gazing into Magnus's eyes as though he would find answers there, but Magnus had no answers to give him.

"Warm. Strange. Not . . . not unpleasant," he added.

"We should get Jem," Alec said.

"No!" said Magnus. "He doesn't know anything about this."

"The Spiral Labyrinth, then," Alec said. *"Someone."*

"No," said Magnus again. "Tomorrow we'll go to the Market and the Palace and we'll get some answers there."

"And if we don't?" Alec was clutching Magnus's shoulder, his grip stiff. Magnus hesitated, and Alec closed his eyes, distressed, brow furrowed. "Why won't you accept help?" he said quietly. "You don't have to deal with this on your own."

Magnus reached up and gently removed Alec's hand from his shoulder, but continued to hold it. "I'm not doing this on my own. As near as I can tell, I'm doing it with a whole baseball team. You, Jace, Clary, Simon, Isabelle, Tian, Jem . . . it's a wonder we didn't bring Maia and Lily with us too."

"Do you wish they all weren't here?" Alec said. "Do you wish I wasn't here? Do you wish I didn't know? About this?"

"No," said Magnus again. Was Alec *angry*? He exhaled slowly. "I told you, I didn't know about the chains—"

"Aren't you worried? Aren't you *upset*?" said Alec, and Magnus realized: He wasn't angry. He was terrified. "You don't have to act cool with me. I'm the person you don't ever have to act cool with."

Magnus smiled and wrapped his arms around Alec, pulling him into a tight embrace. To his relief, Alec let him. "I know that. And you know me," he murmured into Alec's ear, the wisps of Alec's hair tickling his nose with the warm smell of soap and sweat and sandalwood that felt like home. "I try to take it one moment at a time."

He could feel the long exhale leave Alec's body, the tension ease a bit. "Of course I'm worried," he continued in Alec's ear. "Of course I'm upset. I don't really know what's happening, and the only person who might explain it to me is—"

"Unhinged?" murmured Alec.

"I meant Ragnor, actually," allowed Magnus. "Who is possessed by Sammael. But we'll figure it out. Together. Tomorrow. Tomorrow you can help. Tonight I need . . . to unwind." He planted a little kiss on Alec's temple and was pleased to see his boyfriend allow himself a small smile.

Alec turned and put his hand on Magnus's heart, just above the wound. "If you died," he said, "a part of me would die too. So remember, Magnus. It's not just your life. It's my life too."

Someone, long ago, had told Magnus that human beings could never love the way immortals loved; their souls didn't have the strength for it. That person had never met Alec Lightwood, nor anyone like him, Magnus thought, and their lives must have been the poorer for it. The strength of Alec's love humbled him and lifted him up like a wave; he let the wave carry him toward Alec, toward their bed together, toward their interlocked hands as they moved in unison, stifling their cries against each other's lips.

HOURS LATER, MAGNUS WAS SOUND ASLEEP, BUT ALEC remained awake, listening to the insects and the birds sing their night songs. The moon poured creamy light through the window. After a time, he got out of bed, pulled on sleep clothes, and went out.

He walked the perimeter of the house's grounds, along the low brick wall that marked its edge, trailing his fingers. He felt restless and strange. He was worried about Magnus and wanted to *act*, not to sleep, but he couldn't form a plan or even think through steps. He just didn't have enough information.

Jace, unexpectedly, was sitting on the brick wall, watching the sky. He turned to look at Alec's approach. "Can't sleep either?"

"What are you mooning around about?" Alec said. "I'm the one whose boyfriend has a big magical X carved into his chest by a crazy person."

"Everyone's got something," Jace said, and Alec thought that was probably true.

"Maryse asked me if I would take over running the Institute," Jace added casually.

Alec did not say, *I know*, but instead asked, "Are you going to do it?"

Jace hemmed and hawed. "I don't know."

"Why not?" Alec said. "You'd be good at it. You're a good leader."

Jace shook his head, smiling. "I'm good at being the first guy into battle. I'm good at killing a lot of demons. Maybe I can lead that way."

"You don't want a desk job?" Alec said, amused. "You wouldn't stop patrolling, you know. There aren't enough of us for that."

"I just don't think I'm good at the stuff that's part of running an Institute. Strategy? *Diplomacy?*"

"You're great at that stuff," Alec protested. "Who's been putting this idea in your head that you're only good at fighting? It better not be Clary."

"No," said Jace glumly. "Clary thinks I should do it."

"I do too," Alec said.

"None of us have to do it," Jace said. "The Clave would send someone from another Institute, if it was needed. An adult."

"Jace," Alec said, "we're adults. We're the adults now."

"By the Angel, that's *terrifying*," Jace said, with a bit of a smile. "They've let you have a *child*, even."

"I should check in with Mom, actually," said Alec. He took out his phone and waved it around. "And you should go to sleep."

"You too," said Jace, getting up. Before he could escape, Alec had grabbed him in a hug, and Jace, grateful as Alec had expected, hugged him back.

"It's going to be fine," Jace said. "We're going to save the day again. It's what we do." So saying, he headed back in the direction of his room.

Alec watched him go, and then he turned his attention to his phone and called—he almost thought *home*, but no, the Institute wasn't his home anymore. That still felt strange sometimes.

To his surprise, Kadir answered his mother's phone. "Alec!" he said with surprising enthusiasm. "Just the person I wanted to talk to. We didn't want to bother you, but—"

"What?" said Alec, on alert immediately. His nerves were not in good shape. "Is Max okay?"

"Yes, Max is fine," Kadir said. "He is quite a crawler!"

"Yeah, he can crawl pretty fast," Alec said, not sure where this was going. "Hopefully that means he'll be really walking soon."

"Well"—Kadir hesitated—"did you know . . . I mean . . . at *home* does he . . ."

"What?"

"Is that Alec?" Maryse said in the background. There was a clatter, and then she had clearly put him on speakerphone. "Alec, your son is climbing up the walls."

"He can be pretty active, yeah," Alec said.

"No," Maryse said with great calm, "I mean he is *climbing up our walls*. And across the ceiling! And then hanging from the drapes."

Alec pinched the bridge of his nose with his free hand. At home, of course, Magnus could prevent Max's accidental magical adventures with gravity. "I don't think he'll fall," he said doubtfully. "Usually when he does that, he doesn't even notice it's happened and we just wait for him to get back to the ground again."

"Yes, but . . . Alec, the ceilings in the Institute are *very* high."

"I have to walk around with a large cushion all the time just in case," put in Kadir.

"There are some pikes in the weapons room, but nothing long enough to reach," Maryse went on. "There isn't a magic solution? Something in the spell components Magnus brought? Something to . . . to neutralize him?"

"Uh, no, Mom. There's nothing to 'neutralize' him. I told you he was a handful."

"Obviously we would only use the handle end of the pikes, if it came to that," Kadir offered.

"Is he upset?" Alec said.

"Kadir? It's always hard to tell—"

"No, Mom, Max. Is Max upset?"

"Max is *thrilled*," Maryse said, in a tone that Alec strongly associated with his mother talking about Jace. "Max is having an *excellent* time."

"Then you'll just have to keep an eye on him and wait for him to come down," said Alec.

There was a long pause. "Well . . . all right," said Maryse. "If that's all that can be done."

Alec began to say, "You could call Catarina—"

"No, no, no," Maryse said quickly. "We've got it under control here. You go back to your mission and don't worry, all right?"

"Alec," Kadir said, very intensely. "I also must speak to you about *The Very Small Mouse Who Went a Very Long Way*, by Courtney Gray Wiese."

"What about it?" Alec said.

"You did not tell me," Kadir said. "You did not warn me sufficiently."

"We tried," said Alec.

In bleak tones, Kadir recited, "'The finest mouse will go neglected / Who is not often disinfected.'"

"It's hard to really prepare someone for it," Alec said. "You kind of have to experience it for yourself."

"Indeed," said Kadir. "I am glad for *Where the Wild Things Are*, at least. I have learned, after all these years, where the wild things are. They are in this Institute."

Alec said his good-byes and hung up, then gazed up at the clear

night sky. Maryse had raised four kids in an unpadded stone building full of weapons. Maryse had raised *him*, and he had never so
much as broken a bone under her watch. Max would be fine.

Will Magnus, though?

He pushed the thought aside and headed back toward bed.

MAGNUS WAS IN A HUGE, DUSTY HALL. THERE WERE
lights hanging from its ceiling, providing a gloomy yellow illumination, but their pendants, and the ceiling itself, were so far above
him and so shrouded in darkness that he couldn't make them out.

As his eyes adjusted, he realized he was in a kind of courtroom,
an old-fashioned one at that, like something from a hundred or
two hundred years ago. It looked like it had been abandoned
for at least that long. A thick layer of dust and cobwebs covered
every surface, and while most of the carved wooden furniture was
intact, there were chairs thrown here and there that had not been
picked up.

He was dreaming, he thought. Certainly dreaming. But of what?
Of where?

Behind the judges' bench were three seats. The middle seat was
much larger than the others, and a thick gray cloud hung over it,
like a giant Ala demon was perching in it, although Magnus could
see no eyes. To the cloud's right sat Shinyun; to the cloud's left sat
Ragnor.

Magnus lifted his hands and found that the spiked balls that
had been etched into his palms had become real, solid, iron balls,
a few inches across, embedded deeply. Blood seeped from around
them. He held up his hands experimentally and bumped his palms
together, hearing the balls clink dryly in the empty room.

There was a grinding sound that after a moment Magnus recognized as Ragnor clearing his throat. "They're supposed to be so

you can't put your hands together in prayer," he said. His voice was quiet, but it rang in Magnus's ears clearly. "It's a little old-fashioned, but you know how these artifacts are. Lots of symbolism, much less practicality."

"Where are we?" Magnus said. He addressed Ragnor and ignored Shinyun. He had the distinct impression that Shinyun was leering at him, though of course her face was as deadpan as always.

"Nowhere in particular," Ragnor said, waving his hand lazily. "We're just talking."

Magnus strode forward, though he felt heavier than usual, as though his legs were chained to weights. "Talking about *what*? Are you ready to give me any answers? Will you tell me what's going on with this . . . this thorn? The chains on my arms? What you're up to? What you want with the Book of the White? Why you've thrown in your lot with S—"

At that instant Shinyun put a finger up to her lips and shushed him. The noise was deafening, like being drowned in a crashing wave, and Magnus put his hands to his ears, then pulled them away quickly as he felt the iron spikes from his palms poke them.

When the noise died down, Ragnor said reproachfully, "You must not say his name."

"What?" said Magnus incredulously. "*Sammael?*"

The room shook very slightly, disturbing dust clouds into the air.

"Sammael!" Magnus yelled. "Sammael, Sammael, Sammael!"

The room rumbled now and shook like a derailing train. Magnus struggled to keep his footing, but Ragnor and Shinyun remained in their seats, looking impatient.

"*Why?*" Magnus shouted at Ragnor, angry now. "Why him? Why would the great Ragnor Fell ally himself with *any* demon, no matter how powerful? That's not what you taught me. It's against everything you've ever believed!"

"Times change," Ragnor said, annoyingly calm.

"And what's with this . . . this *thorn*? What's that got to do with S—with your Prince of Hell?"

Ragnor laughed now, an unpleasant grating sound very different from the laugh Magnus remembered. "The Svefnthorn? That's entirely Shinyun's doing. It's old magic, Magnus, very old and powerful warlock magic, and it had no master. Shinyun found it, and then it had a master. Our master. The thorn will only help you become who you are meant to be."

He stood now, and Magnus gasped. Ragnor's horns, always so tidy and elegant, had grown and wrapped themselves fully around his head; now they ended on either side of his face, jutting out around his chin like tusks. His eyes glinted like obsidian even in the yellow shadows of the room.

"Shinyun was not lying to you," he went on. "The Svefnthorn is a great gift, one that was lost but, thanks to our master, is now found. It helps us to serve him better. It will help you to serve him better too, in the end."

Magnus tore at his collar and opened his shirt to reveal the wound and its chains. "This is a gift?" he yelled. "How can this be a gift?"

Ragnor chuckled, and it was worse than the grating screech from before. He opened his mouth to speak, but he and Shinyun and the courtroom vanished, and Magnus bolted awake in his bedroom at the Ke house, a scream on his lips and Alec's worried face shining in the full moonlight.

CHAPTER EIGHT

Shadow and Sunlight

MAGNUS WAS STILL SHAKY, BUT HE MANAGED TO PUT ON a brave face through breakfast. He and the Shadowhunters wolfed down Yun's congee before Clary opened a Portal for them back to the Mansion Hotel so they could put on street clothes. Tian pointed out that a team of Shadowhunters in gear trooping through any Downworlder Market wouldn't be seen as friendly no matter their intentions.

Magnus stood in the Ke kitchen and watched out the window as demons scattered from Clary's Portal, then burst into flame as they encountered the daylight. (They had decided to open the Portal out in the courtyard for just this reason.) It was no longer just beetles, Magnus noted—now they were joined by three-feet-long milli-pedes and something that looked like a bone-white daddy longlegs the size of a large watermelon. The Shadowhunters didn't need to engage with them—the sunlight took care of that—but the enigma of why they were appearing at all was annoying Magnus. He should have asked Ragnor and Shinyun about the Portal thing, he thought, when he was in . . . wherever he was . . . in his dream. . . .

Absentmindedly he snapped his fingers in the direction of the dirty dishes, swooping them toward the sink for washing. The first few bowls were already clean by the time he noticed that his magic looked wrong.

The color of a warlock's magic was not especially meaningful, under normal circumstances. It wasn't like a movie, where good warlocks had pleasant blue magic and bad warlocks had ugly red magic. For that matter, it wasn't like a movie where there were "good warlocks" or "bad warlocks"—there were just warlocks, people like any others, with the capacity to do good or bad and the ability to decide anew each time. Nevertheless, Magnus had always been pleased by the smooth cobalt blue of his own magic, which he'd cultivated over a period of centuries. It seemed to him powerful and yet controlled. Soothing, like the wallpaper at an upscale spa.

Today, however, his magic was red. A bright, overexposed red, almost pink, and crackling at its edges with wisps of black curling fire. It still did what he wanted, moving plates in and out of the sink and stacking them neatly, but it certainly looked scary.

With an effort he concentrated on bringing back his magic's normal color. Nothing changed, and he began to grow frustrated. More and more of his concentration moved away from the dishes, and from his friends outside, and toward bending his magic to his own preference. That, after all, was what the color of magic was really about: a warlock's magic was under his own control. It was whatever color the warlock wished it to be.

The glow around the dishes persisted in its tacky reddish haze. Magnus's frustration grew, and finally, when a quiet voice called his name from the door behind him, he lost his grasp completely, and a bowl flew end over end away from the sink and broke as it struck the windowsill.

The magic faded completely. Magnus turned to see Jem standing in the doorway, his face grave.

"Sorry," Magnus said. "But the color—I don't know what it means."

Jem shook his head. "I don't either. Do the others know?"

"This is the first it's happened," Magnus said. "It wasn't doing this yesterday."

"Another thing to research today," Jem said.

Magnus nodded slowly. "I guess that's all we can do. It's a bad sign, though. Are you coming with us?"

"If you wish me to," said Jem. "I said I would help you with the Shinyun situation."

Magnus picked up a bowl. "No need to risk yourself. You said dangerous people were following you—I assume some of them frequent Shadow Markets?"

"Some of them," Jem admitted.

"I'd rather not deal with Tessa's wrath if anything happened to you. Stay here; we can confer when we get back."

At that moment Alec appeared, wearing what for him were going-out clothes: gray jeans, a many-times-washed blue T-shirt that matched his eyes, and a pin-striped gray-and-white shirt with the sleeves rolled up to the elbows. "We should go," he said to Magnus. "The Portal finally seems demon free."

Magnus handed the bowl he was holding to Jem. He ignored Jem's raised eyebrow. "Did you ever have to wash dishes in the Silent City?"

"No," said Jem.

"Then this'll be good practice."

ON THE WAY TO THE DOWNWORLDER CONCESSION, TIAN took them past a huge brick Gothic building, with two spires on either side of its door; it looked like it had been teleported in straight from the French countryside. Alec was used to taking note of houses of worship when he traveled—it was always good to know where the closest weapons cache could be found—and he'd been frustrated by not really being able to identify religious buildings on sight, in this city of so many different mundanes and mundane religions. This building, however, was familiar in a way that made it stand out in a sea of unfamiliarity.

"Is that a *church*?" he said to Tian as they walked.

Tian nodded. "Xujiahui Cathedral," he said. "Also called Saint Ignatius. It's got the largest cache of Nephilim arms in the city, if we need them. But it's also swarming with tourists most of the time, so we don't use it much."

He was right; the place was abuzz with activity. Tourists lined up outside to go in. Some of it seemed to be under renovation, also: scaffolding was wrapped around most of the stained-glass windows along one side.

"Maybe we should stop by and pick up a few more weapons," Simon muttered. "I feel a little naked going into this Market with only one seraph blade and nothing else."

"Just like that dream you have sometimes," Clary said brightly, and Isabelle snorted with a hastily suppressed laugh.

Jace gave Simon a quick sympathetic look. "Maybe Simon is right," he said. "The bad guys seem to be able to find us when they want to, but we can't find them. We should have gone in gear."

"No," Tian said. "This is better. The Institute and the concession are on fairly good terms, as these things go, but the Cold Peace has made everybody more tense. We need to be seen to come in a spirit of friendship."

"We'll see how much they like our spirit of friendship when demons swarm the place," Jace said, and Simon looked over at him nervously.

Alec, meanwhile, looked at Magnus, who seemed relieved that they wouldn't be going into the church. Magnus, like most warlocks, didn't love spending time in mundane religious buildings.

Mundane religions didn't usually have much kindness for warlocks, and that was putting it mildly.

After some twists and turns, Tian led them through an elaborate red gate into a pedestrianized, cobblestoned street. The gate was guarded by two bronze statues: one a rather intimidating wolf on its hind legs, its claws up in either threat or welcome, Alec couldn't be sure; the other a large bat, its wings folded over its body in a way that made it look strangely coquettish.

"Welcome to the Downworlder Concession," Tian said, gesturing proudly.

There was, at least at first, nothing particularly Downworld about the place, although it wasn't like Downworlders had their own styles of architecture. It looked like Shanghai in miniature, really, an eclectic pile of the city's history all built on top of itself. Traditional Chinese curved roofs jostled against Western-style buildings, some looking like they had been teleported directly from the English or French countryside, some all classical columns and marble. And all the people were Downworlders.

The streets weren't crowded this time of morning, but Alec was amazed to see faeries, werewolves, even the occasional warlock walking around, no glamours or illusions at all. He saw Magnus taking it in as well: a place where Downworlders lived freely, without having to constantly hide themselves from the mundane world. It was strange. It was nice.

Tian caught his look. "The whole concession is warded from mundanes," he said. "The arch looks like the entrance to a ruined building, destroyed in the 1940s and never rebuilt."

"Why doesn't this exist anywhere else?" Clary said. "Why aren't there glamoured Downworlder neighborhoods all over?"

Magnus, Tian, and Jace all spoke at the same time.

Tian said, "Shanghai has a very specific and unusual history that allowed this to happen."

Magnus said, "The Shadowhunters would never allow it."

Jace said, "The Downworlders in most places fight each other too much."

They all looked at one another.

"I think it's probably all those things," Alec said diplomatically. Magnus nodded but looked around, distracted.

"Any chance we could grab some food?" he said.

Alec gave him a funny look. "We just had breakfast."

"Research demands calories," Magnus said.

"I could eat," put in Clary. "Tian, is there dim sum?"

"There is a *lot* of dim sum," Tian confirmed. "Follow me."

Though it was in better shape than the neighborhood of old Shanghai that they'd been to a couple of days before, the Downworlder Concession was the same kind of confusing warren of narrow streets. What Alec took to be an alley turned out to be the entrance to a house; what he took to be a storefront turned out to be a road.

Alec trusted Tian—he was a fellow Shadowhunter, he was a Ke, he had been vouched for by Jem—but he couldn't help thinking that there was no way they would be able to find their way out again without Tian's help. He exchanged a glance with Jace, who was clearly thinking the same thing, then reached around to put a reassuring hand on his bow before remembering he didn't have it.

After a few turns, the street opened up onto a larger courtyard, with restaurants on all sides and clusters of plane trees in the center. Tian gestured around him. "Welcome to the dim sum district, so to speak. I don't know how often you eat at Downworlder establishments—"

"Maybe more frequently than you'd think," said Clary.

"Well," said Tian, "there's vampire dim sum, faerie dim sum, and werewolf dim sum."

"Which do we want?"

"We *definitely* want werewolf dim sum," Tian said.

Werewolf dim sum turned out to be not all that different from New York mundane dim sum, except that the tough gray-haired women pushing the carts around were all werewolves. They also spoke no English, but this was, for one thing, also not very different from New York, and for another, easily solved by simply pointing to the stacked steamer baskets and metal bowls as needed. Alec was not the biggest congee fan and had eaten only a small bowl so as not to insult Mother Yun, so he dug into shrimp dumplings, turnip cakes, steamed buns, clams in black bean sauce, stir-fried gai lan—and carefully watched Tian's face and the subtle shake of his head when things came by that were too werewolfish for them: tiny blood sausage, slices of raw red meat, what appeared to be some kind of deep-fried small rodent in sweet-and-sour sauce. Tian tried to stop Magnus from grabbing chicken feet, but once Magnus was contentedly nibbling on one of them, he gave in and ordered some chicken feet of his own. Oddly, so did Jace.

"You like chicken feet?" Tian said, surprised.

"I like everything," Jace said, mouth full of food.

Simon shook his head. "My ancestors fled their home country so they wouldn't have to eat chicken feet anymore. I'm not about to start now. Does anything on the table *not* have meat in it?"

Tian grabbed some vegetable dumplings and mushrooms wrapped in bean curd from the next cart, and the werewolf lady gave Simon a disapproving look.

"Sorry," Tian said. "Even the ones without meat often use dry shrimp or pork fat."

"I'm used to it," Simon said with resignation.

"Also," pointed out Clary, chewing on a steamed bun, "they're werewolves."

Satiated, the team headed out again. As they walked behind

Tian, Alec came over to Magnus and bumped into him affectionately. "Hey, are you all right? You were quiet all through the meal."

"Fat and sassy," Magnus said, rubbing his stomach and smiling at Alec. Alec smiled back but felt an uncertain twist in his gut. The chains, the shining wound—and Magnus had awoken in the night screaming. He had claimed it was only a random nightmare, but Alec wasn't sure.

He also hadn't told the rest of them about the chains on Magnus's body. He wasn't sure how exactly to bring such a thing up.

Where a moment ago Alec had been in good spirits, all of a sudden he felt far away from home, unsettled and on edge. He found himself very aware that he couldn't read any of the street signs or storefronts, that he was half a world away from his child, that there were people here who might hate him for being a Shadowhunter in a Downworlder neighborhood, no matter how friendly relations were. The weight of the Cold Peace and Magnus's wound and the unknowns stacked on top of unknowns came down upon him.

"I wish Max were here," he whispered to Magnus, and that was when the thing with wings swooped down and collided violently with Tian.

MAGNUS WAS DISTRACTED BY THE FEELING IN HIS CHEST; ever since they'd passed through the gate into the concession, he'd felt it. Each time his heart beat, it sent a small throb of magic through his body, and he could feel that throb burst behind his chest wound and extend in spirals along the links of the chains on his arms. It didn't feel bad, but he didn't know what it was, and he didn't like that. He wanted to head straight for the Celestial Palace and bury himself in research; privately he thought talking to Peng

Fang was a waste of time. In the past, he probably would have voiced this feeling. In the past, he probably would have convinced them to skip Peng's entirely and go straight to the bookstore.

He was so lost in thought that he didn't see the shadow pass over them, and he was taken aback when the bird-woman smashed into Tian.

He saw Alec and the other New York Shadowhunters drop back and reach for the few weapons they had on them—except for Simon, who put up his hands as though blocking a punch and looked around as if wondering what to do. Quickly, however, they all realized that Tian didn't seem worried—indeed, he was smiling and laughing.

"Jinfeng!" he was saying, and Magnus realized that the bird-woman had given Tian a quick hug and, while she had moved away, was smiling at him.

She was a faerie, he realized a little belatedly, and a striking one at that: a *feng huang*, a phoenix. The Chinese phoenix was an entirely different faerie from the Western phoenix, and much more beautiful. She was almost as tall as Tian, and her gleaming black hair fell to her feet. Wings of red, yellow, and green spread from her back, rippling in the air; her skin was traced with delicate designs in luminous gold. Her dark eyes, ringed with long lashes, shimmered as she regarded the group.

Jace, Clary, and Isabelle were slowly lowering their weapons in confusion. Simon continued to stare wide-eyed, and Alec, of course, was watching Magnus, giving him a questioning look.

Tian was speaking quietly to the faerie girl. "Oh," she said in Mandarin, "I'm so sorry. Are these . . . who . . ." She trailed off, smiling shyly.

"Would you like to introduce us, Tian?" said Magnus mildly.

"Yes," said Tian. "This is Jinfeng, everybody. Jinfeng," and he continued in Mandarin, "these are the Shadowhunters of New York. And also Magnus Bane, High Warlock of Brooklyn."

The phoenix pulled back, suddenly wary. "I'm sorry," she said again. "I know I—the Cold Peace—"

"It's okay," Magnus said. "We don't like the Cold Peace much ourselves."

"Jinfeng is the daughter of the weaponsmiths I was talking about yesterday," Tian said. "And also"—he sighed—"my girlfriend."

"Ohhhhhhhhhhhh," said Jace. Clary whacked him on the shoulder. Jinfeng nervously moved back over to Tian and put an arm around him. She leaned over and kissed him on the cheek, and he smiled.

"As you can imagine," Tian continued, "we've had to keep our relationship secret when others are around. My family has no problem with our being together, but there are plenty in the Shanghai Conclave who would love to use it against us."

"How do your parents feel about Tian?" Magnus said to Jinfeng. "Or their court?"

Jinfeng turned to Magnus, pleased to have someone other than Tian who could converse with her in Mandarin. "They like him," she said, her feathers rustling a little, "and they trust him. But they don't trust his people." She took in Alec, who had his arm draped casually around Magnus. "How do your people feel about *him?*"

"I don't really have people," Magnus said, "but they seem to mostly like him. And these are all his closest friends and family, right here, and I would trust them with my life." At this, Tian raised his eyebrows. Magnus caught his look and went on, "It's taken a few years, though. I'm vouching for you guys, by the way," he added to the rest of them, this last sentence in English.

"Tell her about the Alliance," Alec said, nudging Magnus.

"My boyfriend wants me to tell you that he founded the Downworlder-Shadowhunter Alliance," Magnus said, and batted his eyelashes at Alec. "If you know what that is."

Jinfeng gave a wry smile. "In Shanghai, Tian and I *are* the Downworlder-Shadowhunter Alliance."

"I thought you said your family approved," Magnus said to Tian.

Tian looked sheepish. "They do," he said, "but that's not the same as allowing us to be public. Much less get married. You must know that I—and they—could get in serious trouble. The Cold Peace forbids even business relationships between the fey and the Nephilim, much less—"

"Sexy business," Magnus agreed.

The rest of their party were standing around politely but beginning to look a little uncomfortable. Simon was checking his phone.

Tian took note and said to Jinfeng, "*Qin'ai de*, I was hoping to talk to your parents. These Nephilim have run into a strange weapon recently and we thought they might know about it. Maybe I could talk to them?"

"You can go on," Magnus said to Tian, in English for the benefit of the others. "I've been to the Sunlit Market enough times that I'm sure I can get the rest of us there."

Tian nodded; he was already scribbling an address down on a scrap of paper from his pocket. "I'm going to go with Jinfeng. Meet us here in two hours, and hopefully Mogan will be willing to talk."

"Who's Mogan?" said Magnus.

Tian smiled. "The smiths. Mo and Gan. Mogan."

"Faeries," Magnus said with a sigh.

He took the paper, and Jinfeng and Tian disappeared down a side street, fairly quickly.

"He seemed pretty happy to get away from us," Isabelle observed as they left.

"Young love," said Magnus. "I'm sure you'd have no idea." He grinned at Isabelle, and she grinned back. "We'll catch up with them later. For now, let's head to the Market."

"We have a very annoying blood sommelier to meet with," Alec agreed.

"And a bookstore," Clary put in eagerly. "Do *not* forget the bookstore."

NOW THAT TIAN WAS GONE, THEY WERE DEPENDENT ON Magnus to navigate, which was fine as far as Alec was concerned. Tian was friendly, and knowing he was also dealing with the complexities of a Shadowhunter-Downworlder relationship made him more sympathetic, but he had felt a little babysat. He knew Shadow Markets; he knew Downworlders. He knew Peng Fang. It was a matter of pride, a bit, that they could handle this errand on their own.

As a guide, of course, Magnus was a bit more hesitant than Tian had been. "You're sure you know where you're going?" said Alec a few times, as Magnus considered two possible paths.

"This way seems familiar," Magnus would say, and stride off in that direction. The others put their confidence totally in the warlock, which made Alec feel like it would be disloyal to raise doubts.

They found themselves, after a few twists and turns, in a dark and narrow alley. Unlike the rest of the concession, which was well-kept, clean, and bright in the sunny late morning, this place felt decrepit, like it was rotting away around them, and it was cast in shadow from the surrounding buildings. The pleasant smells of food and autumn flowers were gone, replaced by a humid, fetid odor, not like the crush of people in a city but like a place long abandoned by anything living.

All of them could sense that something was off. Jace and Clary each drew the one seraph blade apiece they had brought, and Simon stood at the back of the alley, vigilantly scanning all around him. Isabelle stood by him, looking less worried but no less alert.

Alec had his hand on his own seraph blade, though he hadn't yet drawn it. "I think maybe we took a wrong turn," he began to say, but choked on the words as he looked over at Magnus.

Magnus was glowing, an angry scarlet flare around him in the gloom of the alley. His upper lip was curled back from his teeth, and his head was in the air, like an animal sniffing the air for predators. Or prey. His eyes, too, shone in the dark, yellow-green and alien in a way Alec had never thought of them. They were glassy and unfocused—he looked like he was listening to something far away, something none of the rest of them could hear. And it must have been the illusion of the strange light filtered down through the buildings, but he seemed taller, sharper.

"Magnus?" Alec said quietly, but Magnus didn't seem to hear him. There was a skittering noise from behind and above him, but when he whirled around, there was nothing there.

The Shadowhunters made their way down the alley carefully. Jace and Isabelle reached the far end first and waited as Clary led Simon, who looked like a cat with its hackles raised, slowly down the lane, standing shoulder to shoulder with him. Alec waited for Magnus to follow, but he seemed to be stuck in place. His hair was wild and his breathing strenuous, as if he'd been running. Alec gently took him by the hand, and Magnus let him, though when his eyes rolled toward Alec, there was no recognition in them.

Alec felt a jolt of fear through him. Magnus was never distracted, never confused. It was one of the things he loved best about his boyfriend: he knew that if Magnus was forced to walk into Hell itself, he would do so with his hair perfect, his clothes pressed, his eye game on point.

And he had to admit that even now, Magnus *looked* good. His expression may have been hungry and hollow, but it brought out his cheekbones, and Alec for just a moment wondered what it would be like to kiss him while looking into eyes lambent with green and gold. It was a strange combination, this feeling of fear and desire.

He forced himself to walk forward, leading Magnus by the hand. Magnus allowed himself to be led; he seemed to barely notice. Alec held his breath, sure they would be attacked at any moment, but at the end of the alley was another archway, and once all six of them were through it, the sun again shone down and the air was fine and calm. Between one moment and the next, all the peculiarity went out of Magnus and he was again himself. He looked surprised as Alec threw his arms around him, hugging him tight.

"Everybody okay?" said Clary.

"Sure," said Simon, though his voice remained shaky. "Nothing happened, right?"

They all looked to Magnus—of course they did, Alec thought. Even with all their experience, they expected Magnus to have the answers to any mystery. He shook his head, looking grave. "I don't know," he said. "We were walking, and then . . . there were those voices. . . ."

Isabelle and Clary exchanged worried looks. "We didn't hear any voices," Isabelle said.

"What were they saying?" asked Alec quietly.

Magnus looked at Alec helplessly. "I . . . I don't remember."

"You'd think the Downworlders would do something about having an alley from Hell right through the middle of their neighborhood," said Jace.

Magnus shook his head. "I don't know where we were," he said, "but that was definitely not Shanghai."

MAGNUS HAD NOT BEEN LYING. HE DIDN'T REMEMBER what had happened, and he didn't remember what the voices had been saying or whether he recognized who had been speaking. What he didn't say was what he did remember: how powerful he had felt, how strong. Like the rest of them, he had been sure they would be attacked, but he had felt only a contempt for the forces that might attack them, as though he might wipe them away with a wave of his hand. Now he felt a strange emptiness, both relieved and disappointed that his feeling hadn't been tested.

He was the navigator, however, and he tried to put all these feelings aside and concentrate on remembering where they were going. He *had* been here before, but it had been eighty-some years ago—still, he was able to follow the noise, and soon they were passing more Downworlders, all heading in roughly the same direction. Groups of young werewolves, pairs of older vampires huddled under large black umbrellas, and a few faeries, who gave the Shadowhunters worried looks and crossed the street to avoid passing them.

Alec took note. "I don't much like being looked at like the enemy here," he said. "We're all on the same side, Shadowhunters and Downworlders."

Jace quirked an eyebrow. "I believe the Clave's official position is that we are on opposite sides."

"It's ridiculous," said Clary. "How many faeries were *actually* on Sebastian's side in the war? The Queen, her court—it must be a tiny percentage of them. But we've punished them all."

"The Clave punished them all," said Simon. "*We* haven't done anything. We tried to prevent the Cold Peace."

"As long as we can explain that to each of them individually, I'm sure we'll be fine," said Jace.

"Maybe we could get T-shirts made," Simon agreed. "'We Tried to Prevent the Cold Peace.'"

Magnus gestured toward another stone archway. "Through here, I think."

"Our luck with random archways hasn't been great," muttered Isabelle. But they went through anyway, and after a brief moment of eerie radiance that caused them all to catch their breath, the passage shimmered and expanded, and suddenly a tall faerie with a sideways grin and a long brocade jacket was trying to sell them wolfsbane cologne.

The Market square was huge and open, paved with massive slabs of stone. Shadow Markets were usually twisty, labyrinthine affairs, full of makeshift stalls and tents, everyone jockeying for customers' attention and shouting over one another. But the Sunlit Market of Shanghai was an altogether more civilized affair, with stalls and sheds neatly lined up in wide rows, shaded by Shanghai's ubiquitous plane trees. Cafés had outdoor terraces with neatly kept tables, and at the center was a huge fountain with a stone figure at each of the corners. From here Magnus could see a dragon and a bird that looked like Jinfeng, and if he remembered correctly, there were a tiger and a tortoise on the other side. The fountain sprayed in colors: red, yellow, and green, and while the water shot many feet into the air, it all remained precisely within the perimeter of the stone pool. Magnus noted with some interest that he could see the aura of the magic responsible for this, a silver glow that, he thought, would usually have been invisible to him.

He was beginning to get a sense of why Shinyun had thought the Svefnthorn wound was a gift, but given the chains on his arms, it seemed like a gift with a ludicrously high cost. No gift was worth accepting chains as well.

The Market was more well-organized than most, but it was still a bustle of chaotic activity. An elderly vampire who looked half-melted stood under a black velvet parasol and haggled with a Sighted mundane over obsidian stakes. Two warlocks were engaged in what appeared to be a magical drinking game at one of the café tables, and every few seconds miniature fireworks exploded from their fingertips with loud cracks. In front of the fountain, four werewolves were howling in erratic harmony.

Magnus dropped back a step, to murmur in Alec's ear, "The barbershop quartet of the night. What music they make."

"There's one thing I don't get," said Clary. "If the Downworlders have their own district in the city, why do they need a Market? Why not just have permanent stores?"

"They do," said Magnus, leading them through the crowd toward the outer perimeter of stalls. "That's why this isn't really a Shadow Market. It's just a market, like you'd find in any mundane neighborhood."

The outer circle of the market had been all food stalls when Magnus had last been here, and despite decades of upheaval and change in the city, this was still the same. Everywhere was a strange combination of mundane and Downworlder food, with Peking duck and *mapo* tofu, *baozi* and *mantou* laid out in rows next to candied faerie fruit and flowers on sticks. Magnus bought a candied tangerine, then offered it to Alec with a smile. Alec took it, but he was still giving Magnus nervous glances when he didn't think his boyfriend was looking. Magnus wished he could remember what had happened in the alley.

He also wished that the Shadowhunters would be a bit more discreet. They had all, he thought, gotten accustomed to the New York Market, where they were well known and garnered friendly glances from most of the vendors and at least some of the patrons. Here, no matter how good Tian said the relationship was between the Conclave and Downworld, they were still a team of five *laowai* Nephilim.

"We're getting some looks," said Jace, always with a bit more situational awareness than the rest of them. "Maybe we should split up."

"This Peng Fang probably won't want to meet with all of us," Clary said hopefully. "Maybe some of us could just go straight to the bookstore?"

"Ooh, look at the heroes," Magnus said with a little smirk. "Save the world a few times and you start shirking responsibilities."

"Honestly, Peng Fang is *terrible*," said Alec.

"Betrayer," said Magnus.

"I too would like to go straight to the bookstore," put in Simon.

"Fine!" said Magnus. "All of you get out. The bookstore is just through the Night Quarter, where all the vampires are, and to the left. It should be hard to miss. I will handle Peng Fang by myself."

"You will not," Alec said. "You will handle Peng Fang along with me." Magnus thought about objecting, but he'd rather have Alec along with him anyway. Peng Fang could be a lot to deal with.

They sent the other New York Shadowhunters away, and when they were out of earshot, Magnus said, "I appreciate the backup, but you might need to wait outside Peng Fang's. Last time, he clammed up the moment you arrived."

"That's fine," said Alec. "I'm not worried about Peng Fang. I'm worried about you." He peered at Magnus. "You really don't remember anything from the alley?"

"Nothing *happened*," Magnus said, and Alec looked like he was going to respond, but he didn't.

They passed into the Night Quarter themselves, through a huge red velvet curtain. Inside all was dim, lit only by a truly enormous number of candles, in silver holders, and high above them a patch-work of fabric and canvas roofs blocked out any hint of the sun. It was like walking into a very Gothic circus tent.

"Vampires and their candles," Alec said under his breath.

"I know! They're even vulnerable to fire," Magnus said. "But they can't resist. They're like moths, in a way."

He was starting to wonder how they would find Peng Fang's, when he noticed Alec had stopped walking alongside him. He turned and saw his boyfriend looking wide-eyed at something to the side, and followed his gaze. Then it took a moment for him to realize what he was looking at.

There in front of a velvet-draped stall—*Vampires and their velvet, too*, Magnus thought—was a full-size cardboard standee of Alec.

He blinked at it.

The cardboard cutout was in full Shadowhunter gear and had Alec's face. Cardboard Alec was holding up a crystal decanter full of crimson liquid, and a speech bubble emerging from his mouth read, in flowing script, *Mmmm! That's good blood!*

"Magnus," said Alec slowly, "do you think maybe I have brain damage?"

"Wait here," Magnus said, and began striding purposefully toward the tent, magic gathering in his hands.

Before he could reach the entrance, though, a stocky man had emerged from the stall and was extending his arms in welcome, a huge grin on his face. He had hair like a bumblebee who had become a rock star, and he was wearing a red-lined black suit jacket unbuttoned over a T-shirt with an illustration of a steam train on it. The cloud of steam formed puffy gray letters that read HERE COMES THE VEIN TRAIN!

"Peng Fang," said Magnus. "I immediately regret having come to speak with you."

"Magnus Bane!" Peng Fang said. "I haven't seen you in—well, it's been simply forever!"

"It's been three years," Alec said dryly. "You kicked us out of the Paris Shadow Market because you said Shadowhunters were bad for business."

Peng Fang looked thrilled. "And Alec Lightwood! Hey, I'm so glad to see you two lovebirds are still together. Inspiring! A new era of cooperation between Shadowhunters and Downworlders! Here, let me give both of you a hug."

Magnus held up a hand politely. "No touching, Peng Fang. You know the rule."

"But—"

"No. Touching." It wasn't that Magnus objected to hugging per se, but Peng Fang had always been . . . enthusiastic about Magnus. And everyone else. Magnus had laid down the rule early in their acquaintance, sometime in the mid-eighteenth century, and he had never had any reason to lift it.

"What brings you to Shanghai? What brings you to my shop?" He continued smiling broadly at them.

"Never mind that," said Alec, barely keeping it together. "What brings *me* to your shop?" He gestured at the standee.

Peng Fang looked back at it with eyebrows raised, as though he'd just noticed its existence. "My dear boy, you're famous. You founded the Downworlder-Shadowhunter Alliance. You've been a hero of two wars. You must understand how helpful it is for business to let people know that you've been to my shop."

"You kicked me out of your shop!" Alec said, and Peng Fang held up his hands to shush him. Alec ignored this. "*And* you hit on Magnus."

"I hit on everyone." Peng Fang shrugged. "Do not take it personally." He leaned toward Magnus. "You must come through to the shop. I've just gotten my hands on some vintage stuff. Pre-Accords, very hard to come by. I can't say more, but let's say there's something a little . . . fishy about its provenance?" Magnus stared at him. "Mermaid blood. It's mermaid blood," he clarified.

"No, Peng Fang, we still don't drink blood," Magnus sighed. "We've come for gossip."

"You're missing out," said Peng Fang. "Come inside." At the entrance to the stall, he pulled the curtain back with a courtly bow rather at odds with his T-shirt, and waved them inside.

The interior was lined with glass cases, filled with cut-crystal vials and decanters. They glinted in the candlelight, but Peng Fang ignored them. "None of this rubbish," he said, dismissing the vials and taking a candle from atop a large stained barrel. "This stall is just for advertising and selling plonk by the cup." He turned to Alec. "Recent mundane blood, the kind of stuff you'd get anywhere on the street. *You* know what I'm talking about," he added to Magnus.

"I don't," said Magnus.

Peng Fang's smile never wavered. "Follow me," he said. "Let's speak in my office." He pushed a rug aside with his foot, revealing a dank stone spiral staircase that descended into the ground below the stall. Alec gave Magnus a look of concern, and Magnus returned it, but they had come this far, and so they followed Peng Fang down into the depths.

ALEC HADN'T LIKED PENG FANG THREE YEARS AGO, WHEN he hated Alec, and he didn't like him any better now that Peng Fang had decided they were great friends. He already, he thought, had too much going on to be following a shady vampire down an underground passage by candlelight, on the off chance he had useful information. He wished they'd skipped the whole business and gone straight to the bookstore. He kept one hand on the hilt of the seraph blade at his belt, sure that at any moment Peng Fang would turn and lunge for them, either to bite them or kiss them or both.

At the end of the hallway was another red curtain, and when they passed through it, Alec relaxed a little. This was still a cellar, but it was lit with permanent fixtures and the floor, rather than packed dirt, was black marble. A wrought-iron spiral stair headed up, and as they ascended Alec saw that at the top were two doors, one lushly lacquered in red and black and the other painted the same color as the dark gray walls, with a small metal sign reading STAFF ONLY in five languages.

"Excuse me a moment," Peng Fang said, and swung the lacquered door open. Behind it were two ancient vampire women with thin blue-white skin and pale gray eyes, both wearing very old-fashioned widow's weeds. One of them was examining a small crystal vial of blood.

Peng Fang spoke to them in Russian; Alec couldn't understand the words, but the tone was the same unctuous manner he always used, and his smile was wide as always. He ended with a question and looked back and forth between the ladies, who blinked at him.

"V'skorye," he said, and closed the door. "Tasting room," he said to Magnus, who smiled thinly. "Lovely ladies. Been coming to me for years. They're looking to invest in blood futures."

Alec cocked an eyebrow. "So . . . blood that's still inside people?"

Peng Fang clapped Alec on the back and laughed heartily but didn't explain further. He opened the STAFF ONLY door and gestured them inside.

Inside was a huge mahogany desk and a few wing-backed armchairs. In classic vampire style, the lights were very dim, but they had been carefully designed to glitter off the shelves of decanters and bottles that lined the back wall. Peng Fang went to them and began to elaborately select and pour himself a goblet of blood. Magnus dropped into one of the chairs facing the desk and stretched his legs out. Alec remained standing, arms crossed.

Peng Fang turned, holding his goblet. *"Ganbei,"* he said, and took a sip. Magnus and Alec remained silent, and Fang flashed them a toothy, red-stained smile. "What can I help my favorite customers with today?"

"Well, we're looking into a few things right now," Alec said. "The situation with Portals, for example. They've been going wrong all over Shanghai, it seems."

Peng Fang took another sip. "That's not exactly juicy gossip. They've been going wrong all over the world, sounds like. Why you two are investigating, I have no idea; the Conclave's been all over trying to figure it out."

"But you hear things," said Magnus. "All over Downworld. Any interesting theories?"

"Oh, plenty blame the Shadowhunters, of course," Fang said with a dismissive wave of his free hand. "Ever since the Cold Peace, they get blamed for everything. But that's silly, of course. Portals are warlock magic. Let's see. Some say the faeries have been sabotaging them."

"I can't imagine how they'd be able to do that," Magnus said doubtfully.

"Neither can I," agreed Peng Fang, "unless they're in league with somebody very powerful. And I mean *very* powerful."

"A Greater Demon?" said Alec.

"Greater than Greater," said Fang, giving them another grin. "A Prince of Hell. *The* Prince of Hell."

"Not—" began Magnus.

"No," said Fang immediately. "Not him. But close. Sammael."

Alec did his best not to react at all. "Sammael?" he said, chuckling. "Everyone knows Sammael is gone. Has been for—well, basically forever."

"So he's dead," said Fang, though that hadn't been exactly what Alec had said. "So am I, but that hasn't stopped me running a successful international business concern, has it now? You know as well as I do that you can't keep a Prince of Hell down forever. For a while, sure. For longer than I or even you," he added, gesturing at Magnus, "have been around, definitely. But not forever. And Sammael is, after all, the Maker of the Way."

"The what?" said Alec.

Fang looked impatient. "The Finder of Paths? The World-Burrower? The Render of Veils? Any of this ringing a bell?"

"Not at all," Alec said.

Fang made a disapproving noise in the back of his throat and drained the rest of his drink. "What do they teach these Shadowhunters? Sammael, he's the guy who opened the paths from the demon realms into this world in the first place. He weakened the wards of the world, or that's what they say." He reached down for the decanter and refilled his goblet. "So," he went on, "when things go wrong with Portals, naturally people start talking about how Sammael is the source of it."

"Do you believe that?" Magnus said.

Peng Fang smiled. "I don't believe anything unless I get paid for it, Magnus Bane. I've found that to be a good way to keep my head on my shoulders and stakes out of my chest."

"We're also looking for a couple of warlocks," Magnus said. "A Korean woman and a green fellow with horns."

"Oh," said Fang with a distinct change of mood. "Them."

"You've seen them?" Alec said, trying not to sound too eager.

"Everyone's seen them," Fang said. He sounded grumpy. "They've been all over the Market for months. The woman for longer. Nobody likes them much, but they spend like sailors on leave, and they look like they'd kill you just as soon as look at you."

"What have they been buying?" Magnus said.

"Now normally," Fang said, running his finger around the rim of his goblet, "that kind of information would cost you."

"I—"

"But the answer is so simple I can't in good conscience charge you. What *haven't* they been buying? Spell components, plain and fancy. Random antique spell books no one's used in hundreds of years. Cheap blood in bulk."

"Have they bought anything from *you*?" Magnus said.

"Well now," Peng Fang said, a gleam in his eye, "that *would* cost you. But it doesn't really matter. None of the really serious blood magic is accessible to them without some pretty powerful spells. As long as they don't have the Book of the White or anything, we should all be fine."

Alec wasn't able to stop himself from looking over at Magnus. Realizing his mistake, he quickly schooled his features into a bland expression, but Peng Fang noticed immediately. "They don't have it, do they? Right?" He sounded, for the first time, a little less self-assured.

"How should I know?" Magnus said with an impenetrable smile.

"Well, let's hope for all our sakes they don't," Peng Fang said. He drained his cup again and began to fuss with pouring another. "I haven't seen it myself, but people are saying that these warlocks have been bringing demons into the concession. That's strictly prohibited, of course," he added to Alec.

"Has it been reported to the Shadowhunters?" said Alec, already knowing the answer. "Since the relationship between the two is so good here and all."

Peng Fang shrugged. "Nobody's been hurt yet. And nobody wants a repeat of '37." Alec had no idea what this meant, but Magnus frowned. "Gentlemen, it's glorious to see you as always, but I'm afraid that I must tend to my Russians."

Alec was surprised by the abruptness, but Magnus got up immediately and nodded. "Thanks for your time, Peng Fang. We must be off too; we've got an appointment with Mogan."

"The smiths?" Peng Fang sounded surprised. "Don't take this one," he advised Magnus, with a gesture in Alec's direction. "Most fey don't care for Shadowhunters these days."

Magnus was rustling around in his pocket and produced a wad of bills from it. "Some yuan for your trouble."

Peng Fang made a pronounced show of refusing the money. "Magnus, Magnus, we've been friends for so long. I haven't told you anything worth a payment today. That's how much good faith you can have in me. I'm not some two-bit crook like Johnny Rook."

Magnus pressed the money into his hand anyway. Peng Fang tried to hug him again, and with a final no, Magnus headed down the spiral staircase, with Alec following. They retraced their steps back through the cellar and up the stone staircase into the stall.

The ground floor of the shop was dark, but they could still easily see the glass cabinets covered in Chinese labels and their contents. The amount of blood on hand was beginning to get to Alec, and he was happy to go out the front door and back onto the streets of the concession, where it was still a fine, sunny afternoon. "Who's Johnny Rook again?" Alec muttered as they left.

Magnus shrugged. "Some two-bit crook."

CHAPTER NINE

The Celestial Palace

ALEC WAS SILENT ON THE WAY TO THE BOOKSTORE, AND Magnus, for the first time in a couple of years, felt an odd feeling. He felt awkward about the meeting with Peng Fang.

"I really don't know Peng Fang that well," he said. "I've just bought information from him a few times over the years."

Alec nodded, distracted.

"It's just . . . I know there's a lot of sketchy stuff in my past," Magnus went on. What was wrong with him? "I don't want you to worry that any of it will come back to . . . well . . ."

He trailed off, and Alec stopped walking and gave him a curious look. "What's this about?" he said.

"When we were meeting with Peng Fang, I just started to think about how shady it all was, how shady a lot of the things I have to do are. I mean, Peng Fang is harmless, it's just that I'm very big with weirdos. They all think I love them."

Alec grinned affectionately. "It's your devilish charisma," he said. "You can't help it."

"Yeah, but some of the weirdos I know have turned out to be

dangerous. And I know we don't want to put Max in danger," Magnus began, and Alec began to laugh. "What?" Magnus demanded.

"Magnus, I'm the one with the dangerous job," Alec said. "I literally fight demons for a living. We've adopted Max into an incredibly dangerous family situation. I know that! I mean, forget the actual fighting, the monsters, the dark magic. I'm a gay Shadowhunter in a relationship with a famous Downworlder, who is himself the son of a Prince of Hell. My father is the Inquisitor and my parents were members of a hate group. My parabatai has been imprisoned in the Silent City. More than once!"

"When you put it like that," Magnus murmured, "it doesn't sound like a great home environment."

"But it is," said Alec with more force than Magnus would have expected. "I like our life, Magnus. I like that I don't know what will happen next. I like that we get a chance to give Max the kind of life that warlocks rarely get. I like that we'll be doing it together. You remember what the note said when we found Max? 'Who could ever love it?' We could, Magnus. We could love him. We do love him."

Magnus's mind was torn. On the one hand, he was filled with affection and appreciation, for Alec, for Max, for a life he never thought he could have. On the other hand, he thought of the magic growing within his chest, and whatever had happened in the alley. He thought of Ragnor, currently lost in thrall to a demon after hundreds of years of doing only good with his powers.

"How will we ever explain to Max?" he said quietly. "Where he came from. Where I came from. That people will look at him and make decisions about who he is without knowing him at all. That his parents put themselves in danger over and over again, but that we'll always come back to him."

"I think you just said it pretty well," said Alec. "And . . . I don't know. I'm a beginner at this too. But we'll figure it out together. That's the whole idea." He put his hand behind Magnus's head and pulled him in for a kiss. Magnus expected something quick, but Alec kissed him deeply, his mouth slightly open, warm, reassuring, and full of love and desire. Magnus allowed himself to relax into the kiss, but as he did, he felt his tongue pass over his own teeth. They felt different. Were they bigger? Was he growing fangs? What was happening to him?

He decided that he would take things one step at a time, and this step was kissing Alec. Often these days their kisses were casual, familiar, lovely in the way they felt like home. But now they kissed with a desperation and hopefulness, drowning in one another, as they had in the earliest days of being together. After what felt like a long time, Alec broke the kiss and leaned his forehead against Magnus's. "We'll figure this out. We'll figure it all out. We always do."

A werewolf passed by and called out in Mandarin, "Get a room, cute boys!"

Alec turned and waved cheerily to the man. "What did he say?"

"Let's get to the Palace," Magnus suggested. "We've got figuring out to do."

They walked on, holding hands, and for a short time Magnus felt a little more at ease than he had the last couple of days.

MOMENTS AFTER THEY STARTED WALKING AGAIN, A fire-message burst in Alec's face, startling him. He grabbed at it and read it to Magnus.

"'Where are you? Found thorn info. Faeries watching us like we're going to rob the place. Come as soon as you can.—Jace.'"

They hurried down the street, and Magnus followed his dead reckoning until they turned onto an old street in the Market and his favorite bookstore in Asia appeared before him.

The Celestial Palace was the size of a city block, a double-eaved structure that looked like one of the court buildings of Beijing as reinterpreted by faeries. It claimed to be the oldest Downworld business in Shanghai, preceding the concession itself by hundreds of years. Magnus wasn't sure he bought that story—although maybe it was right, since faeries couldn't lie—but it was an impressive piece of old Shanghai regardless, and a show of faerie power. Rather than the brick, stone, and tile that were used to construct its mundane inspirations, the Palace was all colored glass, gold, and glossily polished wood. On either side of the massive double doors, a glass dragon stood guard. They were painted with mercury, and their eyes were huge sea pearls.

As Magnus approached, one of them turned its serpentine head to regard them. "Magnus Bane," it intoned in a voice like stones scraping against one another. "Long time no see."

"Huang." Magnus nodded to it, then turned to the other. "Di."

The one called Di didn't move its head. "Wait."

With a bang, the doors burst open and a small faerie with fox ears ran out, a huge tome under one arm. He bumped into Alec's shoulder, pushing him aside, and took off down the street.

He had made it only a short distance when a prismatic ray of light burst from Di's mouth. It struck the fox faerie, who froze and then vanished in a puff of blue smoke. The tome dropped to the ground. There was a smell like ozone in the air.

Huang regarded Magnus and Alec. "Thus ever to book thieves. Art makes lives worth living, and so theft is the next-door neighbor to murder. They shall be ever cursed, and will never escape the eyes of the Huangdi."

"Noted," said Alec nervously. "We don't steal books."

"It's not personal," put in Di. "It's just business."

"May your trade be always prosperous and your wealth plentiful," Magnus said.

"What he said," agreed Alec.

The eyes of the dragons watched them as they passed through the doors.

ALEC HAD SEEN PLENTY OF WONDERS IN HIS SHORT LIFE so far, but even he had to admit that the interior of the Celestial Palace was something to behold. Despite appearing to be only two stories from the outside, it rose five levels on the inside, each ringed with a balcony boasting floor-to-ceiling shelves containing a seeming infinitude of books. The whole interior was of carved rosewood forming the shapes of twisting vines and branches, and in the center of the huge open space above them, three great spheres of flame hung suspended in the air, giving the whole place a warm glow.

He had been worried that they would have a hard time finding their friends in such a large place, but he caught sight of them almost immediately. Isabelle was perched high up on a ladder, moving easily despite towering heels, his sister fearless about heights as she was about most things. She called down to Simon to move the ladder very fast to the section on blood curses, and screamed, "Whee!" when he did.

Clary came running over, carrying a calfskin book with an unfamiliar symbol stamped on the cover. "We found the thorn," she said. She opened the book on a nearby table, covered with what looked to be faerie cookbooks, and pointed in triumph at the drawing of a thorned spike, below which were paragraphs of runic writing.

"So what's the deal? Why does the sleep-thorn not put people to sleep?" said Magnus.

"That's only what it does to Norse gods, I guess," Jace said. "Look." He pointed to the text. "Do you want me to translate for you?"

"Of *course* you can read Old Norse runes," Magnus said, rolling his eyes.

"I am a man of many talents," said Jace. "Also, my dad was an abusive taskmaster."

"Fair point."

"So," Jace resumed. "The Svefnthorn is made of black *adamas*."

"Which is what exactly?" said Clary.

"*Adamas* corrupted by a demon realm," Magnus said. "Very rare stuff." He traced his finger along the illustration of the thorn. "It ties a warlock to that realm and its ruler, and the warlock draws power from it. Makes warlocks much stronger than usual."

"That doesn't seem so bad," said Alec.

"Until the power overwhelms them, and they either die or are stabbed three times by the thorn and become the willing lackey of the demon who rules the realm," added Magnus.

"That seems pretty bad," Alec corrected himself.

"So it's basically . . . magic meth?" said Clary.

Jace said, "The Spiral Labyrinth forbade its use in . . . wait, let me convert the date . . . 1500 or so."

"Why would Shinyun say it was a *gift*?" Alec said.

"Because she's crazy?" offered Magnus. "The realm has to be Diyu, of course. But why would Shinyun thorn *herself*? Even she isn't crazy enough to kill herself for a temporary power boost."

"Maybe she thinks her demon daddy can prevent her from dying," suggested Clary.

"The question is, how do we prevent *Magnus* from dying?" Alec said. He realized he had curled his hands into fists, and made himself uncurl them.

"Maybe an eldest curse can handle it?" suggested Magnus. "Maybe they think there's something in the Book of the White that would help?"

"I would guess that either you need to go to Diyu as soon as you can, or make sure you never go to Diyu," said Jace.

Alec rubbed his temples with his fingers. "Maybe Shinyun will show up again and we can ask her in between fights with her demon army."

"Simon and Isabelle are supposed to be looking into the whereabouts of the Diyu Portal," said Clary. They all looked over at where they'd last seen the two of them. A stern-looking goblin in rimless spectacles appeared to be angrily lecturing Simon, who was making apologetic gestures. Behind them it appeared that they'd upset a reading circle of toddler-aged hobgoblins. Isabelle saw the others and came over, a stack of books under her arm.

She put them down with a sigh. "Can we come back when we have time to browse? Local history isn't really my thing."

"Did you find anything about the location of the old Portal?" said Alec.

"Not really. Simon was writing down the list of places mentioned, but it just reads like a tourist guide to the city." Isabelle sounded frustrated. "It's like every famous place is rumored to be the site of the Portal."

"Shinyun and Ragnor must know," said Magnus. "They have *some* way of communicating with Sammael, and we're pretty sure he's in Diyu."

"So we're back to hoping they show up," said Clary. "Or checking out every one of these possible locations. Any one of which could turn out to be an open Portal to Hell. Just saying."

Simon came over to join them, running his hands through his hair. "Word of advice, guys, never piss off a goblin bookseller. They are *strict*."

"I hear you've got nothing," Jace said brightly. Simon gave him a look.

"We don't have nothing," said Alec. "We know more about the thorn."

"And I did some reading about Diyu," said Simon. He plonked his stack of books on top of Isabelle's.

"It's Chinese Hell, right?" said Clary.

"Well," Simon said. "Not really. It's maybe more like Chinese purgatory? Souls go there to be tortured for their sins for some amount of time before they get reincarnated. It all seems to be very organized—lots of different hells, each with a different ruler; there are judges, and they decide what hell you go to; and civil servants keeping it all running. Or at least," he added, "it *was* organized, under Yanluo's rule. But Yanluo is gone."

"So now what?" said Alec.

"Reports vary," said Isabelle dryly.

"Nobody knows, because nobody's been there since Yanluo died," Simon added.

"Sammael could be trying to gain energy from all the soul torturing," Alec offered.

"That seems like a lot of work," Magnus said, frowning. "I've never thought of Sammael as the kind to run a civil service. He could just be squatting there."

Clary looked troubled. "I feel like I should ask," she said. "If we find an open Portal to Diyu, are we going to . . . go through it?"

Before anyone could answer, the front doors burst open and Tian came running up to them. He sounded out of breath.

"I hoped I'd find you here," he said, without preamble. "Jinfeng's parents want to see you at once. They said it's important. They said, 'The one with the chains must arm himself.'"

Everyone except Alec and Magnus looked baffled.

"What chains?" said Jace.

Magnus sighed and unbuttoned his shirt, pulling it open to reveal the angry red chains extending from his wound and disappearing into his sleeves. Alec could not say for sure, but he thought they had become more well-defined than before. And had there also been chains extending down toward his legs and up toward his throat before? He couldn't remember.

The other Shadowhunters stared at Magnus.

The bespectacled goblin who had yelled at Simon appeared unexpectedly beside them. He spoke in a hissed stage whisper. "I am sorry, but I *must* ask you to leave. You're disturbing the other customers. They're not used to Shadowhunters in the first place, and now you're taking off your clothes—"

"Got it," said Alec. "We were just leaving."

"The Cold Peace says we're allowed to prevent you from coming entirely," the goblin went on. He had clearly prepared a speech and was going to deliver it no matter what. "But we said no, the Palace is a neutral territory, all of the Shadow World should be welcome. But we *didn't* mean for a whole . . . *squad* of Nephilim to—"

"Yes, yes," Alec said. "We're going." He began herding them toward the doors.

"Also," the goblin continued, "this isn't a *lending library.* Those books are *for sale,* and now we'll have to reshelve all of them—"

Magnus had been slowly buttoning his shirt back up. Now he turned and put his hand on the goblin's shoulder in a friendly manner. The faerie looked at it as if it were a poisonous snake. "Sir, my apologies for my companions," he said. "I take full responsibility. They were only helping me with some of my research. I'm Magnus Bane, High Warlock of New York, and I'm going to buy all of these."

The goblin looked suspicious. "I know of you. You're only the High Warlock of Brooklyn."

"Technicalities," said Magnus. "The point is, sir—may I know your name?"

The goblin sniffed. "Well, if you must know. It's Kethryllianalæmacisii."

"Really?" said Magnus. "Well, anyway, Keth—may I call you Keth?"

"You may not."

Magnus pressed on. "If you'll just ring all of these up and have the bill sent to the Spiral Labyrinth. The books can be delivered to the Mansion Hotel, if you will."

Simon had helpfully piled the books into a single large stack and presented them to Kethryllianalæmacisii, who staggered a bit under the weight, but was clearly not about to lose a decent-size sale to the Spiral Labyrinth. "Of course, Mr. Bane," he said, through clenched teeth. "But if that's all, my staff and I would appreciate—"

"Yes," said Magnus, "we were just leaving."

"Sorry," said Simon to the goblin, who made a hissing noise at him.

Looking a bit dazed, Tian led them out of the store. When the doors opened, a bird in a cage above it sang a snatch of song, haunting and sweet. *"Come away, O human child! To the waters and the wild!"*

On the steps outside, Alec said to Magnus, "Can you really bill things to the Spiral Labyrinth?"

"Let's find out!" Magnus said. "Now, I've heard the one with chains must arm himself, so Tian, lead the way."

CHAPTER TEN

The Black and White Impermanence

THEY FOLLOWED TIAN THROUGH UNFAMILIAR STREETS of the Shadow Concession. Vines stretched in dense tangles between the buildings, forming a kind of canopy over their heads. The light that filtered through to the street below was cool and gentle. The group passed a selkie selling silkie chicken soup, and a fey-made river garlanded with moonflowers in which mermaids sang. Magnus stopped walking and smiled at them, listening. He wanted to see his child. He wanted to crawl into bed with Alec and cuddle and sleep. He let the song flow through his mind, reminding him of visits to China long before any of his companions' grandparents' grandparents were born. He closed his eyes, and after a moment felt Alec's hand on his back—not hurrying him on, just connecting to him.

"'*Chun Jiang Hua Yue Ye*,'" he said to Alec. "'A Night of Blossoms on a Moonlit Spring River.' A song older than me."

He began humming to himself, his eyes still closed. Let the others wait. Why had he never brought Alec here just for a visit? If his friends weren't in danger, he would have drawn Alec down to dance by the glowing river's edge, teaching him the words and the tune.

Instead, the one with chains had to arm himself.

THERE WAS NO MISTAKING THE SMITHY FOR ANY OTHER building. It stood just off the main square of the Sunlit Market, and it was surrounded by a fearsome wall of dozens of long spears lashed together. Which made sense, Alec thought.

Tian led them through a gate in the fence, which opened to his touch with a chime like faerie bells. As they passed through, Jace ran his finger over one of the wavy spearheads admiringly, and Tian noticed.

"Look how the curves of each blade are identical," he said. "The skill of these smiths is unparalleled anywhere in China."

"Would you say those are *qiang* or *mao*?" Jace said.

Tian looked surprised. "Maybe *mao*? But you'd have to ask the smiths. You know Chinese weapons?"

"Jace knows all the weapons," said Clary in a long-suffering tone, but she smiled.

Alec followed Tian inside, expecting gleaming walls of weapons in luxuriant display cases. As much as he teased Jace about his weapons obsession, there was a tickle in the back of his mind about faerie bows, and weren't chain whips a traditional Chinese martial arts weapon? Maybe a gift for Isabelle . . .

Inside, however, he saw no weapons beautifully displayed—in fact, he saw no weapons at all. Instead a very, very old man and woman sat on stools in an empty stone room, lit by braziers. Between them stood a cook fire, bearing a clay cauldron that the woman was stirring.

The Shadowhunters filed into the room and looked around in confusion.

The man and woman looked up. "Oh, Tian!" said the woman. "These must be your friends."

"We hear you're going into Diyu!" said the man.

"We have *not* decided to do that," Alec said hastily. "It was under discussion."

Tian said, "Mo Ye, Gan Jiang, I'd like to introduce—" He took a deep breath and named all of them in a row, from right to left, without taking a second breath. Alec was impressed. "Everyone," Tian went on, "these are Gan Jiang and Mo Ye, the greatest living faerie weaponsmiths."

"Nonsense!" said Gan Jiang. "We're *also* better than any of the dead ones."

"We hear you got stuck with a Svefnthorn!" said Mo Ye eagerly. "We have another Svefnthorn in the back somewhere, if you want it."

"No, we don't," said Gan Jiang. "Don't listen to her. The last time I saw that Svefnthorn, Shanghai wasn't even *founded*. It's somewhere under the mountain, but who knows where? Not me and not her either, I bet."

"Um, honorable . . . I'm sorry, I don't know the right terminology," Magnus said, "but you said something about the chained one and how I needed to be armed? And, well—" He began unbuttoning his shirt.

"Stop!" said Mo Ye. "No need to disrobe. We already know. Here." She reached into the clay pot she'd been stirring with both hands and drew from it two swords, neither of which could possibly have fit into the pot. For all their humble surroundings, Alec thought, faeries couldn't resist a performance.

Mo Ye laid the swords across the top of the clay bowl. They were clearly a match, identical longswords except for their color: one had a blade of deep black obsidian, its hilt shining white metal, and the other was the reverse, its hilt in black and its blade in white.

Magnus looked at them, then up at the faeries. "I'm not really a sword guy," he said.

"They're not *swords*," said Gan Jiang. "They're *gods*."

"They're *keys*," added Mo Ye.

"No offense," said Jace, "but they really look like swords."

"The Heibai Wuchang," said Gan Jiang. "The Black Impermanence and the White Impermanence."

Tian said quietly, in an awed tone, "They guide the souls of the dead to Diyu."

"They *did*," said Mo Ye. "Until their master, Yama, was destroyed."

"That's Yanluo," whispered Tian.

"They flew free of Diyu, unfettered and broken—" said Gan Jiang.

"Until we found them and made them into swords," finished Mo Ye. "You'll need them," she added to Magnus, "to guide your soul to Diyu."

"Again," Alec said. "We're really not sure about going to Diyu. We try to avoid hell dimensions whenever possible."

Gan Jiang smiled at him as if he were a child. "*And* you'll need them if you ever want to get out again."

Magnus hesitated. "I am a man of many talents, but swordplay is definitely *not* one of them."

"And I tell you, when it comes time, you won't need to kill with them," said Gan Jiang. He examined the group with narrowed eyes. "These are swords of mercy and judgment. You, warlock, must take mercy, the white blade—" Mo Ye picked up White Impermanence and went behind Magnus, where she began fussily fastening it to his back with a strap and sheath. Alec smiled at Magnus, who had immediately adopted the neutral expression he wore when a tailor was pinning his clothes for alteration.

"And you, Nephilim, will carry the black." Gan Jiang offered Black Impermanence's hilt to Alec.

Alec was about to say, *Why do I have to be "judgment"?* but the moment his hand gripped the sword, the room and the smiths and his friends vanished, and he was in a different place.

A featureless cracked plain, black and pitted, extended forever to an empty horizon. Above it stretched a red sky, hung with a sun too large and dark as blood.

On the plain was Magnus. Or whatever Magnus had become.

He had not become a monster, not really. He didn't look more like an animal, or a demon. But he had grown to a terrifying height, and when he looked down at Alec, it was with whited-out eyes and no recognition.

This huge Magnus brought his bare arms up, and Alec could see iron chains, affixed to a spiked ball punched through each of his palms. The chains receded behind Magnus into a storm of smoke and flame that trailed behind him.

Magnus still had the freedom of movement to bring his hands together. Jagged, gleaming shards of pinkish-red magic began to coalesce between his hands, and Alec could feel the ground rumble and the power begin to gather.

He held the Black Impermanence before him, and he understood beyond any doubt that only he could wield it. Only he could make the judgment, if it came to it. If Magnus was overcome by the thorn, by Sammael.

Also, the thought of this version of Magnus, all emotion absent, burning with power, wielding a sword of judgment, was a little terrifying.

He held the sword before him, pointing it toward the dark god that had been Magnus, and he said, "Magnus, if you know me, speak to me."

Then he was back in the stone room. Gan Jiang was watching him keenly.

"Obviously I know you," Magnus said worriedly. "Are you all right?"

Alec looked at Gan Jiang, and he nodded. "He's fine," he said. "Bit of a moment with the sword, I think."

"I think your husband's been tested," Mo Ye said brightly to Magnus. "Good news! He passed."

Magnus looked at Alec with concern.

Alec felt himself blush. "We're not married," he said apologetically as he strapped the sword to his back.

"You're not married *yet*," Isabelle piped up.

Gan Jiang laughed. "Do you see rings on *our* hands? And yet Mo Ye and I have been married since before the sea was salt." He leaned into Alec. "Stay with him," he said in a confidential tone.

"I plan to," said Alec.

"Excellent!" Gan Jiang barked. "Now, you must go. We are closing for supper."

This was so abrupt that they all stood around dumbly for a moment.

"You don't have ears?" Mo Ye said. "Get out! We're closed! You're needed in the Market!"

They hustled Magnus and the Shadowhunters out of the room and back onto the street. Somehow, in the short time that they had been inside the faerie smithy, the sun had dropped below the buildings, and it was full dusk. An orange glow passed over the buildings and the trees, and a warm breeze blew gently, carrying the scent of flowers and of the food stalls at the Market nearby.

The door slammed shut, and Alec heard the sound of several latches and bolts being thrown.

"That was surprisingly similar to visiting my grandparents," Simon said after a moment. "Except they would have fed us."

"What happened in there, Alec?" Jace said.

"I had a vision," Alec said slowly.

"A vision of what?" said Isabelle.

"Of what would happen if we fail to stop Sammael, I think."

Jace said, "Did it give you any insight? Into what we should do?"

Alec was looking at Magnus. "Not fail."

"All right," said Jace. "We've got research, we've got swords. What's our next step?"

"Signs are pointing toward us needing to know more about Diyu," said Isabelle. "We could start checking the possible locations for the old Portal. What do you think, Tian? . . . Tian?"

They all looked around. Tian had definitely been in the smithy with them, but he was gone. Alec realized he hadn't seen the young Shadowhunter since before they had taken the swords.

There was a burst of light from the sky above the central Market square. A purple afterimage flashed in Alec's eyes, and he blinked, trying to clear it. Not far away, someone began to scream.

THEY WERE BARELY ARMED. THEY WEREN'T WEARING gear. They hadn't applied combat runes. Magnus had one of their two swords, and he hadn't swung a sword in decades. In fact, he could barely figure out how to untangle it from the complicated shoulder harness Mo Ye had strapped to his back.

But they all ran toward the Market square anyway.

The place was chaos. Downworlders ran helter-skelter in all directions, looking for refuge or escape. Market stall grates and shutters slammed closed. Silhouettes scattered in the dim light; Magnus could hardly tell what was happening on the ground. Far above them, a blackish glow throbbed, like a circle cut out of the sky. It was almost the size of the square itself. And out of the circle came demons.

"It's a Portal," said Isabelle, her black hair whipping in the wind.

"A *dimensional* Portal," yelled Clary, over the sound of chaos. "Not a normal one—this one goes to another world—"

Diyu. They all knew it without saying the word, even before Ragnor and Shinyun stepped free of the Portal and hovered in the air before them, their arms raised and red magic crackling between them. It was the same color that Magnus's magic had become.

Magnus looked up at the Portal. He could see nothing through it, only clouds so dark they were almost black. Long silken threads were emerging from points within it, and down those threads slid dark gray spheres the size of large dogs. As they descended, they unfolded to reveal themselves to be—no surprise, given the day he'd had—huge spiders.

He shot Alec a glance. Alec wasn't the biggest fan of spiders, and Magnus had grown entertained by his unwillingness to deal with even small ones that showed up in their loft, despite also being a heavily armed angelic warrior.

Now Alec drew Black Impermanence and gritted his teeth. "Let's see how well this god-key works as a plain old sword."

Magnus began gathering magic between his hands, disturbed that it was the same color as their enemies'. He was distracted by Ragnor's deep voice, carrying above the chaos. "The host of Diyu is upon you! The courts have judged you unworthy, and you will suffer the tortures of the dead!"

Simon was frozen, gazing in horror at the spiders descending. Behind them, streams of fog announced the arrival of Ala demons, who swooped down, screaming, to chase Downworlders through the narrow passages of the Market. A pack of hellhounds had appeared and cornered a pixie family. Magnus was about to call out for Simon when Jace ran past him, carrying two of the curved-head pikes from the fence outside the smithy, one in each hand.

"Heads up, Lewis! Sorry, Lovelace!" he yelled, and Simon jerked out of his daze just in time to catch one of the spears. He appeared to take a moment to gather himself, and then he and Jace rushed the hellhounds together. One hellhound let a child fall from its jaws as Jace's spear bit into its side. The demonic dog yelped and crashed to the ground; the rest of the hounds turned to face them, eyes red and jaws open, baring rows of jagged fangs.

The lead hellhound went down, felled by Simon. Another hound roared and leaped for Jace, who neatly ducked and used the spear handle and the hound's own momentum to send it crashing through a window.

Xiangliu began to swarm toward Jace and Simon, but Clary quickly appeared to cover them. She lashed out with a glowing seraph blade, whirling around, a blur of light in the fog. In a moment of pause she caught Magnus's eye, then looked up at the warlocks above. Magnus understood her meaning—he had to fly up there and engage with them, just as he had in front of the Institute. In this fight, though, nobody had a bow, and he would be exposed in the air, protected only by his own magic.

Isabelle, meanwhile, had gotten pushed back toward a striped canvas tent by a group of the spider demons. She had only a single seraph blade and no *parabatai* to keep an eye on her. The spiders, sensing her to be vulnerable, leaped. Isabelle spun and kicked one out of the air, but doing so unbalanced her, and she went tumbling back into the tent, which collapsed around her and the spiders.

Magnus cried out and ran toward her, but he needn't have worried. The body of one of the spider demons suddenly emerged from the mess, impaled like a kebab on the end of a steel strut, part of the structure of the collapsed tent. Isabelle appeared, wielding the strut like a quarterstaff, and knocked two more spiders away. Now she held it ahead of her, keeping the spiders at bay, and with her free hand plucked her seraph blade from its sheath and yelled, *"Nuriel!"*

The seraph blade blazed. Isabelle spun and turned the attack on the spiders, pushing them back, when Alec appeared, slicing away with Black Impermanence. Ichor flew.

Shinyun landed amid the demons and produced a massive fireball, which she hurled at Jace, Clary, and Simon, who were fighting back-to-back. Magnus, without thinking, flung himself between the fireball and his friends, and the blazing orb smashed into him, where it disappeared, seeming to sink into his chest. Clary saw and her eyes widened.

"Why are you doing this?" Magnus yelled at Shinyun. "These are Downworlders! They are your people!"

Shinyun turned her impassive gaze upon him. "Witness," she called out, "the opening of a new, permanent path to Diyu!" She drew her hand down, trailing pink flame, and more of the spider demons sprang from her fingers. "*Zhizhu-jing*, my sisters! This is your world now! Prepare the way for your new master!"

"No!" Magnus shouted, and threw himself at the spiders. He thrust his hand at one, and it passed with a *splurch* into the center of the demon's guts. He opened his fist within the demon, which exploded. He glanced at Shinyun and was surprised to see her nodding with approval. This only drove Magnus to more fury, and he grabbed another one of the spiders in both hands and, bringing his palms together, smashed it like a melon.

He stood there, his hands shaking, shocked at what he'd done. He didn't even smash the regular spiders he found in his apartment. Though, truth be told, they deserved it far less than a demon did.

"Magnus!" Alec's voice sounded far away. "Can you close the Portal?"

"Dealing with spiders," he muttered to himself. One had rolled next to him, and he brought his foot down, crushing it. Clear for the moment, he looked up at the Portal and reached for its border with his magic, hoping he could pull it closed.

Ragnor suddenly appeared above him, descending fast. It was the first time Magnus had seen him, other than in a dream, since that night in their apartment—was that really only a few days ago?—and Ragnor looked changed even since then. His eyes, normally dark and kind, glowed from within, and his horns had grown longer and more curled. Spikes had begun to sprout from the horns, and when Ragnor raised his hands, Magnus saw that they were bigger than usual, and tipped with black claws.

"No chance," Ragnor taunted him. "You'll never close it. Not from this side."

Magnus ignored him, concentrating on the lines tying the Portal to the world. He gritted his teeth, feeling magic run in torrents from the nodule in his heart out through the chains on his arms, to emerge from his palms.

"It's not a matter of power," Ragnor said, and he almost sounded like his old self, lecturing Magnus on matters of magical technique and theory. "This is a different magic. An older magic.

"It's your fault, you know," he went on, conversationally. "That we opened the Portal here. We could have picked anywhere, but once our master knew you were in the Market, well, we just couldn't resist."

"Me?" said Magnus.

"All of you," Ragnor said, in a gleeful tone that was chillingly wrong coming from him. "The Shadowhunters especially. The Serpent has a particular fondness for them. He wants all of Downworld to know that the Nephilim can't possibly protect them."

"They seem to be doing a decent job of it," said Magnus. "Ragnor— what's happened to you? Why have you signed on with . . . not just a demon, but the worst evil in existence? You went into hiding to avoid Sammael, and now he's your best friend. You don't have to do this. You don't *have* to do anything. You taught me that."

For the first time, Ragnor appeared to hesitate. Magnus pressed him. "Leave Sammael. Leave Diyu. Come with me. We can protect you—"

But Ragnor was shaking his head. "You don't know," he said. "You don't know what it's like, to be in his presence. You've felt the thorn, but you haven't felt when it's his hand truly wielding it."

"We can reverse it," Magnus said. "We'll go to the Spiral Laby-rinth. We'll get Catarina, and Tessa . . ." He trailed off. Ragnor was smiling a toothy smile that was completely un-Ragnor-like.

"Magnus," he said. "It's too late for me." He put his hand on Magnus's chest, over the X-shaped wound. "It's too late for both of us. You just haven't accepted it yet." He looked up at the Portal in the sky, roiling with demons and a storm, lightning pulsing in the unnatural color of arterial blood. "You can close the Portal from the other side," he said. "From Diyu. But not from here."

He was there one moment and gone the next, ascending into the sky so fast Magnus barely saw him go. Magnus had a lot more he wanted to say, but with Ragnor gone, he could turn his attention back to the Shadowhunters. They were fighting on but beginning to wear down. All five of them had gathered together in the cen-ter of the square, back-to-back, and as fast as they struck down demons, more came to take their place.

Magnus ran toward them—his friends, and the love of his life. He felt the unfamiliar weight of White Impermanence on his back; how did the Shadowhunters carry these heavy hunks of metal around with them all the time? Alec was swinging Black Impermanence before him, knocking Baigujing demons away. Magnus hadn't even seen them enter the fray. Alec called Magnus's name and held up the sword before him.

Magic thrashed in Magnus's chest like a wild animal in a cage. He prepared to feel it thrum along the chains in his arms, as it had been doing, when he had an idea. He concentrated, felt the weight of White Impermanence on his back, and allowed his power to flow from his heart to his spine, to the back of his neck, and into the blade of the sword.

With a crack like thunder, crimson lightning burst from the end of the blade. It sought its twin and passed into the blade of Black Impermanence as Alec held it. Tendrils of magic flared from the lightning, and demons scattered. The dusk was lit up with a hellish red light—but it was a light that could save them.

The demons nearest to the lightning strike simply vaporized. Others nearby burst into flame and fled, screaming. The lightning stopped and for a moment, all was clear and still. In the distance above him, Magnus could see streaks of light: Ragnor and Shinyun descending as fast as their magic would allow.

Magnus closed the distance to the other Shadowhunters, who had grouped together loosely, their weapons out. "Listen to me!" he called. "I need to close the Portal from the other side. From Diyu. It's the only way."

Alec whirled to stare at him. "I'm coming with you. Obviously."

"No," said Magnus, though he saw the look in Alec's eyes, fierce and resolute. "But Max—"

"Magnus," said Alec savagely. "This is *my job*. This is *our job*. We go. We save all these people. *We* close the Portal."

"We're all coming," said Jace. His face was smudged with dirt and blood, his pale gold eyes alight. "Obviously. And then we're all coming back."

"Might as well," said Simon. "What's one more hell dimension?"

"We can't all go," protested Clary. "We can't just leave the Market under attack by all these demons."

Magnus pointed. "Luckily for us, the cavalry is finally arriving."

They looked. At the edges of the square, through the gloomy blue light of dusk, they could see seraph blades lighting up, one after another. Ragnor and Shinyun both stopped descending, still well above the ground, and cautiously moved to face the newcomers.

"Someone found the Conclave," exhaled Isabelle. "Thank the Angel."

"Maybe Tian went to get them," said Jace. "Is he there?"

"We could stay and fight with them until it's done," Simon suggested.

Magnus shook his head and was surprised to see Alec doing the same. Alec said, "We need to get the Portal closed or it won't ever be done." *And we don't want to answer questions about me, or Ragnor,* Magnus thought, and exchanged a glance with Alec, who nodded.

"But how do we get up there?" Isabelle said, turning her face up to the massive tear in the sky.

"I don't know if you've heard," said Magnus, "but my magic power has been highly intensified." He stepped back and looked at them. "Okay," he said. "Everyone bunch up together. Like we're taking a picture."

The Shadowhunters seemed puzzled, but they did as they were asked, shuffling toward one another until they were all pressed together closely. They were all standing on the same stone slab now. Behind them, the figures of Shadowhunters were beginning to engage with the demonic horde. Magnus looked to see if Tian was among them, but he couldn't tell.

Returning to the task at hand, he extended his hands and, with an effort, wrenched the slab out of the ground. It made a terrible grinding noise, but once it was free, it rose cleanly into the air, levitating the Shadowhunters a foot or so off the ground. Bits of gravel and concrete fell in chips, but the slab stayed in one piece. "Okay," Magnus said. "I'm right behind you. Try to hold on."

He couldn't watch. He closed his eyes and crouched down, letting the weight of the slab and its five occupants settle onto the bedrock of his magic.

"Lift with your knees!" suggested Clary.

"Please tell me when this is over," said Simon.

Magnus felt his magic crackle within him. There was so much. It felt—great. Scary, but great.

A whirlwind blew up around him and the Shadowhunters. It quickly gained speed and strength, widening. Magnus waited for it to become powerful enough . . . and quickly found it spinning out of his control.

He saw his friends start to look alarmed as the whirlwind became faster and stronger than he'd intended. Soon it was more like a small tornado than the controlled gust he was aiming for. Lightning shimmered within its eddies, angry and red. Alec yelled Magnus's name, but Magnus couldn't hear him over the noise.

It was now or never. Magnus gave himself over to his power and, with a great whoop, flung the Shadowhunters and the slab into the air. He went with it, pulled into the cyclone as it roared upward toward the Portal.

The concrete slab spun and tilted, and Magnus saw his friends go flying off it. Clary managed to grab Simon's arm, and the two spun together, connected but out of control.

The five of them vanished through the Portal, followed by the slab, which rained broken-off hunks of gravel in Magnus's direction as he rose into the sky behind it.

His momentum would pull him through the Portal no matter what, and he was determined to make the best of the situation. He wrenched his body around in midair and reached out with his hands for Ragnor in one direction and Shinyun in another. The wind caught them, and they too flew toward the Portal, no more in control than Magnus himself.

Tumbling through the air, all three warlocks followed the rocks and the Nephilim through the rupture between the worlds. It glowed like the light coming from Magnus's chest.

Then a darkness covered them, stronger than any light. There were clouds of smoke, and a cold wind, and then there was nothing at all.

PART III
Diyu

† † †

CHAPTER ELEVEN

The First Court

HUNDREDS OF YEARS AGO, MAGNUS HAD LAIN SLEEPLESS
in the City of Bones, among the Silent Brothers. Then as now,
peace had seemed an impossibility.

Magnus's mother had killed herself because of what he was.
His stepfather had tried to kill him for it. Magnus had murdered
his stepfather instead. He didn't recall the time after that very
well. He'd been out of his mind, his powers out of control, a
lost child carrying a storm of magic and rage in his breast. He
remembered almost dying of thirst in a desert. He remembered
an earthquake; falling rubble; screaming. When the Silent Brothers came, he'd stumbled through a rain of rocks toward their
hooded figures, not knowing whether they would teach him or
kill him.

They took him away, but even in their city of peace and silence,
he dreamed of his stepfather burning. He desperately wanted help,
but he had no idea how to ask for it.

The Silent Brothers approached the warlock Ragnor Fell for aid
with this wayward warlock child.

The memory of their first meeting was still crystal clear. Magnus had been lying on his bed in the bare stone room the Silent Brothers had given him. They had done what they could, finding a soft, colorful blanket and a few toys for him to make the space more like a child's bedroom, and less like a prison cell. It was still fairly uncomfortable, not least because the Silent Brothers themselves were so intimidating. Their kindness to him was at sharp odds with their terrifying eyeless faces, and he'd been trying to stop flinching when they entered the room.

He was finally getting used to the monsters caring for him, and then a new monster walked in. The door scraped open, steel on stone.

"Come now, boy," said a voice from the door of his cell. "There's no need to cry."

A demon, the boy thought frantically, a demon like his parents said he was: skin green as the moss on graves, hair white as bone. His fingers each had an extra joint, and curled grotesquely into claws. Magnus scrambled to sit up and defend himself, an awkward preteen in the middle of an alarming growth spurt, limbs flailing and dangerous magic pouring out of him.

Only Ragnor lifted one of his strange hands, and Magnus's magic turned to blue smoke, a blaze of harmless color in the dark.

Ragnor rolled his eyes. "It's very impolite to stare at people."

Magnus hadn't expected this alien being to speak his language, but Ragnor's Malay was smooth and effortless, if accented. "My first impressions are that you have no social grace, and that you are in desperate need of a bath." He gave a heavy sigh. "I can't believe I agreed to this. My first lesson to you, boy, is to never play cards against a Silent Brother."

"What—what are you?" said Magnus.

"*I* am Ragnor Fell. What are you?"

Magnus could barely find his voice. "He said—she called me—they said I was cursed."

Ragnor came closer. "And do you always let other people tell you what you are?"

Magnus was silent.

"Because they will always try," said Ragnor. "You have magic, just like I do."

Magnus nodded.

"Well, then," said Ragnor, "here are the most important things I can tell you. People will want to control you because of your power. They will try to convince you they are doing it for your own good. You must be very careful of them." When Magnus flicked his eyes past Ragnor to the corridor outside his room, Ragnor said, "Yes. Even the Silent Brothers are helping you partly for their own purposes. The Shadowhunters have need of friendly warlocks, even if they might wish they didn't."

"Is it wrong?" said Magnus quietly. "That they are helping me?"

Ragnor hesitated. "No," he said finally. "You are not their responsibility, and they have no guarantees about how you will turn out. You are lucky enough to have been born in a time when Shadowhunters like warlocks, rather than in one of the times in history when they've hunted us for sport."

"So it's dangerous having magic," Magnus said.

Ragnor chuckled. "Life is tremendously dangerous whether you have magic or not," he said, "but yes, especially for people like us. Warlocks don't age like other humans, but we often die young anyway. Abandoned by our human parents. Burned at stakes by mundanes. Executed by Shadowhunters. This is not a safe world, but then, I know of no safe worlds. You have to be strong to survive in all of them."

The child who would be Magnus stammered, "How did you—how did you survive?"

Ragnor came over and sat down on the cold earth floor beside Magnus, their backs against a wall of yellowed skulls. Ragnor's back was broad, and Magnus's narrow, but Magnus tried to sit up as straight as Ragnor did.

"I was lucky," Ragnor said. "That's how most warlocks survive. We're the lucky ones—the ones who were loved. My family were mundanes with the Sight, who knew a little of our world. They thought a green child might be a faerie changeling, and we didn't find out differently until later. Even when they did, they loved me still."

The Silent Brothers had spoken to Magnus in his mind, had taught him a little of where warlocks came from, how demons broke through into the world, forcing or tricking humans into bearing their children.

"And what about your father?"

"My father?" Ragnor echoed. "You mean the demon? I don't call that a father. My father raised me. The other, the demon, has nothing to do with me.

"I know you weren't one of the lucky ones," Ragnor went on. "But we are warlocks. We live forever, and that means sooner or later, we are alone. When others call us the spawn of demons, try to use our power for their own ends, envy us, fear us, or simply die and leave us, we must decide ourselves what we shall be. Warlocks name ourselves, before someone else can name us."

"I'll choose a name," said the boy.

"Then no doubt we will get to know each other better." He looked Magnus up and down. "Your second lesson: the Silent Brothers don't need to wash themselves or their clothes, but you do. You very much do."

The boy laughed.

"Let's keep ourselves sparkling clean from now on, shall we?" Ragnor suggested. "And for God's sake, get some nice clothes."

Later, Ragnor would say he wished he'd never come to the City of Bones that day, and he'd never intended for Magnus to go so far overboard with the clothes. And of course he'd never foreseen the invention of cosmetic glitter.

Magnus had hoped to find peace in the Silent City, but now he understood that such peace was impossible. He could only ask his questions. He hoped Ragnor would give him some of the answers, and then Magnus would give himself a name.

"MAGNUS!"

Alec heard his own voice, echoing out into the desolate space that extended around and above him.

Hell was empty.

Alec lay on his back, out of breath but at least conscious. He'd blacked out as he tumbled through the Portal, he had no idea for how long. He lifted himself up on his elbows, expecting it to hurt, but he seemed uninjured.

There was nothing here. The sky was absent of stars or moons or clouds—no, there was no sky whatsoever. There was no depth or distance, no shades or colors, just a sea of uniform claustrophobic void from horizon to horizon.

Blinking, he sat up and looked around. He was on a vast, blank expanse of gray stone, flat but uneven, with large fissures here and there. The landscape was featureless, rolling away to empty horizons in all directions. The other Shadowhunters were scattered around him, no one farther than maybe fifty feet away. Jace was already standing—of course—and had somehow, miraculously, managed to retain a grip on the spear he'd taken from the smithy. The others were in various stages of rising to their feet. Nobody seemed to be hurt.

Magnus was standing a short distance away from all of them, looking up. Alec followed his gaze and saw a knot of magic in the sky, tangled and chaotic, like a wound sewn up in haste on the battlefield. It crackled blackly, but no demons were emerging from it.

Alec rose and went over to join his boyfriend. He put his hand on Magnus's shoulder. Magnus said, still looking at the messy suture in the sky, "It's not pretty. But I think it'll hold."

Alec pulled Magnus into a tight embrace and held him for a moment, feeling the warmth of his body and the soothing sound of his breathing against him. Then he stepped back. "Shinyun?" he said. "Ragnor?"

"They were right behind me," Magnus said. There was fatigue in his voice, and Alec wondered how much his whirlwind had taken out of him. "I would swear on my life they came through the Portal right behind me. But they didn't appear on this side."

"Well, Sammael is the Master of Portals and the master of Ragnor and Shinyun," Alec offered. "So maybe they went somewhere else."

"Who knows," said Magnus flatly. Despite their success, he sounded defeated.

Isabelle's voice, behind them, suddenly called out, "Simon?"

Alec turned. Isabelle, Clary, and Jace were coming over to join them—all of them looking like they'd been through a windstorm—but there was no sign of Simon.

Clary spun around. "Simon? *Simon?*"

They all looked around them, but it wasn't like there was a hiding place on the bare rock that surrounded them. Simon was gone.

They all looked at Clary. She was holding her arms around herself, her face very pale. Jace put his hand on her back.

"Look for him," he said gently. "Inside yourself."

As Clary closed her eyes, Alec remembered a time, long ago, when Sebastian had taken Jace, and he had searched in vain inside himself for the spark that was his *parabatai*. Watching Clary now, he remembered the pain.

She inhaled sharply. "Okay . . . he's alive, at least."

"You think he went wherever Ragnor and Shinyun went?" Alec said to Magnus.

He expected Magnus to say *who knows* again, but the warlock's expression had sharpened, and he looked a little more present again. "It's possible," he said.

"He *definitely* came through the Portal," said Jace. "I saw him."

Isabelle looked stricken. "He didn't want to come," she said. "To Shanghai, I mean. He thought something terrible would happen. I told him he was being ridiculous." She pushed her tangled dark hair away from her face, her lips trembling.

"Iz," said Alec. "We'll find him."

"We'll have to figure out how to get back home ourselves," said Jace. "And we have no idea how to do that, either."

"*And* we can't leave without the Book of the White," put in Alec. "*And* we have to save *you*," he added to Magnus.

"And we have to rescue Ragnor," Magnus said.

They all looked at him. "Magnus," Clary said gently, "we need to be rescued *from* Ragnor."

"He's not himself," said Magnus. "He's under Sammael's control. I'm not leaving him like that. If there's a way to save me, there's a way to save him."

After a moment, Jace nodded. "Right," he said. "So we need to find the Book of the White, find Ragnor, defeat Ragnor, save Ragnor, find Simon, save Simon, figure out what Sammael's up to, neutralize Shinyun, and destroy the permanent Portal between Diyu and Shanghai."

"I thought we just did that last one," said Isabelle, looking up at the scar in the sky. "Besides—it looks like Ragnor and Shinyun have figured out how to open a big hole between Diyu and our world any time they want."

"Which begs the question," said Jace, "if they can do that, why doesn't Sammael just come through with them?"

Magnus templed his fingers together. "If Sammael *could* come into our world, he would," he said. "So there's some reason he can't pass from Diyu to Earth yet. Probably something to do with the way he was banished. But I don't know what it is."

Jace looked around them, hands on his hips. "Maybe there's an information booth somewhere. You know, like, 'Welcome to Hell'?"

Magnus regarded him darkly.

"Well, we can't just stay here on this rock," said Alec. "Isn't Diyu supposed to be a whole bureaucracy with judges and courts and torture chambers? That can't all be gone, can it?"

"Hang on," said Magnus, and launched himself into the air. Alec watched him, disconcerted. Magnus couldn't *fly*, not normally, but now he was doing it without visible effort. The Svefnthorn in action, he supposed.

In the silence, they watched Magnus swoop around above the stony expanse. Clary put her hand on Isabelle's shoulder, and Isabelle gave her a worried look. "We'll find Simon," Clary said. "He has no part in any of this stuff. There's no reason for him to be in danger."

"Sure," said Isabelle faintly. "He's only *lost* in *Hell*."

Nobody had anything to say to that, and they stood in silence for another minute, until Magnus landed again, his coat billowing out around him elegantly as he descended. Even in a demonic underworld, Alec thought, Magnus had panache.

"This way," he said, and led them off in what seemed to Alec an arbitrary direction. They all followed, bemused.

After a few minutes of walking, during which the landscape didn't change or even suggest that they were going anywhere, Magnus stopped and gestured to the ground. "Voilà," he said.

Below them, invisible from any distance beyond a few feet, there was a large rough opening in the ground. Stone stairs descended from it in a spiral.

"Where do they go?" said Clary.

Magnus gave her a look. "They go down," he said, and started to descend the steps.

Clary gave him a look. "The only person who might have appreciated *that* reference," she said, "is the one we're trying to rescue."

Magnus said easily, "Your comment suggests that you, too, appreciated it in your way."

"At least we'll die sassy," muttered Isabelle as she followed them. Alec followed too, his mind uneasy.

THE STAIRCASE WAS HUNDREDS OF STEPS LONG, TURNING back and forth in a zigzag that kept them going more or less vertically straight down. There was no railing, of course, but Magnus had no idea what would happen if someone fell. He could catch them with his magic, he reasoned, but he hoped it didn't come to that.

For a while, the stairs vanished into haze and smoke below them, with no end. But gradually a huge square shape came into focus below, and as they approached, Magnus realized he was looking down on a walled city.

From above, it could have been a city on Earth, albeit a city on Earth in ancient times. There was an outer wall in stone, marked at regular intervals by towers that, Magnus was sure, were the tops of gates in and out, although outside the walls was the same dark void that surrounded everything else. Inside was a series of courtyards separated from each other by red-roofed buildings that resembled courthouses or palaces.

As they got closer, it became clear to Magnus that he was looking at an abandoned place. All was silent. Nothing moved. When the angle allowed them to get a better look at the towers, Magnus could see that most of them were broken, and here and there on the ground far below, huge boulders of fallen rock blocked the streets.

It seemed at first as if they would descend right into the heart of the ruined city, but this was an optical illusion; when they reached the ground level, they could see that the staircase let them off outside the walls.

The five of them stepped off the final steps into a stone-paved courtyard, just as silent as the plain they'd left above. On three sides the courtyard seemed to end and fall off into nothing, but on the fourth side, two massive *que* towers stood. Their architecture was traditionally Chinese—"traditional" meaning a couple thousand years ago—elaborately carved and topped by flat roof tiles like broad-brimmed hats. As they neared the towers they could see that both were assembled from hundreds, even thousands of bones, from animals and humans alike. One tower shone bleached white, and the other gleamed in ebonized black. Between them, a path curved back and forth like a serpent, leading to an opening in the city walls through which all was dark.

Their steps echoed emptily. The silence was oppressive, the air completely still. They all walked down the winding path; there seemed to be no other way to go. Alec had drawn Black Impermanence and was carefully holding it in front of him, but nothing happened as they passed between the *que* towers.

Magnus wasn't sure what he'd expected when they entered the city walls. The path dead-ended at another large rectangular courtyard, paved in stone. At the far end of the courtyard rose a white, half-timbered building with a hipped red roof, whose doors had been thrown wide. Red paper lanterns, unlit, dangled from the eaves. There was no way around the building; they would have to pass into it, and hopefully through it, before they could continue on.

Once inside, Magnus was reminded oddly of a hotel lobby. Tall stone pillars held up a ceiling so high that it vanished into haze, in a large open space that appeared designed to hold many people at once.

On both sides of the room, tapestries had been hung between a series of tall bronze poles. It looked to Magnus like they had once illustrated some tale, or maybe provided a suggestion of the punishments offered deeper into the realm, but now, other than the occasional face that could be made out, they were indecipherable, covered with dried bloodstains, frayed and torn at the bottom, and faded with age. At the far end of the room was a large but plain wooden desk, with a neat stack of dusty, rotted books and a pile of parchments flaked away to almost nothing. Behind the desk, a tiled wall depicted a surprisingly ordinary pattern of chrysanthemums.

There was no movement, no activity, no wind. Magnus's breathing rang loudly in his own ears; his and his companions' footfalls sounded like knocks upon a massive stone door.

Magnus walked toward the desk, uncertain, and as he did, he saw motion—a thick, stubby tentacle, green-black, appeared from below and flopped onto the desktop.

The Shadowhunters froze. Magnus heard a whisper and the corner of his eye caught the glow of a seraph blade being kindled.

A second tentacle joined the first, then a third. They shifted around on the desktop, leaving bits of slime. Then, acting in concert, they pressed down against the desk and levered into view a slimy head and torso, which rose until the creature was standing up. The tentacles slurped back off the desk and slapped on the stone floor wetly.

The demon had close-set green eyes and a vertical slit instead of a nose or mouth. It opened this slit and made a loud, gurgling noise, thick with slime, which might have been a roar or a yawn.

"Is that a Cecaelia demon?" Jace said, incredulous.

"Mortals!" intoned the demon, in a voice like a drowning man. "Welcome to Youdu, capital city of the hundred thousand hells! Here in the First Court the sins of your life will be tallied, and your punish—" He stopped and squinted at them. "Wait, I know you. Magnus Bane! *What* are you doing in Diyu, of all places?"

Alec said, "What?!" in a very loud voice.

"How do you know me, demon?" demanded Magnus, but a memory was already creeping into his mind, from a few years back. Early in his and Alec's relationship . . . a client who wanted something to do with mermaids . . .

The demon was looking over at Alec. "Hey, is that Alec? So you two crazy kids made it work! Congratulations, guys, really."

"Elyaas," said Magnus weakly. "You're Elyaas, aren't you?"

"Magnus," said Alec, using his most reasonable voice. "How are you and this demon acquainted?"

"You know—Elyaas!" Elyaas said enthusiastically, waving some tentacles around and dripping slime on the desk. "Magnus must have told you about me. We were roommates!"

"We weren't *roommates*," Magnus said sharply. "I summoned you to my apartment. Once."

"But I was there all day! What did you end up getting Alec for his birthday?" Elyaas seemed legitimately pleased to see them.

Magnus turned to Alec with a sigh. "I summoned Elyaas as part of a job, a few years ago. Just standard business stuff, nothing exciting."

"He was trying to figure out what to get you for your birthday," Elyaas said in what was probably intended to be a sweet tone, but just sounded like a man choking to death on a whole octopus. "I always knew you two would stay together."

"No," said Magnus, "you told me he would always hate me in his heart, and that eventually my father would come for me."

There was a pause. Elyaas said, "So I guess that didn't happen."

"Well, my father did come for me," admitted Magnus, "but it didn't go well for him."

"Is this the demon that was dripping slime all over your apartment that day?" Isabelle said.

"Yes!" said Magnus, pleased that someone else could corroborate his version of events.

"Wait, *you've* met this demon?" Alec was giving Isabelle a look of betrayal.

"We're all great friends," enthused Elyaas.

"We are *not*," said Magnus firmly. "What are you doing here?"

"Working the front desk," said Elyaas with a flutter of tentacles that might have been a shrug. "This is the Office of Welcome, where the magistrate—that's me—evaluates your sins and sends you to your appropriate eternal torment. So are you guys married?" he added eagerly. "Got any kids?"

"We have a kid now," admitted Alec, against his better judgment.

"That's *wonderful*," said Elyaas. "I do love children."

"I assume you mean to eat," said Jace.

Elyaas looked disappointed. "You stepped on my line."

"Look, Elyaas, it's good to see you again," Magnus said, lying. "But we're trying to find some friends of ours and we really have to go. So whatever the procedure is for getting through here and into Diyu proper, we're ready to get started."

"Well . . ." Elyaas hemmed and hawed. "Nobody's been through recently, so your friends didn't come this way. In fact, nobody's been through at all, ever, since I started working here." He scratched his head with a tentacle. "I'm not actually sure of the procedure."

"Can we just kill him and move on?" Jace called out.

"That's very rude," Elyaas said. "Just because you're Shadowhunters doesn't mean you're supposed to kill every demon you see."

"It does, actually," Clary said, grimacing.

"This puts our relationship in a very different light," Elyaas told Magnus in tones of disapproval. "I thought we had an understanding. I've never been summoned by the same warlock twice before."

"Twice?" said Alec.

"The first time was way back," Magnus said. "Like, nineteenth century. Elyaas, I promise I'll summon you for a chat later. But we really do need to move."

"Okay, okay. Um." Elyaas picked up one of the rotting books from the desk and opened it with a tentacle. The front cover fell off and onto the floor, and his tentacle came away with pages stuck to it. "Just give me a moment. Why, why did I never learn to read Chinese?"

"Maybe," said Alec, "you could just tell us where to go, and we'll go there, and we'll tell everyone you totally went through the whole thing with the books and the judgment."

"And we won't kill you," added Jace. "This time."

Elyaas considered this. "Okay. But you owe me one."

"No," said Magnus.

"Okay," said Elyaas. "*I* owe *you* one."

"Also no."

"Just go through the door," Elyaas said, waving his tentacles at a tall door that had appeared in the far wall. "It leads to the Second Court, and so on to the others. Your friends must be in one of them. If not, you'll eventually get to the center of Diyu and find Sammael, and maybe he'll help you."

"Not all demons are as helpful as you, Elyaas," Magnus said wearily. "We'll be going." He headed toward the door next to the desk, deeper into Diyu, and the Shadowhunters followed. Behind the door were more stone steps, and Magnus started down them.

"Thanks for coming by," Elyaas said cheerfully. As Alec passed him, he added, "So you're the famous Alec. Hmm."

"What?" Alec snapped.

"Nothing," said Elyaas. "I just thought you'd be better-looking, that's all."

Alec blinked at him. Behind him, Jace stifled a laugh.

"When I heard how he talked about you, I thought, this guy has to have a *ton* of tentacles. Hundreds of tentacles! But look at you." He shook his head sadly. "None at all."

Alec walked on without further comment.

As they descended the stairs, they could hear Elyaas's wet voice fading in the distance:

"How would you rate your welcome experience today? Very satisfied, somewhat satisfied, a little satisfied, a little dissatisfied, somewhat . . ."

AT THE BOTTOM OF THE STAIRS WAS A STONE ARCHWAY leading into a second building much like the first. The archway was three times Alec's height, and its supports were leaning against one another alarmingly. Blocking the way were the remains of two collapsed stone pillars, elaborately carved but now piled in a jumble of hunks of rock, like a gigantic child had been playing with blocks and had failed to put them away.

Magnus seemed ready to magic the stones out of the way, but Alec stopped him. "Let's just climb over them," he suggested, and Magnus agreed, though he gave Alec a strange look. Jace had already begun scrambling over the rocks, and the others followed.

The Second Court was in much worse shape than the First. Or maybe it had been more cluttered to begin with. There was a lot more furniture, some carved of stone, some of wood, all shattered and broken—desks, chairs, tables. There were broken tablets and ledgers, rolls of yellowed parchment abandoned in the dirt. Alec picked his way carefully around the detritus and reached down to pick up a cracked slab of wood with the remains of red and gold paint on it. It might have depicted a face, once.

"It's a battlefield," Jace said, looking around with a practiced eye; Alec thought he was probably right. Here and there abandoned weapons lay—swords, spears, and broken bows—and at the back of the large open courtroom was another table like the one Elyaas had sat behind, but this one was cleaved neatly in two. Five open doors led in various directions out of the room, in addition to the one they'd come from.

The only fully intact object in the room was an oil painting of a young woman in white, hanging on a wall near the broken desk. It had been painted in watercolor, with delicate brushstrokes. The woman was beautiful, Alec thought, and her brightness seemed out of place in these darkened ruins. The painting was marred only by a tear in the canvas across the woman's cheek, a scar that would never fade.

Magnus came to stand next to Alec and look at the painting, and as he did, the woman's face turned within the painting to look at them. Her eyes were empty and white.

"Ack! Evil painting!" Clary jumped back.

The woman's head rolled eerily on her shoulders within the painting, and when she spoke, it was with a voice like the crackling of dry kindling.

"Welcome, lost souls," she said. Alec thought perhaps she would say something about how lonely she had been, but she said only, "Here is where your path will be chosen, and you will pass through the ghost gate to your suffering."

"Great news," muttered Jace.

"Take heart," the woman told him, with a smile that revealed long, needlelike teeth. "When your anguish equals the pain you caused in life, you will be released back into the cycle of living and death. I advise you to face your tribulations with courage. You cannot avoid them, so you may as well go to them with your face raised up."

None of them said anything, and she went on, "All I will require is the standard toll for passage."

"The standard toll?" said Alec.

"Yes," said the woman. "*Yuanbao* are traditional, but these days we also accept the new paper money."

Magnus groaned. "I assume," said Alec, "you don't have any cash on you."

"I have the change from when I bought some faerie tea cakes earlier," Clary said, fishing around in her jeans pocket. "Oh, never mind, it's turned into leaves."

"We don't have any money," Magnus told the painting, "but you see—"

"If you lack payment, you can traverse the Ice Caverns to the Bank of Sorrows," the woman began.

"We're not going to have any money in the bank of Hell," Magnus explained. "We're not dead, you see."

The woman looked taken aback. "If no one has sent offerings of money to you, you may be able to claim remaining funds that were sent to your ancestors—"

Magnus interrupted. "We're not dead! And also, I don't know if you've noticed, but this place is in ruins. Diyu has ceased normal operations. Can't you see this whole court has fallen down?" The woman didn't speak for a moment, and he went on, "When was the last time someone came through here?"

"Magnus—" Jace said. He was staring at one of the side doors, looking through it. "Someone's coming."

The woman spoke, slower than Alec would have liked. "It has been a long time," she said, "and the beadles have done a wretched job of keeping it clean."

"The beadles are gone," Magnus said. "Their master with them. Yanluo, your Lord, was defeated and driven from this place more than a hundred years ago."

"I don't get out much," the woman admitted. "Maybe you are right, but maybe you are a trickster who is trying to sneak through the ghost gate without paying."

"He is right," Alec said. "We just came from the First Court. It's in ruins as well."

"Guys . . . ," Jace said, more urgently. He caught up an abandoned dagger and handed it to Clary. Lifting his own spear, he held it in front of him. They all turned toward the source of the noise. Even Alec could hear it clearly now: footsteps, faint but getting louder, running toward them.

The woman in the painting hesitated. "I'm sorry," she said, "but I must demand payment. Even if there are temporary problems in the machinery of Diyu, they will no doubt be fixed soon. Souls cannot simply pile up forever with no place to go."

"I told you, we don't have any money," Alec began angrily, and then stopped, because through a doorway came the source of the footsteps.

It was Tian. He looked as if he'd been through a wrestling match with a bag of razor blades. His clothes were torn and bloody, his hair tangled, his skin covered in cuts and scratches. Over his shoulder was a torn, stained white cloth that had been gathered into a makeshift bundle.

The woman in the painting turned to look at Tian. "Do *you* have the money to pay the toll?"

"Of course he doesn't—" Magnus began.

"I do," Tian said.

"Tian!" Alec said. "Where have you been? How did you get here?"

"We lost you after we left the smiths," said Clary. "And then the demons attacked."

"Friends, I have been through an ordeal," Tian said wearily. Jace hadn't put his spear away and was watching him suspiciously.

Magnus, too, looked suspicious. "How did you disappear without any of us noticing you?"

"I was seized by demons," said Tian. "The vanguard of the warlocks' army. I stepped outside the smithy to make sure all was safe, and great bat-winged demons swooped down and carried me off.

They pushed me through a Portal almost immediately and I ended up here."

"Why didn't they wait for the rest of us?" Magnus said.

"I don't think they knew the rest of you were there," said Tian. "They must have seen me and just thought I was a random Shadow-hunter in their way." He looked around at them, breathing hard. "I'm very glad to see you all again, even if you are trapped here with me. What of the Portal?"

"It's closed," said Alec. "For now. But Simon disappeared too, and we need to find him before we can leave."

"And, ideally, stop Sammael from doing whatever he's doing," put in Clary.

"And a whole list of other things, actually," said Magnus.

Tian breathed a sigh of relief. "I think I can help." He dumped his bundle on the ground, which made a metallic clank. The fabric fell away to reveal a pile of gold and silver ingots, each about the size of a fist. They were in a variety of shapes—some square, some round, some in the shape of stylized flowers or boats.

"You've been to the Bank of Sorrows, I see," said Magnus, arching an eyebrow.

"I have," said Tian. "There were quite a lot of offerings to the members of the Ke family over the years that have gone unclaimed. The imps who brought them to me seemed happy to have some business." He gestured to the pile below him and addressed the woman in the painting, whose sharp teeth were bared in pleasure. "Honored Hua Zhong Xian," he said, "will these serve as payment for the six of us to pass?"

The woman examined the pile for a moment and then said, "They will."

"Great," said Alec with a sigh of relief. "Thanks, Tian."

"And now the Jiangshi will come to take you to your individual torments," the woman went on.

Through all six doors began to pour a crowd of humanoid creatures, green-skinned with long white hair, their arms extended before them. Their mouths opened to reveal rows of sharp yellow teeth, and they began to emit a low, plaintive wail.

"So, zombies," Clary said. "Now we have to deal with zombies."

"Jiangshi demons," corrected Tian. "But yes, they are very like zombies."

"Oh, come on!" shouted Magnus in exasperation, startling Alec. His eyes flashed in fury, and Alec, who had begun reaching back to draw Black Impermanence, stopped and stared as beams of mottled pinkish-red light, the color of watery blood, fired from each of Magnus's fingers. The beams pierced the Jiangshi, bursting them apart into ichor and ash. Magnus turned, an angry twist to his mouth, and fired beam after beam at the encroaching creatures. Within seconds, they were all destroyed, leaving only a burned smell in the air and the sound of Magnus's hard breathing.

"Well, *damn*," said Isabelle after a moment.

Magnus turned and caught Alec's eye. For a moment, there was no recognition in his expression. His upper lip was curled, revealing teeth that seemed strange, longer and sharper than usual, and then he seemed to come back to himself. When he saw Alec's expression, he hesitated. "I . . . I'm sorry. I got . . . impatient."

Jace said, "All right. Now that we've—" He was interrupted by a new round of the low, keening cries of Jiangshi. "Oh no."

More Jiangshi appeared in the doorways, moving inexorably and mindlessly toward them. Alec was about to speak, but Magnus's fingers lit up with that cruel red light again.

"Wait!" the woman in the painting cried out. Alec thought perhaps Magnus wouldn't hesitate, but he did, breathing hard but holding himself back as she went on: "They will keep coming," she said, "forever, until they are given a soul to take. At least one."

"Call them off!" shouted Alec.

The woman shook her head. "I cannot. I am a servant, no less than they are. We must serve our functions."

"I'll let them take me," said Tian.

"No," said Jace sharply. "You've studied Diyu, you know more about it than we do. We need you to have any chance of getting through this place. I'll go."

"You will *not*," said Clary.

"I'll go," said Isabelle loudly, in a commanding tone. Her voice rang through the room. Even the Jiangshi stopped moving for a moment.

"Isabelle, you can't —" Alec started.

"I'm *going*," Isabelle said. "I'm going, and I'm going to find Simon. I swear I will."

She turned and held her arms out to the Jiangshi. A sort of sigh swept through them, like an exhale of relief. They ceased pouring through the doorway.

"She has chosen," said the Hua Zhong Xian.

Jace whirled to face Alec. "They'll kill her—"

"No," said Magnus in a tense, low voice. "This is already a place of the dead. They assume *she's* dead. Whatever they do, it won't be killing her."

Tears ran down Clary's face. She didn't even try to wipe them away. "Isabelle, *no*."

"Let her go," said the painted woman. "Her choice is irrevocable. Should you try to take her back now, worse will come than the Jiangshi."

"*You* stay out of this," Alec snapped at her. He started toward Isabelle, but it was no use—in the blink of an eye, three of the demons had seized his sister. She put up no resistance. Her eyes were fixed on Alec as the Jiangshi marched her toward one of the doors they had come through. *Don't follow me,* her gaze said. *I love you, but don't follow me.*

"Isabelle," Alec said desperately, "don't do this. Please. We'll find Simon—"

Magnus caught hold of Alec's shoulder. Isabelle was almost at the door. Jace was gripping the spear in his hand so tightly his fingers had gone white. Clary appeared to be in shock.

"Remember, Lightwood girl," said the Hua Zhong Xian. "Go to your torment with your head held high."

Isabelle turned and regarded her. "I swear upon the power of the Angel," she said in a clear voice, "that I will return. I will return, and we will tear down this place. We will scatter the undead to the winds. And I will, personally, tear *you* into ribbons."

Then she was gone.

CHAPTER TWELVE

Ox-Head and Horse-Face

A LONG, TERRIBLE TIME PASSED AFTER ISABELLE DISAP-peared through the doorway. Magnus was vaguely aware that the Hua Zhong Xian had faded and vanished from the painting and left them in silence. Tian, looking lost and uncomfortable, stood with his hands folded. Clary was crying quietly against Jace's chest. He stroked her hair, his worried gaze seeking and finding Alec, who was pacing back and forth across the room, clenching and unclenching his fists.

Magnus wasn't sure if Alec wanted to be comforted or not, but he finally couldn't stand it: going to Alec, he pulled his boyfriend into his arms. For a split second, Alec hung on to Magnus tightly, his hands fisting in Magnus's coat, his forehead pressed to Magnus's shoulder.

Magnus murmured words he hadn't realized he even remem-bered: soft words in Malay, of comfort and reassurance.

Alec let himself shake in Magnus's arms for a only moment, though. He drew away, chin held high, and said, "All right. Now we have *two* people to rescue."

"Three," said Jace, "counting Ragnor."

"I hope you would have rescued me," Tian said mildly.

"We didn't know you were here," said Clary, "and anyway, you've rescued yourself." She smiled at him in a wobbly sort of way, stepping away from Jace. Her face showed the streaks of tears, but like Alec, she had mastered her emotions.

Shadowhunters were good at that.

"We need a plan," Jace said. "We can't just wander around Diyu and hope we find them."

Magnus cleared his throat. "I hate to bring this up, but we also can't just leave Diyu in the hands of Sammael."

"And Shinyun," growled Alec.

"And Shinyun," agreed Magnus.

"It just bothers me that we don't know what Sammael wants," said Clary in frustration.

"To come to Earth and wreak havoc there," offered Alec.

"Yes, but to what end? Why open a Portal to Earth? What's so great about Earth? If he only wanted to rule over Diyu, I think we would just let him."

"Well, the food's better on Earth," Jace said.

Tian was shaking his head. "Sammael does not need a reason. The chaos and destruction he wreaks is for its own sake; who knows why his eye turns in one direction or another?"

"Sammael was slain by the Archangel Michael to prevent him from unleashing Hell on Earth," said Magnus slowly. "He'll want to do what he was prevented from doing so long ago, because it's part of the war."

"The war between angels and demons," said Jace in a rare serious tone. "In which we are soldiers."

"Right," said Magnus. "One thing to remember about Princes of Hell, and archangels, too: they're always playing nine-dimensional chess with worlds as their toys. Just assume the worst."

"True enough," said Tian. "The attack in the Market was a distraction, designed to keep the Shanghai Shadow World focused in one place so Sammael could act elsewhere. But we don't know where."

"We don't know where in Shanghai," said Alec. "But maybe we could figure out where in Diyu. He would pick some central location for his work, right? Not just some random torture chamber. And Shinyun and Ragnor would likely be with him."

"You think we should confront them?" Jace asked. His eyes glittered. Only Jace would be looking forward to confronting two powerful warlocks and a Prince of Hell, thought Magnus.

"I think we'll have better luck figuring out what's going on closer to where they're all acting—Sammael, Shinyun, and Ragnor—than we will out here in a bunch of abandoned courts," said Alec.

"The geography of Diyu is complicated," Tian said after a moment's thought. "Though we are in an underworld, these courts we're passing through actually reside far above the center of Diyu. There, a kind of shadow of the city of Shanghai can be found."

"Like, it's upside down?" said Clary.

"In part," said Tian. "The usual rules of physical worlds don't apply here. What is a mountain in Shanghai might be a deep trench in Diyu, but other places may be reversed in other ways, in color or orientation or even purpose. I was thinking . . ."

"That when I Tracked Ragnor, it led us to a spot in Shanghai where Ragnor *wasn't*," said Alec. "But maybe he's in the mirror spot in Diyu? And maybe we can find that?"

"That's very clever," said Magnus. "My boyfriend is very clever," he added, to no one in particular.

"Except we don't really have a map that will show such correspondences," said Tian. "We probably are best off heading for the heart of Diyu." He grimaced. "As unpleasant as that will be."

"What does heading for the heart of Diyu involve?" said Jace.

"The Final Court, but that won't be a pleasant trip," Tian said. "It's at the center of Diyu's labyrinth—the former throne of Yan-luo. It's at the very deepest point of Diyu, the lowest part of Hell."

"Of course it is," said Clary, sighing.

"Well, perhaps not the deepest. Below the Final Court is Avici." Tian shuddered. "It is the one place in Diyu that terrifies me. Only the worst of sinners are brought there. Those who have committed one of the Great Offenses. Killing an angel, or a Buddha, or one's own parent. They are judged and sent to Avici."

It was probably Magnus's imagination, but it seemed like Tian was looking straight at him. Alec was *definitely* looking straight at him, worry on his face. He knew well that Magnus had struck down his own stepfather—in self-defense, certainly, as he had been trying to kill Magnus, but Magnus didn't know if Diyu cared about technicalities.

"How do we get there?" Magnus said. "The Final Court, I mean, not Avici."

"Diyu is a maze of tens of thousands of hells," said Tian. "If we try to find our way there through all those abandoned chambers, it could take the rest of our lives. But . . ." He trailed off, looking thoughtful.

"What?" said Alec.

"North of Shanghai," said Tian, "south of Beijing, in Shandong Province, is Tai Shan—Mount Tai," he clarified. "Thousands of years ago, it was a place of the dead. Now it's a tourist attraction, but here in Diyu is its darkened mirror, a deep pit receding into shadow. I saw it on my return from the Bank of Sorrows. A road led down to it. I don't know how far it would be, but perhaps deep enough to reach the shadow of Shanghai—"

"Well, it sounds better than wandering through a maze of torture chambers," said Clary.

"Exactly," said Tian with a smile.

They all looked at Magnus, who threw up his hands.

"I don't have any better ideas," he said. "I'm sorry you've all followed me into Hell again."

Clary snorted. "It's easier the second time."

"It's what we do," said Jace. He went to retrieve his spear from where he'd left it leaning against the wall. "Lead the way."

Alec didn't look happy, but he nodded. "Let's go."

"I suggest we put on some Marks," Tian said. "We will almost certainly be getting into some fights."

"Marks work in Diyu?" Alec said, surprised.

"They do," Tian confirmed, and Jace shrugged and took out his stele. Magnus had grown used to a lot of things about spending time with Shadowhunters, but the five solid minutes of drawing on one another that preceded every battle continued to be just a little bit funny to him every time.

"We leave by that side door," Tian added, gesturing, and to Magnus he said, "Your friends are very casual about going where almost no living person has ever been."

"Yeah," said Magnus, "they've been through some stuff."

THE PATH TOOK THEM OUT OF THE SECOND COURT AND into a walled passage. All of Magnus's instincts had told him they were deep underground by this point, but the passage was lined at regular intervals with tall windows that looked out on a vast wasteland far below. The windows had once been elaborate carvings, with faces leering above them, but much of this had eroded away and crumbled.

As Tian, Jace, and Clary went ahead, Magnus hung back to join Alec. "You don't like it," he said. "The plan, I mean. Too vague?"

"No. I mean, it's vague, but I agree we should get to where the action is. And where the Book of the White is. If we can get it away from Ragnor and the others, we can maybe wreck Sammael's plan."

"Or at least ruin his day. You think he's using the Book to figure out how to break through from Diyu to Earth?" said Magnus. It was the same thought he'd had.

Alec nodded.

"Are you angry with me?" said Magnus.

"What?" Alec said sharply.

Magnus stopped walking. "It's just—you're all here because of me. If I hadn't lost the Book of the White . . . if I hadn't been caught by surprise by Ragnor . . ."

Alec snorted. "If I hadn't been in the shower."

"It's not the same," Magnus said. "I shouldn't have kept the Book in Max's room. I should've been more careful about the wards on the apartment."

"Magnus," Alec said, and he put his hand on Magnus's cheek. He looked into Magnus's eyes, and feeling the strange power of the thorn bubbling within him, Magnus wondered what he saw there. "Given that one of the minions of the Father of Demons was holding our kid, and that kid ended up safe in bed at the end of it, from my perspective you handled things perfectly. I'm not angry at you." He sighed. "I'm kind of angry at Isabelle, so let's go rescue her before something terrible happens to her."

"No pressure," said Magnus.

"Yeah," said Alec. "That's why I'm kind of angry at her. Because I hate worrying about someone I love. But I'm not angry at you," he said again. "Clary's right and Jace is right. I'm your partner. They're your friends. We've followed you into Hell before, and we're doing it again, and we would do it a third time.

"Besides," he added with a smile, "a Prince of Hell trying to break through to our world is absolutely our jurisdiction."

He leaned forward and kissed Magnus, gently, slowly, the way he would on a Sunday morning in bed. It was totally at odds with their situation, totally at odds with how either of them felt in that moment. It was wonderful.

"Not the time!" Jace yelled from a little ways ahead of them.

"Always the time," Alec murmured against Magnus's mouth. He called back to Jace, "Just working to keep up morale!"

They hurried to catch up with the others. Magnus felt a little better about Alec, but the uncertainty of where they were going and what they would do there remained in the bottom of his gut like a jagged stone.

And then they saw the pit of Mount Tai.

As they came around a wide curve in the passage, the walls fell away and suddenly they were walking through a wasteland. From their passage, a wide, black ribbon of road jutted off to one side, winding through a blasted wilderness of rock and ruin. In the distance, it glittered darkly—an upside-down mountain, just as Tian had said. Stark, black even against the constant gray background of Diyu, a yawning chasm in the distance that seemed to split open the land.

Magnus could see why Tian had suggested it. No matter how mazelike Diyu's layout might be, this was hard to miss. And it definitely seemed to go a long way down.

Tian led them off the stone and onto the new path, which turned out to be of solid iron. The surface glittered like the scales of a snake, and lining each side of the roadway, twisting loops of wrought iron formed low barriers like thornbushes. Magnus leaned over to take a closer look and realized that these were iron weapons—swords, spears, pikes—melted and bent and re-formed. It must have been an intimidating sight in its heyday, but now, as the path arced back and forth in front of them, huge patches of rust marred the surface, and in many places, pieces of the barrier of weapons had broken off and lay by the side of the road.

They walked slowly and curiously. Magnus could see that once upon a time this had been a real road, signposted, its grounds tended, but now it was just ruination, blasted landscape on all sides. And then there were the demons.

None were nearby yet, but from here they could see a long stretch of the road ahead, and all over were clusters of demons, milling about: the Baigujing skeleton warriors, Ala, and Xiangliu they had fought in Shanghai, plus more of the Jiangshi. There were others whose names Magnus didn't know: huge leopards with horns and five tails, herds of faceless goats with eyes all over their bodies, many-headed bird creatures.

"So many," Clary said quietly.

Tian said, "They used to be responsible for torturing the souls who found their way here. But now there are no new souls coming, and most of them have nothing to do."

"Nothing to do except fight us," said Jace, twirling his spear in his hand. Alec drew his sword, and Clary her dagger. Tian fingered the silver cord of his rope dart, wrapped around his body like a ceremonial sash.

But as they made their way down the path, the demons ignored them. Many of them were a good distance away—the emptiness of the landscape made it difficult to judge how far, and clusters that seemed like they would plainly block the group's way turned out to be hundreds of yards into the wastes. Even when they passed close by, the demons showed little interest in them. In fact, the demons were more interested in attacking one another. Magnus and the others watched as two of the bird demons descended on a pack of Baigujing and tore them apart, flinging human bones away as they feasted. Ala smashed into one another in the sky, creating miniature bursts of thunder and lightning when they collided.

As the minutes passed, most of the Shadowhunters relaxed their grip on their weapons and walked more casually. Only Alec refused to drop his guard, circling the group restlessly, his sword out as if daring any of the demons to come and get them.

Magnus understood. It was its own strange kind of agony to have to walk down this long, long path, thinking of their friends in danger, of their enemies moving forward with their plans, while they could do nothing but traverse the space between. He felt Alec's nervous energy. Alec wanted to *run* down the path, charge ahead toward the inevitable fight, but the way was too far and they needed to preserve their strength.

They walked in near silence. At one point, Alec said to Tian, "Are you sure this is the best way to go?" Tian didn't answer, just walked on.

An hour passed. The iron road wound on.

Two hours.

Finally the smooth road ended, and a massive suspended bridge, of the same iron as the road, crossed a deep crevasse that blocked the way to the pit. On the far side of the bridge, two huge red *que* towers rose, forming a gate to an endless staircase that descended the mountain toward its reversed peak, disappearing into a haze beneath them.

"At least it'll be downhill," Magnus remarked.

Tian nodded. "I've made the walk up the real Mount Tai. It is more than six thousand steps to the top. Except at the top of Mount Tai is a beautiful complex of temples."

"Rather than the deepest pit in Hell," said Magnus.

Tian just looked grim.

Before they could reach the bridge, dark flashes began to burst on the road, like the afterimages from looking at the sun. When Magnus blinked to clear his vision, he saw that two demons had appeared in their path. They had the same greenish skin as the Jiangshi, but where the Jiangshi were gaunt and ragged, these two were massive, heavily built, and well-muscled. One had a human body, but the head of a horse; he carried a chain whip, its links each the size of a human fist. The other, also human in form, had the head of an ox and bore in front of it an enormous, double-bladed battle-ax. The ox let out a tremendous bellow, shattering the strange silence that they had become accustomed to.

The Shadowhunters drew their weapons.

ALEC REFLEXIVELY LOOKED OVER TO TIAN AND WAS shaken to see that a look of terror had passed over his face. "Niutou," he said, "and Mamian."

"Friends of yours?" asked Magnus.

"They are called Ox-Head and Horse-Face," Tian said. "They were the messengers of Yanluo, and guardians of Diyu. There are many stories of Shadowhunters fighting them, in the time when Yanluo still roamed the world."

"If they fought them, we can fight them," said Clary.

Tian shook his head. "They are much weaker in our world. The legends say that they cannot be defeated in their own realm."

"So we turn back?" said Clary.

"It's five against two," Jace said. "I like our odds."

Tian said, "If we want to go forward, we have no choice." He stepped away from the others, giving himself room, and with a few deft turns, unwound the rope dart from his body, grasping its diamond-shaped *adamas* head at the base. Magnus slowly and uncertainly drew White Impermanence from his back and held it before him. It was very strange to see Magnus wielding a sword, Alec thought. It seemed wrong, even perverse. But they were severely underequipped for this fight, and they needed every asset.

"Clary, you've only got a dagger," Jace said quietly, "so you can't get inside their reach. Alec and I will try to tie up the cow and you go behind. Tian, your job is to keep that chain whip off us. Magnus, any protection you can offer . . ."

It was too late for any further planning. With a roar, Ox-Head charged them.

Jace might have been right that it was five against two, but Alec was pretty sure the two were each bigger than all five of them put together. They had no choice but to try, of course—Alec let Jace go ahead to receive the charge with his spear, and he stood ready to slip underneath and strike when an opportunity arose. Out of the corner of his vision, he saw Tian leap at Horse-Face, the rope dart unfurling and bursting out toward his foe like a snake rearing to strike.

Ox-Head's ax struck against Jace's spear with enormous force, and Alec saw Jace shudder as he absorbed the impact. He ran in at an angle, striking at the arm holding the ax, and managed to bite into it with the sword before the momentum of Ox-Head's swing thrust the sword away. There was a cut across Ox-Head's arm, dripping ichor, but it was shallower than Alec might have thought. Still, it did the trick, as Clary executed a controlled roll behind Ox-Head's legs, and with both hands struck out and slashed across each of his Achilles tendons.

Disengaging from Jace, Ox-Head roared a harsh, inhuman cry and twisted around to seek out Clary, but he was slow enough that Jace had time to right himself and approach for another blow. Alec whirled around and saw that Tian had waylaid Horse-Face, leaping and tumbling around him, using the much faster rope dart to prevent his enemy from successfully employing the chain whip. The *adamas* diamond moved in wide, slicing arcs and returned, again and again, wrapping around Tian's body and then unwrapping just as quickly to strike. As he watched, the dart struck Horse-Face in the shoulder, and he jerked back with a raucous braying noise.

Meanwhile, Magnus was being kept busy with other demons. A flock of the many-headed birds had taken note of the fight and decided to join in, swooping down toward the combatants. With a grim set to his face, Magnus held out the sword like a magic wand; over and over, his eerie crimson magic crackled out from the tip of the sword to strike at the birds. They dodged and rolled, and occasionally took a hit, but Magnus was successfully keeping them at a distance, and that was good enough for now.

They were doing fairly well, Alec thought. Jace was using the spear to prevent Ox-Head from winding up for a real strike from his ax. Clary danced around to the side, looking for another opening. But then Ox-Head pulled back, and with a growl leaped backward, sailing through the air to land twenty feet away from the gathered Shadowhunters. He landed on one knee and, holding the ax in one hand, pressed his other fist against the ground. As Alec watched, the wound he'd struck on Ox-Head's arm fizzed and foamed, and in a few seconds, it was totally healed.

"Uh-oh," said Jace.

Alec glanced over and saw that Tian had discovered the same problem: Horse-Face's shoulder injury was also gone, having disappeared as though it had never been inflicted at all.

"Can't be defeated, huh?" he called out to Tian.

Tian looked grim. "Here, the ground itself heals them."

"What do we do about that?" shouted Jace.

"Magnus!" Alec yelled. "Can you get them off the ground?"

"I'll keep an eye on the others," put in Tian, and he spun gracefully, letting the dart extend in a blinding silver flash toward one of the bird demons trying to harry them.

Magnus held White Impermanence in both hands and, with a look of great concentration, flung a wide beam of scarlet light at Ox-Head. Rather than being lifted into the air, though, Ox-Head stood his ground, and the magic flowed into him. He absorbed it, leering, and seemed to grow even taller and stronger before their eyes.

"Um," said Magnus.

"We could use a little of that classic blue magic right about now," said Clary. Magnus looked at her helplessly.

"Any other bright ideas?" Jace called to Tian.

Tian shook his head, wild-eyed. "Stall," he suggested.

Ox-Head swung the ax over his head and brought it down toward Alec, who knocked it away with his sword. Clary flung her dagger, which embedded itself in Horse-Face's chest, but he just yanked it out and threw it back. Clary spun to catch it by the hilt, glaring.

"We are ill-prepared," Tian said.

"You think?" yelled Alec.

Light burst in the sky, above the fray. Alec ignored it, assuming it was just more demons arriving, but then he noticed that Magnus had lowered his sword and was looking up, an unreadable expression on his face.

He looked, and from the blinding light, now dissipating into afterimage, came a horned creature. This one was also green, but a deeper green than the Jiangshi or the guardians they'd been fighting. Huge ram's horns extended from its head, white as bone, and it wore a black cloak that billowed as it descended to the ground. Even Ox-Head and Horse-Face had stopped to watch it.

And then Alec realized. It was Ragnor Fell.

RAGNOR LANDED AMONG THEM. NOBODY SPOKE FOR A moment.

Ox-Head broke the silence, raising his ax tentatively and lowing. Without looking at him, Ragnor raised his hand and waved them upward, and both Ox-Head and Horse-Face were lifted twenty feet into the air, held in a reddish cloud. They flailed around within it but succeeded only in spinning slowly end over end in the air. Horse-Face began to bellow loudly, and Ragnor, with a flash of annoyance that reminded Magnus of the Ragnor he knew, twitched his hand again. The sound stopped abruptly.

Magnus cleared his throat. "So, I suppose this is what I have to look forward to, with the thorning? Bigger horns, mostly?"

Ragnor said, in a voice whose familiarity was unsettling, coming out of his much-altered face, "I'm only here to talk."

Nobody put their weapons away. "So talk," said Alec.

"Are you still Sammael's henchman?" said Jace. "Let's start with the basics."

"Look," said Ragnor. "Everything is already spinning out of control. None of you are supposed to be here. None of this was part of the plan."

"You always did like a plan," noted Magnus.

"So I'm going to help you get out of here," Ragnor went on.

Next to Magnus, Alec breathed a long sigh of relief. "Ragnor," he said, "that's great. With you on our side, we can—"

"Shinyun was never supposed to thorn Magnus," Ragnor went on, ignoring Alec. (This, too, struck Magnus as normal behavior for the Ragnor he knew.) "She never asked permission or even thought about what it would mean for the rest of the plans." He looked scornful. "Any idiot should have realized that with your . . . close ties to the Nephilim, involving you would add an infinity of complications." He looked around at the assembled Shadowhunters with an expression of distaste.

"Yes, Shinyun is clearly deranged," agreed Alec. "So—"

"I can't do anything about the thorning," Ragnor said to Magnus. "No one can. It's not reversible. But I can help you find your way out of here. You're far too much a threat to my master's plans, you see."

Magnus's heart sank. "Your master."

Ragnor looked surprised. "Yes. I believe the whole situation with the Svefnthorn was explained to you already, Magnus. You never pay attention to details. That's always been your besetting sin. My master," he went on, "does not need some hero Shadowhunters and a rogue warlock wandering through his realm, confusing the situation and messing things up. So if you'll allow me." He raised his hands and crimson magic, the twin of Magnus's, burst forth in his palms, which bore the same spiked-circle pattern that Magnus's did.

Magnus felt fairly sure it was a terrible idea to let Ragnor perform unspecified magic on them in his current state, even if he said he was going to help them. For all they knew, he would "help" them by killing them; that was usually the way this kind of thing went. But he didn't have a chance to decide what to do about it, because Ragnor suddenly stumbled forward, blasted in the back by a new jolt of scarlet lightning.

Alec looked over at Magnus, who quickly said, "That wasn't me."

"Ragnor!" They all looked up to see Shinyun, floating in the sky near where Ox-Head and Horse-Face still tumbled lazily in circles. Ox-Head looked like he had fallen asleep. "You will not betray our master."

Shinyun, like Ragnor, had changed in appearance significantly. Her arms and legs were longer, spindlier, giving her a spiderlike look. There was a white aura surrounding her, and though her face was as expressionless as ever, her eyes blazed and glowed with a purplish flame within. Her cloak was cut low over her chest, revealing clearly the X of the thorn's cuts below her throat.

Ragnor had recovered and stood to face Shinyun. "You're making things more complicated," he said, in a lecturing tone. "*Much* more complicated than they need to be. I'm going to take these . . . unexpected factors"—this while waving generally at Magnus and his friends—"and return them to Earth, and then we can get on with things the way we're supposed to."

"Hey," said Magnus, "I've always wanted to be an unexpected factor."

"You used to be an unexpected factor all the time," Clary said. "Used to?"

"Well," she said, "eventually we started expecting you."

Shinyun's eyes glittered dangerously. "You fool. You think they'll just leave us alone if you send them back? You think they'll just let us reopen the Market Portal, not try to come back here? The complication is already done. Now we must deal with it."

"Now *you* must deal with it," Ragnor said grumpily. "Dragging them into this was *your* idea. I'm here to clean up your mess."

Shinyun held her hands up and magic gathered there, the way it had for Ragnor a few minutes ago. She floated toward him. "You forget yourself," she said through gritted teeth. "I am Sammael's first and favorite follower. If not for me, you would never have known the glory of his presence. You would have been swallowed up with all the rest. Show some respect and some obedience."

"I'll show you respect," Ragnor muttered, and leaped at Shinyun, magic blazing out of his hands.

The two warlocks flew into the sky together and commenced brawling with each other. They were clearly both much more interested in besting the other than in dealing with the Shadowhunters.

"We could just leave," suggested Jace. "Start over the bridge . . ."

Magnus felt stuck to the spot, watching one of his oldest friends and one of his more recent enemies clash. They looked less like people and more like mythological creatures. Ragnor went to impale Shinyun with his horns, and Shinyun grabbed them with her spider-like limbs. They grappled and wrestled across the sky. Bolts of scarlet lightning flew. The two of them continued to yell at one another, but their words were indistinguishable under the sound of the fighting.

"Come on," Tian said. "We can make for the pit while they're distracted."

"If we're going to rescue Isabelle and Simon," Magnus said, "I have to try to rescue Ragnor, too."

"He can't be rescued," Tian said firmly. "He's taken the thorn three times. He's part of Sammael now."

Magnus looked at Alec helplessly. "I have to try."

Nobody knew what to do. Magnus stared at the melee above him. Tian's gaze was fixed on the mountain beyond the bridge, and Jace and Clary and Alec waited. Maybe someone would win the fight, Magnus thought, and break the stalemate.

"They're quite a sight, aren't they?" said an unfamiliar voice. Magnus looked over to see that they had been joined by a person they didn't know. He was young-looking, white and slight of build, narrow of face, and he was dressed as though he were a student backpacker who was unaccountably making his way through Diyu: ragged plaid shirt, torn jeans. His hands were shoved in his pockets, like he was watching a parade pass by. *A rare lost soul of Diyu?* Magnus thought.

The only truly strange thing about the man—other than his being present at all—was the old-fashioned Tyrolean hat he wore, in green felt. Sticking straight up out of the band of the hat was a large golden feather, easily a foot long. Magnus was not sure he was pulling it off, but he appreciated the ambition.

"There's really quite enough violence around here," the man went on in a mild-mannered tone, "without those two scuffling like unruly children. Don't you think?"

"I'm sorry," said Magnus, "but who are you? Have we met?"

"Oh!" said the man, in apologetic tones. "How dreadfully gauche of me. I know you, of course. Magnus Bane, High Warlock of Brooklyn! Your reputation precedes you even here. And Shadowhunters! I *love* Shadowhunters."

He extended his hand. "Sammael," he said with a gentle smile. "Maker of the Way. Once and Future Devourer of Worlds."

CHAPTER THIRTEEN

The Serpent of the Garden

EVERYONE STARED. SAMMAEL, MAKER OF THE WAY, ONCE and Future Devourer of Worlds, smiled at them blandly.

"Once and Future . . . ," said Alec.

"Devourer of Worlds," Sammael repeated. "Meaning I devoured worlds in the past, and I plan to devour *more* worlds at some point in the future. The sooner the better."

He was interrupted by yet another crackle of lightning in the sky and looked up at Ragnor and Shinyun, neither of whom seemed to have noticed that he was there. He gave them a fatherly look, sympathetic but frustrated.

"Ragnor," he said. "Shinyun." He spoke in the same casual, quiet tone, but both of the warlocks instantly stopped and jerked their heads around at the sound of his voice.

"My master," called Shinyun.

"Go to your rooms," Sammael said mildly. He snapped his fingers, and with a loud *crack* Ragnor and Shinyun both disappeared from the sky.

"As I was saying," Sammael said into the ensuing silence, "it's been a long time since I devoured a world. I might even be a little rusty," he added with a chuckle. "But your friend Ragnor was good enough to find me *this* place!" He gestured around him. "Kind of a fixer-upper, of course. But so much potential! A massive engine of demonic power, run on the fuel of human suffering. It's just so . . . classic!"

He smiled broadly at them, then turned his attention to Magnus specifically.

"Magnus Bane," he said. "Not just High Warlock but an eldest curse! You know how many of those there are?"

When no one answered, he frowned. "That was not a trick question. The answer is, there can never be more than nine in the whole world: the eldest child of each of us Princes of Hell."

"Who's your eldest child?" Alec said.

Sammael looked surprised. "Well, that's nice," he said. "People so rarely take any interest in me. I don't have one," he confided. "I've been gone for so long that the last of my children on Earth disappeared centuries ago. That's something I'll have to work on, when I get back there." He examined Magnus. "Have you given any thought to the thorn? I'd be happy to give you the third strike myself, if I can wrestle the thing out of Shinyun's hands. She's very possessive of it, you know."

Magnus realized that, without thinking of it, he had brought his hand to the wound on his chest. The chains on his arms throbbed painfully. "I'm not interested in joining your little club, if that's what you mean."

"It is," said Sammael, but he didn't sound particularly upset. "And since the alternative is death, my little club will win no matter what. But I have to say, you'd make an excellent addition to the organization. We don't have an eldest curse yet."

He leaned forward and spoke in a confidential tone. "What I'd suggest is, when you're powerful enough, you just kill Shinyun and take *her* job. You'd get to work with your buddy Ragnor!"

Clary said, "Magnus is already on a team."

"Our team," clarified Jace.

"Yes, I gathered that. My goodness," Sammael said, taking them in, "*Shadowhunters.* This is very, very exciting."

"Because you hate Shadowhunters and want to torture us, I assume," said Jace.

Sammael laughed. Magnus would have expected his laugh to be frightening, or at least intimidating, but he seemed legitimately amused, even friendly. "Are you kidding? I *love* Shadowhunters. I *made* you."

"What?" said Alec. "Shadowhunters are made by Raziel."

"Or by other Shadowhunters," put in Jace.

"Are you kidding?" Sammael said, entertained. "Raziel would never have bothered if I hadn't let all those demons into your world in the first place! *You* exist because of *me!*"

Clary and Jace exchanged confused looks. "But we were created to defeat your demons," Jace said. "Doesn't that mean we're, you know . . . enemies?"

"We are definitely enemies," confirmed Magnus.

"I mean, you're holding two of us in your torture chambers right now," put in Alec, through clenched teeth.

For the first time, Sammael's smile faded, though his friendly tone didn't change. "Well, in a very small number of cases, there might be something personal between us. But dear me, no. I mean, we're on opposite sides of the Eternal War, certainly, but you're . . . well, you're the loyal opposition! I'm happy to wait for the real game to begin. It wouldn't do to destroy you before that."

"Then what about them?" Alec said, gesturing to Ox-Head and Horse-Face, who continued to float haplessly in their bubble cloud, twenty feet in the air and a little distance away.

"Nothing wrong with a test," Sammael said. "Nothing that any Nephilim who are going to put up a decent fight couldn't handle. Speaking of which, they did fail, it seems, so—"

He shrugged and waved a hand at the guardians. As the Shadow-hunters watched, both Ox-Head and Horse-Face became wide-eyed and began flailing again, more violently than before. They seemed to be in some distress.

"They're not even mine, you know," Sammael added. "They just came with the realm."

The two demons thrashed about, visibly in pain. Magnus found himself feeling sorry for them, even though they were literally demons from Hell, and even though they had been actively trying to kill him and his friends only a few minutes ago. It was their help-lessness, their confusion.

Sammael shook his head as if sympathizing with their plight, and then made a wrenching motion with his hands, and both Ox-Head and Horse-Face came apart in pieces.

It was terribly grisly, even for Magnus. There was no magical glow, no bright flash to obscure what was happening. The two demons simply fell apart, their heads and limbs tearing from their bodies, their torsos splitting into several parts. In a shower of flesh and ichor, the wet chunks of what had recently been Ox-Head and Horse-Face fell to the blasted black ground of Diyu in a series of dull, sickening thuds.

Magnus looked back at Sammael, who seemed surprised at the reaction of his audience. The Shadowhunters had unanimously returned to their initial looks of wary horror; these had faded some-what in the face of Sammael's strange friendliness, but were back now. "Don't look like that," Sammael said. "They're not even really gone. They're Greater Demons and they're from here; they'll just regenerate somewhere else in this maze of a place eventually."

"Still, though," said Clary in a small voice.

Sammael held out his hands. "They failed, so they had to be dis-ciplined. I don't see why it's any concern of yours. You were trying to kill them a few minutes ago yourselves, if I recall."

Tian was being very quiet, Magnus noted. He wondered whether the young Shadowhunter hadn't been prepared to encounter one of the most powerful demons in history. Magnus did have to admit that his friends were perhaps more blasé about confronting *yet another* Prince of Hell than most would be. They had encountered Asmodeus a few years ago, for instance. He surreptitiously looked over at Tian but couldn't read his expression.

Turning back to Sammael, he said, "So the demons are gone, Shinyun and Ragnor are gone, it's just you and us. You could just kill us all if you wanted, but you haven't. So what now?"

Sammael said, "Clearly, you should go back the way you came and return to your world. I'm not *entirely* ready to start the war yet, but in fairness to me, you've all had a thousand years to prepare, and I've had only a tiny fraction of that. So, go back—you can just reopen the Portal you closed up so messily when you came in—and I'll see you on the battlefield soon enough!"

He waved good-bye, as if this concluded the conversation.

"We can't go," Alec said. He sounded apologetic, which was a little funny, considering who he was talking to. "We have to rescue our friends."

Sammael squinted at him, as though he couldn't follow what Alec was saying. "How will you *find* your friends, though, little Nephilim? Diyu has thousands upon thousands of hells. I haven't even been to all of them yet. Frankly," he said, putting his hand next to his mouth like he was sharing a secret, "I've heard once you've seen about ten thousand of them, the other seventy thousand or so are pretty much just minor variants on those."

"You're not the first to be interested in Diyu," said Magnus. "Tian here has been studying Diyu for years. He knows his way around."

Alec turned and smiled at Tian, but Tian wasn't smiling back. He really had been totally silent this whole time, Magnus realized.

"Oh, Tian?" said Sammael. "Ke Yi Tian? The Tian standing right there next to you? The Tian of the Shanghai Institute?"

"Yes, obviously that Tian," said Magnus.

The Shadowhunters were all looking at Tian, who was looking straight ahead of him.

"Tian is *my* employee," Sammael said with great glee. "Tian led you right to me."

"That's ridiculous," said Jace.

"Oh?" said Sammael. "So you thought being led down the realm's longest pit to the realm's deepest court was a fine strategy? You thought it was a great idea to go toward *Avici*?"

Magnus shook his head. "This is just trickery. Childish psych-out stuff."

"Tian," Sammael said, almost hopping up and down with excitement, "abandon these idiots, go find Shinyun, and tell her to get started on reopening our Portal to the Market."

There was a pause, and then Tian, of the august and beloved Ke family, lowered his head with a great sigh and said, "Yes, my master." He lifted his head back up and said, frustrated, "I could have just stayed with them. You didn't have to blow my cover now."

"Well, I thought about you leading them to some oubliette somewhere to rot away," said Sammael, "and it just seemed very disappointing not to see their expressions when they found out. I just love that moment. Besides, it doesn't matter: you can abandon them anytime. Leave now, leave later—either way, they starve to death on an infinitely long road that ends at the deepest part of Hell. The warlock dies of his thorn wound or becomes another one of my servants. Nothing's changed," he added reassuringly to Tian.

"Tian," Magnus said in disappointment, his heart sinking.

Tian stepped out of the circle of his fellow Shadowhunters to stand, hunched and bleak, next to Sammael. Sammael let a friendly smile blossom on his face as he slowly reached an arm out, as if they were posing for a picture, and put it around Tian's shoulder.

"TIAN." ALEC WAS THE FIRST TO SPEAK. "WHY? YOU OWE US that much, at least." He looked at Sammael, barely keeping his fury in check. "He does."

Sammael put up his hands. "No, no, go ahead, this part is quite enjoyable for me as well."

Alec didn't care. "Well?" he demanded of Tian.

Tian took a breath. "Do you know what it's like," he said, his voice ragged, "for your love to be illegal?"

Alec threw up his hands in exasperation. "Tian. Yes!"

"Obviously yes," put in Jace. "Big-time."

"No," said Tian, "you can live with the Downworlder you love, Alec. And you," he said to Jace, "well, things worked out for you, which is fine, I guess. Otherwise—look, that doesn't matter."

"Ha," said Jace, with the air of one who had won an argument.

Tian turned back to Alec. "You can adopt a child with the Downworlder you love. I, on the other hand, am not allowed to *see* the Downworlder I love, without breaking the Law. And yes, I know, the Law is hard. It's too hard. It's become so hard and brittle that it has begun to break."

"That's no excuse—" began Alec.

"Have you looked at the Clave lately?" Tian said, bitterness in his voice. "We are a house divided. A house broken into pieces. There are the ones like you, like me, who would prefer peace, who would prefer to work with all of Downworld, to strengthen all of us. Who would put aside the superstitions and the bigotries of our ancestors."

"Jem Carstairs is one of your ancestors," said Magnus quietly. "A man of neither superstition nor bigotry."

"And the others," Tian went on. "The paranoid. The suspicious.

The ones who want the Shadowhunters to dominate, to crush the rest of Downworld under our rule. And especially the ones who call themselves the Cohort."

"The Cohort is just a small group of crazy people," said Jace, incredulous.

"It may be only a few who will identify themselves as such, for now," said Tian, "but there are far more than you might think who agree with them, when they think only friends are there to hear them speak."

"So you *ally* with a *Prince of Hell*?" said Alec.

Every time someone spoke, Sammael would pull an exaggerated face of shock and amazement. He seemed riveted. Alec wished he would stop, but he didn't think it would go well if he asked.

"The war is coming," said Tian, "no matter what I do. The fight between Sammael and the world. And he will find the Shadowhunters divided, scattered, broken on the lies and secrets they keep from one another. They will either fall—and the world will fall—or they will succeed, and the world will be saved. But at least I will be safe, and Jinfeng with me."

"That's his girlfriend," stage-whispered Sammael.

"We know," Clary said.

"And if we win?" demanded Jace. "The Clave is just going to take you back? A traitor who supported their enemy?"

"I like to think of myself as more than just an enemy," Sammael said thoughtfully. "An *arch*enemy at the very least. Perhaps even a nemesis?"

Tian looked stubborn. "I would hope for the Clave's mercy. I would never hope for Sammael's."

"My God," Clary said. "I think that's the most selfish thing I've heard in my life."

"Please," murmured Sammael, "not the G-word." Clary rolled her eyes.

"I've known your family for many generations now," Magnus said quietly. "The Ke family have always been among the most honorable, generous, noble Shadowhunters I have known. They would be very disappointed in you, Tian. Jem would be very disappointed in you."

Tian looked up at Magnus, and for the first time Alec saw a glint of defiance in his eye. "But it's noble to sacrifice for love, isn't it? I've been taught my whole life that that is noble. To sacrifice everything." He looked at Alec. "That is what I have done. Sacrificed everything for love."

Alec didn't know what to say. He didn't have to speak, though, as Magnus said, loudly, "That . . . is *bullshit*, Ke Yi Tian."

Tian looked taken aback. Even Sammael looked a little taken aback.

Magnus's magic flared, red and roiling and furious, shining from his chest and from his hands. He didn't cast any spell, though, just advanced on Tian, a chemical fire raging in his gold-green eyes.

"You are not just some mundane," he said, his voice dangerously quiet. "You are a *Shadowhunter*. You have a duty. A responsibility. You have a high and holy *purpose*, do you understand me?"

He paused like he was waiting for an answer. Tian opened his mouth after a moment, and Magnus immediately spoke again.

"You are the *protector*," he said, "of our world. Ordained by the Angel. Instilled with his fire. Given the gifts of Heaven!" He grabbed Tian's arm and glared into his eyes. "I *know* Shadowhunters, Tian. I've known them for centuries. I've seen them at their best, and at their worst. But I've known others, too, Downworlders, mundanes, and if there is one thing that Shadowhunters must understand, it is that they are *not like other people*.

"They love, they build, they covet wealth—when there is time. When the duty—the *solemn* duty, the *only* duty, the barrier dividing the living creatures of Earth from oblivion at the hands of *literal, actual* pure evil—"

Sammael waved jauntily.

"—allows them to. All love is important. *Your* love is important. And for some people, their love can be the single most important thing, more important than even the whole world.

"But not for Shadowhunters. Because keeping the whole world safe is not everyone's reason for being, but it absolutely *is yours*."

The flare of magic faded. Magnus lowered his head.

Tian stood silently. He did not reply.

"Yeah," agreed Clary faintly from behind Alec.

Alec, however, was staring at Magnus. "I didn't know you felt that way," he said. To his own ears he sounded stupefied. "I assumed you thought the whole holy warrior business was just silliness."

"Even I think it's just silliness sometimes," offered Jace, "and I've literally had evil burned out of my body with heavenly fire."

Magnus's expression softened. He stepped back toward Alec, as though he had only just realized how far he had advanced toward Tian and Sammael. "I try not to take things too seriously," he said to Alec. "You know that. The world is an absurd place, and to take it too seriously would be to let it win. And I still stand by that philosophy. Most of the time. But most of the time," he added, "I am not standing in front of the *actual* Father of Demons, in *actual* Hell."

"Don't forget Devourer of Worlds," Sammael said. "That one is my favorite. I mean, who doesn't like devouring things? Right?"

Magnus turned to Sammael, one finger raised, and for a moment Alec thought, *By the Angel—Magnus is really going to start telling off Sammael, the Serpent of the Garden.* He was still overwhelmed. For one thing, it was quite galvanizing to hear your boyfriend deliver a stirring defense of your importance and righteousness. For another, he was having a difficult time thinking of an occasion when Magnus had been hotter.

Sammael shrugged. "Anyway, have fun wandering aimlessly

around Diyu until you starve to death. Not the way I'd choose to go, but it's your life. Magnus, come with me."

"You have to know," Alec said, "that there's no way we're letting you take him."

Sammael let out a long groan. "Why do you have to do everything the hard way?" He waved his hand in the general direction of the iron bridge beyond, and in front of it, a circular Portal swirled open. Demons—Ala, Xiangliu, Baigujing—began to emerge from it.

He turned to Tian. "When they're done with the rest, bring Magnus to me. I've got things to do." He shook his head as if the whole experience had fatigued him, and vanished with a small popping noise.

For a moment, Alec and his friends stared at Tian. Nobody had anything to say.

Magnus, thankfully, broke the silence. "I know we all have a lot of feelings right now—"

"There's no way you can get through that whole demon army," Tian said. He sounded weary. "Diyu is home to such an infinitude of demons—and Sammael can command them all."

"Then we make for the bridge," Jace said after a moment. "We can't defeat them, but maybe we can break through them. And then on the staircase they'll be squeezed into a smaller space, and only a few will be able to attack at a time."

"Except for the flying ones," Alec pointed out.

"You have a better idea?"

Alec did not.

Clary turned to Tian. "Are you going to try to stop us?" The words were a challenge. Alec was reminded, not for the first time, that in her own way Clary could be as fierce as Jace.

Tian shook his head. "If I stay here, the demons will just devour me anyway. They can't tell the difference. Besides, I have to go find Shinyun and pass along my master's message."

"Great master you've got there," said Alec. Tian didn't reply. He gave them a long look and then walked away, moving quickly and purposefully, cutting across the scorched wasteland. The demons ignored him completely. In a short time he had vanished behind their milling crowds.

"Okay," said Magnus, drawing White Impermanence. "I'll keep the flying demons off us."

"Where to?" said Clary.

"Someplace safer than here," said Jace. "Stay together."

Together the four of them advanced toward the bridge. At the front, Alec and Jace used their weapons to hold off the demons that got in their way; behind, Magnus blasted anything in the air, and Clary held off the demons that tried to flank them.

It reminded Alec of the classical warfare he'd studied—hoplites, squeezed together for protection, making their way through a hail of arrows. It was agonizingly slow going. Ten minutes of fighting brought them onto the iron bridge, but to Alec it looked like the bridge itself would be another hour to cross, stretching off into the indefinite distance. Next to him, Jace struck out with the spear again and again, his face a mask of sweat and ichor. Alec was sure he looked no better.

Once they were fully on the bridge, the demons changed their strategy. This wasn't like the earlier fight; the demons were crowded so thickly that they could barely maneuver themselves, and they quickly realized that rather than trying to break past the Shadowhunters' blades and Magnus's lightning, they would accomplish their aim just as well by forcing them off the edge of the bridge.

"What happens if we fall?" said Clary.

"Remember what Tian said," Jace said. "At the bottom of Diyu is the city of Shanghai, reversed. Whatever that means."

Alec exchanged a look with Magnus, who nodded.

Jace caught their look. "We're jumping off, aren't we?"

"I can protect us from the fall," Magnus said.

"But what about the landing?" Clary said.

"If I only jumped when I knew where I was going to land," Magnus said, "I would never jump at all."

And with that he flung himself over the side of the bridge.

"Are we really doing this?" Jace said to Clary.

Clary hesitated, then nodded firmly. "I trust Magnus."

The two of them, and Alec right after, threw themselves after Magnus. Alec fell backward, watching the bridge recede into the distance, fading into the starless ink of the sky. As he fell he could not help thinking of Tian's face, his expression cryptic, as he had walked away from fellow Shadowhunters who had trusted him.

CHAPTER FOURTEEN

Certain Falling

THEY FELL.

At first they tumbled out of control, and Alec wondered what would happen if any of them drifted into one of the walls of the pit. The sensation of free fall was terrifying at first, the sense of gravity abandoning him, the anticipation of an ending, a violent collision that never came.

And after a few minutes, he found, he sort of became used to it.

It helped that Magnus righted himself first, and then used some magic to gather the four of them, to keep them upright and close enough to talk to one another. And once the bridge was gone from sight, and the path they had been walking, and even the demons, fading into the gray nothing of the background, it was just the four of them, gently falling through the soundless air. Clary's red hair waved gently around her face. Magnus's hands were raised, glowing red, and Alec felt the sensation of nothing under his feet, the illusion of not moving at all as any visual reference disappeared.

"I've made some weird calls in my time," Jace mused, "but spending ten minutes in free fall from one unknown place in a hell dimension to a different unknown place in a hell dimension is pretty reckless even for me."

"Don't feel bad," said Magnus. "It wasn't really your decision."

Clary tugged on a lock of her hair and watched thoughtfully as it floated back up into the air. "I think it's kind of cool."

They both looked at Alec. Alec looked down—although with the lack of features around them, it was hard to keep up and down straight. Far away, in the direction they were falling, outlines glowed dimly. Were they growing larger, closer? It was hard to tell.

Clary and Jace were still waiting for him to speak. "We all made the decision," he said. "We didn't have enough information or enough time. We went with our instincts."

"And what if we're wrong?" said Jace.

"We'll deal with that then," said Alec.

"Even once we land," put in Magnus, "we won't really *know* if we made the right call or not. We'll probably never know if we made the optimal move."

"Sometimes you just go," Alec said. "You know that."

Jace hesitated. It was a strange thing to see on his face, Alec thought, Jace who was always so confident, who went through the world without hesitating or doubting himself. "But that can get people hurt."

"You do crazy, rash things all the time!" Alec protested.

Jace shook his head. "Yeah, but that's just risking *me*," he said. "I can risk *my* safety. It's different to risk other people." He was looking at Clary.

Clary said, "Jace, do you really think when you risk your own safety, that has no effect on anybody else? On me?"

"On your *parabatai*?" Alec agreed.

"On everyone else who has to deal with the consequences?" Magnus grumbled.

"You're one to talk," Jace said.

"Speaking of decision-making," Magnus said brightly, "where are we trying to land, exactly? If those shapes below are Reverse Shanghai, we'll reach them soon enough."

"There must be some place in Shanghai we can go to. In Reverse Shanghai, I mean," said Clary.

"The Institute?" said Jace.

"The church," Alec said, remembering. "Xujiahui Cathedral. Tian pointed it out to us when we were on our way to the Market."

"Maybe it was a trick," Jace said, his eyes narrowing.

"You're suggesting," said Clary dryly, "that Tian knew that we were going to be in free fall, in Diyu, trying to decide what part of Reverse Shanghai we should try to crash-land into, and he pointed out the cathedral so that we would fall into his trap of trying to crash-land into it instead of somewhere else."

Jace hesitated. "I mean, when you put it like that, it does seem a little complicated."

Magnus was moving one hand around below him and looked like he was concentrating. "Saint Ignatius is actually a great choice," he said, "because it's so distinctive. Easy to spot from the air."

"Can you find it?" said Alec.

"Well, there's *something* down there with two big Gothic towers," Magnus said. "That's probably it."

"You think there'll be a weapons cache there, like in the real one?" Jace said.

"Reverse weapons," suggested Clary. "You stab someone with them and they feel better."

"Magnus," Alec said, "are you growing a tail?"

"Not on purpose," said Magnus, but he looked uneasy. Alec had been mostly leaving him alone, letting him sustain the magic keeping them safe without distraction, but now he took a closer look, and the odd inhuman features that had come along with the Svefnthorn seemed more prominent. Maybe it was an illusion, the odd angle he was looking from, the way their bodies were stretched by being in free fall . . . but Magnus's eyes, luminous and acid green, looked bigger than normal. His ears, too, looked a little pointed, like a cat's, and when he opened his mouth, Alec was sure his canine teeth had become longer and sharper.

Magnus looked at him, his brow furrowed in concern, but didn't say anything further.

"Maybe try not to wield too much of your magic," Alec said hesitantly.

"Maybe after we've landed safely?" Jace said, a little frantically.

"Alec," Magnus said. "If it all goes wrong . . . if I . . ."

"Don't think about it now," said Alec. "Get us to the ground. We'll take things as they come."

MAGNUS CONTINUED TO SCAN BELOW HIM, LOOKING FOR the cathedral. He felt magic surge within him when after a minute or two he located it, and he began to slowly surround Alec and Jace and Clary and himself with a protective haze, a bubble that would lower them safely to the black towers waiting below.

His eyes drooped. His vision blurred. Expending a lot of magic was always tiring, but this was something well beyond the usual. The sound of his friends became muffled as he dissociated from the endless free fall, from the void around them. Every particle of his magic he poured into the spell radiating from his hands, protecting, preserving. His mind fell away, and though he remained conscious, and his hands kept up the magic safeguarding them all, Magnus dreamed.

He was home. Home in Brooklyn, in his apartment, just the way they'd left it to come to Shanghai. He was in their bedroom, but he couldn't remember what he'd come in for. On the bed, the maps that they'd used to try to Track Ragnor were still laid out across the rumpled blankets.

I should pick those up, he thought, and reached out to grab them, but then jerked his hand back and held it up to examine it. He wasn't doing any magic, but his hand was glowing brightly anyway. Too brightly: almost too much to look at without hurting his eyes. He squinted and saw that within the dazzling glow, his hand was strange, elongated. It was something like a bird's, with fingers too long for any human and black talons curling wickedly from their ends.

Unsure what to do, Magnus left the bedroom. He had trouble passing through the open doorway and bumped his head somehow, and when he reached up to check, he could feel horns emerging from his forehead, or maybe more than horns, maybe antlers. He knew without seeing them that they were bone white, like Ragnor's, and sharp. He felt for his chest and looked down, trying to see if the thorn wound was there. He couldn't tell; the light radiating from his hand was too bright. Maybe he needed a mirror.

He ducked and went into the hallway, and as he passed Max's room, he looked inside. Alec was there, putting clothes on Max. He looked up at Magnus, and Magnus expected him to cry out in alarm, but he didn't seem to think anything was wrong. "Okay," he said to Max, "arms up!" and Max amenably stuck his arms straight up in the air like he was celebrating a victory. Alec pulled the T-shirt over Max's arms and head and tugged it down. "Wow, great, that's really helpful," Alec said. "Thanks!"

"Wow!" Max repeated—he was in that phase where he tried to repeat most of what his parents said—and grinned at Magnus. Magnus went to wave his fingers at Max and then paused, remembering the glow, the talons.

Instead he just said, "Hey, blue, what's new?"

"Boo," Max said.

"You want to eat?" Alec said. Max nodded, and Magnus watched the little nubs of Max's horns go up and down. Horns just like his.

No. He didn't have horns. But he *did* have horns. Like Ragnor. But Ragnor was dead, wasn't he?

"Magnus," said Alec, "could you grab his cereal bowl and his sippy cup? They're in the dishwasher."

"Sure." Magnus padded down to the kitchen. Why were they still living here when he could barely fit his antlers through the hallway? There was a good reason, but for the moment he couldn't remember it.

In the kitchen, Raphael Santiago was sitting on the counter, swinging his legs back and forth.

"Raphael," Magnus said in surprise. "But you're dead."

Raphael gave him a withering look. "I've always been dead," he said. "You never knew me when I was alive."

"I guess that's true," Magnus admitted, "but I mean now you're dead and not moving around anymore. You're gone. You let yourself be killed in Edom, rather than kill me."

Raphael furrowed his brow. "Are you sure? That doesn't sound like me."

Magnus fumbled at the dishwasher, trying to open it, but his talons were in the way. "Could you give me a hand?" he asked.

Raphael sarcastically applauded.

"You've gotten grumpier since Sebastian killed you," Magnus remarked. "Which honestly I would not have thought was possible."

"Well, I didn't exactly *want* to die. I didn't *deserve* to die," Raphael said. "I was immortal! I was supposed to live forever. And as it turned out, I didn't even make it to a full mortal human life span."

"You didn't, did you," said Magnus. He managed to hook one claw under the lip of the dishwasher and, bending awkwardly, levered it open. It was not his most graceful moment, but he couldn't feel too embarrassed in front of Raphael, who, after all, was dead.

"How's Ragnor?" Raphael said. He was still swinging his legs back and forth from his perch on the counter. It was a very un-Raphael thing to do, and it made Magnus want to shout at him to stop, but that seemed crazy. "Still dead as well?"

"No," said Magnus, but then he stopped. How *was* Ragnor? When he'd last seen Ragnor, it had been in—

—Diyu.

He reached for the cup and the bowl, awkwardly balancing them in his glowing hands. "I have to bring these to Max," he said.

"Try not to claw him up too much," Raphael advised, and Magnus winced. He turned to leave the kitchen, and the cup and bowl slipped from his hands. Though they were definitely plastic—a matched set covered in apples that was Max's favorite—when they hit the tile floor of the kitchen, they shattered into thousands of sharp splinters, as though they had been crystal.

"Whoa!" said Raphael. "I'll just stay up here for now."

The broom was in Max's room. Magnus walked through the shards and felt them cutting up his bare feet (but why were his feet bare?). He looked behind him as he made his way back up the hallway and saw that he was leaving two trails of blood on the hall rug.

At least I still bleed normal blood, he thought.

"Alec?" he said, and Alec came around the corner with Max, now in the front carrier that they'd used to carry him around the streets of Brooklyn in their first few months with him. Max had outgrown the carrier a month or so ago, and they'd been meaning to get a new one. Maybe this was the new one? It looked like the old one.

Also, Max definitely didn't fit. But that was because he had changed. His horns, just adorable little nubs only a few minutes ago, were now jagged spikes, black and shiny like Magnus's talons. A whiplike tail emerged from behind him, hairless like a rat's. It swayed back and forth dangerously, like the tail of a cat preparing to strike.

And his eyes. Magnus couldn't quite describe what was going on with Max's eyes. When he tried to look at them, it was like scratches formed on the inside of his retinas. He had to look away.

"Something's wrong," said Alec.

"Nothing's wrong," Magnus said desperately. "It's just . . . warlocks . . . sometimes you don't know . . ."

"You didn't tell me," said Alec. He sounded flat.

"I didn't know," said Magnus. He began to back away down the hall, stepping again on the shards he'd left behind when he'd approached Alec and Max just now. New jabs of pain arced through his feet.

Alec lifted Max out of the carrier and held him up to look into his face. "I can deal with the claws, and the horns, and the fangs," he said. "But I don't know how to deal with this."

He turned Max back around to show Magnus. Max's face was a frozen mask, expressionless, vacant. *But that isn't his warlock mark,* Magnus thought. *He looks like . . . like . . .*

CHAPTER FIFTEEN

The Lady of Edom

ALEC WONDERED FOR A MOMENT IF HE WAS DREAMING, as Shinyun descended through the space where once a rose window had been set.

He had seen her floating, arms extended, framed in the empty circle, and thought she was a statue for a moment. There was a statue outside the rose window of the real cathedral in the real Shanghai, he remembered.

But then she came floating in and Jace let out a long, frustrated groan. Alec knew how he felt. Had their escape, their daring fall from the bridge, been pointless, if Shinyun could just casually meet them shortly after they arrived?

Sometime during their descent from the bridge, Magnus's eyes had fluttered back in his head and closed. The three Shadowhunters had panicked, preparing to plummet freely downward, but luckily the spell had held. As the tenebrous shapes of Diyu's mirror of Shanghai grew more distinct below them, they had seen the cathedral. It was exactly St. Ignatius's shadow: every detail the same but with all color drained out of it, a picture in washes of dark grays and blacks. It was, thankfully, not literally upside down.

Magnus's protective cloud had brought them to a landing on the church grounds next to one of the transepts, the side arms of the massive cross that formed the overall shape of the building. There was a small side door there, and they helped Magnus inside and arranged him on one of the carved wooden benches they found. Once he was at rest, the magic faded from his palms, and he breathed steadily, as though asleep.

They hadn't been inside the real cathedral, but the interior of the shadow cathedral was sufficiently cathedral-like that Alec thought it was probably laid out the same way. It was strange to go from the eerie inhumanity of Diyu to the very distinct humanity of a Catholic church; at first glance they could have been in France or Italy, or even New York. Only once they walked around, and saw the elaborate wood carving of the pews, the distinctly Chinese tile running down the middle of the nave, did the unique character of Xujiahui come across. Except, Alec realized, for any holy symbol, or saint, or angel, which were missing. There were empty niches and picture rails all over where such things must have been in the original cathedral, but here they had been wiped away. Apparently Yanluo hadn't been a fan. Alec supposed Sammael wouldn't be either.

Returning to Magnus, Alec found him still breathing steadily and, to all appearances, napping. He put his hand on Magnus's shoulder and gave it a little shake. When Magnus didn't react, he gave him a slightly harder shake. He tried to be careful—startling Magnus didn't seem wise either—but no amount of speaking Magnus's name or touching him invoked any reaction.

"Come on, wake up," Alec said urgently. He jiggled Magnus's knee.

"We could throw some water on him," suggested Clary.

"I don't think there's any water," said Jace. "Maybe Magnus can conjure some up. Some food, too."

"If we can wake him up," said Clary.

"Wake up!" Alec said again, and then they heard the rustle of movement and turned to see Shinyun descending toward them through the blank hole where a window should have been.

She landed lightly, her elongated limbs folding under her, giving her an eerie insectile appearance. Jace drew his spear, and Clary her dagger. Alec continued to nudge Magnus, more and more desperately.

"I don't want to fight," Shinyun called out. Nobody moved to put their weapons away.

She approached, and they stood their ground. "Is Magnus . . . asleep?"

"It's been a long day," said Alec dryly.

"He suffers without the third thorn," she said.

"He'd choose to die."

"It's very interesting," said Shinyun, "how many people choose not to die, when the final decision comes." She eyed them. "It's usually because they worry about the effect it will have on others."

"Not a problem for you, I guess," said Jace.

"No," she agreed. "I understand the nature of power too well to allow myself the kind of sentimental attachments that tether most people to the world. A world that will fail them, in the end."

"You're wrong," Magnus said faintly.

Alec helped him sit up. He blinked his eyes, larger and more luminous than they had been, so familiar to Alec and yet becoming more alien with every passing hour.

"You're wrong," Magnus said again. "Those so-called sentimental attachments—they are where strength comes from. Where real power comes from."

"It amazes me," said Shinyun, "that you would think that, even after living four hundred years. After outliving so many. Knowing you'll outlive all of *them*." She gestured at the Shadowhunters.

"Not at this rate," Magnus said lightly, gently running a hand down his front, as if checking to make sure all his organs were still inside.

Shinyun ignored this. "You know that time is a cruel joke, that it takes everything from us eventually. Time is a machine for turning love into pain."

"But there's so much fun to be had on the way," murmured Magnus. He shook his head. "You can say it prettily, but that doesn't make it true."

Shinyun sighed. "I didn't come here to argue philosophy with you, Magnus."

"I didn't think you did," Magnus said. "I guess I assumed you came here to taunt us and lecture us."

"No," said Shinyun, a frown in her voice. "I came to tell you where to find your friend Simon."

"WHY IN THE WORLD," SAID MAGNUS, "WOULD YOU DO that?"

He had been embarrassed, when he came to, that he had fallen into some kind of trance. Already the memory of his dream was fading from his mind, and he could remember only tiny snippets: Raphael Santiago's legs dangling from his kitchen counter. Max holding up his arms to help Alec put his shirt on. Blood trails on the rug.

"I don't have to explain myself to you," Shinyun said.

Alec folded his arms. "Then you'll understand why we wouldn't trust anything you'd tell us."

"Would you trust anything *we* tell *you*?" Magnus added.

"I would," said Shinyun, "because you are all so painfully without guile that you think telling me the truth will somehow win me over. Like I will have no choice but to respect your integrity and high principles."

"Aw," said Magnus, "you know you respect my integrity and high principles secretly."

Shinyun let out a long and annoyed groan, a strangely expressive sound coming from her motionless face. "Do you want to know where your friend is or not?"

"Not unless you tell us why you're offering your help," Jace said.

"Because I am annoyed," said Shinyun flatly.

"Annoyed at us? Annoyed at Simon?" said Magnus.

"Annoyed at Sammael," Shinyun snapped. "For months every moment has been dedicated to his grand master plan, the ultimate payoff for all the work he's done, all the work *I've* done, and then you show up and he becomes totally distracted by some stupid petty grievance."

"You mean *Simon?*" said Clary, aghast. "So Sammael grabbed him when we first came through the Portal? What is Sammael *doing* to him?"

"And why Simon?" demanded Alec.

"They've *definitely* never met before," said Jace. "I know Simon goes to some weird parties in Brooklyn, but it's still impossible." He glanced at Clary. "It is impossible, right?"

Shinyun threw up her hands. "Ragnor and I are trying our best to implement his schemes for the invasion of the human world, running around this dank pit like lunatics, ordering demons around who are *not* the most responsive underlings—"

"Yes, yes, hard to find good help these days," agreed Magnus hurriedly. He stood up, testing his legs. He was fairly steady; it seemed he had already recovered from the outpouring of magic he had committed on their way down to the cathedral. Recharged by the thorn? He couldn't know. "What is the Father of Demons doing to Simon and why?"

"He has shut himself into some random torture chamber to torment one Shadowhunter who is in no way a direct threat to him. It's ridiculous. It needs to stop."

"Agreed," said Clary immediately. "Point the way."

"So you're going to take us to save Simon," Alec said, making sure he fully understood, "so that Sammael stops being distracted and gets back to the business of destroying the world."

"Yes," said Shinyun. "Take it or leave it."

"Wait," said Magnus. "I need to ask you something first."

Shinyun cocked her head a little to the side. "Oh?"

Magnus hated to ask Shinyun any questions about himself, his thorning, his current state. He had no reason to believe her answers, for one thing. And she would use it as an opportunity to lecture him again. But he didn't understand what was happening to him, and behind that incomprehension lurked fear.

"You said I was suffering from the thorn," he said, "but that's not true. I'm getting stronger. My magic is getting more powerful. I don't understand."

"You don't understand?" said Shinyun.

Magnus said, "I don't understand how, without a third thorning, I die. If you ever had the slightest fleck of mercy in you," he pleaded, "you have to explain. So at least I know what will happen. Will I suddenly weaken? Will I wither away?"

"No," Shinyun said. "You will simply take on more and more of the thorn's power without being fully bound to its master. Your magic will grow stronger, and wilder, and less in your control, and you will become a danger to yourself and the people around you. If they don't abandon you, they'll surely die themselves."

Magnus stared.

"So I'll feel better and better and better," he said. "Until I suddenly feel much worse?"

"No," said Shinyun. "Until you suddenly feel nothing. *That* is why everyone takes the third thorn. The choice is no choice at all. Now, shall we go get your friend?"

A glow emerged from her chest, the same red as Magnus's magic. With the ease of a master painting a line, she drew a Portal in the air with her index finger. It opened on a chamber of black obsidian spikes. In the background, a pool of something red bubbled. "Hmm," she said. She gestured with her finger, and the view through the Portal changed. Now they were looking at a huge white stone plate toward which a gigantic millstone descended. "Not that, either." She gestured again and then again, flipping through different destinations.

"Hell of Iron Mills . . . Hell of Grinding . . . Hell of Disembowelment . . . Hell of Steaming . . . Hell of the Mountain of Ice . . . Hell of the Mountain of Fire . . ."

"Lots of hells, huh," said Magnus.

"Can we hurry this up?" said Alec.

Shinyun gave them a withering look and kept browsing.

"Hell of Worms, Hell of Maggots, Hell of Boiling Sand, Hell of Boiling Oil, Hell of Boiling Soup with Human Dumplings, Hell of Boiling Tea with Human Tea Strainers, Hell of Small Biting Insects, Hell of Large Biting Insects, Hell of Being Eaten by Wolves, Hell of Being Trampled by Horses, Hell of Being Gored by Oxen, Hell of Being Pecked to Death by Ducks—"

"What was that last one?" said Jace. Shinyun ignored him.

"Hell of Mortars and Pestles, Hell of Flensing, Hell of Scissors, Hell of Red-Hot Pokers, Hell of White-Hot Pokers, ah! Here we are." Through the Portal seemed to be a limestone cave, dense with stalactites and stalagmites, a great mouth of fangs. Loose iron chains lay scattered across the ground like a nest of sleeping snakes.

"What's that one called?" Alec said.

"No idea," said Shinyun. "Hell of Wasting Time Torturing Someone Unimportant. Go through before I regret this."

They kept their weapons at the ready and passed single file through the Portal into the cave.

The interior of the cathedral had been dank and musty, but cool. By contrast, the cave was scorchingly hot, and dry like the inside of an oven. Magnus followed Alec, Jace, and Clary as they picked their way around the stalagmites jutting from the ground toward an open area a little distance away. He noticed, to his mild surprise, that Shinyun had followed them through the Portal and trailed behind them.

After a short walk Sammael came into view, pacing back and forth, hands behind his back as though he were deep in thought. Magnus looked around, but it took a moment before he was able to spot—

"Simon," Clary whispered, her voice a dry thread.

In the center of the clearing, Simon hung, spread-eagle. His wrists were manacled to iron chains that stretched to the ceiling of the cave, his ankles similarly chained to great iron hasps sunk into the ground. Only as Magnus got closer did he see that being chained up was the least of Simon's problems.

A dozen sharp blades hung around Simon, hovering in the air. They whirled and shifted, now random, now in patterns—clearly operating at Sammael's will.

Simon had several slashes across his body already, and as they watched, one of the knives lurched at tremendous speed and cut across his arm. He winced, his eyes closed, but Magnus could see he was using all his energy to hold himself very, very still, as the other blades danced inches from him.

Besides the suspense, Simon must already have been in tremendous pain, but he was silent, his jaw set, even as blood dripped down his skin. His eyes had opened wide when Clary cried out: he stared at his friends now, almost blindly, as if he feared they might be a dream.

Sammael turned and started, but as if pleasantly surprised. "You're just getting the full tour of this place, huh?" he said. "I don't know, I like some of it, but Yanluo and I have a *very* different design sensibility. Luckily, this is only a temporary situation until I move to your world and take that as my realm."

Clary lunged at Sammael; Jace caught at her arm, hauling her back. Her teeth were bared. "What are you doing to Simon?" she snarled. "What did he *ever* do to you? You've never even met him before."

Sammael laughed heartily. "What a question! No, this gentleman and I hadn't met before earlier today. I noticed him coming through the temporary Portal my warlocks opened at the Sunlit Market and had him brought here. Because, you see, I know *of* him. I know a lot about him. We're just getting started knowing each other now."

Clary called out, "Simon, are you all right?"

Without changing his tone, Sammael said, "Simon, if you answer her, I will put out your eye."

Simon, wisely, remained silent, and Magnus realized that Sammael really was just getting started. Cutting Simon up a little, threatening him with whirling magic knives, wasn't Sammael's torture. It was an appetizer. An amuse-bouche. This was Diyu. He could cut Simon up for a good long while before he moved on to worse things.

Sammael scowled at Simon, and Magnus was surprised by the look of real, pure hatred that crossed Sammael's face. Magnus had begun to wonder if Sammael was so removed from being a person that he was more like Raziel—a force of will beyond understanding, incapable of human emotions like pettiness or spite. He had thought that maybe Sammael was less like a demon and more like a weather pattern, or a god, too monumental and too unearthly to be comprehended.

But now he realized he had been wrong. Sammael was in every way capable of human hatred. In every facet of his expression, he hated Simon.

"I know that he was not always of the Nephilim," said Sammael. "I know that he was born a mere mundane, but that he then became one of the Night's Children. And in that form, he committed the greatest of crimes.

"He struck down Lilith, First of All Demons, Lady of Edom, and the only love I have ever known in all my long existence."

Clary gasped. Alec said, "Oh," very quietly.

With a flourish, one of the blades drew a red line across Simon's stomach. Clary winced violently. Magnus was horribly impressed with Simon's ability not to cry out. In his position, Magnus was pretty sure he would be screaming.

"I don't know how a mere vampire could have prevailed over her," Sammael went on. "If I had heard the tale from anyone but the Lady herself, I would never have credited it. But it was she herself who told me. I was so close, so close to returning. I was drawing myself free of the Void. I had been searching for one who might find me a realm I could rule. And then, cutting across the worlds, I heard my beloved's scream of rage. Her fury could have powered a universe." He sounded admiring. "She cried out that she had been struck down. She was fading. She would be gone from the world for eons. The force of her rage revived me, sent me whirling back from the Void into these material realms, where things have form and meaning. I again had a living embodiment, and I vowed two vows."

Magnus was listening, but he was watching Simon, who was following Sammael with his eyes.

"It was pain and rage that drove me from the darkness," Sammael went on. "All I wanted was to be with Lilith again, but, irony of ironies, it was by her own passing that I was able to return."

"I don't think you're using 'irony' correctly," said Magnus. "Well, maybe it's situational irony."

Alec flashed him a look. But Sammael was on a roll and wasn't paying any attention to them.

"My first vow was to finish what I started; to rain fire and poison upon Earth, to lead the armies of demons to whom this universe truly belongs by right. My second was to see the murderer of Lilith conquered, and to see him suffer for what he did."

Simon spoke thickly. "It wasn't my intention—"

Sammael interrupted. "I'm not surprised this one would try to talk his way out of his just punishment, but honestly, I really thought he would come up with something better than 'I didn't mean to defeat the mother of all demons, it was an accident.' I suppose," he said, "she tripped and her heart fell directly onto the end of your blade."

"Something like that, actually," said Clary. "It *wasn't* Simon's fault. It was my fault, if it was anyone's."

Sammael rolled his eyes. Before he could speak again, Shinyun interrupted. "My Lord Sammael," she said. "I respect your need for closure, but this seems like too small a task for someone of your stature and importance. We have a war to plan, troops to muster."

"Plenty of time for all that," Sammael said, waving his hand dismissively. "Once I have had my fill of satisfaction from this creature's pain."

"You won't be satisfied," Simon said. "Eventually you'll have mashed me into paste and then what? You still won't have your girlfriend back."

"Why can't you just leave him to be crushed to powder with the rest, when our hordes flood Earth in blood?" Shinyun said. She sounded frustrated. "If you want to punish everyone individually who's done something bad to someone you know, that's going to take a very long time. Time we don't have."

Sammael sighed. "Shinyun, you know I hold you in high regard. You're very good at organizing demonic forces, and you brought me Ragnor Fell. You have a great work ethic, and you seem to truly enjoy your job. But you don't understand. You can't understand. Only Lilith, perhaps, would understand, and I hope that somewhere, somehow, she sees what's happening here and smiles." His expression turned dreamy. "I do so miss her smile. And those snakes she has for eyes. They always liked me."

"Yes, my master. I will try to understand." Shinyun closed her eyes in acquiescence, but she did not seem happy.

"Now," said Sammael, "neutralize Magnus until I'm ready for him, and give these others to the courts of Diyu for processing."

"I thought you were going to let us wander around until we starved," said Alec.

"I was," said Sammael, "but apparently members of my staff have decided to arrange meetings for us during your period of starving and wandering. I was looking forward to thinking of you all sometimes, dying alone on a featureless rock in a world with no stars. It takes a lot of the pleasure out of it if I have to actually talk to you." He shrugged. "So let Diyu decide where you end up. Have some torture for your troubles. They're very good at it here, when you can get them to show up for work."

Shinyun turned around to look at Magnus and the Shadowhunters. She gave a small shrug.

"What exactly was your plan here?" Alec hissed at Shinyun. "I assumed you had something better than just trying to talk him out of it. If he wouldn't listen to you, why would he listen to *us*?"

Shinyun hesitated. "I thought he would be embarrassed."

"I don't think he embarrasses easily," Magnus said. "Have you seen his hat?"

"Are you going to take us back to the courts?" said Jace, and Shinyun looked uncertain, but whatever she would have said, it was lost in a sudden tumult: the buzz of hellish magic, like a swarm of bees, and the roaring of water.

Before Magnus could see what had caused the ruckus, a long tongue of orange flame, straight as an arrow's flight, appeared and sliced cleanly through the iron chains binding Simon's ankles. Sammael looked up, unpleasant surprise blooming on his face. The knives stopped whirling and hung in the air, waiting.

The tongue of flame reappeared, cutting Simon's arms free, and Simon fell with a nasty thump to the ground. He rolled over as best he could, considering that his hands were still shackled, and Magnus was relieved to note that he was still conscious.

Clary and Jace were running toward Simon, and Magnus was gathering his magic—he didn't even yet know for what purpose—but Alec was standing dumbstruck, looking up with an expression of complete astonishment.

Through a Portal of storm clouds and rain had come Isabelle. She carried a blazing whip in one hand, and was riding on the back of a tiger. A very *large* tiger, even by tiger standards.

Magnus had to admit that even he was surprised.

The orange flame had been Isabelle's: as Magnus watched, she reared back and struck again with the whip, whose length burst with fire.

Isabelle whooped a warrior's cry as the gigantic tiger landed in the clearing and gave a roar that shook the very foundations of the cave. She dismounted from the tiger and ran toward the spot where Simon knelt, Clary beside him. She immediately joined Clary in trying to free Simon's wrists and ankles from their shackles.

Then another figure came leaping through the Portal, and while Magnus would have guessed that "Isabelle Lightwood riding a giant tiger" would be the most surprising thing he would see that day, he had to admit that this was a close second.

Drenched to the bone, his hair and clothes matted to his body,

Ke Yi Tian landed in a crouch on the ground. He straightened and ran directly for Shinyun, swinging the diamond blade of his rope dart in a tight circle as he ran. The glitter of *adamas* was a strange sight in this murky place, but Magnus found it oddly uplifting, even if he didn't yet understand what was going on.

Shinyun raised her hands at almost the last moment, and Tian's dart was deflected away, bouncing off a barrier visible only as a crimson smoke whose color Magnus was becoming familiar with.

Sammael had stepped back. Magnus had assumed he would soon start fighting, but he continued to hesitate. He was watching the tiger, Magnus noticed. Sammael turned to say something to Shinyun, and then with one finger drew a Portal in the air. It glimmered darkly, as though absorbing all the light from around it, very different from the Portals Magnus was used to seeing opened by warlocks. With a last look at the tiger, Sammael went through the Portal, but it didn't close behind him. Instead, a stream of Baigujing skeleton warrior demons began spilling out of it.

Clary and Isabelle were unprepared to immediately start fighting, as they were busy freeing Simon, but the rest of them responded instinctively, pulling out weapons and readying themselves for battle. Jace clambered onto a nearby rock, his spear out, and leaped off it, directly onto the nearest of the skeletons. They both collapsed on the ground and rolled around, but Magnus couldn't focus on what was happening there. Tian had begun striking the skeletons with his rope dart, and Alec had engaged too, his sword flashing.

A new skeleton was still emerging from the Portal every few seconds, so Magnus ran toward it, drawing red sigils in the air with his fingers as he went. He reached the Portal and began frantically to dismantle it.

Luckily, a Portal made by Sammael seemed not all that different from a Portal made by anyone else. Within a minute or so, he'd folded up the magic and closed it off.

Between Tian, Alec, and Jace, the last few skeletons were quickly dispatched. The tiger even took a swipe at a few, when they got close enough, but mostly it seemed content to let everyone else do the work.

When the last of the skeletons was gone, silence fell in the strange cave. Only Shinyun still remained, with her hands raised, keeping a magic barrier between her and the rest of them. Tian stalked toward her, spinning the dart at his side with murder in his eyes.

"Tian," Alec said, approaching him, "she isn't going to attack us."

"I'm not," confirmed Shinyun. "For the moment I have enough other problems." She kept the barrier up, though.

Clary and Isabelle had succeeded in getting Simon free from the remainder of his bonds, but that didn't mean he was in good shape. Blood was seeping sluggishly from Simon's wounds. None seemed deep, but there were many. Isabelle was cradling his head in her lap, stroking his hair as Clary drew *iratze* after *iratze*. Alec was helping Jace up; one of the Baigujing had gotten in a good blow before Jace dispatched it, and his shoulder was bloody. He winced as he stood.

"Okay, Tian," Magnus said, coming to join them. "So are you in league with Sammael, or not? I'm starting to get confused."

"I'm not." Tian shook his head. "And now he knows it. I've been waiting for the right moment to act on the knowledge I've gained, pretending to ally with him." He nodded at Simon. "I knew that if you ended up in Diyu, Simon would be taken. And when Isabelle also went . . . it seemed the right time."

"You *knew* Simon would be taken? And you let it happen?" Clary wasn't looking very forgiving.

"You must have known what Sammael would do to him." Isabelle didn't sound too pleased either.

"I also have a *lot* of questions for Tian," Alec said. "But maybe we should leave this particular hell first?"

"I'd like that," said Simon. Isabelle and Clary were helping him upright. Many of his wounds were closing up, but he was still pale and shocked-looking. "It's been a day."

"It's not over," Jace said grimly, leaning against Alec's shoulder. "I think my foot is broken."

Alec took his stele out.

Shinyun said abruptly, "I am summoned. I go to speak with my master, who I am going to try to get back on track." She looked around at all of them. "Why do you make everything so complicated?" she said, as if to herself, and then she vanished into the dark of the cave.

Alec, having runed Jace—the break was a bad one, pushing against the force of his *iratzes* like an insistent hand—put his stele away and glanced around. "Okay," he said. "What's with the tiger?" The tiger, who didn't seem all that interested in anything going on now that Sammael and his demons had departed, had lain down and was licking its front paw with a massive pink tongue.

"Oh!" Tian went back over to the tiger and leaned down. "Thank you, Hu Shen," he said in Mandarin. "The Nephilim of Shanghai owe you a favor."

Hu Shen yawned and stretched, then stood up. He lay one enormous paw on Tian's shoulder and gazed at him for a moment. Then he trotted away, disappearing into the depths of the cave beyond where they could see.

"A great faerie of legend, Hu Shen," Tian said as they watched him go. "A guide for lost travelers. Sometimes it is useful to be on good terms with the fey."

"Will he be all right?" Clary said.

Tian looked in the direction Hu Shen had gone. "Faeries aren't bound by the same rules as the rest of us. And he's been around much longer than any of us. Even you," he added, nodding in Magnus's direction.

Clary had gone over to Jace and was talking to him in a low

voice, clearly concerned. Jace was standing on one foot, looking irritated, and using his longspear as a kind of crutch. "I really am fine," he said, "but it might be a while before it's healed. I won't be too speedy until then."

"No more wrestling skeletons today," Alec said. "I hope."

"I'll be *fine* in a few hours," repeated Jace. Magnus was entertained to see how annoyed he was at having suffered an injury, and how quick he was to change the subject. "What was that weapon you were using?" Jace asked Isabelle.

"Flame whip," Isabelle said happily. Jace reached out a hand and she slapped it away. "Well, don't *touch* it," she scolded. "It's hot."

"I think we could all use a bit of time to catch up and heal our broken feet. And exchange information," Magnus said. "Especially information about what game *you've* been playing, Tian."

Tian had the courtesy to look chagrined. "I am sorry. I will explain."

"Hey, guys?" said Simon. "Time to go? I'd really like to not be here anymore. You know, in the torture cave."

Magnus thought that was an excellent idea. "I'll bring us back to the cathedral," he said, wiggling his fingers.

Tian's eyebrows went up. "Xujiahui? I wondered if you'd get there."

Magnus nodded and, with a wave of his hands, opened a Portal. It glimmered blackly, with the same uncanny light as the one Sammael himself had opened earlier. Magnus exchanged a look with Alec.

"That doesn't look right," said Clary, and Simon looked hesitant. But they could all see the interior of the cathedral through the Portal's aperture, and none of them wanted to stay in the cave. There was nothing for it but to step through, and hope that Diyu and its masters would give them a moment's rest. They all, Magnus could see, desperately needed it.

CHAPTER SIXTEEN

The Phoenix Feather

THEY FOUND THE CATHEDRAL UNTOUCHED, AND THEY set up camp in the apse, where the altar would have been in the real building. Here, of course, there was no altar, just an expanse of cracked white marble. Simon, Isabelle, Clary, and Jace perched on the marble steps that led down toward the pews, while Tian sat in the first row and Magnus leaned casually against a pillar.

Alec paced back and forth across the apse, restless and worried. Magnus had summoned some nourishment for them, which he had promised was safe—plain bowls of rice in broth, and capped thermoses of water. They didn't taste like much, but everyone had wolfed them down anyway.

Though Alec would have liked it if Magnus could have been convinced to take more than a few bites. Instead, he was gazing at Tian, a shimmer of concentration in his gold-green eyes. "So, Ke Yi Tian," he said. "What's the story? With you and Sammael?"

With a sigh, Tian put aside his empty bowl, nodded once, and told his tale.

* * *

I WAS FIRST APPROACHED BY JUNG SHINYUN AND RAGNOR Fell in the Sunlit Market, months ago. Already there had been mutterings in the Downworlder Concession about these two warlocks, neither of them locals, who had come from nowhere and instantly became regulars. The Shanghai Conclave took an interest, and since I knew the concession well, I began keeping an eye on them. What vendors were they visiting? What were they buying? Did they meet with anyone?

In retrospect, I think that they were surveying the Market itself, learning how well and in what ways it was surveilled and defended. So all my careful recordings of their purchases of bird entrails and quartz crystals were probably irrelevant. But at the time, they were only persons of interest, newcomers to keep an eye on.

Unfortunately, as it turned out, Jung and Fell were keeping an eye on *me*. And I've grown . . . incautious about my relationship with Jinfeng. I'm lucky enough to live in a place where Downworlders and Shadowhunters are on good terms, and Jinfeng and I are lucky enough that both our families approve of us. So where I should have been vigilant, I was unguarded. Vulnerable.

One day in the Market they found me in a dark corner. They told me they knew about Jinfeng and me, and that they could get me in trouble. I told them my family knew, that the Shanghai Conclave supported me. But then they spoke of the Cohort.

ALEC KNEW OF THE COHORT. SCATTERED AMONG THE Clave were a small number of Shadowhunters who not only thought the Cold Peace was a good policy, but believed that it was the first step toward the return of the ultimate supremacy of the Nephilim over all of Downworld. Where Valentine Morgenstern and his Circle had argued that only by making war on Downworlders could the Shadowhunters be "purified," the Cohort took a more subtle approach, proposing new rules to restrict the rights of Down-worlders, often in small, localized ways. The danger of the Cohort, as far as Alec was concerned, was not that they would start a new Mortal War, but that the rest of the Clave would allow them to make these small changes, not noticing the larger dangers until it was too late. As yet they were still a small faction, but Alec's father kept a close eye on them, and there was a growing worry that their numbers were increasing, however slowly.

Tian and Jinfeng's relationship *was* illegal, under the Cold Peace, and Alec knew that its discovery and exposure to the larger Clave could well bring down not just Tian himself but his family's control of the Shanghai Institute, and destroy the careful balance that had been achieved in the city.

Tian took in the grim look on their faces and said, "I see you understand."

Alec nodded. "Go on."

Tian continued.

SOUTHWEST OF SHANGHAI, ONLY A HUNDRED MILES OR so away, is the city of Hangzhou. Its Institute is run by the Lieu fam-ily. The husband of the head of the Institute there is Lieu Julong, and while he is not officially a member of the Cohort, it is well known among the Shadowhunter families of China that he is sympathetic to their cause. It is also well known that the Lieus would seize upon any opportunity to damage the reputation of the Ke family, in the hope of gaining control of the Shanghai Institute for themselves.

Shinyun knew this. She spoke of Lieu Julong by name. She said that my family would be forced to turn me over to the Clave for violations of the Cold Peace, if they wanted to keep the Institute. I said that they would never do such a thing, but in my heart I knew

I would never allow them to lose their influence and their positions because of what I had done.

I asked the warlocks what they wanted of me. They wanted information—about the Institutes of China, their defenses, the number of Shadowhunters in each Conclave, the relations between the Shadowhunters and Downworlders in those cities as I understood them. I provided it all to the best of my understanding. I told myself that I was not giving away any crucial secrets, that all of this was knowledge they could find out on their own, even if I refused to help.

A month passed, perhaps two. Jung and Fell continued to be frequent visitors to the Sunlit Market, and one day they again waylaid me. They took me to a cellar on an anonymous street in the concession, where they'd set up a kind of office and laboratory.

The moment I saw their headquarters, I knew I was in terrible danger. They made no attempt to blindfold me or otherwise hide their work from me. And their work was as terrible as you would think. What I saw in a single glance there was enough of an Accords violation to sentence both warlocks to languish in the Silent City for eternity. I assumed they had brought me there to kill me.

Instead they told me everything. That their master was Sammael, Father of Demons, that they were working to bring him back to Earth to resume the war that had been delayed a thousand years ago when he was defeated by Michael. And that now I, too, worked for him.

I said no, of course not, I would never. And they said, you will, or we'll tell your family that you've already provided us with intelligence about Shadowhunters, their numbers, their strengths, their weaknesses. You are already a spy for Sammael, they said. You only have yet to admit it to yourself.

* * *

MAGNUS LOOKED AGHAST. "THE FEATHER IN SAMMAEL'S hat," he said. "It's a phoenix feather, isn't it? Is it Jinfeng's?"

Alec didn't know the finer points of faerie magic, but he knew the feather of a phoenix gave you power over that phoenix. Tian shook his head violently. "No. *No.* I agreed that I had no choice but to do as they asked. Their next request *was* the feather of a phoenix—they obviously wanted me to betray Jinfeng, so that I would fall deeper into corruption. Instead I took Jinfeng into my confidence—the only person other than you here who knows the whole story—and she brought me a phoenix feather from the tomb of one of her ancestors. I told Jung and Fell that it was hers."

He looked around. "You understand, I thought I would take advantage of the situation. I was allowed into Diyu and began to learn its layout, its structure, its rules. I thought, at least this could be useful to me, if I ever find a way out of this trap."

"It *was* useful," said Isabelle. Alec looked at her, and she looked back, her dark eyes clear and shining. Simon, who was leaning his head on her shoulder, smiled up at her. "The Jiangshi took me through to yet another court, and there was an old guy there with kind of a melted face? He yelled at me in Mandarin for a while, and when I didn't say anything, he opened a panel in the wall and sent me through."

"Which hell did they send you to?" said Alec.

"The Hell of Silences," Isabelle said.

"Could be worse," Jace said. Alec thought of the Hell of Boiling Soup with Human Dumplings.

"It was the top of a tower, a little platform surrounded on all sides by a thousand-foot drop onto metal spikes," Isabelle said conversationally. "They hung me from a chain and strapped a metal rod around my neck, with spiked forks at both ends. One end poked into my throat, the other into my chest, so if I spoke, or even nodded my head, I would be impaled on both. Demons watched over me and laughed while I struggled."

"Oh," said Jace.

Simon drew Isabelle even tighter to him.

When Alec had first met Simon, he would have laughed uproariously at the suggestion that his sister would someday hold on to him tightly, that she and Simon would find affection and reassurance in each other. Of course, at that time he would have laughed at the suggestion that he and Magnus Bane would be raising a child together too. They had all changed so much, in such a short time.

"I was only there for a few minutes," Isabelle went on. "Tian found me. The demons watching over me let him get close, and then, uh, then a giant tiger showed up and killed them."

"Once Sammael's eye was no longer on me, I called upon Hu Shen for assistance freeing Isabelle," Tian put in.

"That must have been so cool," murmured Simon.

"I made sure we brought the tiger," Isabelle said. "I knew you'd be disappointed if you missed it."

Simon kissed her on the cheek. She blushed a little—very unlike Isabelle, Alec thought with amusement. Very unlike Isabelle most of the time, anyway.

"You know the rest," Tian said. "Sammael's probably planning to spend today moping around Diyu, complaining about how terrible it is and ordering his two warlocks around. And now he knows I'm his enemy too."

"Believe me," said Simon wearily, "when Sammael decides to be demonic, he has no trouble bringing the evil."

Alec nodded. He had been startled by his first meeting with Sammael; he had been so friendly, and so unthreatening, but the sight of Sammael's face as he sliced up Simon's body had reminded him of who they were dealing with. "He's still the most dangerous thing here."

"He also seems to have a strange interest in you, Magnus," put in Tian. "I suppose it's because you were thorned by Shinyun, but it seems to me if he wanted more warlock minions, he could probably find willing ones."

Magnus shrugged. "I guess I'm already here?"

"So Sammael is here preparing," said Clary, "but what's he preparing for? What's his plan exactly?"

"Sammael is prevented from entering Earth by wards put in place by the Archangel Michael long ago," said Tian. "As near as I can tell, he's got Jung and Fell working on finding something in the Book of the White that will let him get around the wards."

"Is that possible?" said Jace. "Is there something in the Book of the White that could do that?"

They all looked at Magnus. "Probably," Magnus said grimly. "Yes. No wonder the Portals on Earth are all malfunctioning. Sammael's minions have been fiddling with the walls that keep dimensions separate."

"So why haven't they figured it out yet?" said Clary.

Tian looked thoughtful. "It seems to me that Sammael thought Diyu would be a much better source of power. It used to be, under Yanluo, of course; by design it is a dynamo that transforms human suffering into demonic power. But the machinery has been broken for almost a hundred and fifty years. Not only is it difficult for Jung and Fell to draw on its power to fuel their magic, but the demons who used to run Diyu have grown used to freedom and chaos. Sammael can't whip them into shape by himself." He shook his head. "Shinyun thinks that with enough power granted by the thorn, she could hold the entire host of Diyu under her magical compulsion, but she isn't there yet."

"So we have a little time," said Alec. "Are we safe here?"

Tian nodded. "Sammael doesn't think we're any real threat, and he's dependent on his underlings to keep Diyu under observation. Demons don't like coming to churches, even in demon Shanghai."

"Okay," said Jace. "So what's the plan? Rest up and then go after Sammael?"

"Or go after Shinyun and Ragnor," said Clary. When she saw Magnus's face, she said, "We can't let them figure out how to allow Sammael to enter our world. We just can't."

"Would getting the Book away from them stop Sammael's plans, though?" said Simon doubtfully.

Tian shook his head. "It would delay them, but they would find some other solution, I'm sure. There's a lot of dark magic in the world."

"We still can't just leave it with them," Clary said. "Or leave things the way they are."

"Okay," said Alec. "So where do we find the Book? Or Sammael? *And* Sammael, rather?"

Tian looked uncertain. "He doesn't really have a home base here. He wanders all over the realm." He adopted a confidential air. "He's kind of a micromanager."

"Then what?" said Jace, frustrated. "Back to the iron bridge? Back to the courts? Demand to be taken to him?"

"We draw him out," said Magnus. "Use me as bait."

"No," said Alec instantly.

"Shinyun has some weird thing about me and the thorn," Magnus said. "She's been taunting me since this whole thing started, telling me that in the end I would choose to take a third wound from the Svefnthorn rather than die. If I go somewhere and make a lot of noise, demand to speak to Shinyun, she'll show up. From there we can get to Sammael. Or he'll get to us."

"No," Alec said again.

"It can work!" Magnus said.

"Magnus," said Alec, "what happens if she actually thorns you again? You'll fall under Sammael's control. And then it's all over. For . . . everyone," he added quietly.

"She won't," said Magnus. "She can't. I have to choose the third wound, and I won't do that."

"But you'll lie to her and say you will," Alec said.

Magnus actually smiled a little, clearly pleased at how well Alec knew him. "Right. Then she'll probably want to do some complicated ritual with a bunch of chanting, you know her. She'll light a million candles. It'll take forever. Plenty of time for our attack."

Alec's heart was beating too fast. "What if she doesn't? What if it doesn't?"

"Alec," Jace said carefully. "I don't think we have a better idea. Magnus is right. The rest of us, we can just stay in the cathedral until we die of starvation, as far as Sammael or his minions are concerned. They don't think we can really do anything to disrupt their plan. We can kill some demons, sure, but two thorned warlocks and a Prince of Hell? We're just some foot soldiers in the faceless infantry of the opposing army."

"He'll find out he's wrong about that soon enough," said Isabelle.

"I mean, yes," said Jace. "Fine point from Isabelle. But when Sammael met Magnus, he tried to *recruit* him. He offered him Shinyun's job! Magnus is the only one who can get their attention, who might be able to defend himself if one of our three buddies attacked." He nodded toward Simon. "Sorry, no offense intended."

"None taken," Simon said with a weak smile. "I'm not really at a hundred percent right now."

Alec didn't know what to say. A terrible thing was going through his mind, an anxiety he had never really felt before, or allowed himself to feel. A conversation with Max, a horrible conversation, about how Magnus wasn't going to be back, how it was just the two of them now. *A risky plan, a long-shot plan, but we thought it would be fine. . . .*

"We'll all have eyes on Magnus while this is happening," said Jace. As usual, he knew Alec well enough to read the trepidation in his eyes. "He'll never be in any real danger. We've fought off

Shinyun before, we can again, and Magnus is right—he'd have to choose the thorn this time. That's why she hasn't bothered to try thorning him since we've been in Diyu."

Alec sighed. With an effort, he decided to wait on the morbid fantasizing and focus on the moment at hand. "Okay, okay. I agree it's probably our best bet."

"So now what?" Clary said.

Simon yawned. "I don't know about anyone else, but I could use some sleep. It's been a long day for me—dim sum, the Market, being hung from chains and lacerated with magic flying knives. I know that's a normal weeknight for most of you, but I'm pretty worn-out."

"Also, my foot bones need to knit," said Jace. "And I don't suppose you know where we could find some better weapons," he added to Tian.

"Flame whip!" said Isabelle.

"More flame whips would be acceptable," allowed Jace, "though they're not my first choice."

Tian said, "As a matter of fact . . ."

AT THE END OF ONE OF THE TRANSEPTS WAS A SMALL room. It was obviously a private chapel in the real cathedral, but here, of course, all signs of religious practice were missing, so it echoed emptily as Tian led Alec, Jace, and Clary into the center. Jace hopped along with his spear as a cane, keeping his weight off his foot. Magnus had come along too, Alec thought in order to let Simon and Isabelle have a little time to themselves, not because he cared at all about weapons. Alec stood against the wall and watched with vague interest while Tian got down on the ground and knocked on a few of the stone floor tiles, listening. After a few false starts, he reached down and carefully lifted the largest tile out of the floor, revealing a chamber below it framed in wood. In the chamber was a pile of oilcloth bundles.

"It's nothing like you'd find in the real cathedral," said Tian apologetically, "and they won't be runed, so you can hurt demons, but you'll need to make the kills with seraph blades. But . . ."

Jace made a happy noise. Tian started retrieving the bundles from the chamber.

Alec said quietly, "Tian, why didn't you tell us that you had been forced to work for Sammael? You trusted us enough to tell us about Jinfeng."

Tian looked at Alec with surprise. "I would think that was obvious. I knew you wouldn't disapprove of a relationship with a Downworlder, but there was always a chance that the connection between me and Sammael could get back to the Clave and they'd step in, and Jinfeng would be harmed. My family might be harmed too."

Clary snorted. "What?" said Tian.

"It's just . . . *we're* the ones who keep stuff from the Clave," she said.

"It's true," said Alec. "We're not exactly known for keeping the authorities up to date on our plans."

"For instance, we didn't tell the Council we were coming to Shanghai," agreed Clary. "I thought we had an understanding."

Tian looked amazed. "Alec, your father is *the Inquisitor*. I think I've trusted you all quite a lot considering I only met you yesterday. Wow, today has been a long day."

"He's got a point," said Jace. With the handle of his spear, he had pushed the oilcloth aside, uncovering a two-handed sword with an immense broad curved blade, like a cross between a scimitar and a machete. He gingerly nudged the tip with his good foot. "As does this. Clary? *Dadao?*"

Clary took it and went to the other end of the room, where she stepped through a few two-handed sword forms, her bright red braid whipping around her head as she spun through a series of forward cuts, ending with the sword elegantly held downward. She flashed them a smile. "I like it."

Jace was staring. Alec patted him on the shoulder.

"There's something about a tiny girl with a gigantic sword," Jace murmured.

Clary came back over. Jace visibly restrained himself from grabbing her and kissing her, and instead went back to the pile of weapons at their feet.

"It just bothers me," Alec said to Tian. "The distrust, the secrets. Mine, yours." He furrowed his brow. "The Shadowhunters are supposed to be this ironclad institution, the bulwark between humans and demons, the first and last line of defense. But instead we're just riddled with secrets. I used to think it was just me and my friends who were keeping things from the Clave, but you know what I've realized? *Everyone* is keeping things from the Clave."

"Are you saying I should have trusted you more?" Tian said, sounding nettled. "Even though I'd just met you?"

"*Yes,*" said Jace, and both Alec and Tian turned to see what he meant, but it turned out he'd just uncovered a weapon—two hardwood sticks linked with a length of iron rings. One of the sticks was clearly a handle, while the other was much shorter and was covered all over in short iron barbs. He looked up at them with glee. "*Morning star.*"

"Okay, that's *definitely* a flail," said Clary.

"Let me have this one," Jace said. "It'll be good in case I have to fight before my foot heals completely. I can spin this around and keep demons off me."

"You're not *useless* in a battle with a broken foot, you know," Clary said. "You're good at strategy and tactics."

Jace shook his head, smiling. "We all know the main thing I have going for me is my sumptuous, lithe physicality. Without that," he added, "who am I?"

Clary rolled her eyes. "You *are* the guy who figured out how to break us into Sebastian's fortress in Edom. For one thing."

"Sure," Jace said, "one thing."

Clary smiled. "Remember, your most sumptuous muscle is your brain."

Tian watched this interaction with amusement. "I don't think you should have trusted us more, by the way," Alec said to him. "Any more than we would have trusted you with all of our secrets after such a short time." He sighed. "It's just . . . it's getting worse, among Shadowhunters. Less and less trust. More and more secrets. I don't know how far the system can bend," he added, almost to himself, "before it breaks."

Jace turned up a surprisingly decent horn bow, with curved, double-bent ears, and a quiver of arrows. He offered it to Alec, who took it but said, "I'm going to give this to Simon. I've got Black Impermanence, after all."

They headed back down the transept toward the nave, their feet echoing on the stone floor. Magnus broke the silence unexpectedly, his voice low and steady. "My father is a Prince of Hell, Asmodeus," he said to Tian.

Tian stopped walking and blinked at him.

"It's just something I think you should know," Magnus said. "Before we go into battle with Sammael. He's mentioned me being an eldest curse a few times. And Jem said Shinyun was after Tessa because she was an eldest curse. It makes me think it matters to them, who my father is."

"Oh," said Tian. He thought about this for a moment. "What does that mean for our plans?" he asked.

"I don't know," Magnus said. "Maybe nothing. Maybe Sammael thinks there's some power he can extract from me. Or maybe he thinks he's some kind of uncle to me. I just—like I said, I thought you should know."

He started walking again, and after a brief hesitation, the rest of them did too. Alec saw Jace and Clary exchange troubled looks.

"That's terrible," said Tian. "I mean, for you."

Magnus looked at him with surprise.

"You never asked to have a Prince of Hell as your father," Tian said. "And now it probably means you'll have Greater Demons and Princes of Hell bothering you . . . well, forever."

"Regularly," agreed Magnus.

"What can you do about it?" Tian said.

"Nothing," said Magnus. "Live my life. Protect my family."

"Be protected by your family," Alec put in.

"And friends," added Clary.

They walked in silence for another moment. "Thank you," said Tian. "For deciding you trust me enough to tell me. I will tell no one."

They turned toward the apse, where Simon was gazing out one of the windows at the nothingness outside. Isabelle was at the other end of the room.

"It's up to you to decide if you need to tell anyone," said Magnus. "To decide who *you* would trust. That's how trust works." He paused. "Also, Jem knows and would be happy to answer any questions about it. He's got some experience in this area."

As they approached the apse, it was obvious that Isabelle was not happy. She was watching Simon from across the room, her brow knitted in worry. Her arms were folded tightly over her chest.

"Izzy?" Clary called.

Alec wanted to go to Isabelle, his instincts for protecting his sister kicking in, but he was still awkwardly holding the bow and arrows he'd found, so he went to give them to Simon first. Jace went with him, for which Alec was grateful. Magnus and Tian hung back uncertainly.

"Simon," Alec offered as they approached. "I found you a bow."

"Great," said Simon, without turning around. "A souvenir. Let's go home."

Alec and Jace traded looks. Jace spoke first. "What are you talking about, Simon?"

"I want to go home," said Simon. "You should want to go home too."

"Of course we *want* to go home," said Alec cautiously. "But we can't go yet. Sammael still has the Book of the White, and we need to—"

"We're all back together," Simon said dully. "We're all safe, for the moment. There's no reason to stay here."

"We don't have a way back," said Alec. "We'll need to find one."

"So let's find one," said Simon in that same flat tone. "That should be the plan. Find a way to leave. Then leave." He looked up at Jace hopefully. "Come back with reinforcements. You love reinforcements."

"Magnus is still in danger," Alec said. "We have to figure out how to deal with the Svefnthorn."

"Well," said Simon, "maybe it would be easier to find a solution somewhere other than *literally in Hell.*"

Clary was walking over with Isabelle. She looked wary. "Simon," she said. "This isn't like you."

"This isn't even your first trip to a hell dimension," Jace pointed out.

Simon turned around now, and Alec had expected to see tears, given the tone of Simon's voice. But there were no tears. Instead Simon's face burned with barely contained rage.

"It's too much," he said quietly. "It's too much gambling with people's lives." He wouldn't look at them. "With all your lives."

"Simon . . . ," said Clary again. "We've been through so much already and we're okay. You've been undead, you've been invulnerable. You're one of the only people alive to have seen an angel, and you've been in the presence of two different Princes of Hell. You killed Lilith!"

"The Mark of Cain killed Lilith," said Simon in a colorless tone. "I just happened to be there."

"Being a Shadowhunter—" Alec began to say, but to his surprise, Isabelle stopped him with a glare.

Simon lifted his head. He looked lost, distant. "We went through the Portal, gambling we'd be able to get back. You gave yourself to the demons," he added to Isabelle. He sounded sick. "You were gambling you'd be able to get away. Tian pretended to betray us. Gambling he'd be able to save Isabelle once Sammael wasn't watching him."

"But that all worked out," said Jace. "I mean, I guess we don't *know* how we'll get back from Diyu yet, but given all the Portals everywhere . . ."

"It's too much gambling," said Simon. "You can't win every time. Eventually you lose."

"But not yet," said Alec.

Simon glowered. "In May," he said, his voice shaking, "I watched George Lovelace die screaming. For no reason. He drank from the Mortal Cup and he burned and he died. He was no different than me. No less worthy of Ascension. If anything, he was more worthy than me."

No one spoke.

"It was the final lesson of the Academy," he said quietly. "Shadowhunters die. They just . . . die for no reason."

"It's a dangerous job," said Jace.

"George wasn't doing anything dangerous," Simon ground out. "He didn't die in a noble act of sacrifice; he didn't die because a demon got the better of him. He died because sometimes Shadowhunters die, and it isn't *for* anything. It just is. That was the lesson."

"Isabelle was rescued," said Alec. "*You're* rescued. Tian is okay."

"This time!" Simon laughed. "Yes, this time it worked out. What about next time? And by the way, next time is *tomorrow*. How do you do it?" he said, looked around at them helplessly. "How do you risk yourself and everyone you love, over and over again?"

Isabelle went to Simon and put her hands on his shoulders. He looked up into her eyes, searching for something there. Alec knew what he himself would say: that this was the gig. That being a Shadowhunter was a high and lonely task, that being chosen for such a purpose was a gift and a curse, that its risk was precisely why it was so important, that he had fought with Simon for years now and Simon was definitely, obviously worthy of being one of the Nephilim. He thought of Isabelle, her ferocity, her intensity, her commitment, and he expected her to say something like what he himself would say.

But she didn't. Instead she put her arms around Simon and hugged him tightly. "I don't know," she whispered. "I don't know. It doesn't always make sense, my love. Sometimes it makes no sense at all."

Simon made a low, choked sound, and buried his head against Isabelle's neck. She held him there, still and silent.

"I'm sorry," he said. "I'm sorry."

"He has to understand," Alec said very quietly.

Isabelle gave a tiny nod of her head. "He does understand," she said. "Just—give us one second, okay?"

Clary bit her lip. "I love you, Simon," she said. "I love you both."

She turned and walked away, and the others followed: as Simon's *parabatai*, in an odd sort of way, it was Clary's call. Alec could hear Isabelle murmuring softly to Simon, until they had moved far enough away that the sound disappeared.

"Isabelle's right," Clary said, once they had returned to the nave. "Simon knows—he's just hurting. It's only been a few months since he lost George." She leaned against one of the stone walls. "I wish I could do more. Be a better *parabatai*. Fighting alongside someone you love isn't just about fighting more effectively. It's also about supporting each other when things go wrong."

"We know exactly what you mean," Alec said, looking at Jace. "And you are a good *parabatai*, Clary. Watching you and Simon together—"

"It's like seeing the two of us," Jace said, indicating himself and Alec. "Strength and beauty. Perfect harmony. Skill and intuition, exactly matched."

Alec raised an eyebrow. "Are you strength or beauty?"

"I think we all know the answer to that," said Jace.

"You really are a very strange group of people," observed Tian.

Jace grinned. Alec knew he'd been trying to lighten the mood, and he'd succeeded. "Maybe we should find somewhere to sleep. I thought I saw some larger benches, down the other transept."

"How will we know to wake up?" Alec said, realizing. "It's not like the sun's going to rise down here."

Clary perked up, drawing her stele. "Let me see your arm," she said. Alec held it out and she scrawled a shape he hadn't seen before onto his arm, a circle with a number of radiating arms of different lengths curving in a spiral from its center. Clary counted under her breath as she drew it, then said, "There. Something I've been working on. Alarm rune. It'll go off in seven hours."

"Or you could use your phone," said Jace.

Clary shrugged. "Runes are more reliable. Also cooler."

"The Alliance rune is still your best work," said Alec, smiling.

"They can't all be world-savers," said Clary. "Sometimes you just need to wake up on time."

"No, I mean, it's the thing you were talking about," said Alec. "It lets us share our strength with each other. Not just our strength—our vulnerabilities, too."

Clary looked over at Magnus and then back at Alec. She smiled a little, though she was still clearly worried about Simon. "Well . . . I'm glad I could give that to you."

Jace took her hand, drawing her close. His arms went around her. Clary laid her head against Jace's shoulder, and he closed his eyes; Alec knew what he was feeling, for he felt it himself, whenever he was with Magnus. That inner wonder at the enormity of love, how the joy of it was so intense it was nearly tinged with pain. Jace rarely spoke of his feelings, but he didn't need to: Alec could read them on his face. Jace had chosen Clary to love, just as Alec had chosen Magnus, and he would love her forever and with his whole heart.

Jace brushed his lips against Clary's hair and released her; she took his hand. With a crooked smile, Jace mouthed "See you" to Alec, and headed off with Clary into the dark shadows in the depths of the cathedral.

"I suppose I should bid you good night as well," Tian began, then paused. Isabelle and Simon had descended the steps into the nave. They were holding hands, and Simon looked a little abashed.

"Sorry about that," he said.

"Don't worry about it," said Alec. "You said it yourself. It's been a day."

Tian and Magnus stepped back a bit, giving Alec a moment with his sister and Simon. Alec thought he saw the tracks of recent tears on Simon's face. It didn't make him respect Simon any less; in fact, he thought, he might respect him a little more.

Simon looked at him steadily. "I think I just have to get used to not being invulnerable anymore. It's not like being a vampire—or having the Mark of Cain—was a nonstop party, but it was a nice insurance policy. That's gone now." Simon straightened his shoulders. "I signed up to fight," he said. "I wanted to be a Shadowhunter so much. So now I am, and now I fight. It would be great if you didn't have to constantly work to preserve the things and the people you love, but . . . you do."

"That's being a Shadowhunter," said Alec.

Simon shook his head. "No, that's being a person. At least as a

Shadowhunter my work involves exotic travel and awesome hand-to-hand combat."

Isabelle kissed him on the cheek. "Never doubt that you are a badass, sweetie."

"See?" said Simon. "My life rules. My girlfriend has a flame whip! That's a true statement I just made."

"You two get out of here before my brotherly instincts kick in," Alec said, and the two of them went off to find someplace private to rest.

Alec looked around and saw Magnus engaged in conversation with Tian. Magnus had White Impermanence free of its sheath, and Tian was speaking intently while gesturing to it. Curious, Alec went to join them.

Magnus looked up as he joined them, and Alec was startled yet again by the changes in him. His face seemed narrower, his features sharper. His eyes glowed luminous green in the dim light. There was something hungry in his look, like a vampire who had not fed in a long time.

Alec knew that hunger was for the Svefnthorn's third strike, and he shuddered. It was easy to celebrate that they had saved Simon, that Tian hadn't betrayed them, that he had rescued Isabelle. That they were, at this instant, out of harm's way. It was easy to assume that they would find some solution for Magnus, some way to draw the thorn out of him, some loophole in the magic. But Simon was right: Sometimes things went bad. Sometimes there was suffering. Sometimes there was death. It was too late for Ragnor, for Shinyun, but what about Magnus?

Tian said, "May I see your sword?"

Alec shrugged and drew Black Impermanence. He handed it to Tian, who held the two swords next to one another and examined them.

"Do you know what it is you're wielding?" he said to both of them.

Alec thought. "Gan Jiang and Mo Ye . . . they said they weren't swords—they were gods."

"They're clearly swords," said Magnus. "Alec has been cutting through demons with his all day."

"They also said they were keys," said Alec.

Tian rolled his eyes. "They like being cryptic, Gan Jiang and Mo Ye. I guess they think it's their prerogative, given their age. I don't know what it means that they're keys," he admitted. "But they *are* gods. I meant to talk to you about it before . . ." He trailed off, not saying, *before Sammael revealed that I was working for him.* "But if we're heading toward a confrontation . . . you should know something of what they are. They may be our strongest weapon in this place."

"Maybe this is a stupid question," said Alec, "but if they're swords, how are they also gods?"

"The Heibai Wuchang," said Tian, "were a god in black, and a god in white, and long ago, they were responsible for escorting the spirits of the dead to Diyu. There are hundreds of stories about them, from all over China, but they are from long before the Nephilim, so we have no idea which, if any, are true."

"All the stories are true," Alec murmured to himself, and Magnus heard and quirked his mouth in a small smile.

"The faeries say that the Heibai Wuchang grew tired of being constantly bothered by mortals, who sought them out to ask for their wishes to be granted, and they retreated into these swords." Tian shook his head. "I don't know what it means that we have brought them back to their original home in Diyu, but if the smiths thought it was wisdom to do so, they must have had a reason."

"Maybe they thought the swords could hurt Sammael?" Alec suggested.

"Maybe they unlock a door and then we kick Sammael through it?" Magnus offered.

Tian said, "I don't know. I just thought that you should know what it is you're wielding. *Who* you're wielding." He held up the black sword and handed it back to Alec. "Fan Wujiu. Meaning: *there is no salvation for evildoers.*" He handed the white sword to Magnus. "Xie Bi'an: *be at peace, all those who atone.*"

"Some disagreement between the two of them, I see," Magnus said.

But Tian shook his head. "I don't think so. In some stories they are referred to as one being. Whatever they are, they are supposed to be in balance with one another."

"Aw, just like us," Magnus said, winking at Alec.

Alec *did* think of himself and Magnus as in balance, at least under normal circumstances. But was that still true? The thorn had invaded Magnus's body, had thrust him in the direction of its will—of Sammael's will, Alec reminded himself. Magnus was still Magnus, of course, but he *was* changing, and they didn't know of any way to change him back.

Alec strapped Black Impermanence—Fan Wujiu—back on and said to Tian, "Thanks. Now I'm prepared just in case my sword suddenly turns into a dude."

Tian said, "You never know." He looked out on the open space of the cathedral stretching behind them. "We should get some rest. This may be our only chance for it before we have to go back to the fight."

"There aren't going to be a lot of comfortable places here for shut-eye," said Magnus.

Tian said scornfully, "We're Shadowhunters. We can manage to rest even in the depths of Hell."

He made his way down the steps and disappeared deeper into the church. Alec turned to Magnus and said, "Shall we find a place to sleep too?"

"Let's," said Magnus, a small gleam in his eye.

* * *

THE OTHERS HAD GONE TO THE FAR ENDS OF THE cathedral's main floor, it seemed, so Magnus directed Alec downstairs, into the vaults. Magnus lit a globe of light to guide them down the stone steps and into a small room off the hallway that extended the length of the building. The globe of light was bright and scarlet, and washed the color from Alec's face as he walked next to Magnus, quiet and seemingly lost in thought.

The room was probably an office, in the real cathedral, but here in Diyu it was just another empty box, with a marble floor and whitewashed stone walls.

"Cozy," said Alec. "Do you think you could summon some comfy blankets?"

Magnus cocked an eyebrow. "From where, exactly? I got the rice and water from offerings to the dead, but the pickings are slim down here for luxury items."

Alec shrugged. "The . . . Hell of Comfy Blankets?"

Magnus thought. "I could . . . summon one of those nine-headed birds and we could try to pull off its feathers? No, they probably wouldn't smell very good. *Wait.*"

"What?"

Magnus giggled to himself and summoned himself a blanket from the one place in Diyu whose occupant he knew would prioritize a pleasant sleep experience.

A red brocade duvet popped into the room, in a puff of crimson smoke. It was lined with gold tassels.

"Is it a coincidence," said Alec, "that the duvet is the same color as your magic?"

"I . . . don't know," said Magnus.

He summoned a couple of pillows as well. Alec looked pleased.

They settled themselves down on the ground and placed themselves in their usual sleeping positions. Strange things, sleeping positions, Magnus thought. They get set at the beginning of a relationship, when nobody is thinking about it, and then they are set forever. But now it was true: if Magnus was in bed, as long as Alec was lying directly to his right, there was something of home, wherever he was.

"Before you put out the light," Alec said.

Magnus waited for the rest, but when it didn't come, he said, "Yes?" Alec looked hesitant. "What is it?" He was beginning to be a little alarmed.

"Before you go tomorrow . . . to be bait."

Magnus blinked a few times. "Are you having trouble finishing your thoughts?"

"No," said Alec, sounding put out. "I think we should use the Alliance rune."

"What Alliance rune?"

"*The* Alliance rune," Alec said. "*Clary's* Alliance rune. That allows a paired Shadowhunter and Downworlder to share power."

Clary had invented the Alliance rune three years ago, in the Mortal War, to give Shadowhunters and Downworlders the ability to fight as a pair, sharing their skills and their strengths. Magnus vividly remembered the eve of battle years ago. He'd been jangling with nerves, the prospect of death on the battlefield before him, and he'd felt heavy with sorrow. He'd told this young Shadowhunter he loved him, but he didn't know how that Shadowhunter truly felt about him, whether their relationship could endure or whether it was as impossible as he feared.

He'd watched the rune forming on his own skin, the intricate lines and curves of an angelic rune something he never would have thought he would bear.

But now—now it was Magnus's turn to say, *"No."*

"You don't have to do this alone," insisted Alec. "You should take some of my strength. I should take some of the burden of the thorn."

"We have no idea what it would do," said Magnus. "What it would mean for you to take some of this weird magic. It's connected to Sammael somehow, and you're full of, you know, angel magic. You might explode."

Alec blinked. "I probably wouldn't *explode*."

"Who knows what could happen? Neither of us is exactly an expert on this particular magical artifact."

"Still," said Alec mulishly. "I think we should do it." When Magnus didn't say anything, he added, "If I'm going to let you go out there and demand to be attacked, at least let me share some of the burden with you."

Magnus looked into Alec's eyes. "If something happens to me," he said very quietly, "Max will need you."

"If we put the rune on and something's going wrong," said Alec, "we'll scratch it out. It'll be fine."

Magnus sighed. "I have to give in on this," he said, "because I said 'it'll be fine' about the bait thing and you agreed, right?"

"There are some who would consider that a valid argument, yes," said Alec.

Magnus stretched out his arm. "Okay. Why not one more totally irresponsible thing before we close out the day?"

Alec drew the strokes of the rune with attentive care, and Magnus felt the same wonder as he had years ago, the same calming of fear. On the eve of battle, amid the darkened spin of a strange infernal city: it made no difference where they were. They would fight and live and die together.

As Alec finished the last loop of the rune on his own skin, Magnus watched him carefully. After a moment he said, "How do you feel?"

Alec looked uncertain. He lifted his arm up and held it out for Magnus to see. The Angelic Power rune on the inside of his forearm was glowing, a dark but definite red color.

"That's new," he said.

"Other than that?"

Alec waited. "Nothing," he said. "I feel fine." Experimentally, he drew a quick Awareness rune on the same arm, just a simple loop and line. They both watched it for a long moment, but it just seemed to be a regular rune, behaving normally.

"It seems to be okay," said Magnus.

"It does," murmured Alec. Then he leaned forward to kiss Magnus.

Magnus kissed him back, expecting a simple good-night kiss, but instead Alec reached out and tangled his hands in Magnus's wild hair, pulling him closer and deepening the kiss into something much stronger, something wild, almost ferocious.

Alec's arm slipped down and wrapped around Magnus's waist, pulling his boyfriend on top of him. Magnus growled low in his throat: the feel of Alec's body stretched along his always made him wild. He kissed Alec deeply, reveling in the scrape of his stubble, the softness of his lips; Alec gasped and clutched at Magnus's back, pulling him closer, as close as they could be.

Magnus paused. "How do you feel?" he said, his lips moving against Alec's.

Alec thought. "Worried about you."

"No," said Magnus, rolling them both over, so Alec was on top of *him*. "I mean, how do you feel about *this*?"

He slid his hand down and did a thing he knew Alec liked.

"*Ohhh*," said Alec. "Oh! Uh, I'm definitely interested in *this*. But still worried about you," he added. His beautiful eyes looked directly into Magnus's. "Just keep it in mind. You're my heart, Magnus Bane. Stay unbroken, for me."

"Noted," said Magnus, doing the thing he knew Alec liked again, and put out the light.

CHAPTER SEVENTEEN

Heibai Wuchang

IT WASN'T A BETRAYAL, MAGNUS TOLD HIMSELF; NOT really. But he knew that he would never get a chance to do what he wanted to do, with the Shadowhunters along with him. He could probably have convinced them to let him and Alec go together, but . . . as much as he didn't want to admit it, Alec would be a liability in this situation too, for what he had in mind.

And Alec would never let him go on his own.

Alec would be right, probably.

But Magnus knew what he was doing. At least, he thought he knew what he was doing.

Alec slept on in the pitch-black of the cathedral office. It had been perhaps five hours since they had fallen asleep, but when Magnus woke up, he had done so feeling energized, rested, ready to go.

He would go and come back before Alec even noticed, he told himself.

Magnus had always been good at seeing in the dark, and in the last few days his vision had become even keener. He needed no illumination to guide him as he dressed in the lightless room, careful to remain quiet as he strapped his shoulder harness on.

With a gesture, a darkened surface appeared before him, a shimmering mirror. In that dark glass, Magnus saw his own face. He saw the darkness writhing at his throat and in his eyes. The worst was the razor gleam of his teeth, the way they seemed to pull his face into an entirely new shape.

Magnus knew a mundane story about a witch's mirror that had broken into pieces: when a piece lodged in a child's heart, that heart would turn to ice. He could feel the magic of the thorn twisting in his chest, as if it were a key opening a door he'd tried to keep shut. He didn't need to glance down at his hands to see the veins standing out in red and black, or the marks of chains growing stronger. He could *feel* the subtle, terrible alteration of his being as his blood itself changed.

He had to do *something*. This was something.

Before he left, he held out a hand and gestured toward himself. Slowly, without a sound, Black Impermanence rose into the air from where Alec had carefully laid it down next to him. Careful not to disturb Alec or even the blankets, Magnus turned the sword in the air and floated it toward him. He held his breath, but in a moment Fan Wujiu was in his hand. He waited to see if he would explode; the smiths hadn't said anything about being worthy to wield both swords at once.

Nothing happened. Maybe the Alliance rune, he thought, made him able to wield Alec's sword. Maybe the rules were slipperier than some faeries had let on. Maybe both. He started breathing again and carefully placed the Black Impermanence on his back, next to its twin.

At the door he turned and looked back at Alec. And at the top of the stairs to the nave, he looked for a long time at the breathing quiet of Xujiahui. They were in the depths of Hell, and this cathedral was only the shadow of something real. Nevertheless Magnus felt the hush of holiness, of faith like a light in the darkness. It pervaded the cavern of the church, even here a sanctuary. Perhaps their last sanctuary.

FOUR HUNDRED YEARS AGO, MAGNUS HAD HAD ONLY one friend in the world: Ragnor Fell. Ragnor had taught him what it was to be a warlock: power, yes, the ability to twist space and time to your own ends, yes, but also loneliness, constant danger, a life of wandering. A warlock would never find a warm welcome, Ragnor told him. Even other Downworlders would not trust him. Shadowhunters could capture him, torture him, kill him with impunity. Vampires had clans and werewolves had packs and faeries had courts, but a warlock stood always alone.

There was a time when Magnus found himself in the city of Leonberg. Magnus did not like Leonberg. He had seen very little of the Holy Roman Empire, but based on his experience here, he was prepared to call it grossly overrated: the weather cold and damp, the food heavy and dull, the people suspicious and parochial. He had come at the request of a minor landholder who wanted Magnus to improve his crop yields and the fecundity of his pigs, for much more coin than such magic deserved. Magnus had executed the task in a matter of about fifteen minutes, and now sat drinking insipid beer in the garden of an insipid bar. This bar had a lovely view of Leonberg's prison tower, which squatted like an angry troll under a gunmetal sky. He sighed, he drank, he dreamed of magic as yet unmade that would allow him to disappear from this place and reappear in a warm, cozy place, perhaps Paris, or somewhere in southern Italy.

His reverie was disrupted by a commotion from the direction of the prison. A group of men in local livery were dragging a disheveled woman out. They hustled her around the side of the prison and vanished from sight. As they did, Magnus noted that the woman was glamoured, and that under the glamour she had blue skin.

He sipped his beer. His hand shook. In his mind, Ragnor's voice told him sternly that he should look out for himself, that he had nothing to gain from risking his own well-being for a stranger.

He sipped his beer again.

With an abrupt decisive movement, he slammed his glass down on the table, stood up, cursed loudly in Malay, French, and Arabic, and strode purposefully in the direction of the prison and the blue warlock.

Centuries later, he could still remember her screams as her hair caught fire. He broke into a run as he heard a man's voice sternly proclaim that by the order of the Leonberg judiciary, the woman was guilty of witchcraft and cavorting with devils, and was therefore sentenced to be put to death by the flame.

There were a few locals there to gawk, but witch burning was no longer much of a novelty in these parts, and the day was unpleasant. Nobody got in Magnus's way as he charged toward the bonfire, now spreading orange gouts of flame well above the blue warlock's head. Nobody stopped him as he spoke words of magical protection, unsure whether they would even work, or as he braced a boot on the stacked crackling wood and vaulted up into the pyre.

His flesh may have been protected, but his clothes immediately caught fire. He shrugged off the discomfort and grasped hold of the ropes binding the woman, dissolving them with sparks of blue magic. The woman wheeled her gaze toward him and caught sight of his cat's eyes. She had a look of terror mingled with surprise as he wrapped his arms around her and made to leap off the pyre.

"Hello," he murmured in her ear. "When we hit the ground, please roll back and forth to put the flames out."

Without waiting for her reply, he jumped, taking her with him. They thudded into the cold mud next to the bonfire. While it did put out the flames, by the time they stood up their clothes were blackened and falling off, a development Magnus had not antici-pated. He could, of course, summon up new clothing, but these didn't seem the sort of people in front of whom it was wise to do magic.

The soldiers overseeing the execution had been frozen in bewil-derment so far, but now were recovering themselves and drawing their swords.

Magnus looked at the woman. "Now what?" he shouted over the roar of the fire and the exclamations of the crowd.

The woman goggled at him. *"Now what?"* she yelled. "This is *your rescue!*"

"I've never done this before!" he yelled back.

"How about we *run?*" the woman suggested. Magnus stared at her stupidly for a moment, and she shook her head. "Good God, I've been rescued by an idiot!" She turned toward the crowd and held out her hands, and billows of blue smoke emerged from her palms, spreading in thick clouds quickly. The soldiers' yelling became more confused.

"Yes! Good idea!" Magnus said. The woman rolled her eyes and ran. Magnus followed, wondering how fast they could find shelter and whether that tailor in Venice would have enough of that bro-cade material to make him a replacement for his coat.

Ragnor caught up with them many hours later, at a tavern on the road to Tübingen. By that point they had found new clothes and Magnus had learned some things about the woman he'd rescued. Her name was Catarina Loss; she had come to Leonberg to treat an outbreak of plague; she had been caught laying glowing hands on a patient and had been immediately arrested as a witch. Leonberg, she explained, was just mad for witch burning.

"Everywhere in Europe is mad for witch burning," Ragnor said, ill-tempered. He was angry at Magnus, but equally obviously liked

Catarina, and the two of them had quickly fallen into as pleasant a rapport as Magnus had with either of them. Unfortunately, their favorite topic so far was how stupid Magnus had been for attempting the rescue.

"I saved your life!" he protested.

"And a very careful, understated saving it was," Ragnor said. "How do you think I found you? Within minutes the whole area was buzzing with rumors of a vile magician swooping through the sky over Leonberg on a black cloud, flying through flame and carrying a foul witch out of the fire meant to sanctify her."

"So we stay out of the Holy Roman Empire for a while." Magnus shrugged, grinning. "I won't miss it."

"It takes up half of Europe, Magnus."

"Very overrated, Europe."

Catarina interrupted this to put a hand on Magnus's arm. "Thank you, though, truly," she said. "It is terrible to be a warlock in these times."

"I am fairly new to the experience myself," said Magnus. "But Ragnor here says we must go our own ways."

"We can rescue one another, though," said Catarina. "Since no one else will rescue us. Not other Downworlders, not mundanes, and certainly not Shadowhunters."

"May they all rot in hell," put in Ragnor. But his expression softened. "I'll go fetch us a great deal more to drink. And I'm not against traveling together, for safety. For now. I don't generally hold with making friends."

"And yet," said Magnus, "you were my first friend."

Catarina gave him a small smile. "Perhaps I will be your friend too. Someone has to stop you from making a complete fool of yourself."

"Hear, hear," said Ragnor, draining his glass. "You're an idiot."

"I like him," Catarina told Ragnor. "There is something

righteous about someone who doesn't turn away from danger, even when he should. Someone who sees suffering and will always choose to plunge into the flames."

By morning, they were all friends. The whole world had changed since then, but that hadn't changed.

MAGNUS'S KNOWLEDGE OF SHANGHAI GEOGRAPHY WAS A little rusty, and he was turned around in the starless emptiness of Diyu, but since he could apparently fly now, he let himself drift over the reversed city until he found what he was looking for.

The temple was small and, like everything else in Diyu, ruined. It had been a humble building to begin with, a simple one-room structure of ochre-stained brick walls, its roof plain and undecorated. Back in actual Shanghai, it had probably been built for a single family.

There was a mark across the side, a slash of black paint that looked familiar. It was the same design that had been graffitied on the side of the modern apartment complex that the Tracking rune had led them to, in their initial hunt for Ragnor.

Magnus climbed the steps and peered into the open front door.

The room inside was fairly bare. An oil lamp hung from the ceiling, illuminating the plain wooden chair where Ragnor sat, glaring, in a shabby robe belted over trousers. He had evidently been expecting Magnus.

"You stole my blankets," he said sourly.

"And a couple of pillows," Magnus said. "You know how hard it is to find any kind of textiles in this place?"

"I know very well," said Ragnor. "Unless you like sleeping on old tapestries crispy with bloodstains."

Magnus looked more closely around the room. There was a simple platform in one corner, which Magnus assumed had been

Ragnor's bed before Magnus had stolen all the linens off it. There was a small wooden table, on which was, not surprisingly, the Book of the White. Ragnor's chair had been placed facing the front door, as if Ragnor had been sitting and waiting for hours. He might have been.

Magnus stood in the doorway. He hadn't really made a plan that went further than this. "I wouldn't have guessed that you would have done it," he said cautiously. "Taken the third thorn of your own free will, I mean."

"Sorry to disappoint you." Ragnor's eyes gleamed. "When it came to it, I decided that I didn't want to die. Nor should you."

"Well," said Magnus, casting his gaze around at the dingy interior of the temple. "Now that I've seen the perks that come with the job, how could I resist?"

Ragnor sighed.

Magnus could stand it no longer. "When you faked your death. In Idris. You told me you would contact me," he blurted. "And then you didn't. I assumed—"

"You assumed that Sammael had caught me," said Ragnor. "You were right, of course."

"I assumed you were dead," Magnus said.

Ragnor shrugged. "I could have been. For a while, I might as well have been."

It was so strange, talking to Ragnor like this. He sounded like— well, he sounded like *Ragnor*, Magnus's first and oldest friend, who had done more than anyone to make Magnus into who he was. But Magnus could see the star of red light gleaming against Ragnor's chest, and he knew that as gruff and familiar as Ragnor's demeanor might be, he had become Sammael's creature, maybe irrevocably.

His curiosity was too great not to continue this conversation, though he knew he might not have time, that perhaps Shinyun or Sammael even now knew he was here. But he had to know. The question had eaten at him for too long now. "What happened?" he said.

"Shinyun happened," Ragnor said. "Take a seat."

There was another plain wooden chair next to the open door, and Magnus dragged it over and sat across from Ragnor, like he was interviewing him on a talk show.

"Sammael was looking for me," Ragnor said. "He was still mostly Void, and looking for a demon realm in which he could become embodied and make his plans. My name reached his ears."

"I remember," Magnus said. "So you faked your death during the Mortal War and fled."

"Quite. Most people didn't believe it could be the real Sammael who had returned, but Shinyun did. She found me, and she stuck me in a cage."

"A *cage*?" said Magnus.

"A cage," confirmed Ragnor. "It was not my most dignified moment. This was before Shinyun had sworn fealty to Sammael, you understand. But she knew about him. She knew about the way he'd been banished, knew he was able to return in brief, faint bursts. Knew he'd been looking for me. I was the bait she thought she could attract his attention with." He smiled bitterly. "It worked."

Magnus was uncomfortably aware of the concept of "bait" as a central axis of his and his friends' own plan.

Ragnor went on. "She told me about how she had met you and Alec Lightwood, how she had been rejected by Asmodeus. How, in the end, you took pity on her. And rather than bringing her to the Spiral Labyrinth, or letting the Nephilim have her, Alec let her go."

Magnus let out a deep breath. "Alec *is* the one who let her go," he said, "because he is a better person than almost anyone else I know. He told me about it when we got home from Italy. I think we both hoped that Shinyun would take that mercy as an opportunity to rethink her choices. To think about a different path than just seeking the most powerful entity available and declaring her loyalty to it."

"Well, it didn't work," Ragnor snapped, in a way that was so ordinary for him that Magnus almost smiled. "Shinyun understood that mercy to be from both of you, and she understood it as a pointed message about your power over her. A mockery of her. That holding her life in your hands, and letting her go, was toying with her. The way a cat toys with a rat."

"What did you think?" Magnus said quietly.

Ragnor snorted. "I thought you had done her a totally undeserved favor, and the least she could do was show some gratitude. She didn't like that."

"I bet she didn't," said Magnus.

"When Lilith died, it drove Sammael from the Void and into Shinyun's arms. So to speak. He ordered Shinyun to recover the Svefnthorn. And you know what happened next." Ragnor shifted in his chair. "Shinyun and Sammael came to me together, with the thorn. Before Sammael struck me the first time, he told me it would increase my power, and that I would need that power to find him a realm. I refused, because at that time I did not fully grasp either Sammael's or the thorn's power and thought that some other path might exist than serving him. It didn't, of course."

Magnus said nothing.

"He struck me a second time, drawing a Greek cross upon my heart. I felt power surge within me. It was . . . a heady experience. I became briefly intoxicated with power and burst the bars of my cage. I meant to make my escape, but Sammael stopped me." He smiled, as if nostalgic for a beloved memory. "I should have known better than to challenge him.

"Shinyun demanded to be thorned as well. Sammael allowed her to take the thorn, but he explained the way the thorn's magic worked: that she would need a third strike, and to become his servant forever, or the thorn would burn her very life out. She grabbed the thorn and took the third wound upon her without hesitation."

"And you?" said Magnus.

"I resisted, of course," Ragnor said. "I was frustrated, and willful, and did not yet understand the situation. Once I did, I took the thorn willingly. I did not want to die, after all." He gave Magnus a stern look. "You do not want to die either, Magnus. There is no reason to martyr yourself to the cause of the angels just to make a point. We are Lilith's creatures, after all, you and I, and it is fitting that we serve her eternal consort."

"I won't betray Alec," Magnus said. "Or Max."

"There's no need to betray *Max*," Ragnor scoffed. "He is Lilith's child just as much as either of us. He would thrive, on Sammael's Earth. As for Alec . . . well, that's your mistake, I suppose. I told you long ago, many times, that the life of a warlock is a lonely one, and that pretending otherwise leads only to sorrow. And now here is that sorrow, come for you as we both always knew it would."

Magnus was silent, watching the play of light on the bare floor. After a long time, Ragnor sighed. "The rest of the story you can guess. I used my increased power, I found Diyu for Sammael, he took it over, and he began his preparations for war."

"Ragnor." Magnus leaned forward. "Even if I can't save myself . . . I can save you. You don't need to remain here in Diyu. You don't need to serve Sammael—or anybody else. I can free you." *I think. Maybe.* He stood up from the chair, and slowly he drew the two swords, the White Impermanence and the Black, from where they were strapped to his back.

He had a hunch. It was a very vague hunch, but he'd acted on less. Rarely when the stakes were this high, though.

He briefly worried Ragnor would attack him, but the other warlock didn't move. "If by that you mean you can kill me, I think you'll find you can't, here in Diyu." Ragnor's voice was melancholy.

"I am under too much of Sammael's protection, and this place too full of his power."

"I'm not going to kill you," said Magnus, although he had to admit that if someone said that to him while pointing two swords at him, he probably wouldn't believe them.

"Even if you could release me from the thorn," Ragnor said, "you cannot *save* me. I have done too much, under Sammael's command, to atone for now. Neither the Spiral Labyrinth nor Idris would ever allow me my freedom, even if the Archangel Michael came down and slew Sammael a second time, in front of my eyes." He looked curious. "I hope *that* wasn't your plan."

"No," said Magnus. He turned the swords so that he was holding them with the flats of both blades toward the sky. "Do you know these swords?"

"I don't," Ragnor grumbled, "but I bet you're going to tell me about them."

"This one," said Magnus, holding up the black sword, "says that there is no salvation for evildoers. This one"—he held up the white—"says that those who atone will be at peace."

"So they contradict one another," said Ragnor. "Is that meant to be somehow meaningful?"

But Magnus wasn't listening closely. He felt his magic flow in and through the swords, and he thought, *Heibai Wuchang. Master Fan, Master Xie. Your home has been taken, and the magic of the Svefnthorn flows through this place, where it was never meant to be. Your king Yanluo is gone, and he will not return. But if you drive the Svefnthorn from this warlock before you, I will release you back into Diyu, to serve it however you desire. Only do this one thing for me.*

After a moment, Ragnor said dryly, "Is something supposed to be happening? Your eyes are closed."

Magnus felt the swords jerk in his hands.

His eyes flew open. A glow had formed around the swords, not the crimson radiance of the thorn's magic but something totally different, white smoke and black smoke intermingling in the air between them.

The swords wished to be together. Magnus felt them pull toward each other, like magnets. He watched in fascination as they transformed, from inert, inanimate objects to moving, visibly living things. As though they had never been inanimate at all, but only sleeping.

Magnus hoped they didn't mind too much that they had been stuck through a number of disgusting demon bodies in the past couple of days.

He released the hilts of both swords, and they drifted in the air toward one another, each seeking its mate.

In the middle they joined, blade alongside blade, and then they began to bend and twist around one another. Ragnor was simply staring at the swords, a look of utter astonishment on his face. He made eye contact with Magnus, and Magnus shrugged to indicate he didn't know what was happening either.

Light poured from the swords, and as their spinning and writhing ceased, Magnus could see that where there had been two there was now only one sword. He was sad to note that it was not actually twice the size of the other swords, but it was impressive regardless. The entire hilt was bright black horn, with the cross guard carved into twisting shapes that quite closely resembled Ragnor's horns— his old horns, not the new spiked monstrosities that the thorn had made. The blade was of bone, smooth and long and, Magnus could tell, very sharp.

He had just enough time to admire the sword's beauty before it plunged forward and ran Ragnor through.

Ragnor was thrown backward, his robe falling open. Magnus could see the third thorn mark now, a line cutting through the "Greek cross" of the first two wounds. The sword had plunged into the center of the convergence of scars, light shimmering out from the place the metal entered Ragnor's flesh.

Magnus dropped down to his knees immediately, next to Ragnor. His old friend didn't seem able to see him—his eyes were staring straight ahead, filmed with a white blindness. Ragnor's back arched, and the sword began to slide deeper into his chest, sinking slowly down. An acrid cloud of red mist drifted upward from the wound. It became denser and fuller, and then it was pouring from Ragnor's eyes, too, and his nostrils, and his open mouth.

Magnus leaned back. He didn't know if breathing the magic fog was actually a problem, but he thought it was better not to risk it.

The sword penetrated through Ragnor's chest up to the hilt, and then just kept going, the hilt, too, passing through his chest as if through water. The red mist came out of his chest in spasmodic coughs, and then the sword was gone, and the red mist dissipated, and Ragnor was still.

For a moment, there was only the sound of Magnus's breathing, terribly loud in his own ears.

But Ragnor wasn't dead. His chest, Magnus saw, was rising and falling. Not a lot. Not powerfully. But enough.

After what felt like a very long moment, Ragnor blinked his eyes open. He looked around until his gaze found Magnus, over to his right.

"You," said Ragnor, "are a terrible fool."

Magnus cocked his head, unsure what this statement said about Ragnor's current evil-or-not-evil status. He did note that Ragnor's horns were back to their normal size. His eyes and his teeth, also, seemed more familiar.

"You had the power of gods in your hands," Ragnor said. "They spoke to me. You could have wielded them in any number of ways against Sammael. And you *wasted* them on, of all things, un-thorning *me*."

Magnus laughed, unable to stop himself. He leaned over and grabbed Ragnor into a tight bear hug.

"I assume," said Magnus after a moment, "that you're tolerating being hugged for this long because you are suffused with your love for me as your dearest friend and also your savior, and not because you are too weak to get away."

"Think what you like," said Ragnor.

Magnus pulled away and examined Ragnor's chest from several angles. The thorn scars were, as far as he could tell, completely gone. Unfortunately, so were the swords.

Ragnor drew himself up onto his elbows. "The Black and White Impermanence," he said, shaking his head in disbelief. "Where in all the realms of this universe did you get them?"

"You'll forgive me," said Magnus, "if I don't say. I'm only around seventy-five percent sure you're no longer under Sammael's thrall."

Ragnor shook his head somberly. "It was the wrong call, Magnus. Saving me. You'd have been better off using the power of the Heibai Wuchang to stop Sammael, or even to delay him or change his plans. I'd be better off left behind here. I told you, I've done too many things that cannot be atoned for."

Magnus held up his two palms and mimed balancing a scale. "No salvation for evildoers. Those who atone, be at peace. I'm sorry, Ragnor, but the death gods have decided, and they say, be at peace."

"Do you believe everything death gods tell you?" said Ragnor sternly.

Magnus helped him to his feet. "Are they gone, do you think? Did I . . . did I use them up?"

Ragnor said, "You can't keep a god down, Magnus. They are Black and White Impermanence. You know, impermanent. After a time they'll re-form in Diyu, I'm sure." He looked around at the temple, as though he'd just noticed how dilapidated and grimy it was.

"Ragnor," Magnus said, "was stealing the Book of the White absolutely necessary? Did Sammael demand it?"

Ragnor looked over at the Book on the table and started, as though he had forgotten it was there. Then he turned back to Magnus and barked a laugh. "No. It was Shinyun's idea."

Magnus's eyebrows went up. "He *doesn't* want it?"

"Well, no, he does," Ragnor allowed. "He wants us to use it to weaken Earth's wards, the ones put in place after he tried to invade the first time. So he can get back in." He gave a wry look. "But Shinyun was *very* committed to the idea of retrieving it."

"Because she wanted to come visit me?" Magnus said.

"Not everything is about *you*, Magnus," Ragnor said sternly. "Although yes, Shinyun has . . . complicated feelings where you're concerned. But I think she wanted the Book for her own purposes. She may be Sammael's favorite pet, but I know her, and she definitely is playing her own game, separate from Sammael's."

"That's exactly what I said!" Magnus exclaimed, gratified. "I said those exact words, 'playing her own game.' So, *what* game? A hedge against the possibility of his failure?"

"Setting the stage for her own success," Ragnor said. He stood up. "My stars," he said, "I can't believe I accepted this kind of accommodation just because I was willing to serve Sammael. What a dump."

"I can't promise it's any more comfortable," said Magnus, "but let me take you back to Saint Ignatius. Well, Reverse Saint Ignatius. All the Shadowhunters are taking sanctuary there."

Ragnor hesitated. "I suppose I must," he said. "Atonement has to begin somewhere. And Sammael isn't going to just let me go back home." He looked a bit lost. "My home . . . ," he said. "I can't return there anyway."

"Let's go," Magnus said. "We can discuss your future when we get there."

Ragnor retrieved the Book of the White. He pressed it into Magnus's hands, and Magnus took it. He didn't feel like he was finally receiving one of his possessions back; he felt like this was just the latest laying of this burden on his shoulders. Nevertheless, he carefully shrank the Book down to a manageable size and tucked it away in his pocket.

As soon as they left down the path away from the temple, Magnus could tell that Ragnor was in a weakened state. He walked slowly and placed his feet carefully, as though he wasn't sure they would reliably obey him.

After a few minutes of walking in silence, in the dark, with Magnus at least fairly sure they were headed the right way, Ragnor spoke up. "Magnus, I don't know any way to undo the thorning. Now that the swords are gone, I don't know how it could be drawn out of you. Or Shinyun, for that matter, not that she wants it removed. You'll still be stuck with the choice, soon enough, to join Sammael or die."

"Then I'll die," said Magnus.

"You won't," said Ragnor with a sigh. "No one chooses to die, when there is a choice to live. You rationalize. You justify."

Magnus said nothing. There had been a change in the dead air of Diyu. Where before all had been stillness and oppressive silence, now a slight wind had picked up. It blew faint white noise into the silence, and unpleasantly hot air in irregular gusts around Magnus's face. Ragnor noticed it too, his head lifting when it started, but after a moment his eyes returned to the ground and he resumed walking.

"So," Ragnor said, "Max." He cleared his throat. "Your son."

"He's named after Alec's brother," Magnus said. "The one who was killed by Sebastian."

Ragnor gave him a wry look. "Did you know, Sammael showed up in the first place because he was trying to reach Valentine Morgenstern's son, Sebastian? Lilith suggested that Sammael seek him out. Said they had similar goals. Anyway, apparently Sebastian was dead well before Sammael could have found him. That would have been interesting."

"'Interesting' is one way to describe it," said Magnus. He paused. "Ragnor. One thing that happened, that you probably don't know." He just had to say it quickly. "Raphael . . . he died."

Ragnor stopped walking, and Magnus stopped beside him. All around them blew the faint, dry wind of Diyu, smelling of iron and char.

"Valentine's son, Sebastian," Magnus said. "He, uh, he took over Edom."

"Oh, I know," Ragnor said, his eyebrows raised. "I didn't hear the end of it. You think Sammael would be here if he could be in Edom? He loves it there. But—Raphael."

Magnus took a deep breath. "Sebastian was holding us both prisoner. He ordered Raphael to kill me. Raphael refused. Sebastian killed him." He looked at Ragnor, who appeared to be going through all the stages of grief at once, his expression flashing rapidly stunned surprise, sorrow, anger, thoughtfulness, and back. "He was paying back his debt to me, he said. For saving his life."

Ragnor took a long breath and collected himself. "Every war has a body count," he said bitterly. "And if you live long enough, you'll see too many friends become part of that body count. Poor Raphael. I always liked him."

"He always liked you," said Magnus.

"I get the sense," said Ragnor after a moment of silence from both of them, the roar of the hot wind of Diyu the only sound in the world, "that it is a good thing that Sammael wasn't able to meet Sebastian."

"I don't know if they would have been able to collaborate," Magnus said. "Neither of them are exactly good team players."

"How did you come to adopt Max?"

"It's a long story," said Magnus, "which I will tell you in full once we are safely out of Hell."

"Well, tell the short version," Ragnor said impatiently. He began walking again, and Magnus followed.

"Another warlock baby abandoned," said Magnus flatly. "Another horrified parent. They left a note that said, 'Who could ever love it?'"

Ragnor snorted. "The oldest warlock story."

"He was left at Shadowhunter Academy," Magnus said. "I was a guest lecturer there. We ended up going home with Max."

"Truly," said Ragnor, "this is the culmination of your foolish dedication to rescuing people."

Magnus gave him an incredulous look. "*You're* one to talk."

"Not that I'm not grateful," Ragnor allowed.

"That's not what I mean," Magnus said. "I don't mean *now*. I mean you're one to talk because all those hundreds of years ago, *you* rescued *me*. You idiot."

The wind was picking up and, worryingly, growing hotter. They walked along the darkened streets, past empty black shells of buildings Magnus couldn't have identified—presumably, they corresponded to buildings in Shanghai, but here they resided in complete shadow and could barely be distinguished from the landscape around them.

Ragnor said gruffly, "Well, at least that's one more warlock who will grow up with loving parents. Who know about Downworld." Magnus knew that coming from Ragnor, this was effusive praise. "Pity about the Shadowhunter influence, though."

"Hey," said Magnus. "I was taught by the Silent Brothers, you know."

"Yes, and look how *that* turned out," said Ragnor.

Magnus was silent for a time and they walked. Even here in

Hell, there was something companionable about walking alongside Ragnor, as he had done so many times before. Even with the thorn burning in his chest, even with no clear way back home.

"I'm going to marry Alec, you know," he said after a while.

Ragnor raised his eyebrows. "When?"

"I don't know. Not yet. The Shadowhunters wouldn't acknowledge it, but we're hoping that will change."

"How would it change?" said Ragnor in a dismissive tone.

"Because we'll change it," said Magnus.

Ragnor shook his head. He looked weary. Magnus suspected that at some point, the full horror of what he had done would strike Ragnor. Right now he seemed insulated by shock. "Where you got your hopefulness, I have no idea. I certainly didn't teach that to you."

"When we can get married and have it recognized, then we'll do it," said Magnus. "Only then. When it's legal for me to marry Alec. For Tian to marry Jinfeng."

"For Shinyun to marry Sammael," Ragnor said dryly, and Magnus choked a laugh, until they turned the next corner and the laugh was cut off.

Ahead of them stood St. Ignatius. It was blowing away.

Here, the hot wind they'd felt before was stronger. It danced around their heads, and, whipped into a frenzy, tore pieces of the cathedral loose and hurled them up into the empty sky. Huge chunks of marble and brick tore free, making a racket of grinding, crashing, and scraping noises. One of the two spires was gone, disappeared into the whirlwind. But what really worried Magnus was the roof.

The roof was missing—no, not missing. The roof was now in pieces, free-floating, huge boulders of tile and stone, as though some great creature had come and torn the church open, like a child unwrapping a present. The chunks of roof hung in the wind, suspended and drifting. It was hard to tell for sure, but if Magnus squinted, he thought he could see a human figure flying around the rocks, swooping and climbing.

Ragnor called, "Alec!" and Magnus looked back at the ground, where Alec, his Alec, was running full tilt toward them, soot on his face. He was yelling something, but Magnus couldn't make it out.

Only as he got closer could he be understood. "The swords!" he was yelling. *"We need the swords!"*

CHAPTER EIGHTEEN

Avici

ALEC DIDN'T KNOW WHAT HAD BECOME OF HIS FRIENDS. He had been awoken by a tremendous sound, like an earthquake, and by the time he had made it up the stairs, the roof had been torn off the cathedral. Above him, against the inky black curtain of Diyu's sky, two figures cavorted. One of them was Shinyun, who in addition to her elongated limbs had now sprouted a pair of broad insectile wings, iridescent and veined, like a dragonfly's. She looped around the floating pieces of the cathedral's roof, clearly enjoying herself.

The other figure was Sammael. He was hard to miss, as he was now easily three times the size he'd been on the iron bridge, floating above Shinyun and looking perfectly at home suspended in the air. He peered into the cathedral from above, occasionally pushing away rocks that drifted into his vision.

Alec had thought it would be unwise to run across the entire length of the cathedral, directly in view of Sammael, to reach his friends. He had to hope that they were seeking some kind of safety. But where was Magnus? He had departed voluntarily: his clothes and shoes were gone. But why had he taken Alec's sword as well as his own?

The wind, though it was not too strong for him to resist, seemed to be harming the church, which was beginning to come apart in pieces. Alec had known he had to get out of the building, skirting around to avoid being seen until he'd found a low enough opening in the rapidly decaying walls. He hurled himself through it in a forward roll, curled up to protect his head. He'd felt the hot, corrosive wind on him, and then he was clear.

The Alliance rune had burned on his arm, and he had felt Magnus's presence, not far away. He could see Magnus's glow in his mind, even through the dark and the wind. He ran toward that glow.

Now he had reached Magnus and, to his surprise, Ragnor, who looked subdued and embarrassed at the sight of Alec. For a moment Alec had worried that perhaps Magnus had been struck a third time by the thorn, that he was with Ragnor because, like Ragnor, he had been lost. But then, as he approached, Magnus and Ragnor began talking at the same time, and it was clear that Ragnor was out from under Sammael's control, somehow.

Magnus explained quickly about the swords, that they had saved Ragnor, that they were now gone. When he finished, he hesitated and said, "Are you angry?"

"Of course I'm not angry that you used the swords to save Ragnor," Alec said. "I'm a *little* angry that you didn't tell me you were leaving and didn't take me with you."

"I didn't want to wake you," Magnus began, but Ragnor stopped him with a hand on his arm.

"Domestic squabbles *later*," he said sharply. "Look." He tilted his chin toward the church.

Human figures, distant and small, were tumbling end over end upward in the wind of Sammael's windstorm, becoming visible to

Alec as they cleared the walls of the cathedral. Sammael was gathering the Shadowhunters to him, he realized, drawing them up to join him in the fire-tinged sky. Jace, Clary, Simon, Isabelle, Tian . . . all of them identifiable more by the silhouettes they made with their weapons than anything else.

"We have to get to them," Alec said.

"We may not have a choice," said Magnus. And indeed, Alec felt the unpleasant hot wind lick at his body as well, wrap itself around his legs, tugging at him like insistent hands. "Hang on," said Magnus, "I'm going to—"

The wind carried Alec up into the air, the horizon whirling around him in a dizzying rush. He had always wanted to be able to fly, but this was not at all how he'd imagined it. The currents of air swirled around him, spinning him like a top. He tried to reach for his seraph blade—it was thrust through his belt—but he couldn't get a grip on the hilt.

Then movement stopped, and while it took Alec a moment to reorient, he realized that he hung suspended in the air. The wind continued to whip around him, but he at least was no longer at its mercy.

He looked around and realized that Magnus and Ragnor were still with him, or at least nearby. They also floated in the air; Magnus's hands were raised, his arms tensed, and crimson-white light poured from the centers of his palms. In the distance, the other Shadowhunters still tumbled around and around like clothes in a dryer; Alec could tell it was taking all Magnus's strength to maintain his and Alec's stability.

Shinyun hovered nearby, watching but not engaging. Alec wondered why. Surely they were helpless. Surely if Sammael wanted them eliminated, now would be the time. . . .

He turned again to look at Magnus. His worry must have shown, because Magnus made a series of head movements that Alec interpreted as conveying that he was doing his best but that he couldn't reach the others with his magic from here.

Sammael was drifting over toward them, his hands folded in a mockery of prayer. He seemed totally unaffected by the wind, presumably because he was causing it.

Stupid, Alec was thinking. *Our plan was so stupid.* Baiting Sammael into fighting them would have been a *terrible* idea. He may have looked like a mild-mannered mundane, he may have talked like a game show host, but he was—of course—a supremely powerful demon. They were outmatched, Alec thought, and only Sammael's lack of interest in killing them had kept them alive so far. It was a chilling thought.

"Hey!" Sammael said with a wave, as he got closer to them. "How's everybody doing over here?"

Before anyone could answer—not that Alec had any idea how to answer—Sammael looked at Ragnor and jerked back in an exaggerated performance of surprise.

"Holy cats!" he exclaimed. "The thorn's gone. How did you pull off *that* little trick?" he said to Magnus. "Ragnor," he went on, "didn't we have some good times? Weren't you looking forward to ruling the world with me? At least a little? Come on, you wanted to a little bit."

Ragnor looked unimpressed. "You kept me in a cage and stabbed me several times. I was hardly a willing recruit."

"To be fair," said Sammael, "Shinyun kept you in the cage."

He turned back to Magnus. "I hope you aren't planning to try to remove the thorn from Shinyun, too."

"I don't think she wants it removed," said Magnus.

Sammael laughed. "You said it, buddy. I wasn't even going to thorn her, you know that? Did she tell you that? I thought, no way she could take it. But she insisted. Demanded it. Demanded from me, the greatest of all demons!"

"Second-greatest," said Ragnor quietly.

The Prince of Hell narrowed his eyes. "Well. We don't talk about *him*." He looked over at Shinyun, hovering near the still-struggling Shadowhunters a short distance away. "You know," he confided, "if I let her, she'd just kill all of them."

Alec cleared his throat. "So why won't you let her?"

"Oh!" said Sammael. "Because I came up with a plan. Just on the way over here, can you believe it? Popped right into my head."

He waved his arm, and far below them, the ground began to shake. For a moment, Alec wasn't sure what he was looking at, but then he began to grasp it. All around the cathedral's walls, fissures were opening in the ground. The cathedral itself tilted and shifted dangerously, and then, with a great crash, its front half and back half fell into one another with a tremendous crash. Dust and smoke began to rise into the burning wind.

The cathedral didn't have time to fully collapse. While its walls were still lurching toward one another, the entire stretch of land around the cathedral fell, as though into a sinkhole. A slab of stone the size of a city block came loose from the streets around it, and the cathedral groaned and swayed and fell into the hole.

With a dazed horror, Alec watched it fall, tumbling through a voidlike darkness. At the bottom of that void was a lake, red and black, like molten rock.

The cathedral smashed into the lake of fire with a boom that went on and on. Jace, Isabelle, and the others had stopped spinning: Alec could barely see them through the smoke, but they all seemed to be watching in silence as the church settled into its new position, halfway submerged in lava, one broken tower still jutting up at an angle like the hand of a drowning man.

Alec looked over at Sammael, who caught his eye and waggled his eyebrows. Alec looked farther over at Magnus, who continued to keep his hands up, holding the three of them—Alec, Ragnor, and Magnus—steady in the air.

Now that the billow of dust was beginning to spread and drift, Alec could see that the lake below was not as featureless as he'd first thought. Around the sinking cathedral were tall columns of stone that rose high above the lake's surface, and here and there stone platforms connected by bridges and staircases. The cathedral had smashed through some of this infrastructure, but a lot of it remained, now modified by the slabs of brick and marble that were all that remained of the church.

"Behold," said Sammael. "The Hell of the Pit of Fire. An elaborate labyrinth of tortures, where condemned souls try to maintain their footing on an ever-shifting tangle of connected platforms as they dip in and out of burning flames. I moved it under the cathedral here, just for funsies."

Alec looked at the lake below him. Nothing appeared to be moving around the lake, except the slowly dissipating dust cloud from the cathedral's impact. He looked back at Sammael.

"Well," Sammael said, "it's not operational now, obviously. It's been closed for repairs for a hundred and fifty years, give or take. That's the problem with Diyu. That's the *problem, Ragnor*," he snarled. "It's supposed to generate all this demonic energy from the torment of souls, but the machinery is broken and the souls are gone, so *none of it works!*"

With those last words he brought his hand down in a violent gesture, and the distant silhouettes that were Alec's friends went tumbling down, down, through the sinkhole, through the air, and came to a landing on top of the cathedral tower. Alec held his breath, but he didn't even need to search inside himself for his connection to Jace to know it was intact: the Shadowhunters were clearly still alive, brought there safely by Sammael. They clung to the tower and scuttled around it; they were much too far away for Alec to tell what was happening.

Sammael giggled and waved his other hand. Down by the lake,

far below, three Portals opened, and tiny figures began to emerge from them. Demons, he thought, by the way they moved. He exchanged an alarmed look with Magnus.

"You see," Sammael said, as though conveying a wonderful secret, "I figured it out. I can use *their* souls and make them fight some demons, and use *that* power. It won't be a lot, nothing like what Diyu must have produced in its prime. But enough to make the Portal I want."

"You still can't pass through to Earth," said Ragnor. "The Taxiarch's wardings are intact—"

Sammael grinned merrily. "The Portal isn't for me," he said. "It's for Diyu."

"What?" said Alec. It was all he could come up with in the moment.

Sammael rubbed his hands together. "That's right. I'll need the energy of all your friends' souls to open a Portal *the size of all Shanghai.*" He did a little dance in the air. "I'm a genius. I seriously am. There wasn't enough energy in Diyu to break the Taxiarch's wardings, right? So I started to think: Where can a guy get a big burst of evil energy like that? I was collecting all this information from Tian about enemy forces and where they're headquartered and all of that business and then I realized, hey, I'm *Sammael.* I'm the Master of Portals! I can send *anything* through a Portal. So *blam!* Shanghai gone in an instant, and Diyu in its place. Or at least a chunk of Diyu the size of Shanghai." He laughed. "Think about it! A whole human city swallowed up by a demon city. Absolutely guaranteed to provide me enough energy to break through the wards."

"Can he do that?" Magnus said to Ragnor. "Swallow up the whole city?"

Ragnor looked ill. "He's certainly going to try."

"Please don't talk about me like I'm not here," sniffed Sammael. "It's very impolite."

"He's also going to torture our friends. That's part of 'trying'!" Alec said to Magnus. "Magnus, send me down there—"

"No," Sammael said sharply. "If I wanted any of you down there with them, I would have *sent* you down there with them. *We* have unfinished business," he said to Magnus. "Thorny business. But," he added with a wink, "is there any other kind?"

There was a loud noise, and Alec felt a rush of wind on his face. The lake of fire, the ruins of the cathedral, the rest of Shanghai's shadow surrounding the sinkhole, all went black, and for the second time in Diyu, Alec fell through nothing, toward nothing, surrounded by nothing.

THIS TIME HE FELL FOR ONLY A FEW SECONDS, AND WHEN he stopped, he didn't land, really. He was floating in the air above the ruins of Xujiahui Cathedral, then he was falling, and then he was standing somewhere else.

He looked around. Magnus was here, and Ragnor, and—looking a little puzzled—Shinyun. And Sammael, of course, who had thankfully returned to human size.

As abandoned and broken-down as the rest of Diyu was, this place seemed to have been forgotten entirely. It had the silence of a tomb that had been sealed for thousands of years and was never intended to be opened again. In a realm of abandoned chasms, Alec knew, felt in his body, that this was the deepest and most lonesome.

Up close, Shinyun really was looking very spidery, Alec thought—her limbs elongated and multiply jointed, her face narrowed, sharpened. Her lack of expression was always uncanny, but now that her movements seemed less human, it gave her the look of an alien creature studying them, trying to decide whether to crush them. Her lambent eyes peered at them in the dark, her head tilting back and forth like a snake examining its prey.

Not that Magnus was looking much better. His eyes were larger than normal and seemed to glow of their own accord. The chains that bound him were starkly clear on his arms, and the spiked circles harsh on his palms. He seemed elongated too, in almost serpentine fashion, taller and skinnier than he'd been.

It was remarkable, Alec thought, that Ragnor was by far the most human-seeming person here other than himself, and he had actual horns on his head.

Alec had no further time for observations, because Shinyun starting yelling. "The Svefnthorn cried out!" she called into the echo of the vast empty space they found themselves in. "It told me—it has been insulted. Disrespected. Injured." Her gaze found Ragnor, who gazed at her with loathing. "Ragnor. Why would you do this? Why would you reject the greatest of gifts?"

"If I recall," Ragnor said, as if the effort to speak was almost too much for him, "I turned down your gift, and it was given to me anyway, without my consent. I think you'll find that isn't what most people mean when they say 'gift.'"

"Now, now. Welcome!" interrupted Sammael. His constant ebullient tone was starting to fray Alec's nerves. "Welcome to Avici."

Alec looked at Magnus. Magnus nodded slightly, as though this was what he'd expected.

It wasn't what Alec had expected at all. What he knew of Avici was that it was Diyu's lowest hell, the one reserved for only the worst offenders. Given what he knew of hell dimensions, he'd expected fire, molten lava, the screams of sinners burning in the purifying flames. Or ice, perhaps, an endless expanse, with souls frozen, unmoving, for all time.

Avici was just . . . empty. They were standing on something, surely, but that something was black and featureless, indistinguishable as any particular material. It was nothing: not rough, not smooth, not level, not undulating. In all directions around them it stretched on and on, forever. At the horizon only the faintest of blurry haze marked the change from land to sky, the same empty sky that surrounded all of Diyu.

Perhaps the punishment of Avici was just to be here, alone, with no sounds, no sights, no wind blowing, only bare floor and bare sky. Just you and your mind, until your mind inevitably fizzed and burned and melted.

"I know what you're thinking," Sammael said. He threw out his arms and adopted a look of puzzlement. "Where's all the stuff?"

Alec exchanged a glance with Magnus.

"When I got here, I thought that too," Sammael went on. "I thought, ooh, very clever, very good, the worst punishment for the worst sinners isn't"—he gestured upward, presumably indicating all the other hells—"having your tongue ripped out, or being run over with wagons or boiled in cauldrons. It's just to be here with yourself and nothing else, right? But *then*," he continued, "I got to talking to some of the locals, and I learned that that wasn't it at all. This was Yanluo's . . . workshop. This was his atelier. He made it empty so he could bring to it anything he wanted, because those who came here had earned *customized* tortures."

He laughed, that grating, false laugh. "That's right, for the VIP clients, Yanluo believed in getting in there and getting his hands dirty himself. Some of the demons say that he made it such a light-less black so that no matter what he did here, how much he dismantled human bodies, how much he maimed and lacerated and butchered, nothing would ever stain Avici."

He threw his arms out again. "It's all stain, you see," he said with pleasure.

Alec said, "So it doesn't . . . stay empty? You bring things in? Like . . . torture things."

Sammael looked offended. "*I* don't do anything," he said. "Or at least I haven't. I didn't make this realm, you know. Blame Yan-luo for how it works. Do *I* seem like I would make *my* deepest hell a big blank space? I'm really much more the waterfalls-of-blood, abstract-sculpture-of-viscera type. But to answer your question, yes, the excellent thing about Avici is that I can bring in whatever I want. For instance, I can stick *this* quisling in a cage, where he belongs."

A theatrical wave of his hands, and spikes of wrought iron shot up around Ragnor. It was fast, but Alec was surprised that Ragnor didn't even move as the cage closed around him.

"Ragnor!" Magnus said. "You're still a *warlock*, come on. You don't have to let him just . . . capture you."

Ragnor tilted his eyes toward Magnus, and Alec was astonished by the depth of self-loathing he saw reflected there. "I can't," he said. "I deserve this, Magnus."

"That's not the way things work," Magnus said, clearly frustrated. "You can make up for what you've done, but not like this. Not by letting yourself be trapped."

"I told you," said Ragnor. "I've betrayed myself too much now. Gone too far, done too many things that can't be undone."

Sammael looked back and forth between them, visibly entertained.

The iron bars closed over Ragnor's head with a clanging sound. He barely seemed to even register their presence, looking purposelessly into the middle distance.

"All right," said Sammael, as though he'd been waiting for the Ragnor situation to be dealt with. "The Book, if you please, Shinyun."

Shinyun looked around as if unsure of herself. "Ragnor had it."

Sammael rubbed his forehead with his hand. "In other words," he said, "now Magnus has it."

"Maybe not," Magnus suggested. "Maybe it's still back at

Ragnor's place." Sammael gave him a withering look, and Magnus shrugged. "Worth a try."

"Please," Sammael said to Shinyun, "go get my Book back."

Her dragonfly's wings quivering on her back, Shinyun walked toward them. Magnus held up one hand, scarlet light blossoming from its center. "I'm not giving you the Book, Shinyun."

Shinyun kept approaching. "Magnus, I know you. I know both of you," she added, nodding to Alec. "You believe in mercy. You believe in forgiveness. You believe in not doing things that you can't take back."

Alec was watching Sammael, who stood a little apart from the rest of them, his arms folded, watching with keen interest. It was strange: Alec was sure Sammael could do any number of terrible things to them, or just turn Magnus upside down and shake him until the Book fell out. But he didn't; he was happy to let Shinyun do the work, even though she was much less powerful than him.

It occurred to Alec that most of the powerful people he'd fought were at pains to demonstrate that power. Valentine, Sebastian, Shinyun herself, Lilith . . . They wanted respect. They wanted fear.

Sammael didn't seem to care about any of that. As if his power was so great that he didn't care if it was disrespected. As if in his mind, his victory was so inevitable, so assured, that the question of the Book of the White was only of minor interest.

"You won't attack me," said Shinyun, "unless I attack you first. So what will you do when I close the distance between us"—she was staring at Magnus—"and try to take the Book? Will you run? There's nowhere to run. Or will you let me take it, like you let me pierce your heart with the thorn?"

Magnus looked at Shinyun unhappily. Then a bolt of crimson lightning burst from his palm, and Shinyun flew backward, struck by the force of his magic.

"Wow!" said Sammael. "Did you see *that*?"

* * *

SHINYUN WAS RIGHT: MAGNUS DIDN'T WANT TO ATTACK her. He wanted her to understand that there were ways of making things happen other than violence and its threat. He had given her a chance. He had given her, he thought, probably too many chances. Shinyun didn't want to learn. She didn't want to change.

He was heartbroken at how lost she was, filled with compassion for this warlock who had learned too early that the world only pays attention to brute strength, that empathy was weakness.

But that didn't mean he was going to let her get close enough to him to take the Book. Or stab him with the Svefnthorn again.

She wasn't expecting the first burst from his hand, and fell back. Alec charged toward her, reaching for his seraph blade, but she quickly regained her footing and shot up into the air. She flung her magic at Alec, and a huge blast of it drove him to one knee. Shinyun came screaming down at Alec, the Svefnthorn drawn like a rapier, ready to strike.

Magnus knocked the thorn aside with his own wave of energy, and Alec rolled out of the way. Magnus reached out to summon something—anything—from elsewhere in Diyu. A sword from a fallen Baigujing warrior. The chair from Ragnor's temple. A chunk of masonry from a crumbled hell court.

Nothing came. Apparently the power to summon things to Avici was Sammael's alone—Magnus was sure that if Shinyun could, she would be summoning demons and lava and who could guess what else. Sammael had picked an excellent place to leave Magnus at a disadvantage. Most warlock magic wasn't about channeling raw power into violent force, but about manipulating the world to your own advantage. But here there was no world to manipulate. And unlike him, Shinyun had a weapon.

Alec was on his feet now. His seraph blade was in his hand. He shot a look of contempt at Sammael.

"Michael," he said, and as the sword blazed up with holy flame, Sammael visibly flinched at the sound of the archangel's name.

Magnus felt a wave of pride. Not everyone could diss a Prince of Hell so artfully.

Blade in hand, Alec lunged at Shinyun from behind, and she took off into the air again, swooping around in a wide arc. At its height she drew an elaborate many-pointed star in the air with the Svefnthorn, and flames poured from it. Magnus rapidly threw up spells of protection, and the fire bounced harmlessly off Alec.

But Shinyun was still circling, and soon she would find a new opening. Magnus looked at Alec and then up at Shinyun.

"Go," Alec said urgently. "I'll be fine."

The strength of the Alliance rune and Alec's faith and the thorn humming through him, Magnus took to the air himself.

"The more you use your magic," Shinyun said to him, "the closer you get to losing yourself completely. The changes will accelerate."

In the void above Avici, Magnus fought Shinyun. She was determined to attack Alec, recognizing that he was the more vulnerable target, and also knowing that Magnus would protect him above all else. Magnus flew defensively, getting in Shinyun's way, blocking her magic, distracting her. But with the full power of the thorn behind her, Shinyun was more than a match for him. And Alec couldn't touch Shinyun unless she got close, which she was clearly not about to do.

Worse, as he fought, Magnus could feel the magic of the thorn flowing in and through him. It gave him power, but power that was alien to him, something separate from him. He could feel its hunger, its desire to fill him until, inevitably, it replaced him.

"If you just gave yourself to the thorn," Shinyun yelled in frustration, "there'd be no need for any of this."

"Yes," Magnus said through gritted teeth, "that's kind of the whole point."

They grappled there in the empty sky, neither able to attain a real advantage over the other. "Shinyun!" Sammael called. "I noticed you haven't gotten the Book back yet. Do you need some help?"

"No!" said Shinyun angrily. Magnus took the opportunity to knock her off balance.

"I don't know," said Sammael. "It sure looks like Magnus is keeping it away from you. Let me just give you a hand."

"No!" screamed Shinyun again, but Sammael was already reaching out with his hand, and while he remained where he was, it grew and extended and grabbed hold of Magnus, plucking him from the sky and smashing him down into the rough plain of Avici. One moment Magnus was flying toward Shinyun, and the next he was on his knees on the ground, next to Sammael. Sammael was leaning his hand, now normal size again, on Magnus's shoulder in a casual, avuncular fashion, but Magnus found he was unable to move from its grip.

"You're cheating," he said, looking up at Sammael.

Sammael frowned, seeming puzzled. "My dear curse, how could you still think we were playing a fair game here?"

Magnus spun around, Sammael's hand biting hard into his shoulder. The breath left Magnus's body in a single, hard exhale. *No,* he thought, and then: *I should have known.*

Shinyun had hold of Alec. She stood behind him, grasping him around the neck with her arm and holding the point of the Svefnthorn to his chest. His seraph blade lay in front of him, guttering like a spent match.

His face was impassive, his blue eyes steady. He could have been looking out over a beautiful landscape, or studying a subway map. Magnus had seen Alec frightened—had seen him in every phase of vulnerability, clear and open as a summer sky—but Alec would never show such a thing before Shinyun and Sammael.

"Oh, *interesting*," said Sammael with delight.

"Magnus!" Shinyun's voice was hoarse and cracked. "I demand that you take the third blow from the Svefnthorn. I *demand* it. Or I will kill the thing you love best." Her eyes were wild, monstrous, more inhuman than ever.

She twisted the point of the Svefnthorn against Alec's ribs, over his heart, and Magnus felt it like a stab to his own gut. The thorn was warlock magic—there was no way it could be anything but death for a Shadowhunter.

He had no options left. If he took the thorn, Shinyun won: he'd become a willing minion of Sammael, and maybe the whole world would be destroyed. If he refused the thorn, Alec would be murdered before his eyes, he himself would die, and Sammael would go on toward the war he wanted.

"Will you spare Alec?" he said quietly. "Promise you'll let Alec go, and I'll do it."

She glanced at Sammael; he shrugged. "You have my permission. It's not like this one Shadowhunter poses any real threat. I can't guarantee his safety once the invasion of Earth starts, of course," he added. "That's a different story."

Magnus nodded. Alec was looking at him, his gaze still steady, still unreadable. Magnus wondered what would become of his love for Alec after the thorning. Would it vanish like it had never been? Would he love only Sammael? Or would he still love Alec, but demand that he also turn to Sammael's side?

But the choice between him and Alec both definitely dying, and only one of them dying, was no choice at all. Max was waiting at home. Better one parent than no parent. The calculus of it was self-evident, the conclusion inevitable.

Before Shinyun could act, though, Alec was moving. He was reaching out, and he was wrapping his hand around the blade of the

Svefnthorn, and he was grimacing with effort and resolve, and he was thrusting the Svefnthorn into his own chest, piercing his own heart. From where he knelt, Magnus could see the thorn run all the way through him, emerge through his back, and remain there. Alec's eyes were still open, still wide, still staring right at Magnus.

Magnus opened his mouth to scream, and crimson magic exploded from Alec's chest, from his back, a blinding flash that turned the permanent night of Avici briefly to day. In the glare, beyond sight, still under the iron grip of Sammael's hand, all Magnus could see of Alec were his eyes, clear and bright and filled with love.

CHAPTER NINETEEN

The Endless Way

BY HIS NATURE, ALEC DIDN'T LIKE ACTING ON HUNCHES. He liked to study a situation, make a plan, and execute the plan. It got him teased by Jace, by Isabelle, who both believed in jumping off a cliff and somehow sewing a parachute on the way down. They acted on instinct, and usually it turned out all right. But Alec didn't have the same kind of faith in his own instincts. He believed in gathering intelligence, doing research, being prepared. (To be fair, Isabelle and Jace also believed in those things; they just believed other people should do them, because they were boring.)

This was a fine strategy for most Shadowhunting missions, but sometimes it all fell apart. Sometimes there was a no-win situation, where your only choice appeared to be between dying one way and dying a different way.

Diyu, and Sammael, and Shinyun had all confounded Alec's ability to organize and plan. Shinyun's motivations were so confused and contradictory that Alec was sure she herself didn't understand them. Diyu was a surreal ruin. And Sammael acted as though it was all just a distracting game, as though nothing they did could have any meaningful effect.

For this whole mission they'd been working on hunches, mostly Magnus's hunches. A hunch that Peng Fang would know something about the warlocks in the Market. A hunch that the cathedral would be in Diyu and would be safe. A hunch that the Heibai Wuchang could be used to save Ragnor.

So Alec had acted on an intuition of his own and asked Magnus if they could use the Alliance rune.

Now, faced with the choice of losing Magnus in one fashion or losing him in another, he acted, plunging the Svefnthorn into his own heart. He only had time to register the surprise on Shinyun's face before everything exploded.

Crimson light burst, so intense it whited out Alec's vision. He felt a harsh, burning energy pour into him, caustic and alien in his chest. He could feel his runes heating up, as if by friction, as if abraded by the demonic magic of the thorn, like a meteor falling through the upper atmosphere. All except the Alliance rune, which sizzled on his arm. The power of Sammael and the power of Raziel battled within his own body, but he could feel the Alliance rune absorbing the friction, smoothing it, teaching the different magics to cooperate.

Alec's vision was beginning to clear. He could see the desolate black space of Avici, the tableau of Shinyun, Sammael, Magnus, all watching him, Magnus's face a mask of horror.

I'm alive, Alec realized. He was a little surprised.

Shinyun jerked the thorn back. She looked nearly as horrified as Magnus, as the thorn slid free of Alec's body. It was painless. There was no blood on the thorn, and when Alec glanced down, he saw no mark on himself to show where it had pierced him.

Shinyun had staggered back. She held the Svefnthorn out in front of her, staring: it glowed red, like iron heated in fire, and with some astonishment Alec saw that the thorn's glow was visible to him in Magnus and Shinyun, too. In each of their chests hung a miniature star, a fireball made of magic, spinning madly behind the wounds the thorn had made. Shinyun's fireball was somewhat larger than Magnus's, but more importantly, a thick rope of magic extended out of Shinyun's wound, terminating in the middle of Sammael's own chest. Magnus had no such rope connecting him to Sammael—presumably because he had not suffered the third strike from the thorn.

Alec shivered; he could feel the magic leaving his body, his Alliance rune cooling. He had to act before it was gone completely. Still kneeling, he flung his hand out toward Magnus and called the thorn's power to him.

It was like trying to restrain a wild horse. The fireball in Magnus jerked, leaped, shook. Beyond the realm of conscious thought, Alec reached out to it. Soothed it. Coaxed it. And with a gentle motion, he tore it from the tendrils of Magnus's own magic that held it in place, the magic he knew, blue and cool and beloved. He reached, and the fireball left Magnus's body.

As soon as it was freed, it expanded in size, becoming the only illuminating star in Avici's sky. It spun above them all, a fireball several feet wide, crackling with power. Alec could feel its instability, its desire to find a new resting place. It yearned to be within his own chest, but without another wound from the Svefnthorn, it would find no purchase in him. So for a moment it spun freely, and for a moment all of them present only stared.

Sammael recovered first, of course. He had taken his hand off Magnus's shoulder and was looking up at the orb. Magnus remained on his knees. "Excellent!" Sammael said, laughing. "Great work. I love an unexpected turn, don't you?" He seemed to address this question to Ragnor, who didn't lift his head to acknowledge any of what was going on. Sammael squinted up at the orb. "Shinyun, if you could be a dear and grab that thing and bring it to me, we can get on with our plans."

Shinyun was also watching the orb. She didn't respond.

"Hello?" Sammael said after a moment. "Shinyun Jung? My loyal lieutenant? Get the orb?"

When Shinyun turned around, she wasn't looking at Sammael. She was looking at Magnus. Staring at him, white-hot hatred in her eyes.

"I will never understand you," she said, in a quiet tremor that suggested she was barely keeping herself from a complete meltdown. "Never have I seen someone so determined to throw away their birthright. We are *warlocks*, Magnus Bane. We are the *children of Lilith*."

Alec tried to ignore the frothing magic boiling through his body and focus on Magnus. He could *feel* the rotating sphere of magic above them. Magnus had been looking at it, a little dazed, but now his attention was on Shinyun as she stalked toward him, her wings out and twitching dangerously.

"The power of the thorn is the greatest gift that a warlock can receive," she said through gritted teeth. "It is the power of our father—our *actual father*, Magnus, not just the demon that made us individually—the one without whom our race would not exist at all. I found that power. I offered you that power. Despite all you did, despite your rejection of Asmodeus . . . you showed me mercy. And this is how I repaid you."

Her voice broke with anguish. "And *this* is how you repay *me*?"

"Shinyun," Sammael said, a hint of alarm creeping into his jovial voice. "I get that you and Magnus have some unresolved stuff, but really, he's irrelevant to the larger plan."

Magnus looked over at Sammael. "Well, that hurts a little."

Sammael threw up his hands and affected a bewildered look. "I didn't even know you existed. I mean, once I understood that you were Asmodeus's eldest curse and already had two thorns in you, well, I wasn't about to just ignore the possibility of your service."

"So I wasn't part of your plans . . . at all?" Magnus said, incredulous. "But you went after my oldest friend . . . and the warlock who tried to drag me into Asmodeus's control three years ago."

"You'll forgive me," said Sammael, "if I think of Ragnor Fell as 'the most knowledgeable expert alive on the subject of dimensional magic' first, and your 'oldest friend' second. As for Shinyun, *she* came to *me*."

Magnus looked helplessly over at Ragnor, who shrugged.

Shaking his head, Sammael said, "I don't know how to tell you this, but not everything is about you, Magnus. As for you, Shinyun," he said, reaching out toward the orb, "I'm very disappointed in you—"

"Everybody *shut up!*" Shinyun yelled, and even Sammael seemed startled. The orb had been drifting toward Sammael's open hand; Shinyun suddenly shot up from the ground, her new wings flapping, and caught the orb out of the air as if it were a basketball.

Sammael said, "*Shinyun,*" sternly this time.

She cast one wild glance at him, then thrust her hand forward, punching through the surface of the orb. At once it emitted a high-pitched shriek and began to deflate like a balloon. Alec slapped his hands over his ears and realized, no, not deflating. The six-pointed wound over Shinyun's heart was absorbing the magic, drawing it in like a deep inhale. As they all watched, the orb grew smaller and more oblong until, with a popping noise, the entirety of it disappeared into Shinyun.

"Uh-oh," muttered Sammael.

Shinyun hovered motionless where the magic had been, glowing with crimson fire. After a moment, she began to emit a strange shaking sound. After another moment, she threw back her head and

Alec realized: she was laughing. A dreadful laugh, a cackle of rage and mockery.

Her face began to crack.

Lines appeared, spreading from her mouth into her cheeks, fissures opening around her eyes and on her forehead and down her chin. The planes of her face began to separate, and Alec felt his stomach drop. Shinyun's features separated, broke, snapped like something behind the mask of her face was punching its way out.

With a great roar of triumph, inhuman and ancient, she burst, in a shattering of limbs and lines and eyes and wings and teeth . . .

Her eyes were now twice the size they had been, and Shinyun herself twice the height. Her limbs spread like a great water insect's, and her wings, now a dark blood-red, flapped slowly behind her. Her face, no longer frozen in place by the arbitrary maledictions of the warlock mark, twisted in glee. Her teeth were bright and sharp, with a pair of fangs, like a tarantula's. At her back was a long, whiplike tail, and at the end of the tail, a nasty-looking iron barb. The Svefnthorn itself.

Alec watched in horrified fascination. Shinyun had become the thing she loved most—a demon. A Greater Demon, Alec was sure.

She screamed that unearthly scream again, and the ground of Avici began to shake below their feet.

"Shinyun!" Sammael called. "Marvelous new look! I think maybe we've gotten a little off task, though. If you'll just come down and we can decide what to do with—"

In a flash of motion Shinyun was hovering above Sammael and Magnus, her tail flicking dangerously back and forth.

"I thought you were the ultimate power," she said to Sammael. Her voice was still recognizably her own, though it was slashed through with high-pitched scratches and a kind of skittering that Alec realized was her breathing. "But you aren't."

Sammael looked offended. "If you know of a demon more powerful than me, feel free to let me know so I may pay him homage."

"You may be the greatest of the Princes of Hell," Shinyun spat, "but you're so much weaker than I realized. You're as dependent on others as these idiot humans." She gestured with a clawed hand at the others. "You're dependent on Diyu. You're dependent on souls being tormented to give you power. You're dependent on *me*."

"If you've decided that Sammael, of all people, is not powerful enough for you . . ." Magnus shook his head. "You're one hard-to-please lady, you know that?"

"Apparently, of all the beings here," Shinyun said, "*I'm* the only one who understands true power. True power is to depend on no one, on nothing. If I cannot trust anyone else to rule over me, then I will rule myself. And I will rule alone."

With that, she circled upward, away from them. She opened her mouth and exhaled a wide cone of crimson light into the dark. When the glare cleared, it formed a Portal, the surface a silver mirror whose destination Alec couldn't make out. With a last scream, Shinyun flew through the Portal, which closed around her, and was gone.

The ground was rumbling even harder now. Alec noticed that at some point he'd fallen and was crouched on the ground. Magnus was making his way over to join him, moving carefully on the suddenly uneven terrain.

Sammael looked around with some disappointment. "Well, that's it for Diyu, I guess. She's going to bring the whole place down around us." He sighed. "That's how the cookie crumbles, I suppose."

Magnus had reached Alec. He was helping him up. Alec was only dimly aware. The whole world was shaking around him, shaking and wobbling. Or possibly he was shaking and wobbling?

He looked up to see that Sammael had come over to join them for some reason. "Magnus, I'm sorry we aren't going to be working together. And I'm sorry you both are going to die in the deepest pit in Diyu when miles and miles of underground city and courts and temples come crashing down on top of you." He frowned. "Come to think of it, I have no idea what'll happen to humans if they die in a dimension for the already dead. Well, whatever awaits you, good luck with your future endeavors. If you turn out to have any."

"You're just leaving?" Alec said.

Sammael looked surprised. "Did I not make that clear? I have to go find another realm." He shrugged and added, almost to himself, "What an unusual several days it's been."

Then, blipping out as though he'd never been there, he was gone.

THE MOMENT SAMMAEL VANISHED, MAGNUS DROPPED to his knees beside Alec. He pulled Alec toward him almost violently, pressing his hand over Alec's chest, pushing aside the collar of Alec's shirt so he could reach the place the thorn had pierced him and run his fingers over it.

There was no wound, no indication that anything had happened to Alec at all, and most of his runes seemed normal. The Alliance rune, however, had disappeared entirely.

Magnus continued stroking Alec's chest where the thorn had entered, until Alec, with effort, said, "Not here, my love. Ragnor is watching us."

A sound broke from Magnus's chest, half laugh and half sob. He grasped Alec's hair in one hand and showered kisses all over his face, crying and laughing at once. Alec's eyes were open, and reflected in that midnight blue, Magnus saw a gleam of gold. His own eyes, watching Alec in return.

"That was very brave, what you did," Magnus said. "Also completely reckless."

Alec smiled weakly. "I've been working on being more brave and reckless. I found a really great example to follow."

"We can't *both* be brave and reckless," Magnus said. "Who will watch out for us?"

"Eventually, Max, I hope," said Alec with a grin.

"If you two have a moment." Ragnor's voice came drifting through the void. "Do you think you could stop mooning over each other and get me out of this cage?"

Alec's look of love suddenly turned to alarm. "Magnus. The others. The Hell of the Pit of Fire."

Magnus jumped up. "It never ends, does it," he said. He ran over to Ragnor, who was sitting grumpily cross-legged on the ground, tapping impatiently at the bars of his prison.

Magnus reached for his magic, and he felt a woozy disorientation, like missing the last step on a staircase. There was an emptiness in his chest, and while he knew that the thorn's power had come from a terrible enemy, the enemy of all humans, he understood why Shinyun had clung to it, had allowed herself to be warmed and comforted by it. It wasn't love, but if you didn't know the difference, it might have felt like love.

With a few gestures he shattered the bars of Ragnor's cage and helped him to his feet. Ragnor looked at Magnus for a minute, then turned to look past him and said, "That was *very* stupid."

Alec was making his way over to them, a little slow but walking steadily. When he got close, Magnus put his arm around his waist. "Maybe I need to make more thorough introductions here." He cleared his throat. "Ragnor, this is Alec Lightwood, my boyfriend and co-parent. He just saved my life and, by extension, yours. Alec, this is Ragnor Fell. He is a terrible jerk to everybody, even when he's not under the mind control of a Prince of Hell."

"I've heard a lot about you," Alec said.

"I haven't heard about anything for years, except creepy evil plans to rule the world," Ragnor said, "but now that I'm back from that, I expect Magnus will bore me to tears with stories from my absence." He looked at Alec again. "How *did* you survive the thorning? Anyone who wasn't a warlock should have died from the overflow of demonic magic. And there aren't any warlocks who are Shadowhunters, except—" He peered suspiciously at Alec. "You aren't Tessa Gray in disguise, are you? This isn't some elaborate prank you've been playing on poor Magnus? If it is, Tessa, you and I are going to have *words.*"

"Of course not!" Alec said, offended.

Ragnor squinted even harder at him. Magnus sighed. "I've been in the same room with both of them, Ragnor. He's definitely not Tessa."

"Then how—"

"Later," said Magnus. Only then did he fully grasp how much Ragnor had missed, and how much more he needed to be told. The Alliance rune. The Mortal War. The Dark War! And smaller, more personal things. Malcolm Fade was the High Warlock of Los Angeles. Catarina was still in New York, for now.

One thing at a time. "Ragnor," he said, "can you get us to the Hell of the Pit of Fire, where the other Shadowhunters are? We need to try to save them."

Ragnor shook his head. "I'm sure it's too late," he said. "But I'll open the Portal and we'll see. At least we can take whatever's left of them back to Earth."

Alec looked stricken. Magnus patted him on the shoulder. "Don't take it too seriously," he said. "Ragnor's just like that."

Ragnor twiddled his fingers, the extra joint on each of them making his movements intricate and alien even to Magnus. Within a moment a door opened in the nothingness of Avici, through which orange flames leaped against black rock. It seemed to be quaking in the same way Avici was.

Magnus looked to Alec. "Are you ready to fight again?"

"Not really," Alec said, drawing his seraph blade from his belt. "But here we go."

"Right." Magnus charged through, and Alec followed close behind.

They emerged onto a rocky platform suspended high above the lava pools below. A stone staircase led down to more platforms and the rest of the labyrinthine landscape. Magnus was not happy to note that nothing was visibly keeping their platform in the air, and the earthquake that was rumbling through Diyu was even stronger here.

"Okay," said Alec. "Let's save our friends."

"Or what's left of your friends," Ragnor muttered. "Wait. Where *are* your friends?"

They seemed to be scattered. Far below them, on a fairly broad plain, Simon, Clary, and Tian were fighting some of Diyu's various demons. Separated from them and somewhat elevated was Isabelle, and even higher, on a separate platform, was Jace.

Alec looked puzzled. "What's going on?"

"Well, Jace's foot was broken, so I guess they found a safe place for him," offered Magnus.

"And why is Isabelle by herself?" Exhausted by magic he might have been, but Alec still jogged down the staircase ahead of them, weapon at the ready.

Ragnor gave Magnus a look. "You're not going to *jog*, are you?"

Magnus raised one eyebrow. "In these shoes?"

They descended the staircase, and the one after that, with the decorum appropriate to warlocks who had defeated a Prince of Hell that day. Or at least, they had been in the same place as a Prince of Hell, and they had made him leave first.

By the time they reached Jace, Alec had clearly already exchanged some words with him and looked much less concerned.

"So you haven't all been devoured yet, I see," said Ragnor.

"No, they've got it all under control," Alec said, excited. He gestured at Jace. "Tell them!"

Jace looked at him sideways. "I was about to. We've got it all under control," he went on. "I can't really fight right now, so Clary helped me up here so we could see as much of the battlefield as possible, since the paths are so irregular and confusing. But *then* we noticed that the demons had the same problem we did. They could really only get to us on a set number of paths, and three people could cover two paths each."

Magnus raised his eyebrows.

"So Simon, Tian, and Clary went down there to do that. We put Isabelle on the middle platform because she's the only one whose weapon has any reach, so she can handle the occasional flying dude."

Alec seemed near tears. "I'm very proud of you," he said to Jace. "You actually made a plan."

"I'm good at plans!" Jace said.

"You are, actually, good at plans," Magnus said. "It's just usually you're yelling them behind you as you sprint toward danger."

"But you used your sumptuous brain and you're all okay!" Alec said, thumping Jace on the shoulder. He looked over at Ragnor. "Take that, pessimism guy!"

Ragnor furrowed his brow. "Well, obviously I'm glad everyone is still alive."

"I should mention," said Jace, "the ground started shaking a little while ago."

"That would be Shinyun," said Magnus. "It's a long story. Also, luckily for you I brought the world's leading expert in dimensional magic, and he's going to Portal us right on out of here."

Ragnor gave Magnus a sour look. "I suppose I am, but I'm going to need your help."

"Great news," said Magnus, and he jumped off the platform. He floated slowly down to the plain, waving at Isabelle as he passed.

"Magnus!" said Clary, lopping the head off one of the Baigujing skeletons. "Good to see you!"

"I'm going to say something," Simon said in Clary's direction, "and I don't want you to get mad."

Clary let out a long, beleaguered breath. "Go ahead. I guess you've earned it."

"Magnus," Simon said with a smirk. "Nice of you to drop in."

Clary sighed again.

"I've got good news and bad news," said Magnus. "The good news is I'm here to Portal us back to Earth. The bad news is that I need Ragnor's help, and he's taking the stairs all the way down."

Ragnor, indeed, was strolling down the staircase at a leisurely pace. As Magnus watched, Jace overtook him, which was impressive given that he was walking with a crutch.

The demon horde was beginning to flag, it seemed. New demons appeared from the Portals less and less frequently, and both Jace and Isabelle joined their friends to mop up what remained. Perhaps the demons had noticed Diyu's imminent collapse and fled for their lives; perhaps once Sammael and Shinyun were gone they had no reason to obey their orders.

Eventually, Ragnor deigned to join them. He and Magnus quickly worked together to set up a Portal; it occurred to Magnus how very much he'd missed working with Ragnor.

And when the Portal opened, he was relieved to see it glow a familiar, cheering blue.

CHAPTER TWENTY

The Soul of the Clave

IN 1910, CATARINA LOSS'S SON EPHRAIM DIED. BY THAT time, he was an old man with children and grandchildren of his own. Catarina hadn't seen him for decades; he believed that she'd died when he was only in his thirties, in a shipwreck.

Magnus had been living in New York at the time, in a smart apartment in Manhattan across the street from the old Metropolitan Opera House, the one they tore down in 1967. A telegram came: *No. 2, the Bund, Shanghai*, it said in Catarina's hurried hand. So Magnus fetched his gloves and his hat and he went.

Number Two, the Bund, turned out to be the home of the Shanghai Club, a little bit of English elitism dropped right in the heart of China, in the form of a squat marble baroque revival building in which Shanghai's British elite hobnobbed, drank, and for a short time, essentially ruled the mundane world. The building was new, though the club was not. It was a funny choice for Catarina. She knew as well as Magnus that it was open to white men only. This was Catarina being mischievous, in her way. She sometimes enjoyed glamouring herself into the private spaces of rich mundanes, delighting in her ability to stand totally outside their world, to have a drink with an old friend in the face of those who wouldn't allow them entrance under normal circumstances.

The whole place was palatial in a way that was also a bit grotesque. Magnus walked through a cavernous columned Grand Hall, past taipans and diplomats, utterly pleased with themselves. And why not? They were living like royalty at the heart of one of the oldest kingdoms in the world. They had no reason to think it would ever end—and at the time, Magnus wondered himself how long it could last. Not much longer, it turned out.

But for now, here were expensive cigars and brandy, fresh newspapers, and a library rumored to be larger than the city of Shanghai's. Magnus was unsurprised to find Catarina in it.

Though no one but Magnus could see her, she was elegantly put together as always: her dress was a slender column of white satin, with a black lace overlay and butterfly sleeves. A black velvet sash waistband completed the affair. Magnus thought he saw the hand of Paul Poiret, the famous designer, at work; Magnus wondered if Catarina had managed to outdress him.

She was seated in one of the club chairs, gazing at the shelves across from her as though she was studying their spines from a distance, though they were too far for Magnus to read. He sat down in the chair opposite Catarina and said, "So what's the plan? Are we tearing this whole place down in the name of freedom and equality?"

Catarina looked up at him. There were dark circles beneath her eyes. "I had to watch a man die here once," she said.

Magnus leaned forward sharply. "What?"

"It was a few years ago," she said. "I was here, in the library, and a man fell to the ground, writhing in pain. A medic was called, the other club members gathered around their mate, but none of them had any medical training or knew what to do—they argued about whether to elevate his legs or elevate his head, whether he should be prone or supine—and he died there, before any doctor or nurse could reach him."

She looked distant. "Could I have saved him? Magically or otherwise? Could the mundane doctors, if there had been one here? I don't know. Maybe he would have died regardless. But what could I do? I couldn't simply appear to them as if from a dream; they'd think somebody had poisoned the punch."

"Do they still serve the punch?" said Magnus.

Catarina raised an eyebrow. "You think I am being morbid."

"I think," said Magnus, "that the fact that mundanes die, and we can't save them, isn't something you just recently learned."

Catarina sighed. "It's not that we can't save them," she said, "it's that we can't save them even if we love them very, very much." There were tears in her eyes now. He knew better than to say anything; instead he simply took her hands in his.

After a moment she said, "For mundanes, it is considered the greatest of tragedies if a parent outlives their child. For warlock parents it is an inevitability. I always thought it was strange that most warlocks spend their lives alone, without attachments, without ever putting down roots. . . ."

Magnus let her trail off and said, gently, "If you had it to do over again, would you choose not to do it?"

"No," Catarina said without hesitation. "Of course I would do it again. No matter how many times I was made to choose, I would choose to adopt and raise Ephraim again, to see him become a man, to have children and grandchildren of his own. However hard it was. However hard it is now."

"I've never had a child," said Magnus, "but I know what it is to lose someone you love, for no better reason than that all humans must die."

"And?" said Catarina.

"So far," said Magnus, "life seems to me to be a matter of choosing

THE LOST BOOK OF THE WHITE

love, over and over, even knowing that it makes you vulnerable, that it might hurt you later. Or even sooner. You just have no choice. You choose to love or you choose to live in an empty world with no one there but you. And *that* seems like a truly terrible way to spend eternity."

Catarina didn't quite smile, but her eyes glistened. "Do you think vampires go through this kind of thing too?"

Magnus rolled his eyes. "Of course they do. I've found you can't get them to shut up about the topic for even a moment."

"Thank you for coming, Magnus."

"I would always come," he said.

Catarina wiped her eyes with her hand. "You know," she said, sniffling a bit, "this club contains the longest bar in the world, downstairs."

"The longest *bar*?" said Magnus.

"Yes," she said. "It's at least a hundred feet long. It's called the Long Bar."

"The English are good at luxury," Magnus said, "but they don't always make creative naming decisions, do they?"

"You'll see," said Catarina. "It's *very* long."

"Lead the way, dear lady."

AS THEY TUMBLED FORTH FROM THE PORTAL, ALEC AT first was sure that Portals were still malfunctioning. He expected the busy streets of Shanghai, but they seemed to have ended up in a patch of trees, towering and narrow and densely planted, their leaves beginning to change from pale green to yellow to orange. Nearby Alec could see the moon reflected on water.

It was dark, which surprised him, but he wasn't quite sure how many hours they had spent in Diyu, and knowing how bizarre dimensional travel could be, there was probably some time dilation effect. He could probably ask Ragnor.

"Where have we ended up?" Alec called out. "Are we close to Shanghai?"

He turned to see Jace raise his eyebrows at him in surprise. Wordlessly Jace gestured to the view behind him.

Alec took a few steps, and through the trees, very suddenly, were the lights of Shanghai, sparkling in every color. "Oh," he said.

"There are these things called 'parks,'" said Jace.

"It's been a long couple of days," said Alec.

"People's Park," said Tian. He gestured to the water Alec had noticed before, which he now could see was a small pond with banks of carefully arranged stones. Lilies floated, black against the glassy surface. "That's the Hundred Flower Pond there. A good choice," he added to Ragnor and Magnus.

Ragnor nodded in acknowledgment. "I thought it would be quiet, this time of night."

"What time *is* it?" said Clary.

After a moment of peering at the sky, Magnus said, "It's about ten thirty."

"You can tell the time from the sky?" said Alec, amused.

Magnus looked surprised. "You can't?"

"Hey, guys?" said Simon. "Can we take a moment to, uh, just quickly celebrate that we won, and nobody died? Because I don't think we should just let that go without mentioning it."

"Hear, hear," said Isabelle, punching the air in victory. "Hooray for us. We beat a Prince of Hell."

"Well," said Ragnor, "to be fair, you all saved Magnus and me from the Svefnthorn—Alec specifically, obviously—and then Shinyun went mad and began wrecking Diyu, so the Prince of Hell left to find a different realm, and he'll definitely be back at some point. Shinyun, also, is a loose end, as she is now some kind of dragonfly-spider thing."

Everyone paused to soberly consider that for a moment. Finally

Simon said, "But everyone lived. Magnus saved you. And Alec saved Magnus. And my girlfriend saved me *while riding on a giant tiger.*"

"Yes," acknowledged Ragnor, "the day has not been a complete loss."

Alec smiled, but he was tired of being away. And he felt a pull toward home, one that he wasn't used to, but that now beckoned him with an incredible force. *Max. Max.*

He tried to catch Magnus's eye, but Magnus had come up to Tian, who looked as weary as the rest of them. "Would you say good-bye to Jem for us? And give him all our regards?"

Tian looked surprised. "You're leaving?"

Magnus nodded. "I really feel like we didn't have time to explore Shanghai in the way I'd have preferred, but I hope you won't take it as an insult if we New Yorkers head home straight from here." Magnus looked over and caught Alec's eye. "I'd like to see my kid."

"Of course not." Tian smiled. A light had come back to his dark eyes that Alec hadn't even realized was missing before. "I'm going to go see Jinfeng. She'll be pretty happy to hear I'm not going to be spending time in Diyu anymore. Ragnor—" Ragnor turned to him, surprised. "As far as I know, you're the only person alive who has been stabbed by Heibai Wuchang and survived. There might be some interesting side effects."

"Excellent," said Ragnor mournfully. "Something to look forward to in my coming years of shame and anonymity."

Tian turned to face the others. "Thank you all, by the way, for all that you have done. And for keeping my and Jinfeng's secret."

"And thank you, Tian," said Simon, reaching to shake the other boy's hand. "For saving Isabelle. For helping us."

There was a chorus of assent. "The Cold Peace won't last forever," said Alec. "We'll keep working to make the Clave see reason and bring it to an end."

"I hope they will," said Tian, "but I know you're not the only influential force within the Clave these days." He put a hand on Alec's shoulder. "You must understand how much of an inspiration you are," he said firmly. "Your family—the two of you and your son—just by existing, by being so prominent in the Clave, you are doing much. *Your* family—if the Clave is to survive, that is their future. It must be."

"No pressure, though," said Alec with a smile. "And you're an inspiration yourself. Don't forget it."

Tian inclined his head. "It's only a matter of time before there's a real fight for the soul of the Clave. If we don't want the Cohort's vision to become reality, we will have to be involved. To be loud, even if we would prefer not to be."

"You're a good guy, Tian," Alec said. "I'm glad we're on the same side."

He wasn't the loud one, in his family. He was the quietest by a good margin. But Tian was right. And he was going to do some thinking.

Ragnor and Magnus had started preparations on a Portal home, though Ragnor seemed to be letting Magnus do most of the heavy lifting. His argument was that he was recovering from three strikes by a Svefnthorn, whereas Magnus was only recovering from two.

"You know who should open this Portal? Clary," Magnus grumbled. "Nothing that bad happened to her on this trip."

"I'm not entirely comfortable with that girl's ability to open Portals," Ragnor said, with a nervous glance in Clary's direction. She had Jace's arm around her, and was laughing with Isabelle. It was amazing how resilient people were, Magnus thought. "I find it . . . theologically confusing."

"That," said Magnus in breezy tones, "is why I never think about the deeper meaning behind anything." Ragnor's look told him that the other warlock knew very well that wasn't true. "So where are you headed?" he said. "Back to Idris? Tidy up your house for the first time in years?"

Ragnor hesitated. Magnus rolled his eyes. "Don't tell me you're going to keep pretending you're dead. How well did that work last time?"

"The mistake I made," Ragnor said, "was in trying to disappear completely. That just made me seem more suspicious." He gave a paranoid look behind each of his shoulders. "There's going to be a lot of heat on me for a while. Shinyun and I were . . . not careful about being seen in the Sunlit Market. I'll be a person of interest to much of Downworld, and possibly some Shadowhunters as well. Not to mention, Shinyun herself is still out there. Sammael, too, eventually."

Magnus sighed. "Ragnor, do you know how many hits my reputation has taken over the years? I'm still working. Nobody's thrown me into the Silent City. Nobody's hauled me up in front of a faerie court."

"That's different," said Ragnor. "You weren't working for a Prince of Hell."

"Ragnor, not long after you faked your death I was being accused of running a cult for Asmodeus."

"You *did* start that cult," Ragnor said, frowning. "It was one of your less funny jokes, as I remember."

"Then you'll be happy to know I was duly punished for it," Magnus said.

Ragnor paused in his magical machinations. "No, of course not." He sighed. "Maybe you can take that kind of heat, Magnus, but I can't. More to the point, I don't wish to. I did bad things, working for Sammael. Actual bad things, that I can't now take back. Just bringing Sammael to Diyu should probably be a capital offense."

"You were mind-controlled!" said Magnus.

"But I chose to take the third thorn. I *chose* that. I need time. To atone, I suppose. I've been dead for three years; I need to take some time to think of who Ragnor Fell will be when he comes back to life."

Magnus didn't say anything for a while as they finished the Portal. "Will I still hear from you? Because if I don't, I'm going to assume Shinyun has captured you again and I *will* come for you."

"Only you could make the promise of rescue sound like a threat," grumbled Ragnor. "But yes, I expect you'll have frequent dealings with the new me."

"Well, that's something," Magnus said. He paused. "I didn't tell Catarina."

"Nothing?" said Ragnor.

"Nothing. But that's not fair to her. I'll tell her when I see her next. It would mean a lot to her to know you're all right."

Ragnor looked surprised, but pleased. "Really?"

"Yes," said Magnus. "You idiot. She cares, more than almost anybody. There are so few of us, and—" He stopped. A terrible thought had occurred to him. "Oh no," he said. "You're not going to use that stupid alias again?"

"First of all," said Ragnor, "I am not going to take naming advice from somebody who could have chosen any name in the world and went with 'Magnus Bane.' Second, yes, I *am* going to use that name."

"I wish you wouldn't," said Magnus.

"It's only appropriate," Ragnor said with a wink. "I am now, after all, but a Shade of my former self."

Magnus let out a long groan.

AFTER SAYING GOOD-BYE TO RAGNOR AND TIAN, ALEC and the rest of them stepped through the Portal and walked out into a cool autumnal morning in New York. Unfortunately, they were standing in an alley near the Institute, which was redolent with the smell of garbage.

"Ah," said Simon, "home."

THE LOST BOOK OF THE WHITE

"Magnus," said Jace, "why didn't you just open the Portal directly into the Institute?"

One of the things that Alec had come to enjoy about raising a child with Magnus was that it was adorable when Magnus, the most self-assured, levelheaded man he knew, looked uncertain and awkward. And having a child greatly increased the frequency with which Magnus looked uncertain and awkward.

This was one of those times. Alec wanted to grab him and kiss him, but it did seem like a strange moment for it. "I didn't want to maybe wake up Max," Magnus said with a shrug.

Once they got inside, Max was quickly located, crawling happily around on the rug in Maryse's study while being watched by Maryse, Kadir, and unexpectedly, Catarina. Rather than greeting any of them, Alec found himself discarding his usual self-possession and running to scoop Max up from the ground and hold him tightly. Max was pleased, but clearly puzzled by the intensity of Alec's affection. After a moment he gave in and began laughing and wriggling happily. Magnus came over and stroked Max's head affectionately, looking a bit distracted.

Jace and Isabelle had gone to hug Maryse; Simon and Clary were chattering to Kadir and Catarina. Holding Max, Alec leaned into Magnus, savoring the circle the three of them made—here, surrounded by their family and friends. He had risked his life and been thankful to get home safe many times before, but this was different. This was painful and beautiful and terrible and perfect.

Fairly soon, Jace, Clary, Simon, and Isabelle excused themselves to go clean up—they were all streaked with dirt and grime. Alec knew he didn't look much better, but he didn't care—he bounced Max in his arms while Magnus dragged Catarina off for a conversation. Alec assumed he wanted to tell her about Ragnor—they had been close for centuries, and she would need to know the whole saga, starting with his not being dead and ending with . . . wherever he was going now.

For their part, Maryse and Kadir seemed happy, both to have watched Max and also to return the baby to his parents. Max, too, seemed sanguine enough. He bounced contentedly in Alec's arms.

"Wasn't too bad?" Alec said, smiling.

"No!" said Maryse. "Not at all. Nothing I couldn't handle."

"I can't help but notice," Alec said, "that your arm is in a sling. Also," he added to Kadir, "that you have two black eyes."

Kadir and Maryse exchanged glances and then returned to their sunny smiles. "Nothing to do with Max," Maryse said breezily. "Just a bit of an accident hanging a picture on a high wall."

"Uh-huh," said Alec. "So definitely nothing to do with Max?"

"The very idea is ridiculous," said Kadir solemnly.

"We had an excellent time watching Max," said Maryse firmly. "And we greatly look forward to doing it again."

"Again!" agreed Max. Alec chucked him under the chin.

"Hey, kiddo," Clary said. She and Jace had returned, changed and scrubbed. Her red hair shone. Alec noted that Jace was still carrying his spear from Diyu; apparently he'd grown fond of it. Clary ruffled Max's blue hair. "Keeping out of trouble?"

"Boof," Max confided. He high-fived Jace.

"That's a fine spear, Jace," said Kadir. "Though I prefer a *naginata*, myself."

"Okay," said Jace. "Mom, Kadir. Clary and I were talking. And I think . . . I'm willing to run the Institute, but only if I can do it with Clary. Both of us together."

Maryse seemed delighted. "I think that will work out fine." She looked over at Alec. "Did you help convince him?"

Alec shook his head. "Nope. He decided on his own. Have you told Isabelle and Simon yet?" he added to Jace.

Jace and Clary exchanged a glance. "We went to Isabelle's room," Jace said cautiously, "but they seemed to be, uh, busy."

"That's my sister," said Alec. "I didn't need to know that." He looked over at his mother, who was, or was pretending to be, deep in conversation with Kadir.

"At least you didn't have to *hear* it," said Clary.

The corner of Jace's lip twitched. "I guess Simon has realized that rather than dwelling on life's uncertainties, you should spend quality time with people you love."

"Dear God," said Alec, "I am removing myself and my baby from this conversation."

He headed across the room to Magnus, still deep in discussion with Catarina. She looked stunned, but managed to smile as Alec approached them carrying Max.

Max held his chubby blue arms out to Magnus. "Ba!" he said.

"Oh, here," Alec said. "Take the little guy for a minute." He prepared for the handoff.

Magnus backed away, hands raised as though warding something off. "No, you . . . you keep him for now. I'll, uh, I'll just . . ."

"What?" said Alec. "What's wrong?"

Magnus looked around hectically. "I've just . . . I've been very monster-y recently. I'm still a little rattled from that. I don't want to, you know . . . drop him. Or anything."

"Magnus," Alec said. "You aren't monster-y. You're Magnus. Take your kid."

"Excuse us, Alec," said Catarina, and caught hold of Magnus's hand. "I need to borrow your boyfriend for a moment."

CATARINA THRUST MAGNUS INTO A CHAIR IN THE HALL-way. He was still slightly dizzy; she had advanced on him and dragged him away from Alec and Max with startling force. Sometimes he forgot how strong she was.

She stared at him intensely. "Don't do this," she said.

"What?"

"Don't do this self-loathing, 'wah wah I'm a monster' thing. It's unbecoming."

Magnus hesitated. "You didn't see Shinyun. I got very close to becoming a monster. It's a complete fluke that I was saved."

Catarina looked at him skeptically. "I thought it was a very clever plan executed by your boyfriend."

"Well, yes, but it was a guess on his part. He didn't know it would work. I'm still not sure why it *did* work."

"And so suddenly after hundreds of years you've decided that, what, you're a danger to the people you love? Because you're a warlock and warlocks have demon parents? You've gone through this before, you know, and come out the other side. You don't need me to give you the speech about how we're defined by what we do, not what we are. I've heard you give that speech yourself." Catarina's look was compassionate, but Magnus could feel her aggravation in the set of her shoulders. They really had known each other a very long time.

"It's different now," Magnus said. He paused. "Do you remember the Shanghai Club? In 1910?"

Catarina nodded slowly. "It was just after Ephraim passed away."

"I asked you if raising him had been worth it," Magnus said. "You gave so much, and he lived a good life . . . but then he died anyway."

"Ah," said Catarina with a small smile. "That's why it's different now."

Magnus nodded sheepishly.

"Magnus, you are *surrounded* by people who love you. I didn't let Ephraim go until I made sure he too was surrounded with love. His living to a ripe old age, dying in his bed surrounded by his family—I was so sad when he died, but it was also a victory. I had saved that boy. I had raised him into a man. He had lived, had loved others. He had exactly what I wanted him to have."

"But Max," began Magnus, and Catarina waved her hands.

"Magnus, I hate to sound like Ragnor, but you *are* an idiot sometimes. I am telling you that you are doing good, that you are doing the right things. Your loved ones, your family, will be there to save you when you need saving. And they will be there to help save Max, if he needs saving. You have to trust in that." She gave him a wry smile. "You are literally the person who taught *me* that."

Magnus shook his head, overwhelmed. "You're right. It's just hard to remember sometimes. It feels so different now, with Max. My responsibility to him is so huge, so much bigger than any responsibility I've felt before."

"Yep!" said Catarina, folding her arms. "We call that 'being a parent.'"

Magnus held up his hands in surrender. "Okay," he said. "Okay. You win. And since you're my oldest friend, or one of them . . ."

"You're going to ask me for a favor, aren't you?" said Catarina in a resigned tone.

Magnus reached into his torn and tattered jacket and drew out the Book of the White. "Bring this to the Spiral Labyrinth for me, will you?" he said. "I think I'm done looking after it for now."

IT WAS ALWAYS STRANGE FOR ALEC TO LEAVE THE INSTI-tute, to say good-bye to his mother and Isabelle and Jace and . . . *return home*. The Institute had been his home for so many years, and while he'd settled into Magnus's apartment being *their* apartment, there was still always a brief moment, as they departed, when Alec felt like something was off.

Back at home, Magnus called the Mansion Hotel in Shanghai and arranged to have all their things placed into storage, from which he planned to teleport them home when the hotel staff weren't looking. Alec played with Max, who crawled happily around the living room, enjoying the quiet of being home. Presently, Magnus returned and scooped up Max, who protested briefly before giving up, breaking into a beaming smile, and immediately beginning to chew on one of Magnus's buttons.

"They're pretty, aren't they?" Magnus said.

"You know," said Alec, "I always got that our job was saving the world, but it's way more terrifying now that Max is here."

"Excuse me," said Magnus, "maybe *your* job is saving the world. My job is harder to summarize, but a significant portion is just about looking good."

"Oh," said Alec, "so when the world needs saving, you're not going to show up and save it? Sure, that sounds like the Magnus I know. Hey, Max!" he added, and Max briefly paused in his intent chewing to look over at Alec. "Is that your *bapak?* Can you say *bapak?*"

"He doesn't say *bapak* yet," Magnus said in a whisper. "Don't pressure him."

"It's weird," said Alec. "It's a weird life. But it's the life we're made for, I guess. And the life we choose."

"Bapa!" Max yelled loudly, waving an arm. Behind him, one of the curtains in the window burst into flame. Alec sighed, grabbed a couch cushion, and went to beat the fire out.

"Our other job," said Magnus, "is to keep Max from burning down this whole building until he's old enough to control his magic."

Alec smiled. "After Sammael, that seems almost possible."

"Bpppft," said Max.

"Bapak?" Alec said again.

Max frowned in concentration, and then began chewing on the button again.

MUCH, MUCH LATER, WHEN ALL WAS DARK AND QUIET IN the apartment, and they were all back in their own beds, Magnus awoke from fitful dreams. Very carefully he freed himself from the grasp of Alec's arm, crept out of bed, threw on a sweater over his silk pajamas, and made his way across the hall and into the other bedroom.

Almost immediately, he saw two very blue eyes peering at him over the edge of the crib. The lurking eyes reminded Magnus of a time he'd seen a hippo lying in wait with *its* eyes just above the waterline.

Magnus strolled toward the crib. "Hey there, you," he whispered. "I see someone who shouldn't be up."

There was a growing twinkle in the blue eyes, as though Max had been caught with his hand in the cookie jar but was hoping to find a co-conspirator to cut in on his illicit cookie deals. When Magnus approached, Max lifted his arms, in silent demand to be scooped up.

"Who's a wicked, rule-breaking warlock?" said Magnus, complying with the request. "Who's my baby?"

Max squealed in delight.

Magnus lifted his son up high. Then he tossed Max into the air in a shower of iridescent blue sparks and watched him laugh, perfectly happy, perfectly trusting that when he came down, his father would catch him.

THE SOUND OF SONG RUFFLED THE CALM OF ALEC'S slumbers. He could've easily let himself roll over in their silk sheets and fall back into the luxurious warmth of sleep, but instead he pulled himself to the surface of awareness. He was still drowsy, but the song was sweet, and it made him want to see.

When he slid open the door and peered into Max's room, he did. Magnus was dressed for comfort at home. In fact, he was wearing one of Alec's sweaters, the thick worn fabric slipping to one side on his narrower shoulders. As with most things, Magnus made it look good.

"Nina bobo, ni ni bobo," he was singing in his deep, beautiful voice, an Indonesian lullaby, much older than Magnus himself. He rocked their child in his arms. Max was waving his hands as though to conduct the song, or to catch the firefly-bright and cobalt-blue sparks of magic floating around the room. Magnus was smiling down at Max, a small, tender, and impossibly sweet smile, even as he sang.

Alec meant to let them be and return to bed, but Magnus paused in his song and tossed Alec a glance as though he knew he'd been watching.

Alec leaned in the doorway of the bedroom, resting his hand over his head against the doorframe. "Is that your *bapak?*" he said to Max.

After some consideration, Max said, *"Bapak."*

The look Magnus gave Alec was golden as a coin, as Nephilim wedding cloth, as the morning light through the windows of home.

Epilogue

IN A PLACE BEYOND PLACE, THE PRINCES OF HELL gathered.

A request had come, making the veils of the worlds reverberate with the sound of their brother's voice. That it was a request, and not a command, was itself surprising.

Some came out of loyalty. Some out of curiosity. Some came because if the others were coming, they were certainly coming as well.

"I know we don't talk much," Sammael began.

They settled down and gave him their attention. They were a motley sort of crew, he had to admit, from Belial—appearing, as he most often did, as a beautiful pale-haired man—to Leviathan, who was more of a dark green serpent, with sleek scales and arms that could be charitably described as tentacle-adjacent.

"I know we mostly go our own ways," Sammael went on. "We only see one another to fight, over territory, over power. That's how it's been, since the beginning."

That was how it was at present, as well. Belphegor and Belial had ignored each other completely since they arrived, each refusing to acknowledge the other's existence. Leviathan and Mammon had decided to sit in the same chair, each arguing that it was the only cosmically large chair present and as the most sizable of the princes he deserved it more.

Sammael considered explaining to them that the chair was only a metaphysical construct and there could just as easily be two chairs as one, since they were in a place beyond place and all that. But he didn't like to get involved.

Asmodeus, obviously the strongest of them by most measures, still maintained his loyalty to Sammael. Luckily for Sammael. When he bowed his head in acknowledgment of Sammael's superiority, the others took note, and Sammael didn't think he would have too much trouble with them.

"If that's the way it's always been, then that's the way it's supposed to be," said Astaroth. There was nodding from the others.

"Recently," Sammael said, "as some of you surely know, the love of my life, the great Mother of Demons, Lilith, was killed by humans on Earth. It has *destroyed* me," he went on sharply. "I grieve with a grief to make stars collapse."

Azazel rolled his eyes.

"I see that, Azazel!" Sammael snapped. "None of you perhaps understand, as you believe love is incompatible with the goals of the demonic realms. But I am here to tell you that you are wrong," he said. "Lilith was the greatest of my strength," he said, choking up a little. "And only now that she is gone do I feel a part missing from me."

There was a silence. Belial said, "Sammael, have you brought us all here, disturbing our activities across the entire universe, in order to tell us that *love is real*?"

"No," said Sammael. "Well, okay. Love *is* real, so if you're capable of taking any insight from that, there it is. But no, I have a more concrete reason for gathering you.

"Recently," he went on, "I had a series of strange encounters with humans—with warlocks and Nephilim—in the broken courts of the realm of Diyu."

"Diyu?" rumbled Mammon. "Yanluo's old place? We had some *parties* there."

"Yes," said Sammael, "and you should see the state it's in now. *Not. Good.*" He gave them a significant look. "But that's important to my point. All my plans there came to ruin."

"You have brought us here," said Belial, his diction as elegant as always, "to tell us that love is real and that you are terrible at your job?"

Sammael ignored this. "I failed not because I lacked power, and not because the realm of Diyu was unable to serve me. I failed because I did not account for the power that a group can have, working together and having each other's back."

The other Princes of Hell exchanged puzzled glances.

"I really found it quite inspiring," Sammael said. "And so I come to you with a proposal, dear brothers.

"Too long have we gone it alone. If we are ever to truly achieve our larger goals, we must recognize that we are more alike than we are different. We must put aside our old grievances, forget them, and work together."

Asmodeus looked astonished. "You mean—"

"*Yes,*" said Sammael. "I want to talk about Lucifer."

Acknowledgments

I WANT TO THANK NAOMI CUI FOR HER THOUGHTFUL read of the manuscript. Otherwise, this acknowledgments section is a little different from most. Ordinarily, I use this space to thank my friends, my family, and my cowriters and editor. While I am deeply grateful to all of them for providing a nurturing community for *The Lost Book of the White*, this time I want to use this space to acknowledge my readers.

Dear readers, thank you for sticking with me and Magnus and Alec and all their friends. Thank you for sharing stories, adventure, and magic with me. Your enthusiasm and affection for the inhabitants of the world of Shadowhunters and Downworlders never ceases to amaze me. I am so fortunate to have readers who are as thoughtful, joyous, and delightful as you. Thank you for being a part of my story. I couldn't imagine it without you.

—C. C.

I'M NOT SAYING THE ELDEST CURSES PUT A SPELL ON ME or anything, but before I worked on this series, I had zero children.

ACKNOWLEDGMENTS

We welcomed Hunter to the world while I was working on *The Red Scrolls of Magic*, and then my second son, River, while working on *The Lost Book of the White*.

Coincidence? Mayyyyyybe.

I'd like to think that this has less to do with correlation or causation, and more to do with the fact there was just an abundance of joy and love in my life during those Eldest Curses years. It came from my growing family, and it came from my work writing Magnus and Alec's (and Max's!) adventures. It was especially entertaining to witness Magnus and Alec go through the same growing pains we went through raising a family. How else do you juggle bottle-feeding, daycare, and (writing) magical battles all at the same time?

So, above all else, this book is dedicated to family—my family and families everywhere—as we balance love, happiness, and the incredible adventures of raising these magical creatures we call children. To my lovely wife, Paula, my partner, for helping raise two wonderful boys. To Hunter, my inspiration and teacher of patience, I will forever be your DJ and dance partner. To River, my joy and faith in humanity, you're going to conquer the world one day. To the rest of my extended family, thank you; you are my tribe. To my agency family at Scovil Galen Ghosh Literary, for always having my back with their unwavering support. To the family at Simon & Schuster, for producing this amazing book the readers are holding in their hands.

A special shout-out to Cassie, my writing family. Thank you for allowing me front row seats to witnessing your creative genius.

Lastly to the Shadowhunter family: you are the reason we tell these stories. Thank you for your love and trust.

A final thank-you to Magnus and Alec and Max. Congratulations on your amazing family. We should totally hire a babysitter for the kids and double-date sometime.

—W. C.

Turn the page to read

In Dreams Begin,

A BONUS STORY FEATURING

TESSA AND JEM.

———◆———

MAGNUS BANE WAS SCHEMING.

To an untrained observer, the High Warlock of Brooklyn wouldn't look like he was doing much of anything at all. For one thing, he was wearing purple silk pajamas. For another thing, he was in bed, leaning back against a pile of pillows with a spell book open in his lap.

Beside him, Alec Lightwood was stretched out on his side, deeply asleep. Earlier that day, Alec had taken their son, Max, to the Brooklyn Botanic Garden. This had been at Magnus's request—he wanted Max to have ample opportunity to tire himself out before bedtime. It worked almost too well. Max had made fast friends with a werewolf toddler named Eliza, and the two of them tore around the gardens blissfully for about three hours straight, Max crawling while Eliza ran, albeit unsteadily. Eliza's mother had been quite surprised the first time Max levitated. Luckily, he was glamoured, so only she and Alec noticed.

Though not possessed of much vocabulary, Eliza clearly wanted Max to levitate her as well. Fortunately, Max did not yet have that sort of skill. Alec and Max returned home happy, covered in mud, and—best of all—exhausted. Magnus really wanted them all to sleep through the night.

Magnus shifted position and peered across the room at the mantel clock atop the dresser, a hideous thing covered in putti that Ragnor had given him years ago. The room was lit only by a candle that burned with a blue flame on the table beside him, but he could make out the numbers. It was one forty-five a.m. Surely that was late enough. Surely even the Shadowhunters and Downworlders of the West Coast would be turning in. He'd given Catarina and Jem and Tessa a heads-up, after all, and as for the Blackthorns and Emma Carstairs, they were kids! And not even babies, with their bizarre and erratic relationship to sleep. Surely they would be asleep by now, worn out from running around on the beach or whatever it was that the residents of the Los Angeles Institute did all day. Yes, it was time.

Snuggling a little farther under the blanket, Magnus looked fondly over at Alec's sleeping form, his black hair like spilled ink across the ivory pillowcase. He closed his book and set it on the bedside table. He mentally reached within, feeling about for a particular pocket of magic folded away deep inside, a self-contained bubble. It had been two weeks since he'd been freed from the influence of the Svefnthorn, and while the markings on his skin had faded, his teeth had shrunk back to their normal size, and the overcharged magic of the artifact had left his system, this one reserve of magical energy had lingered.

At first, Magnus had considered hanging on to it as a sort of insurance policy. A little extra magic went a long way, especially when the magic was this potent, and Magnus was quite certain that he and Alec and their friends would have plenty more dangers to face in the years to come. That was their job, after all. But clinging to the magic out of fear of imagined dangers didn't feel good.

It felt like letting demons have a small victory over him, playing right into their scaly, demonic hands. No, instead he had resolved to use the power in a decidedly un-demon-sanctioned manner—to create joy.

Magnus shut his eyes. Oneiromancy, the study and practice of dream magic, had never been one of his specialties. But with the added kernel of power from the Svefnthorn, he felt quite confident that he could pull off this one feat, even as complex as it was. The trickiest part, it seemed to him, was holding himself in that drowsy state between waking and sleeping, while maintaining enough awareness to cast the spell. He lay back against the pillows, letting his eyelids flutter shut for just a moment. . . .

WHEN MAGNUS OPENED HIS EYES AGAIN, HE WAS STANDING in the middle of Blackfriars Bridge, the panorama of London spread out around him in all directions.

He took a deep breath of river-tasting air. The sky was a dark violet, the sun only just beginning to rise. There was no traffic, which was a distinct advantage of throwing a party on a dream bridge rather than on the real thing. There was a warm breeze in the air, and the Thames danced beneath it, silvery in the dawn light. Had he ever noticed wind in a dream before? Magnus wasn't sure. He admired the view from the bridge—it seemed just about right, though he hadn't been here for a couple of decades. Perhaps some ugly new construction had taken place since then, but who would fault him for omitting that?

"Magnus!"

He turned and saw two figures hurrying toward him. It was Tessa and Jem, both in what Magnus assumed was their pajamas. Tessa's were gray with white rabbits on them. Jem's were dark-green-and-navy-blue plaid. They were barefoot, but that wouldn't matter on a dream bridge. He started to smile as they got closer and he could see that they were both giddy and laughing, a hint of disbelief on their faces.

Tessa threw her arms around him, knocking him off-balance. He marveled at how solid and real she felt.

"It's working!" she said in wonder.

"A magical discipline unexplored is always worth exploring," Magnus said, stepping back. "I may be late to the game with onei-romancy, but I plan to make up for my tardiness all at once, right now. Is that what you're planning to wear to your wedding?"

"It's not traditional, but neither was the yellow cotton shift dress I wore for the courthouse wedding. And I do love bunnies," said Tessa. "I'm all right with it if Jem is."

"I would marry you if you were wearing a barrel," said Jem.

"But why *would* I be wearing a barrel?" said Tessa.

They were both grinning at each other stupidly. Magnus decided something needed to be done; he wasn't sure how long his magic would hold out.

"I won't have it!" he said. "If I'm to throw you a dream wedding, you must be properly dressed for the occasion. It's in my contract. I do hope you read the fine print."

He snapped his fingers, and Jem's pajamas were replaced by an exquisitely cut black suit. Magnus aimed for something that suggested the style of the Shadowhunter gear Jem had worn long ago, in the first years he knew Tessa. Wedding runes were intricately embroidered on the lapels in gold thread. As Jem marveled at the excellent fit, Magnus turned his attention to Tessa.

"I know," he said, "a wedding dress is a highly personal choice. But as our other guests will be arriving momentarily, and time is of the essence, I'm going to take a stab at it."

"You have my express permission," Tessa said.

Magnus snapped his fingers again, and then Tessa was wearing a beautiful sleeveless gown of pale silver, with a full skirt that reminded Magnus of the first time he'd met her, at a vampire ball. A couple more flicks of his fingers, and her hair rearranged itself beautifully into an updo, with a few tendrils loose around her face. One more gesture, and Tessa's familiar jade pendant appeared around her neck—as did the pearl bracelet she always wore, a gift from Will on their thirtieth anniversary.

Tessa looked startled, reaching up to touch her hair, then brushing her hands over the gown. "How do I look?"

Jem looked very young again as he gazed at her, his dark eyes full of emotion. *"Ni hen piao liang,"* he whispered. *You are very beautiful.*

Magnus turned away to give them a moment—and felt familiar arms close around him.

Alec kissed Magnus on his forehead—being slightly shorter than Magnus, he had to pull Magnus down a bit to do it, which Magnus didn't mind at all—and muttered, "You're a sentimental bastard, aren't you?" in his ear.

But he was grinning all over his face as he turned to greet Tessa and Jem, congratulating them. They both looked delighted to see him.

"So let me get this straight," Alec said. "You, me, Tessa, and Jem will all remember this with perfect recall. For the other guests, they'll remember it at first, but then it will fade away, the way dreams do?"

"That is correct. They won't recall it the way we will, but their souls will be present, and glad for it. Well, mostly glad for it," Magnus said.

"What do you mean, '*mostly*'?" Jem said nervously.

"I mean that I'm not sure how Church will feel about the whole thing."

"Church!" Alec and Jem exclaimed at the same time, and turned to see the grumpy Persian cat sauntering toward them down the center of the bridge.

Tessa laughed. "Well, he does sleep twenty hours a day. I suppose we shouldn't be surprised."

"I took the liberty of adding him to the guest list you gave me," Magnus said. "I'm trying to get on his good side."

"Why?" Alec asked, incredulous. "He's a *cat*."

"So he won't hate me forever when I do *this*." Magnus snapped his fingers, and a silver bow in the same fabric as Tessa's dress appeared around Church's neck. Church's eyes widened for a moment. Then he sat down, and after a moment, became very focused on cleaning his front paw.

"Now," Magnus said, "I simply must get this bridge decorated."

"It's decorated perfectly," said a voice from behind him. Turning, he saw Clary, who was holding Max. Behind her was Jace, followed by Isabelle and Simon, who were leaning together, whispering conspiratorially. Jocelyn and Luke were there, looking slightly unkempt, and Magnus remembered that they were in the process of remodeling a barn at Luke's farm so Jocelyn could expand her painting studio. Ragnor and Catarina had also appeared, as well as a whole gaggle of kids—the Blackthorn clan. Julian and Helen, Tiberius and Livia, Drusilla and Octavian. Emma Carstairs was with them, though she broke away from the group immediately, running to hug Clary. They were the same height now, Magnus noticed with amusement. Max had escaped from Clary and was riding on Alec's shoulders now, babbling a story to Helen Blackthorn and her wife, Aline. They looked very amused, though it was unlikely they understood even a quarter of what he said.

Maryse and Kadir were there too, already deep in conversation with Jocelyn and Luke. Kadir hadn't been on the guest list Jem and Tessa had given Magnus, because they didn't really know him, but Magnus had added him as Maryse's plus-one. It never hurt to butter up your boyfriend's mother, especially when she was willing to babysit for days at a time.

A couple of Silent Brothers had appeared—Enoch? Shadrach? Magnus was slightly embarrassed to admit that they all looked alike to him, now that Jem was no longer counted among their number as Brother Zachariah. Magnus hadn't known if the Gregori would be able to attend, since they didn't normally sleep. One of them—Enoch?—inclined his hooded head slightly at Magnus, acknowledging this mad thing he was doing as worthwhile. At least, that was how Magnus chose to interpret the gesture.

Octavian was climbing Jace like a jungle gym. Clary was talking with Julian and Emma, while Tiberius stood near his older brother, looking around at London with fierce curiosity in his gray eyes. Livia and Drusilla were perched on the railing of the bridge, Livia chatting animatedly with Simon and Isabelle, Drusilla looking around shyly. Catarina went to lean beside her, asking her a question. Magnus looked at the motley assortment of clothing on the assembled group. Mostly casual, though there were more pajamas as well. Magnus made two sweeping gestures, and all at once everyone was looking very sharp in formal attire. Even better, they barely seemed to notice the change. Magnus was impressed. Oneiromancy—who knew!

A hand gripped his arm. It was Tessa, who looked close to tears. "Magnus. I can't believe you're doing this for us. I . . ." She trailed off, at a loss for words.

Magnus regarded her fondly. "Tessa, most people's idea of a dream wedding is not a literal dream wedding. But since yours is, I am happy to oblige. Shall we get this show on the road?"

Jem and Tessa took their places on either side of Magnus, and the guests gathered around. The sun had climbed well above the horizon, casting rays of warm light between the long shadows of the wedding guests.

"Dear friends," Magnus said to Jem and Tessa, "we are honored to share this moment with you, and I am doubly honored to be given the chance to speak. Several hundred years ago I got very drunk and woke up an ordained minister. Today I have decided that doing so was a wise choice after all."

Jocelyn snorted, then looked embarrassed. Luke grinned at her.

"Joking aside, it is impossible to stand here with you all and not feel that there is some greater plan at work, some greater force that has brought these two souls across more than a century to be joined as one."

Clary's eyes were glistening. Jace reached into his pocket and offered her what looked like a handkerchief but was more likely a soft cloth for polishing blades. She gave a wry smile of recognition, and sniffled into it.

"I debated which customs to follow in officiating this wedding," Magnus went on. "Whether to conduct a Shadowhunter ceremony, or a warlock ceremony, or even a mundane ceremony, for many worlds have been united in the two of you. But none of these traditions seemed quite appropriate on their own. So I've attempted to tailor a ceremony that will honor your unique paths."

Magnus nodded to Jem, who reached into his pocket and produced a gold ring. Jem had requested a single word etched around the outside of it: *Mizpah*.

"It has been said," said Magnus, "that when two people are at one in their inmost hearts, they shatter even the strength of iron or bronze. Theresa Gray, are you at one with James Carstairs in your inmost heart?"

Tessa's eyes were wide, her face serious as she gazed at Jem. "I am," she said, offering her hand to him. He slid the ring onto her finger.

Then Magnus nodded at Tessa, who produced another ring, this one from thin air. Magnus had to suppress the grin that threatened to break his calm officiant expression. It delighted him that Tessa was engaging in a small amount of oneiromancy herself, and Jem looked as pleased by it as Magnus felt. This ring was the exact match of the first, and he knew what it said as well: *May the Angel watch between me and thee when we are absent from one another.*

"James Carstairs—Ke Jian Ming—are you at one with Theresa Gray in your inmost heart?"

"I am," Jem said, delight visible in his dark eyes. Tessa put the ring on him, and they stood for a moment, holding hands and smiling at each other like they couldn't quite believe this was happening.

"For I am persuaded," said Magnus, and Jem and Tessa both looked up at him, recognizing a piece of the old Shadowhunter wedding ceremony, though he had altered the wording, "that neither death, nor life, nor angels, nor demons, nor principalities, nor powers, nor things present, nor things to come, nor height, nor depth, nor any other creature, shall be able to separate these two." He stretched out his arms. "Therefore I am overjoyed to declare this marriage consecrated, here in the presence of your friends and family. Tessa Gray and Jem Carstairs, you are married, and the world is better for it. You may kiss each other, not that you really need my permission."

The assembled crowd cheered as Jem and Tessa kissed, a kiss that had been long delayed. The kiss continued, and Magnus slowly backed away, joining the cheering audience. "Let's give them a moment," he said, and happy chatter swelled around him.

Magnus noted that Alec was looking very foxy in his Armani suit, laughing with Maryse. Ragnor and Catarina were cackling over something, glad to be reunited now that Ragnor didn't have to pretend to be dead—or at least, didn't have to pretend with *them.* Clary had her arm draped over Emma's shoulders, and Jace was arguing with Simon about how to properly tie a necktie.

Tiberius and Drusilla were watching this argument as though it were a tennis match. Julian had lifted Octavian up so he could look down at the river flowing by beneath. Isabelle was joking with Livia, who was giving Max a piggyback ride. It was a miraculously good wedding.

Here they were, his friends. They'd literally gone into Hell twice with him now. He found himself reflecting on how much had changed. At first his life had felt like Magnus against the world. Then for years and years it had been Magnus, Catarina, and Ragnor against the world. Now his community was a much larger group, one that had spread wide enough that instead of Magnus and his friends against the world, it felt like Magnus and his friends, a *part* of the world. Probably the best part of the world.

It was a good feeling.

"Look!" a girl's voice cried. It was Drusilla, pointing up into the sky, eyes wide with wonder. There was a collective gasp as the crowd saw what she had spotted.

Two figures flew overhead, riding a translucent white stallion with two gold hooves and two silver. One of them was a blond boy in ragged clothes, who looked down at the Blackthorns and waved. The figure in front of him was harder to make out—a gentry faerie in clothes just as ragged, only he was as translucent as the horse. The blond boy must be Mark Blackthorn, Magnus marveled. He'd "invited" the whole family, not knowing whether those who rode with the Wild Hunt could be summoned by dream magic. He had his answer, but it came with another mystery. Who was this companion, so close to Mark that they would appear together in a dream?

The riders made a circle overhead, while the Blackthorns shouted and waved, and Mark waved back, smiling an odd smile down at them. Then they faded away into the morning air.

Magnus saw with relief that Jace, Clary, Simon, Isabelle, and

Alec had all moved in around the Blackthorn kids, giving them an opportunity to talk about what they had just seen—their stolen brother, visiting so briefly.

He glanced over and saw Tessa and Jem still standing by the railing. There was a shimmer beside them, at the edge of the bridge, and the hair on the back of Magnus's neck rose.

He knew Will Herondale had never haunted the mortal world, because he had lived and died happily and had no unfinished business among the living. While Magnus didn't subscribe to any specific set of beliefs about reincarnation or an afterlife, he had always had a strong sense that Will was waiting on the other bank of a dark river—be it Lethe, or some other border between the living and the dead. He was there among the green grass, the sky above as dark a blue as his eyes, waiting patiently for Jem and Tessa to join him, that he might lead them by the hand to whatever wonders lay beyond the veil.

The philosophers of ancient Greece had believed dreams and sleep to be the twin of death: Morpheus and Hades, standing side by side. And here, in that space, Magnus would not have been surprised if Will stretched out his hand to those he had loved best in life—to Jem and Tessa.

He was, after all, a Herondale, and very stubborn.

Alec sidled up to Magnus, leaving the Blackthorns in the capable hands of his siblings and their partners. The kids seemed to have taken Mark's appearance as a sort of wedding favor created especially for them.

Alec twined an arm around Magnus's waist and pulled him close, kissing him on the temple. "It was very kind of you to use the last of your Svefnthorn magic on this," he said.

Magnus leaned into Alec. "Well, it wasn't enough magic to send us to the moon, or get us into the front row at the Alexander McQueen runway. So I figured, next best thing."

Alec smiled at him pointedly. "*Actually*, I happen to know that you did it because you are an incredibly kind person, and that is one of the many things I love about you."

"Oh dear," Magnus said, turning to face him. "You know all my secrets."

Then they were kissing, and kissing in a magical dream turned out to be just as perfect as kissing in the waking world.